For Mark, Rupert and Tim

Instructions for Mummification

You will need:
1 cadaver
1 embalmer's board with at least four raised cross struts
20 litres date palm wine
1 curved iron hook
small bowls and vessels
a large quantity of linen swabs
1 obsidian blade
4 Canopic jars
400 lbs natron – a naturally occurring salt compound
frankincense and myrrh
2 pedestals, equal height
100 yards good quality untreated linen
2 litres tree resin

You may find that some of these items are difficult to procure. If you need to, use the closest alternative that presents itself, though it may be detrimental to the process.

1. Place the naked cadaver face up on the embalming board and wash the body with date palm wine.
2. Insert the iron hook into each nostril in turn. Use it to break

through the cribriform plate of the ethmoid bone. Rotate the hook thoroughly throughout the cranial cavity to liquify the brain.

3. Turn the cadaver over so the brain can drain out of the nostrils into a small bowl.

4. Attach strips of linen to the iron hook and use them to swab out the cranium until no more brain tissue can be retrieved.

5. Pour tree resin into the cranium via the nostrils.

6. Use the obsidian blade to make a three-inch incision on the left side of the abdomen.

7. Remove the abdominal and thoracic organs – spleen, liver, kidneys, pancreas, gall bladder, intestines, lungs. Leave the heart in situ.

8. Pack the removed organs into the four Canopic jars with natron.

9. Cleanse the abdominal cavity with palm wine and pack the space with linen-wrapped packages of natron, frankincense and myrrh.

10. Spread a deep layer of natron on the embalming board, filling the spaces between the cross struts. Lay the cadaver back on top and cover it entirely with the remaining natron.

11. After 35 days at room temperature, the natron will have set hard like baked salt. Break the natron away from the cadaver, which will now be desiccated.

12. Rest the cadaver across the two pedestals, one at the head and one at the feet, and wrap it as tightly as possible in a basket-weave pattern. Fingers and toes should be individually wrapped. As you do this, paint the linen strips with tree resin to ensure they stay in place. Include amulets and good luck tokens among the bandages.

The mummified cadaver is now ready for interment.

I

The Embalmer

There's a man. A man who believes he's immortal. Or at least on his way to immortality. He's followed the instructions, point by point. He's making his way along the sacred path, so he can take his place among the gods.

Ra, the sun god.

Amun, the invisible one.

Isis, the mother.

Apophis. The Great Serpent. His god, the one he worships.

If he succeeds in what he's doing, he'll become one with Apophis. He'll become the living incarnation of the Great Serpent. And in death, he'll become immortal.

The man stands in front of the altar and sighs. He extinguishes the candles with the softest touch of his fingers, relishing the burn to his mortal flesh. He won't need it much longer. He bows his head and whispers the name of his god.

'Apophis. God of snakes. Watch over me and protect me.'

He makes a soft hissing noise, as he walks across the stone floor of the shrine to where the mummified woman lies, so beautifully wrapped, in her casket.

The night's work is ahead of him. With the sacrifice he's made, he'll announce his arrival to the world. A new god moving among them. He checks off the list of what he'll need with the stub end of an ancient

3

pencil. Small teeth marks pit the wood – he remembers chewing on it as he struggled with homework. All those years ago. He can still hear the other boys' laughter in his ears.

He banishes the thought. There will be no more laughter at his expense.

Tonight he will announce his arrival by unveiling his creation. She'll be put on display for all the world to see. To admire. First, he must move her to the loading bay, then into the back of the van. The casket isn't heavy – the pale, voluptuous flesh of a month ago is gone, transformed by the mummification process into a dark, leathery hide stretched taut over her bones. Her pretty, plump cheeks are now hollow and her fat fingers have turned into claws. She's as light as a feather.

He smiles. He hisses, pressing the two tips of his bifurcated tongue against his bottom teeth.

The journey to immortality has begun.

It's just a matter of sacrificing the right people.

In the right order.

And a certain person last of all.

2

Gavin

It was Gavin Albright's second day on the job. The new team member. And it was not what he'd expected, mainly because he'd had to step into a dead man's shoes. Even if it wasn't technically the case, it certainly felt that way. DC Tony Hitchins had been murdered by the so-called Poison Ink Killer just a few weeks ago and now Gavin had joined the team – anyone could be forgiven for thinking it was to fill the gap. Still, at least he didn't have to come to work wearing a uniform any more.

He looked across to where Detective Inspector Francis Sullivan was talking animatedly with DC Angie Burton, his new partner. Burton had returned to work for the first time since being injured during the chase for the Poison Ink Killer. Her return was the reason why the whole team had ambled over to the Mucky Duck for a couple of pints at the end of the shift.

Sullivan was young and forward-thinking, and he had a growing reputation as a hands-on DI, a man of action. Gavin thought they were about the same age, thirty, but the boss certainly looked younger than him – his short red hair and boyish features against Gavin's receding hairline and heavy beard. But Sullivan was already a DI – on the fast track – and in the last two years, he'd apprehended two of Brighton's most horrifying killers. He was scarred as a result of it, quite literally. There was

5

a black gulley on his left cheek, where he'd been gouged with a poison-laced tattoo iron.

'Albright?'

Gavin stopped scratching his beard and turned his attention back to what was happening in the pub. Rory Mackay, Sullivan's sergeant, was beckoning him across to the table he was sharing with Sullivan and Burton. Mackay was a short man, with just the first sprinklings of grey in his cropped hair. He had a reputation as a solid and experienced detective within the station, but Gavin had heard rumours of resentment when Sullivan leapfrogged him to DI.

'Call come in – domestic disturbance ongoing in Kemptown. You two take it?' He nodded at Gavin and Angie.

Angie frowned from behind her untouched pint. She didn't look well – pale and drawn in the face, skeletal body, older than her thirty-four years – and Gavin wondered if she was really ready to come back to work.

'Seriously, boss?' She was appealing directly to the DI.

'Come on, Angie. You know what night it is – uniforms are all busy with rogue trick-or-treaters. We need to pick up the slack.'

'We'll take it,' said Gavin, earning an eyeroll from his partner.

'Good man,' said Rory.

Routine stuff for someone with Angie's years of experience maybe, but still a hell of a lot more interesting than anything he'd been involved in as a constable on the beat. He was happy to go, even if she wasn't thrilled at the prospect. He knew she – and the whole team – had just lost a colleague in the most harrowing circumstances, and of course he was sympathetic. But her return seemed to cast a pall of gloom over everyone.

'Straight back on the horse,' said Angie, with a sigh. There were dark circles of grief under her eyes.

'If you don't feel ready . . .' said Francis.

She shook her head. 'No, it's fine. Come on, Gavin. Let's

get it done.' She pulled an elastic off her wrist and drew her shoulder-length brown hair into a tight ponytail. It made her look even more severe.

Gavin read out the address Rory texted to him as he and Angie walked up the road to where Angie had left her car.

'I know that address,' said Angie.

She glanced back over her shoulder and Gavin looked round too. The boss was leaving the pub and heading off in the other direction.

'What?' said Gavin. There was something in the way in which she'd quickly turned her head back.

'The address. It's Marni Mullins's house.'

The name was familiar to Gavin but he couldn't think why. 'Who's she?'

'It's none of our business,' said Angie, striding forward.

She wasn't making sense.

'What information do we have?' said Gavin, climbing into the passenger seat.

Her car was small and the top of his hair practically brushed against the roof interior. He had to extend the seat belt to its full length to get it around him. At six foot three, he was almost a foot taller than Angie, and maybe twice her bulk with his rugby-player's physique.

'Not much. A neighbour called the police – screaming, crashing.' She started the engine and put the car into gear.

'And you know the people who live there?'

'Marni Mullins is a local tattoo artist. This isn't the first DV call to her address.'

Gavin heard her dislike for Marni Mullins in the tone of her voice.

'Violent husband?'

Angie shook her head. 'No, it's not Thierry Mullins who's the problem. It's her. She drinks, throws stuff around, has a go at him.'

7

'So what's none of our business?'

'It's nothing. She was involved in the Tattoo Thief case.'

'Ah,' said Gavin, finally making the connection. 'She's the one who was linked to the boss in the newspaper?' He remembered the grainy picture of the boss emerging, early morning, from the house of a woman who was apparently a witness in an ongoing case. It had been the talk of the station for weeks.

'Fake news.' She said it a little too quickly, then changed the subject. 'Good to have you on the team, Gavin. The boss thinks you're a bit of a legend since you helped him arrest Jered Stapleton.'

'Just did what I was told,' said Gavin with a wry smile. 'But thanks.' He was proud of the role he'd played in the apprehension of the Poison Ink Killer. 'Angie, I know from the rest of the team you were close to Tony Hitchins.'

Angie didn't respond. They were turning the corner into Great College Street.

Had he put his foot in it?

'I just want you to know, I'm not trying to step into his shoes or anything. I'm not here to replace him – I was scheduled to join the team anyway.'

Angie shook her head. 'It's fine. I understand.' She pulled the car into a space by the pavement. 'We're here.' She sounded relieved to draw a line under the conversation.

They were about two doors down from the house number Rory had given them, but Gavin could already hear noises from inside. A woman was shouting – the words indistinct – and the front door was opened, then slammed, twice in quick succession. A middle-aged man in a cardigan and slippers came towards them on the pavement.

'You the police?'

'Yes,' said Gavin. 'Did you call it in?'

The man nodded and looked at the house. 'Bloody fed up with them, I am,' he said. 'Should just let 'em do each other in, then

8

we'd get a bit of peace around here.'

'Thank you for calling,' said Angie. She strode up to the door of the Mullins house and rang the bell.

The shouting was louder by the door and Gavin could hear a multitude of swear words, in English and in French. The second time Angie rang, the door opened and a short, dark-haired woman peered out at them. Her face was flushed and her eyes widened.

'I know you,' she said, addressing Angie. 'You can fuck right off.'

She started to shut the door but Angie leant against it with her shoulder.

'Mrs Mullins, calm down.'

As they went into the hall, Gavin saw a tall black man leaning on the newel post of the stairs. Thierry Mullins.

'I know what I saw, Thierry.' Marni was going to continue arguing, regardless of the presence of two police officers in the house. 'It was Paul. He's back here.'

'Paul's dead.'

'He's not. He's here. He wants to take Alex away from me. Fuck you, Thierry, for not believing me.' She launched herself at her husband and began to pummel his chest.

'*Merde*! Not again.' He grabbed the top of her arms.

'Mrs Mullins,' said Angie. 'Step away from your husband.'

Marni pulled away from him, unsteady on her feet, tears welling in her eyes.

Thierry sneered. 'What's wrong now? Not the policeman you were hoping for?'

With a yelp of anger, Marni lunged at her husband.

'Gavin!' shouted Angie.

Gavin blinked and made a grab for Marni, but he was too slow to stop her from connecting with her intended target.

Her knee. Thierry's groin.

Ouch.

3

Wednesday, 1 November 2017

Francis

Francis took the call on the way into work. A cryptic, garbled message about a break-in at the Booth Museum of Natural History on Dyke Road. Great. He hadn't had coffee yet and he was having to go out of his way because the uniform who'd arrived first on the scene couldn't be sure whether a crime had been committed. Or whether there was a body or not.

The Booth Museum was an anachronism. Francis knew it well – everyone who'd grown up in Brighton knew the Booth. It was a good, old-fashioned, glass-display-case museum, with no interactive videos and no buttons to press. It didn't spoon-feed its visitors an education and nowadays it couldn't compete with the aquarium or the i360 viewing tower. There was just row upon row of exquisitely – if now a little faded – stuffed birds, harking back to an era when birdwatching included killing one's quarry and putting it in a glass case for posterity.

When he arrived, he parked on a yellow line opposite the entrance. There was a patrol car already drawn up outside the museum, blocking a bus stop. At eight thirty, the museum wasn't yet open for business, so he had to tap on the main door to be let in. The uniform officer who'd requested assistance opened the door, and led him up a short flight of steps into the reception area.

Francis looked around. The walls were completely lined with square and rectangular glass cases containing stuffed birds in dioramas of their natural habitats. They looked stiff and dusty – there was nothing lifelike or natural about them. Apart from their eyes. Francis remembered them from school trips. Dark and beady, they followed you malevolently as you walked past. He'd never been a big fan of dead birds.

At the centre of the rear wall there was a broad wooden counter with a till at one end, and in the centre of the floor were several shelving units containing books, postcards, keyrings, pencils, polished stones and model dinosaurs – all the usual museum shop tat calculated to separate young visitors from their pocket money. The stock didn't seem to have changed since he was a boy.

A young man in a wrinkled suit and round glasses was coming towards him.

'Hello, I'm Nathan Cox. I'm the assistant manager here.' His voice had a nervous tremor, but he stuck out a hand.

Francis shook it as briefly as he could. The man's palm felt clammy against his own.

'DI Sullivan.' He resisted the urge to wipe his hand on his trouser leg. 'Tell me why you called us.'

'I arrived here at about half past seven,' said Cox. 'We don't open until ten, but I find it's the best time for getting anything done, before the public arrive. Especially before the school parties come through the door.' Nathan Cox grimaced. 'I like it when it's silent, and all I can hear is the echo of my own footsteps.'

Francis pursed his lips. Surely his time could be better spent elsewhere.

'This morning, I felt almost immediately that something was ... not wrong, but different. I came in through the back door and I felt certain someone had been in here since I'd locked up last night.'

'What made you feel that?' said Francis. 'Any signs of a break-in?' He looked around, taking note of a large open case with sand spilling out, near the entrance, and there seemed to be some sort of mess on the reception counter.

'No, nothing like that,' said Cox. 'Just a hunch. I'm very sensitive to the atmosphere of the place. The air ... dust had been stirred up.'

'Can we get on? What is it I'm supposed to be looking at, Mr Cox?'

'Yes, sorry. I came in at the rear entrance and dropped off my coat and bag in the staff-room. It was half dark – we have to keep the blinds on the skylights shut to stop the exhibits from fading. I switched on the lights and walked through the small dinosaur gallery up at the far end. It all looked perfectly normal. Then I came down the long gallery, checking the exhibits on both sides. Everything seemed fine. The Victorian parlour in the middle was the same as ever. But when I came through to the reception area here, I saw it immediately.'

Francis raised his eyebrows. 'It?'

Nathan Cox pointed at the case to the left of the entrance, the one Francis had noticed earlier. 'There.'

Francis looked. Inside the case he saw what appeared to be an ancient Egyptian mummy on a wooden plinth, covered with brightly coloured hieroglyphs. It stood on several inches of fine, golden sand. To one side of the plinth there was a row of three clay jars, the tops of which had been shaped into the heads of Egyptian animal gods.

It wasn't real – even he could tell that. The bandages wrapped around the mummy were too white and fresh-looking. The whole thing was too perfect. Real mummies were dirty and stained, battered-looking. This looked like a new display, probably for the school groups.

'So what's the problem?'

'The mummy,' said Cox with a sniff. 'It wasn't here when I

locked up last night, and we had no contractors booked onsite. That case usually holds a pair of white-tailed sea eagles.'

'And where are they now?' said Francis.

Nathan Cox looked around frantically. 'I have no idea. I don't know why this is here or who did it. My boss isn't here yet . . . she might know something.'

'So why exactly did you call us, rather than waiting for your boss to arrive? Are you sure this isn't some kind of Hallowe'en prank?'

Cox didn't answer him.

Francis went closer to the case and peered inside. His nostrils were assaulted by a smell that combined camphor, pine, incense and rosemary. It wasn't unpleasant, though there was a sharp after-tang that caught in the back of his throat.

The linen bandages were wrapped around the mummy in an intricate pattern of overlapping and intertwined bands. There were small clay figures tucked among the folds. Where the body's face would have been, there was a curved wooden lozenge, painted with a woman's features, the eyes heavy with kohl, the lips dark red and sensual. He wondered who she was. It was probably a copy from an original mummy, a woman who lived in ancient Egypt and whose remains were actually mummified. Was she somewhere in a museum now?

He prodded the mummy with his finger, wondering what it was stuffed with. Straw probably – it rocked slightly on its plinth. It seemed quite light, given the size of it. He stepped to one side and squatted down to examine the jars, his feet crunching on grains of sand as he moved. The jars wouldn't be original either – real ancient burial jars were priceless museum pieces, he knew that much. He couldn't remember the names of the Egyptian gods, but the jars were all about storing the organs of the deceased, ready for when they needed them in the afterlife. There was a dent in the sand at the end of the row.

'Was there something here?' he said, looking up at Nathan Cox.

'Yes.' Nathan looked at him and then looked at the counter. Francis followed his gaze. There was an overturned clay pot, a painted wolf's head, a scattering of lumpy white powder and something that looked like an old leather pouch, stiff and brown, a few inches in diameter. Francis straightened up and went over to it. The wolf's head had pointed ears and a long narrow snout. It wore the typical striped headdress of the Egyptian pharaohs, and though the body of the jar was unpainted, the head was picked out in gold and blue and black. He studied the powder spilled across the counter and became aware of a new smell, the sort of musty reek of long-abandoned basements or church crypts.

'What's all this?'

'I opened up one of the jars. I wanted to know what was in them. To be honest, I thought it would be empty, but it wasn't.' His voice cracked. 'I think that's part of a body?' He ended the sentence with a high inflection, making it into a question.

Francis looked at what Nathan was pointing at, the thing that resembled old leather. It was almost black, and the surface looked parched. He bent and sniffed the air close to it, pulling a face.

'There's no reason to think it's human,' he said, straightening up. 'We've had some of these turn up, apparently with cat remains inside.' Both Cox and the PC grimaced. 'I'll call our pathologist to come and take a look – and at the other jars,' he continued, waving in the direction of the display case. 'In the meantime, I think the museum should remain closed, just in case this is a crime scene.'

He called the city's head forensic pathologist, Rose Lewis, and told her about the jar. She wasn't impressed when he described it to her.

'I've seen enough mummified cat entrails, thank you,' she said.

'This is the third Canopic jar called in this month, complete with mummified body parts.'

'Seriously?'

'Don't worry, they're not human – cat parts.'

It was as he'd thought.

'Someone mummified cats? Were they ancient?'

'I don't think so, but I'm not wasting tests on them.'

'So basically this call-out is a waste of my time?'

Rose laughed. 'If you're there, you might as well pick it up for me.'

'There's still the question of what's inside the mummy,' said Francis, glancing over at the Egyptian tableau. 'Probably totally fake with nothing inside, but I think we need to treat it as a crime scene until we've got some explanation.'

'Okay, fair enough – I'll come down.'

He put the phone back in his pocket.

'Nathan,' he said, 'you said you're the assistant manager?'

Nathan nodded.

'Who manages this place and where is he?'

'She. Alicia Russell. She should be in by now.' Nathan looked around as if expecting her to materialise. 'I can go and check the staff-room at the back.'

'Please.'

By the time Rose arrived it was approaching opening time and Nathan had put up a notice at the main entrance to say the museum would be closed. There was still no sign of Alicia Russell – she hadn't arrived for work and wasn't answering her phone.

Rose was dressed in running gear, and she'd recently had her auburn hair cut into a short, sharp bob. There was still a sheen of sweat on her forehead, making Francis all too aware that he could hardly remember when he'd last exercised. But at least she came armed with coffee.

Francis took a long-overdue mouthful of it and directed her towards the reception counter.

'That,' he said, pointing at the desiccated pouch, still sitting amid the pile of powder.

Rose inspected it from a number of angles, before pulling on a pair of latex gloves.

'This was in the jar?' she said.

Nathan Cox nodded.

Rose walked across to the mummy. The door of the glass case was still open, and Rose leaned inside, sniffing the air thoughtfully. She looked down at the other three jars and frowned.

'Francis?' Her voice struck a note of concern.

'Yes.'

'How big do you think a cat's stomach is, especially when it's been dried out during mummification?'

He looked across at the object on the counter. He could see her point. The coffee in his mouth became bitter and he pulled a face.

'Exactly,' said Rose. 'That's not any part of a cat. I suspect that's a human stomach. Which means this is a crime scene.'

4

Wednesday, 1 November 2017

Francis

Francis walked the length of the empty museum. The long-dead birds followed him with their glass eyes and he had the uneasy sensation that he was breathing in dust from their carcasses. At the end of the gallery, a huge stuffed bat with papery wings seemed to be flying right at him, its sharp rodent teeth poised to pierce his skin. Harmless enough, but he'd always found the place a bit creepy – even before the discovery of the stomach.

The uniformed officer who'd taken the original call was standing by the door of the staff-room.

'Any other staff members arrived for work yet?' said Francis.

'There's a girl who sells the tickets and runs the shop. I've asked her to wait in here.'

Francis went into the staff-room – there were a few chairs, a coffee table, and a small kitchen unit with a sink and a kettle. It didn't look welcoming or relaxing. A girl was sitting nervously on the edge of a wooden chair. Nathan Cox stood with his back to her, staring out of the window. The view was a brick wall. He turned round as he heard Francis coming in.

The girl looked up, wide-eyed and flustered, as Cox introduced her. She looked about eighteen, though she was wearing the sort of frumpy floral dress that Francis would have expected to encounter at a church council meeting. Heavy-rimmed glasses obscured her eyes and her brown hair was tied back in a high ponytail.

'This is Martina Russell.'

Francis waited, then gave her a nod of encouragement. 'What do you do here, Martina?'

'On reception four days a week, one day helping Alicia in her office.' Cox gave the information before the girl had the chance to speak.

Martina Russell nodded in agreement.

'Russell?' said Francis. 'Are you related to Alicia?'

'She's my aunt.'

The sour look that flashed across Nathan Cox's face didn't go unnoticed. Francis wondered what it signified.

'Do you know any reason why she hasn't arrived for work this morning?'

The girl looked up, surprised. 'It's Wednesday, right?'

Francis nodded.

Martina shook her head. 'She never said anything to me about not coming in. Maybe she's caught in traffic.'

'She's nearly two hours late and she only lives in Shoreham,' said Nathan Cox. It was clear from his tone that he had little time for Martina. 'And she hasn't phoned in.'

'Does she keep a diary here?' said Francis. 'Maybe she had a meeting somewhere else.'

Martina nodded, then shook her head. 'Yes, there's a diary in her office. But she didn't have a meeting. I would have known about it.'

'Can you show me her diary?'

When Martina stood, Francis saw that she was wearing chunky, schoolgirl-style sandals with white ankle socks. He couldn't decide whether she was being ironically fashionable or whether ideas of teen glamour had completely passed her by.

He followed her through the back area of the museum and into a small gallery displaying animal skeletons and fossils. At the far end there was a door. Martina pulled a bunch of keys from the pocket of her dress and opened it.

'This is her office,' she said, showing him in. 'We keep it locked if no one's in it – members of the public are nosy, and they'll try any door.' She seemed more animated now they'd left Nathan Cox behind.

The office was anything but grand. In fact, it seemed decidedly poky to be the office of the director of the museum. Obviously, space was at a premium. The impression wasn't helped by the amount of clutter – two small desks and a row of bookcases were overflowing with documents, newspapers, books and folders. There was a vase on the windowsill. The chrysanthemums it held were brown and wilted. Martina picked up two empty coffee cups from one of the desks, but it was too little, too late.

'The diary?' said Francis.

The girl put down the cups and lifted a pile of papers on the other desk. Despite the mess, she'd known exactly where her boss's diary was. She flicked through the pages and then held it out to Francis.

'Look – there's nothing in there for today.'

'And you have no idea where she might be?'

Martina shook her head.

'When did you last see her?'

'She was here at work the day before yesterday. Yesterday was her day off, so I didn't see her. But she never said anything about being late in today.'

Francis turned back a few pages. 'There's nothing in here relating to new exhibits or anything Egyptian. What about last night or yesterday during the day? Any indication she had plans?'

'She said she was looking forward to a quiet day at home,' said Martina.

'And you don't know anything about the mummy or who brought it here?'

'No.' Martina looked momentarily stricken. 'Nathan said that jar had a part of a body in it. Is that true?'

'We don't know yet,' said Francis. 'It will have to be examined in the pathology lab.'

'A human body?'

'I really can't discuss it,' said Francis. He turned towards the door.

'Wait,' said Martina. 'If there's a real human inside that mummy . . .' Her voice tailed off.

'What?'

'Could it be Alicia?' She blurted out the words as if she'd had to force herself to say them.

It wasn't a possibility Francis wanted to admit in front of the girl. He shook his head and made his escape.

Outside, he took a deep drag on a cigarette, his first of the day. He was supposed to be giving up. He'd promised his sister, Robin, that he would cut down. Only a call from Rory just now had triggered the familiar cascade of adrenalin and anxiety that came with the mention of a certain name.

'Something you should probably know, boss,' Rory had said.

'Yeah? What?'

'That call-out that Gavin and Angie took last night – it was to Marni Mullins's house.'

Shit. He didn't say anything.

'Cautions issued to her and Thierry Mullins. Apparently, she was kicking the shit out of . . .'

'I don't need to know the details, thank you, sergeant.'

Marni Mullins and her broken marriage. How long was it going to limp on for?

'God, not you too? The whole bloody department's smoking now.' Rose was standing in the doorway, frowning. She'd always been vocal in her anti-smoking stance – but, of course, she'd seen enough of the internal evidence to know what she was talking about.

Francis stubbed it out.

'Something in here you need to see,' she said.

He caught her arm as she turned to go inside.

'What d'you make of Nathan Cox? Is he telling the truth about the mummy suddenly appearing?'

'Can't see why he'd lie about it,' said Rose. 'What's weird is the missing manager, though. No sign of her?'

Francis shook his head. It was weird.

They went inside and ducked under a ribbon of crime scene tape that blocked the way into the reception area. Beyond it, a CSI was photographing and inspecting the other three Canopic jars. Another one was fingerprinting the glass case and taking more photos. Rose led him across to the cabinet, where the other three Canopic jars had been moved off the sand and onto the floor. She bent down and pointed at something with a gloved hand. Francis squatted to see it clearly.

It was a small paper scroll, tied with what looked like straw or raffia. She snapped some pictures from different angles.

'I didn't see it before,' said Francis.

'It was round the back of one of the jars.'

'Can we unroll it?'

Rose picked it up and took it to the reception counter. She photographed it again, then carefully untied the binding. Francis peered over her shoulder as she unrolled a square of coarse, thick parchment. As she held it flat, he could see two symbols, drawn in heavy black ink.

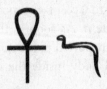

'Hieroglyphs,' said Francis.

'What do they mean?'

'Damned if I know.' He shrugged. 'A snake ...'

Rose let the parchment roll up again and dropped it into an evidence bag.

'What else have you got?' he asked, peering cautiously at the contents of the first jar that were still strewn across the counter.

'This,' she said, indicating the object with a gloved finger, 'is a human stomach. There appear to be other bodily remains in the other three jars, but I don't want to empty them out until I'm back in the lab.'

The withered brown pouch didn't look like a human stomach to Francis, but he supposed the drying process must have discoloured and shrunk it.

'How old do you think it is? Ancient or ... recent?' The latter didn't bear thinking about.

'Hard to say. I can't date it in the normal way. I'll have to run some other tests on it. But these jars clearly aren't antiquities.'

Francis studied them. All four were clean, with no dents or scratches to suggest hundreds of years buried in a tomb.

'And this? Is it salt?' he said, pointing at the scattering of white crystals.

'Probably,' said Rose. 'The Egyptians used a naturally occurring salt compound called natron for drying out their mummies. This lot certainly isn't ancient Egyptian, so I doubt that it's actually natron.' She shrugged. 'We'll have to assess it in the lab to know for sure.'

'And what about the mummy?' He walked over to the glass case to give it a closer look.

'I think we've got to accept the possibility that there's a mummified body inside it. As soon as the crime scene team is finished, I'll have it transported to the morgue.'

If there was a dead body inside the mummy, who the hell could it be?

And who put it there?

5

Wednesday, 1 November 2017

Gavin

Gavin had just sunk his teeth into the first bite of a Subway Meatball Marinara when Francis's call came through. Tomato sauce squelched from the side of his mouth and onto his keyboard. Great. He answered with his mouth full and chewed his way through the conversation, finally hanging up with a new set of instructions, the first of which was to go and find Angie.

He finished the sandwich, and grabbed the cardboard cup of coffee from his desk. He'd been working through the lunch hour, typing up a statement on the disturbance at the Mullins house the previous evening. He was determined to keep on top of things and make a good impression with his new boss.

He found Angie in the canteen. She seemed to be lunching on a solitary packet of cheese and onion crisps, staring into the distance with a distracted look on her face. Not even eating the crisps.

'Just had a call from the DI,' he said, moving to stand in front of her so he could catch her attention. 'Wants us to go and check out the home of . . .' he glanced down at the note he'd taken, 'Alicia Russell, director of the Booth Museum of Natural History.'

'Sure,' said Angie, her expression unchanging.

She stood up. Gavin towered over her – he was six foot three and she barely reached up to his shoulder. She crumpled up the half-empty crisp packet and dropped it into a bin as they left the canteen.

'What are we looking for?' she said eventually as they headed out of the station.

'She's missing from work and they think they've got some human body parts at the museum.'

'Hers?'

'Who knows? We've got to see if we can locate her.'

They took Gavin's car this time. Although it wasn't new, it was new to him and after a couple of years in marked cars, he was delighted with the slate-grey Audi he now got to drive around in.

'We're heading for Shoreham,' said Gavin, as he pulled out of the police car park onto Kingswood Street.

They turned left onto Grand Parade, then circled Victoria Gardens to head north. Gavin could feel Angie watching him as he negotiated changing lanes. Her gaze fell to his hands on the steering wheel, taking in the wedding ring he wore on his left ring finger.

'Is your wife pleased about your new job?' she said, as they turned onto the main road that would take them out towards Shoreham.

'Husband in fact – Harjeet.' He glanced across at her with a grin. 'I call him Harry. Yeah, he's pleased for me. He knows exactly how much I wanted this. Are you married?' He hadn't heard any mention of a husband.

'No.' She didn't expand her answer.

Gavin didn't want to pry, so he changed the subject. 'So, Francis Sullivan. I heard he's good to work for.'

She brightened up at the mention of the boss. 'He is,' said Angie. 'He's done a lot for me. Especially since ... what happened in the sewers.'

'What exactly happened?' said Gavin. The stories he'd heard about the chase for the Poison Ink Killer through Brighton's

Victorian sewer system had sounded horrendous.

She shook her head. 'I'd rather not . . . It's taking me a while to adjust back at work, and I really need to put the past behind me.'

That was fair enough. She'd lost her partner and now she was having to get used to working with someone new.

They reached Shoreham some twenty minutes later and located Alicia Russell's house. She lived in a quiet 1970s estate called Greenacres, a few streets back from where the River Adur twisted on its path down to the sea. Hers was the left-hand property of a pair of semi-detached houses, with a neat lawn and a garage. There was no car on the drive, so Gavin parked across it and they got out.

Rather than being at the front of the house, the front door was set in the left-hand wall. They walked up to it, and after confirming they had the right house number, Angie rang the bell. They waited in silence, Gavin rehearsing in his mind what he would say when Alicia Russell opened the door. No one came, so Angie rang the bell again.

'I don't think she's in,' said Gavin. 'We should check with the neighbours, when they last saw her.'

There was no one in at the adjoining house, and the woman who lived opposite her wasn't much help.

'A few days ago,' she said, with a shrug. 'Maybe at the weekend?'

'Did you talk to her?' said Angie.

'Not that one,' said the woman, looking across at Alicia's house over the rim of her glasses. 'Kept herself to herself.'

'She lives on her own, right?' said Gavin.

The woman nodded.

'Did she have a boyfriend? Anyone who came round regularly?'

The woman's face tightened into a frown. 'I'm not a curtain twitcher and I don't keep tabs on my neighbours, young man.'

'No, I wasn't suggesting you were . . .'

A telephone sounded in the woman's hall.

'I've got to go,' she said, and she pushed the door shut, effect- ively expelling Gavin from where he stood on the threshold.

They went back to Alicia Russell's house.

'Let's take a look round the back.'

'Sure.'

There was a path running down the side of the house, with a gate at the end. They skirted past a row of dustbins and Gavin tried the gate. It opened, and Angie followed him through it into a small back garden, half paved, half lawn, with a couple of shrubs along the back fence. Gavin walked across to the double patio doors at the back of the house and peered inside.

'I can't see anyone.' He rapped on the glass.

Angie came up beside him and looked in.

The ground floor was an open-plan kitchen-living room. The space was cluttered with furniture, and untidy. No, untidy wasn't quite right. Something had happened here. There was a coffee table on its side, magazines splayed out on the floor beside it. A coffee cup seemed to have rolled, or been kicked, under the sofa. On the kitchen counter, there was a broken glass.

'Does that look like blood to you, on that glass?' said Angie.

It did.

A handbag hung over the back of one of the kitchen-table chairs. On the table itself, the remnants of a meal – a plate with knife and fork akimbo, and a glass half full of water. A meal interrupted? A black cat jumped down from investigating the remnants, disturbed by Gavin's knocking. It came towards the glass door and as it got closer, they could hear its pitiful cry.

'The cat's distressed,' she said. 'No one's seen Alicia since she left work on Monday, and something clearly happened here.'

'But no sign of a break-in?'

'Someone she knew, then.'

'I'll see if I can get in,' said Gavin. 'You might want to call the RSPCA.'

'You shouldn't,' said Angie. 'We haven't got a warrant.'

'Come on,' said Gavin, 'we're saving the bloody cat. And she might still be in there.' He tried the patio doors. 'It's not even locked,' he said, sliding open one of the doors. 'That's strange.'

The cat rushed towards them and snaked around Gavin's legs as he stepped inside.

Angie went straight to the kitchen area. There were two cat bowls on the floor, both empty, one overturned. She quickly filled one with water at the sink, then put it down. The cat ran over and drank greedily.

'Looks like she's been alone here for a couple of days,' she said.

Gavin was inspecting the glass on the counter. 'It definitely looks like blood. And it's dried. Whatever happened, it was a day or two ago.'

Angie pulled a pair of latex gloves out of her pocket and put them on. Then she took the handbag off the back of the chair and put it on the table.

'Mobile phone, purse, keys,' she said, pulling items out of the bag and placing them on the table. 'Where would she go for a day or more without taking her bag?'

'She wouldn't. Come on, let's check the rest of the house.'

There was no sign of Alicia Russell anywhere, and the upstairs – two small bedrooms and a bathroom – looked undisturbed, apart from a rank smell of cat's urine in the master bedroom.

'Something's not right about this,' said Angie, as they came back into the kitchen. 'She's been taken, hasn't she?'

Gavin was looking in the cupboard under the sink.

'What are you looking for?'

'Cat food.'

Angie nodded. 'I'll call the RSPCA. But first I'm going to call the CSIs. Alicia Russell is missing – which makes this a crime scene.'

6

Wednesday, 1 November 2017

Marni

Marni scrambled out of the car. For one horrible moment she'd thought Francis Sullivan was going to try to kiss her. But when he didn't, she decided it wouldn't have been horrible at all – and she leant towards him, her intention clear.

Their lips met. Kissing Francis was just as she remembered it. It wasn't a long kiss, but it was good. They broke away from each other, then neither of them knew quite what to say. So she scrambled out.

'Bye,' she said, slamming the car door. 'Thanks.'

For what? For spending an hour with her in the pub while Thierry retrieved the last of his bags? How fucked-up was that? She approached the house with some trepidation, desperately hoping Thierry would be gone.

Francis wound down the window and leaned across to speak to her.

'Dinner, maybe? Next week?'

She stopped and turned back to him, taking a deep breath. 'I don't know . . . Sorry, Frank, I'm not sure this is the right thing for me . . .'

Go away – was what she wanted to say. Bloody men.

She'd made him drop her at the corner – she didn't need Thierry or the neighbours to see her being delivered home by

Francis Sullivan. It was almost dark as she walked slowly down the street, thinking about the kiss. Did she want more than that? Did she want Frank Sullivan? They'd had something going on the previous year, after she'd helped him identify the Tattoo Thief, but it had fizzled out. Then Thierry had come back on the scene and things were good with him. For a bit.

'Fuck,' she said out loud, startling a piebald cat in one of her neighbour's front gardens. She simply didn't know what she wanted. Not Thierry, though. That had replayed itself like a broken record.

Because her side of the road was in deep shadow, she didn't see that the front door was open until she was nearly upon the house.

Damn the man!

'Thierry?' she called, stepping inside.

As she slipped off her leather jacket, she heard a thud and a masculine grunt from the kitchen. The door was shut. So was the door to the living room and she heard Pepper launching himself at it, and barking, on the other side.

'Alex, is that you? What's going on?' she called, hanging her jacket on its hook.

'Marni . . .'

It wasn't Alex's voice. It was Thierry. But it didn't sound right. At the same moment, she saw that Thierry's cases were still lined up in the hall. Why hadn't he taken them by now?

'Marni, get out!' There was a note of desperation.

She hurried to the door and pushed it open.

The scene that unfolded before her made her heart stop.

In the dark kitchen, two men struggled on the floor.

She knew them both. She knew them both far too well. But in the darkness, she couldn't work out which twin was which.

A metal blade flashed, and fear struck like lightning.

It was happening again. Her past crashing forward into her

present. But this wasn't the past. This was here and now, in her kitchen.

Paul. Thierry. One of them had a knife.

She screamed. 'Thierry, get away from him!'

She stood paralysed as they writhed on the floor in front of her. They were both grunting, arms and legs thrashing as each struggled to overpower the other. The hand holding the knife moved in a steep arc, only to be stopped by another hand catching it by the wrist. The knife clattered to the floor.

Marni lunged for it but a dark fist snaked out of the melee and grabbed it.

'Thierry?'

'Get out!'

She wasn't going to leave him.

Another grunt. Whoever had been on top a second ago was now underneath. Then they flipped again. Which was Paul? Which was Thierry? She lunged for the light switch, but stumbled on one of their ankles. She heard a gasp, followed by a long moan. Blood spattered across her legs and her hand, hot and heavy. The men stopped moving and she could smell the ferrous taint of fresh gore. The floor was slick as she went towards them, a black pool spreading over the tiles.

One man was alive. One man was dead.

And in the dark, Marni couldn't tell which.

7

Thursday, 2 November 2017

Francis

The house that Francis Sullivan called home didn't belong to him. It was his father's house. But Adrian Sullivan had chosen a new life in Thailand ten years ago, and now he had a second wife and a young son, leaving the ornate Tudor Gothic house abandoned like his family. Standing in a terrace on Wykeham Place, on the hillside below St Catherine's Church, it had once been a refuge for former prostitutes, the irony of which wasn't lost on Francis. Now, however, it was the spacious family home where he had spent alternate weekends through his teenage years, and which he'd moved into on his return to Brighton.

'You up yet?' he called, as he scooped ground coffee into the machine.

He was talking to his sister Robin who, after years of struggling with MS in a flat on her own, had finally taken up Francis's offer to move in with him. She'd been there for three days – her presence in the house still a novelty for both of them.

'Just about,' came her voice from the hall. She pushed open the door and came in, still in her dressing gown and using a stick to help her walk.

'Off to work?' she said, dropping heavily onto one of the kitchen chairs.

'In a minute. Coffee?' It was good to have some company

31

he supposed, but she'd already made her mark. Nothing in the kitchen was as he'd left it and his reassuring drift of post, bills, takeaway menus and newspapers that usually spread from the worktops to the kitchen table was gone. There was a vase of flowers on the table and a bowl of fruit on the counter.

'Please.'

He put a cup down on the table in front of her. 'But no more tidying, Robin.'

Robin grimaced, biting on her top lip. 'It was a mess, Fran.' She shrugged. 'At least there are flat surfaces now to put things down on.'

It felt uncharitable to wish he'd never suggested the move, but it was his house. He took a breath, about to speak, and then remembered that it wasn't, and that Robin had just as much right to live here as he did. And after the events of the previous summer, she needed his support – not least to help mend a broken heart and the crippling shame she felt over her involvement with a man who had turned out to be the Poison Ink Killer.

His phone vibrated in his pocket.

'Rory?'

'Boss.'

There was an ominous pause. Francis turned his back on Robin and waited for Rory to continue.

'Yes?' he prompted.

'There's something you should know.'

'Spit it out, sergeant.'

'Marni Mullins is being held on suspicion of murder.'

'What the actual . . . ?'

As the words tumbled into his ear, Francis gripped the edge of the granite counter, attempting to anchor himself in the reality of a moment ago.

'What? Who did she . . . ? I'm coming right now.'

He heard Robin put down her cup as he bent forward to lean on the worktop for support.

Ten minutes later, Francis was intercepted by Rory in the corridor of the station's custody suite. It wasn't his intention to talk to Rory first – he wanted to get to Marni as quickly as possible. But his deputy effectively blocked him from going further. His expression was grim.

'Hold up, boss. Let me tell you what happened first.'

'Who is she supposed to have murdered?' said Francis. He couldn't keep the disbelief out of his voice.

'Thierry.'

Francis stumbled back against the wall.

'No. No way.'

'Stabbed him, in the kitchen at Great College Street.'

'No.' Francis shook his head adamantly. 'She wouldn't have . . . She loved Thierry.'

'When did that ever stop anyone?' said Rory. 'You need to sit down.'

Francis ignored him. 'I want to see her.'

'Let me give you the facts first.'

Rory led him into one of the interview rooms and closed the door.

'When did it happen?' said Francis. 'Who brought her in?'

'Early yesterday evening.'

'She was with me.'

'For God's sake, boss. She was found by a neighbour, cradling Thierry's body, with a bloody knife in her hand.'

'It wasn't her.'

'She said, and I quote, "What have I done? What have I done?" and she had his blood all over her clothes. You can't give her an alibi. She was there, at the scene of the crime.'

Francis's head spun and he clapped his hands to his face.

'Thierry's dead?'

'Yes.'

'I was with her, Rory. I dropped her off at her house, no, at the corner of the street, at just after seven.'

'Angie took the call at seven thirty, brought her in under suspicion.'

Francis shook his head in disbelief. 'She took that decision fast.'

Rory drew himself up to his full height, though he was still several inches shorter than his boss.

'She made the right decision in the circumstances,' he said firmly.

'That'll be for the CPS to determine. If it comes to that.' He glared at his subordinate. 'Which it won't.'

Rory lowered his brow. 'Mullins was found with the body and holding the murder weapon. Her hands and clothes were covered in his blood. There was no one else at the scene.'

'What does she say about it?'

'She hasn't been interviewed yet.'

'No one's seen her yet? For fuck's sake, Rory. I'll go talk to her.'

He left the interview room and went along the corridor to the row of rooms where they held individuals after arrest. Rory followed him.

'Which room?'

The heavy doors had small reinforced glass panels. Francis peered through each one as he went past. Most of them were empty, but there were a couple of young men lying on the flat, hard beds that were the only furnishings. Finally, he came to the cell in which Marni languished.

He stared in through the glass. She was lying face down on the floor, her head rested on her folded arms, not moving. He could see dried blood on her hands. Her hair was a tangled mess, her clothes were rumpled, and she seemed to be missing a shoe.

'Marni!' he gasped, trying the door handle. Of course, the room was locked. 'Get this door open, sergeant.'

He banged on the door to attract her attention, but she didn't move. 'Marni!'

'I don't think so, boss,' said Rory, placing a hand on Francis's arm. 'If you were the last person to see her before it happened, you're an important witness in the case. There's no way you can talk to her.'

'She needs to see a doctor,' said Francis.

'She's been seen by the duty doctor,' said Rory. 'She came in in a state of shock. She's been sedated, which is why no one's interviewed her yet.'

'What about her meds? You know she's diabetic?'

Rory shook his head. 'No.'

As Francis turned to face him, the custody sergeant on duty hurried towards them.

'Open this door,' said Francis. 'Help her onto the bed, and get her some water.'

'Yes, sir.'

Francis addressed Rory. 'Get the doctor back here. Tell him she's Type 1 diabetic – she uses insulin. He'll need to check her blood.'

Rory glanced at the custody sergeant, who was fiddling with his keys in the lock. 'Just get the doctor, sergeant,' he said. Then he pushed Francis back hard against the wall.

'You can't be on this case, boss. You can't speak to her. Got that?'

'Damn you,' said Francis, pushing Rory out of his way. But he knew Rory was right, and he turned up the corridor towards the exit of the custody suite.

'Stay away from her or I'll take it to the chief.'

Rory Mackay. He might be right about the propriety of Francis getting involved, but it also proved one thing – he was still Bradshaw's boy.

'I'll keep you posted,' the sergeant called after him.

'Too right you will.'

What the hell had happened after he'd dropped Marni off?

35

8

Thursday, 2 November 2017

Marni

The thin prison mattress on the concrete base offered no comfort, the threadbare blanket no warmth. Although she was avoiding sleep, Marni kept her eyes tightly closed. She'd dreamt she was back in a police cell. She'd dreamt she'd been arrested. She'd dreamt there'd been blood on her hands. And she wouldn't open her eyes, just in case it wasn't a dream.

Thierry was dead.

She sat bolt upright.

'No.'

The pain of realisation ripped through her. Thierry was dead. Images – memories – flashed in front of her eyes. Thierry's blood on the floor. The back door slamming shut as Paul ran out. That awful woman cop who she hated. A bearded policeman dragging her away from Thierry's body. Blue lights flashing on the short drive to the police station.

'No. No.' She shook her head frantically, as if vehement denial could reverse what had happened. It hadn't happened. It couldn't have. Those were false memories. She was still dreaming. She'd wake up in a minute.

But she didn't.

Her mind joined up the images into a coherent narrative and her world disintegrated around her.

The door to her cell opened and she looked up.

'Francis!'

'Shhhh, I'm not supposed to be in here.'

That didn't make sense. She stood up to go to him, but he took a step back from her.

'What happened, Marni?'

'It was Paul.'

'What do you mean?'

'Paul was there, in the kitchen, when you dropped me off. They were fighting.'

'But you said Paul was dead, didn't you?'

Marni shook her head. 'No. Thierry thought he was dead. Thierry thought he'd killed himself. But I never believed that. And I was right.'

'Why did he come back?'

'He's obsessed with me, I think.'

'Still? Even after all that's happened?' Francis appeared to doubt what she was saying.

'He couldn't get over the idea of having a family. Me and Alex. He was always jealous of anything Thierry had, ever since they were children – and it got worse as they got older.'

Francis stared at her, an incredulous look on his face. 'But Alex is, what, twenty now? That boat has long sailed.'

'You have to believe me, Frank. I didn't do it.'

'I want to believe you.'

But he evidently didn't. And if Francis Sullivan didn't believe her, who the hell would? She dropped down onto the bed, her head in her hands, overcome once more with the enormity of what had happened. Thierry was dead. It didn't matter what happened next. But then a thought struck her.

'Francis, does Alex know?'

Francis shrugged. 'Would he have been back to the house?'

'He's staying at his cousin Liv's at the moment.' She stood up again. 'You have to get me out of here. I need to go to him.'

'I can't get you out. A family liaison officer will visit him, and tell him what's happened.'

'A stranger, for God's sake? His father's dead. You're in charge around here, aren't you?'

Francis took hold of both her hands. 'Okay, Marni – I'll go and talk to Alex, but I can't have anything to do with this case. I dropped you off just before . . . it happened.' He paused awkwardly as if he didn't know how to refer to it. 'That makes me a witness.'

'You mean you won't help me?'

'I'll do what I can, but my hands are tied.'

Marni pulled away from him. 'No, it's my hands that are tied. Now why don't you fuck off? And don't come back till you're on my side.'

She turned her back on him. He didn't believe her. He thought she'd done it. And now he was going to let her rot in a police cell, while her son had to cope with his father's death on his own.

She'd thought Sullivan was one of the good guys. It was funny how wrong you could be about people.

9

Thursday, 2 November 2017

Rose

Rose was beginning to wish she hadn't taken the call.

'Do me a favour, Rose,' Sullivan had said. 'You're the assigned pathologist for Thierry Mullins's murder, right?'

'Yes.'

'When you go to the house, will you take a look round for me? Marni didn't do it. There was someone else there, and I need somebody I can rely on working the scene.'

This was wrong on so many levels. For a start, this wasn't Sullivan's case. Furthermore, nothing had been found so far to suggest that Marni Mullins wasn't guilty, whereas there was a lot suggesting that she probably was. Policing wasn't about searching for the evidence you needed to fit your hypothesis. Quite the opposite. And she knew how he felt about Marni.

So why did she now find herself in her car, driving towards Great College Street, working out how to do what he asked? Because she had a soft spot for the man – and she was stupid. After all, it wasn't as if she had time to spare – not with a potentially mummified corpse waiting for attention in the morgue. She'd have to work as quickly as she could.

The scene-of-crime officers were already hard at work by the time Rose arrived. She'd been held up doing the post-mortem of a drunk driver who'd wrapped his car around a tree in the early hours of the morning up on the South Downs. Of course, they knew the cause of death, but she still needed to catalogue the internal injuries he'd sustained and record his blood alcohol level. As soon as he was safely back in his refrigerated drawer, she'd driven down to Kemptown.

The Mullins family lived about halfway along Great College Street in a small terraced house with a yellow front door and a bay window. Rose recognised the white CSI van parked outside, and a constable was standing watch at the open door. Rose showed her ID and went inside with her bag of kit. She was already wearing a white paper scene-of-crime suit, but on the front step she slipped shoe covers over her trainers so she wouldn't tread dirt into the house.

She knew from Francis that the kitchen was the scene of the crime, but she could see that the investigators had been busy taking prints from the front door, the living-room door and all the way down the hall. Here, they'd laid down metal stepping plates to protect the integrity of the floor. They would have photographed everything and taken samples from the blood spatter and stains around the kitchen. She was here in her official capacity to examine Thierry's body and organise its removal to the morgue. Unofficially, as Francis's spy.

She'd never been to Marni's house before, but the kitchen spoke to her of the woman she knew. There were watercolour versions of Marni's signature chrysanthemum tattoos hanging on the wall, a battered, kilim-covered armchair in one corner, empty wine bottles on the kitchen counter and a half-smoked spliff in an ashtray on the island unit. But these were fleeting impressions. Rose's attention was immediately snagged by a body, lying in the centre of the floor between the door and the kitchen island. She recognised him immediately – it was Marni's ex-husband, Thierry Mullins, who she'd met on a couple of occasions during the Tattoo Thief case.

She got out her camera and started taking pictures. The crime-scene team would already have done this, but she wanted her own record, from every conceivable angle. Thierry was lying flat on his back, his legs bent awkwardly to one side. Rose had read the arrest report and she knew the body would be just as it settled when Gavin and Angie had pulled Marni away from it. From him. His eyes were closed and his face looked at peace, but that wasn't a true reflection of how he must have been feeling when he died. Muscles changed after death – first they relaxed, then contracted with the progression of rigor, then relaxed again as the muscle tissue began to decompose – that included the facial muscles, which is why some corpses looked like they were gurning and others looked terror-struck.

She measured the body temperature and checked the rest of the muscle groups for rigor, but she already had a good idea of the time of death from the time of Marni's arrest. The first paramedics on the scene, called by one of the neighbours, confirmed that he had literally died just a few minutes before their arrival. She pulled up Thierry's blood-soaked T-shirt to expose the stab wound in his chest. She probed it with a sterile spatula to estimate the depth of the wound and its angle. The single puncture was deep enough to kill him, the blade passing cleanly between two of his ribs to pierce his heart. A fraction higher or lower and the tip of the knife would have hit bone, and Thierry might well have survived the attack. It had travelled into him at a downward angle, which suggested to Rose that his attacker was possibly his height or taller. But it didn't necessarily prove that. Thierry could have been bent, seated, kneeling or even lying down when the blade went in, or a short person could have simply struck with a raised arm.

The trajectory of the wound further suggested that the killer had been right-handed. She didn't know if Marni was right- or left-handed.

After looking at the wound, Rose turned her attention to Thierry's hands to see if there was any evidence of trauma. Had he fought back? Were there traces of his killer's skin or DNA under his fingernails? His right knuckles showed signs of fresh abrasion, so he hadn't gone down without a fight. Rose would need to alert the investigative team to check whether Marni had any corresponding bruising. She slipped paper evidence bags over each hand and secured them with tape around his wrists. She would inspect underneath his nails once she was back at the morgue.

Rubbing her back, Rose stood up and looked around the kitchen floor at the pattern of the bloodstains. Around Thierry's body it was a mess. He'd bled heavily from the moment he'd been stabbed and someone – himself or maybe Marni – had pulled the knife out of the wound while he was still alive, causing even greater blood loss. She'd been careful to look at him without treading in any of the spilt blood, but a range of footprints tracking from it to the door and even into the hall suggested that others hadn't been. The paramedics for certain, and no doubt Gavin and Angie hadn't been able to avoid treading in his blood when they'd taken Marni into custody. The CSIs would have close-up photos of all the footprints and would be eliminating them by comparing them to the footwear of everyone present.

Rose watched the two officers working. One was dusting the back door-handle for prints, while the other was retrieving DNA evidence from a number of wine glasses. They were both wearing masks, so it was difficult to tell which was which.

'Ken?' she said.

'Yes,' said the man by the back door.

She went over to him, skirting around the smudges of dried blood.

'Anything I should know about?'

42

He finished dusting the area he was working on, then lowered his face mask.

'Yes.'

He stepped away from the door and across to an area of floor close to Thierry's body.

'Look here,' he said. Rose looked to where he was pointing. 'See that?' He was indicating a tiny smudge amid a row of three splashes of blood. Rose bent down and examined it. There was a straight line of red, about an inch long, with a shorter line jutting out at right-angles to one side. 'It's a partial footprint.'

Rose nodded. 'You could be right.'

'So far it doesn't seem to match any of the other prints in here and we've accounted for all the feet that were on the ground.'

'So there was someone else here after he died?'

'After, or as he died.'

Was this what Francis had hoped she'd find?

'Does it repeat anywhere?' said Rose, glancing around to look for another print.

'Yes. He or she walked in this direction,' said Ken, pointing towards the rear of the kitchen. 'There's a faint imprint of it here, and then another small mark just there.'

'Heading towards the back door? You been outside yet?'

Ken shook his head and Rose looked out at the Mullins's garden. It was a tiny postage stamp of grass, bordered by narrow flower beds in which someone had planted a few scrubby bushes. Low walls separated it from the gardens on either side. Could someone have got away out here?

Rose went outside, examining the back step and the small patio for traces of blood.

Ken stuck his head out of the door. 'We'll get to it, don't worry.'

The body was her remit, not investigating the scene. That was clearly his inference.

Rose ignored him and continued to look around. There was

nothing. But a plant stalk in the right-hand bed had been recently snapped and there was a scuff mark in the dirt that clung to the lower part of the wall. Rose peered over into the next-door property. This garden had been paved over, so there was nothing to indicate whether someone had jumped over and run through it.

Rose pulled her mask off her face and clambered over the wall. She looked around nervously. Technically, she was trespassing, but the house seemed quiet. Its occupants were probably at work. She looked back towards the Mullins house. Ken had disappeared back inside. She climbed over the next wall and the one after that. The final house had been extended at the back and there was just a narrow pathway between it and the property it backed on to. She squeezed through the gap and opened the gate at the end. She came out and found herself in a small private car park, the entrance of which brought her onto Abbey Road.

Had whoever left the partial footprint in Thierry's blood come this way to escape the scene? Was that person the killer? She turned left into Abbey Road, then left again to go back along Great College Street to the front of the house.

Could Francis actually be right about Marni's innocence?

10

Thursday, 2 November 2017

Alex

Francis Sullivan was the last person in the world Alex expected to hear from. He hated the man and he thought the feeling was mutual. But now this cryptic message from him. His mother was at the police station and he needed to go there. No explanation. No reason why. He listened to it a second time. There was something weird about the DI's voice.

He tried his mother's phone but there was no answer. After a couple of attempts, he tried his father, but Thierry wasn't picking up. The police station was a good fifteen-minute walk from the flat he shared with his cousin Liv and by the time he reached John Street it was already dark. He pulled open the door to the main entrance with a horrible feeling of foreboding. Nothing good ever happened in this building. Why had the message come from Francis Sullivan and why hadn't his mother called him herself? He was scared of what he was about to discover.

The desk sergeant was busy – he was on the phone and there were two people waiting impatiently at the counter. Alex hung back and then sat down on a grey metal seat that was screwed to the floor. His leg jittered compulsively, even when he rested his folded arms across it. What did Sullivan want?

The sergeant's call was interminable. One of the men waiting for him gave up and went towards the door, giving Alex a sympathetic look.

'They don't give a shit,' he muttered as he left the building.

Alex pulled out his phone and wondered whether to call Sullivan. It would save him hanging around here for hours. He dreaded what he would hear but he couldn't stand the waiting.

'Hello, DI Sullivan? It's Alex Mullins.'

He didn't have to wait. Within three minutes, Francis Sullivan was ushering him into an empty interview room.

'What's going on?'

'Sit down, Alex.' The inspector's face was grave.

Alex shook his head and remained standing. 'Where's my mother?'

'You need to sit down,' said Sullivan, his tone firm.

They stood staring at each other until Alex bad-temperedly pulled out a chair and plonked himself down in it.

'Okay. I'm sitting.'

Francis Sullivan pulled out the chair opposite him and sat down too.

'Alex, when did you last see your mother?'

'A couple of days ago. I dropped into her studio.'

'And your father?'

'What is this?' Why didn't he get to the bloody point? 'Where's my mother?'

Francis took a deep breath.

'I'm afraid she's being held in the custody suite.' He looked pale and there was a tremor in his voice.

'Why? What's the charge?'

Alex had never seen a police officer look so sick. The short pause before Sullivan spoke dragged into something longer. Finally he summoned up the courage to speak.

'She's been arrested on a charge of murdering your father. I'm sorry, Alex – your father is dead.'

The words were out. The box was open.

Alex couldn't unhear them. But nor could he digest them.

'No.' He shook his head. 'No. No. You're wrong. That can't be right.' His father dead? His world imploded. He felt dizzy but he stood up, staggering against the hard edge of the table. 'She didn't. She couldn't have.'

Francis was instantly on the same side of the table as him, taking him by the arm and trying to make him sit again.

'Get off me. I need to go to her.'

'Alex, wait. Please.'

They were struggling now, as Francis gripped both of his upper arms.

'Let me go.'

'Alex, sit down.'

Alex felt himself being pushed back down into the chair and he couldn't find the strength to resist. He kicked back with one of his legs and the chair toppled over and skittered across the floor. But the momentum of their two bodies was unstoppable. Alex sprawled backwards, landing against one of the table legs and sliding down it. Francis lost his balance and came down heavily on top of him.

They rolled apart, both panting, then Alex started to cry.

His father was dead.

Francis clambered to his knees, put an arm around Alex's shoulders and pulled him in against his chest.

'I'm so sorry, Alex.'

Alex fought for breath. There was a sharp pain in his chest, and he gasped like a fish floundering on the deck of a boat. Black dots crept into his peripheral vision. What was he doing here? The room spun and as he finally caught his breath, he heard himself calling for his mother …

The floor was cold against his cheek. He opened his eyes and the

47

room was side on. He heard footsteps and Francis Sullivan came into view. He had a paper cup in his hand, which he put down on the floor nearby.

'Take a couple of deep breaths.' Francis helped him to sit up, then offered the cup. 'Drink some water. When you feel better, we'll go and see your mother.'

'You know she didn't do it, don't you?' said Alex.

'Nobody knows anything yet. Two of my officers were called to her house and found her cradling your father's body.'

The enormity of his father being dead hit him again, and he coughed as the water went down the wrong way. He felt like he was choking.

Francis held him while he fought for control, taking the cup from his hand, and patting him on the back.

'No,' said Alex. 'I can't believe that.'

'I need you to talk to her,' said Francis. 'She was in shock and said some foolish things at the scene, which was why she was brought in.'

'What d'you mean?'

Sullivan shook his head. 'She'll tell you what happened. Then you tell me.'

Alex whipped his head round to look Francis in the eye.

'I'm not going to help you build a case against my mother.'

'Jesus, Alex. That's the last thing I want to do – and I'm not even working the case. But if she's innocent, I'll do everything in my power to prove it. Surely you know that?'

Alex had never trusted Francis Sullivan and had been deeply suspicious of his mother's relationship with the policeman. It was Sullivan's fault that he'd nearly drowned in Brighton's sewers, and the DI had tried to pin one of his unsolved murders on a member of the Mullins family once before. Why should this time be any different?

'I'll talk to her alone,' said Alex.

Francis helped him to his feet.

'Are you okay now?'

Alex stared at him. He'd just heard that his father was dead. His mother was accused of murder. He was anything but okay. He didn't answer.

'Come on,' said Francis.

They went down to the custody suite and the sergeant on duty led them along the corridor to where his mother was being held. Glancing into the empty cells they passed brought a rush of memories. He'd been held here himself, more than once, and he hated the thought of his mother being caged in here. He made a mental note to call Jayne Douglas, the family lawyer, as soon as he left the station.

'Has she seen a lawyer yet?'

The sergeant stopped by one of the doors and peered through the rectangle of glass.

'Not yet,' said Francis. 'She's spoken to no one. She was brought in last night and she's due to be interviewed shortly. She needs to get her story straight, and I thought you should be the first person she sees.'

Alex wondered whether this was a cynical ploy to get his mother to talk, or whether it was genuinely a sign that Francis Sullivan cared for his mother. He suspected the former.

Francis stepped back to let Alex go in first.

'Mum?'

His mother was sitting on the bed, slumped awkwardly against the wall. She half opened her eyes when Alex spoke. Her skin looked grey and dirty, and patches of dried blood had turned brown on her clothes.

'Mum.' Alex rushed over to her, knelt in front of her, and pulled her into a tight embrace.

Francis and the custody sergeant crowded into the tiny room.

'Marni, how are you?' said Francis.

Marni pressed her face into Alex's shoulder without answering.

Alex looked around. 'Can we have some time alone?'

'Sure.' Francis bundled the other policeman outside and closed the door.

'Mum? What happened? Is Dad really dead?' Alex was struggling to keep a grip of himself, but he needed to stay strong for her.

Marni said nothing, but just clung to him, her shoulders shaking and her sobs muffled by the padded down jacket he was wearing. He stroked her back but she showed no sign of stopping crying. Minutes passed. Tears rolled down Alex's cheeks and he bit down hard on his lower lip. He was desperate to know what had happened but she remained silent.

He extricated himself from the hug and took both her hands in his. She wouldn't look at him.

'Tell me, Mum,' he said.

'Paul did it,' she said.

'Paul?'

'I came back to the house and he was there, fighting with your father in the kitchen.'

'What was Dad doing there?'

'He came by to collect his stuff. I wanted him out of the house.' She began to cry again. 'But if he hadn't come for it just then, he wouldn't have run into Paul. He'd still be alive.'

The door opened and Francis Sullivan came in. Alex looked round at him, willing him to go away. Marni pulled away from him, glaring at the DI.

Alex stood up and turned to speak to him.

'Anything?' said Francis.

'Yes.' Alex got up and they both went outside into the corridor. 'She said Paul did it – my father's twin. So how is it that she's ended up in a cell and Paul's nowhere to be seen?'

Francis took a deep breath. 'The duty sergeant took a call from one of your mum's neighbours. She'd heard screams and the sounds of a fight coming from the house. We sent a fast response car and the PC found your mother sitting on the kitchen floor, with Thierry in her arms. He was already dead, from a knife wound to the chest. Marni was holding a bloody knife. It came from the knife block.'

'But what about Paul? Was he there?'

'There was no one else there, Alex. None of the neighbours have admitted to seeing a man fitting his description.'

'But he fits my dad's description, so if they saw him, they would just assume it was my dad.'

Francis shrugged.

'But you don't believe she did it?'

'I don't know what to think,' said Francis slowly. 'We won't know what happened until she's been interviewed and all the forensic evidence has been evaluated.'

'It was someone else. There must have been an intruder in the house. And if she says it was Paul, that's who it was.'

'Alex, we need more evidence than just your mother's word. You know that.'

'So what happens now?'

'She needs a lawyer. Can you give me the details of your solicitor?'

Alex nodded and pulled out his phone. 'Jayne Douglas. I'll send you her number. But I'll give her a call too.'

'Thanks.' Francis paused. 'Have you got anyone you can be with? Anyone you can call? I don't think you should be alone right now.'

'I think Liv's at home.' He had no idea, but it didn't matter. He needed to be alone, whatever Francis Sullivan thought. His father was dead.

'And I'm sorry, Alex – I'm going to need you to come to the morgue for a formal identification of your father's body. Can you let me know when you feel ready to do that?'

Alex turned on his heel and left the station.

He would never be ready for that.

II

The Embalmer

Ca·no·pic jar | \ kə-ˈnō-pik- : a jar in which the ancient
Egyptians preserved the viscera of a deceased person usually
for burial with the mummy.

*Like any worthy achievement, immortality requires sacrifices to be
made. Human sacrifices. The first had involved the long and complex
process of mummification, but the man can't wait another forty days
before announcing his second victim. He needs to send a message to
the world – and to one man in particular.*

*He feels the weight of the Canopic jar in his hands. The curved
surface is smooth enough. It had taken several attempts to get the
shape just right – slightly bulbous at the top and then narrowing a
little towards the opening. He'd used a potter's wheel for the base of
the jar. He puts it down, then picks up the lid of the jar to examine
it. The head of Duamutef, one of the four sons of Horus. This was the
jackal-headed god of the East. One son for each compass point. One
son for each jar. He'd modelled the four heads out of clay, and once
they'd been fired, he'd painted them, carefully matching the colours to
pictures of the real things.*

*The Duamutef jar was always used to store the deceased's stomach.
He sprinkles a layer of natron into the bottom of the jar.*

The woman is watching him, straining against the ropes that

52

secure her to the chair. She's been useful to him so far, and she'll be even more useful to him presently. In death. He can smell her fear – rank sweat and urine. Three days in the same clothes. He doesn't mind the smell. He hisses at her. Her head thrashes from side to side.

But before he starts the ritual he needs to pray.

Then he'll write his missive.

And after that, he'll be ready to make the sacrifice.

The wind at the top of the cliff cuts through him like a knife as he gathers what he'll need from the back seat of the car. It's her car, a red Golf. It's a few years old and it hasn't been cleaned often enough. The dirt seems ingrained into the paintwork, the windows so dusty that it's hard to see in – apart from the two semi-circles on the windscreen made by the wipers. He's parked it at the top end of the dirt track that leads up to the cliffs. Out of the way, where nobody comes. There are tall hedges on either side of the track, the only view a strip of slate sky between them.

The interior of the car is a mess – chocolate wrappers, water bottles, takeaway coffee cups clutter the passenger footwell. A newspaper and a raincoat on the back seat. On the floor, a pair of high heels, kicked over and half under the seat in front. There's a cardboard pine tree hanging from the rearview mirror, but it's so old that it does nothing to mask the smell inside the car.

The smell of a woman approaching death.

She's curled in a foetal position in the boot, still tied at the wrists, ankles and knees with lengths of steel-core PVC washing line. It's blue, and couldn't be more mundane. The knots are large and clumsily tied, but it makes no difference. She can't reach them. The dark skirt suit and white blouse she's wearing are crumpled and soiled. Her hair's tangled and snagged on the coarse nylon carpet that lines the boot.

He opens the hatchback and stares down at her.

This woman did wrong by him. She chose another over him when

53

he would have been perfect. He offered all that she needed. He bends down, bringing his face close to hers, remembering how it felt. The sense of rejection. Again. A familiar feeling that, after this, he'll never have to experience again.

His muscles tense as his anticipation turns to anger.

He thinks about how he's been able to make use of her. He thinks about the terror in her eyes when she realised it was him who had stepped silently into her kitchen. How she must have regretted being careless with the lock. She was pliable, begging for mercy, begging for forgiveness and doing everything he asked. Giving him the keys without needing to be asked twice. Had she thought that he'd let her live if she was compliant? If she made herself useful?

A bird flies across the strip of sky between the hedges. Its cry pierces the air like a whistle. He steps back from the car and looks up at it. It's a guillemot and he smiles. He makes his hand into the shape of a gun and points it at the bird. 'Pop!' The bird wheels higher and disappears from view. The man's not in a hurry, so he walks beyond the car and further up the track. As it crests the gentle incline, the hedges give way to open ground and he can see the sea – and other birds in the distance. Gulls, terns, another guillemot. Or perhaps it's the same one.

He walks to the edge of the land and looks down. The quickest way to kill her would be to push the car over the edge. The car would drop a hundred feet to shatter on the stony beach. The woman's body would be pulverised in the wreckage. Smashed like a watermelon dropped from a window.

But that isn't part of the ritual.

He walks back towards the car. He lifts the woman from the boot and drags her, struggling, to a level area at the edge of the cliff. He ties her wrists and ankles to four small wooden stakes so she's spread-eagled on the grass. He cuts her crumpled clothes away, carefully, carefully – he doesn't want to cut her by accident. He places the Canopic jar beside her. The bag of natron. The block of wax with which he'll seal the jar, once it's done.

54

He blindfolds her. Her eyes have been darting this way and that like a frightened horse's, and he doesn't want to see them any more.

He wonders if it will be painful. On balance, he thinks it will be. He wonders what thoughts will go through her head in those final few moments. Will she see a white light coming towards her or will she just see blood? Will she see at all?

He calls upon his god, Apophis, the Great Serpent, to guide his hand. He takes a deep breath and picks up his knife.

He will secure his future by stealing hers.

12

Friday, 3 November 2017

Francis

Francis shifted on his chair but it made no difference – the pain was excruciating. Heartburn and black coffee weren't a good mix. Thankfully, a call from Rose served as a distraction.

'Got something?'

'I've X-rayed the mummy.'

'And?'

'You'd better get down here.'

In typical Rose fashion she disconnected without telling him more – but it was obvious enough. He took a last, unenthusiastic bite of his sandwich and called Rory.

'Meet me in the car park in five. There's a body in the Booth Museum mummy.'

They drove the ten minutes up to the mortuary in silence. There was a hangover of tension from a sharp exchange when Rory had arrived in the office. Frustrated that Marni Mullins had refused to answer his questions when he interviewed her, he had accused Francis of meddling in the case. Francis didn't care to be lectured by his subordinate and had given Rory some unsolicited advice on how he ought to be running the investigation. It hadn't gone down well.

Francis considered strategies for keeping an inside track on the case as he waited for the lights to change on

Gloucester Place. He owed it to Marni to do what he could to help her.

Rose was waiting impatiently, and by the time they walked in, she had the mummy laid out on one of the stainless-steel cutting tables, ready for investigation. They hurriedly pulled on white lab coats, grabbed masks and went over to her.

'Let me show you the X-rays first,' she said.

She directed their attention to a set of X-ray films pinned up on a lightbox attached to the wall nearby. The first was of the mummy's head and thoracic region. Francis could quite clearly see a skull and vertebrae, and further down the clavicles, scapulae and breast bone of a human skeleton. A number of other slides showed the rest of the skeleton.

'Look here,' said Rose, pointing to a dense area in the centre of the skull, 'there's some obvious damage to the cribriform.'

'The what?' said Rory, peering hard at the image.

'It's the plate of bone that separates the brain from the nasal cavity. The ancient Egyptians would break through it to remove the brain.'

'You think this a genuine Egyptian mummy?' said Francis.

'Not at all. But on the evidence of the Canopic jars, I assume the body's been mummified in the traditional manner, in which case I would expect to see just this sort of damage.'

Rory let out a low whistle.

'What else can you see?' said Francis. 'Is it a man or a woman? And anything that suggests how they died?'

'I can't be sure, but I think, from the size of her, this is probably a woman,' said Rose. 'We'll be able to see when we unwrap her. The X-rays don't tell us anything about the cause of death – all the other bones are intact.'

On the worktop below the X-rays, four stainless-steel trays held the four Canopic jars and their contents. Francis looked at the blackened remains, the stomach and a selection of other

57

organs, all crusted with salt. Parts of them reminded him of biltong and one bit looked like a piece of black pudding months past its sell-by date. A faint whiff of dried-out meat mingled with herbs hung in the air.

'What about these?' said Francis. 'Do they tell you anything?'

'I've sent tissue samples for testing. When the results come back, we'll know if they're a match for each other and for the body inside the mummy. I'll check the stomach contents later and look at cells under the microscope. The liver,' she pointed at the tray that had reminded Francis of black pudding, 'looks as if it was quite fatty. But with the drying-out process, it's hard to say how healthy or how old the woman was.'

They went back to where the mummy lay on the table.

Francis stared down at it. To all intents and purposes, it looked just like the Egyptian mummies he remembered from his school textbooks – the bandages were wrapped tightly and interwoven into a geometric pattern of chevrons all around the body. At the front of the head, a painting of a woman's face, Egyptian in its artistic style, was held in place by a frame formed from additional strips of linen. At intervals, there were what looked like small figurines tucked between the bands. But there was one huge difference. All the ancient Egyptian mummies Francis could remember seeing were dusty and dirty, the fabric discoloured, stained and worn in places. This mummy was new – as pristine as if it had been wrapped the previous day.

'Where do you start?' said Rory.

Rose gave a wry smile. 'No instructions included,' she said. 'But I was thinking about it last night when I couldn't sleep. I think it makes sense to simply cut right through the bandages in a straight line, starting at the feet and going up to the crown of the head.'

'You wouldn't just unwrap it the way it was wrapped up?' said Francis.

'Look,' said Rose. Using a gloved finger, she tried to loosen one of the bandages near the mummy's shoulder. She couldn't get her finger into the gap between the strips and Francis could see there was some sort of yellow waxy substance in the crack.

'What's that?'

'The Egyptians used tree resin to stick the bands in place. I won't know exactly what this is until I've had it analysed in the lab, but whatever it is, it makes unwrapping it bandage by bandage virtually impossible.'

Rory pulled on a pair of latex gloves. 'Can I?' he said.

'Be my guest,' said Rose.

Rory touched the mummy, feeling the bandages and, like Rose, trying to pry one from its neighbour. Francis did the same.

'No wonder the ancient ones stayed intact for so long,' he said. The fabric felt quite solid to the touch, making it seem that the body was encapsulated rather than simply wrapped.

Rose selected a pair of bandage scissors from her instrument tray. The sturdy blades were set at an angle to the handles, to make it easier to cut clothes off a dead body, and the bottom blade had a flattened, rounded tip to stop it piercing the skin beneath. She went to the foot of the mummy and spent a couple of minutes attempting to insert the rounded blade under one of the strips of linen. Finally, with a slight cracking sound, she managed to prise two of the bandages apart. Having tucked the lower blade into the gap, she tried to start cutting her way through the fabric.

'God, this is going to be difficult,' she said. She wrestled with the scissors for a while, using both hands and leaning right into them to apply as much pressure as possible. Red in the face, she let Rory take over. He found the material just as intractable.

Francis watched them struggle. 'What if we applied some heat?' he said. 'Would that soften the resin?'

'Good suggestion,' said Rose. 'I've got a hairdryer up in my office – let's try that.'

Rory dropped the scissors back onto the instrument tray with a sigh of relief. Rose returned a couple of minutes later with a small travel hairdryer, but it was enough to do the job. She focused the jet of hot air on the area of wrapping they'd just been trying to cut, and when Rory picked up the scissors again, this time he was able to slowly slice his way through the warm, and now tacky, strips of linen.

Rose moved the blast of heat up the body, and slowly and carefully they were able to dissect the mummy's outer shell. When they reached the painted board covering the face, they worked their way around one side of it until they were able to proceed up the centre of the forehead and over to the crown. Rose then instructed Rory on slitting the covering at each end out towards the sides. Finally, the three of them were able to fold back the layers of linen to either side to reveal an inner shroud made out of the same material.

Rose carefully placed the painted face on a metal tray on the trolley next to her. She looked down at it.

'I wonder if it's a good likeness of the woman inside,' she said.

'There's only one way to find out,' said Francis.

This time the garment scissors worked without a hitch and a minute later the three of them were looking at the shrivelled, hollow-cheeked, sunken-eyed, leathery face of what was clearly a female cadaver. There was no mistaking that this was a real human body – they knew that from the X-rays already – but it was shocking to look at the desiccated remains knowing that she'd probably been alive a short time ago.

'How long does it take to mummify a body?' said Rory.

'I read up on it last night,' said Rose. 'If you follow the method used by the Egyptians, it takes about forty days.'

'So that would give her a date of death sometime in late September?' said Francis.

Rose shrugged. 'Certainly, she's not an ancient Egyptian, but who's to know exactly when she was mummified? She could have been like this for several weeks or months, or even longer.'

'But September would be the latest she could have died?' pressed Francis.

Rose conceded his point with a nod.

'Right – that means it's not Alicia Russell. She was at work at the Booth Museum on Monday.'

'So if it's not Alicia Russell, who the hell is it?' said Rory.

'And where does that leave Russell? Rory, we need to redouble our efforts to find her. This turns up and she goes missing ... there's got to be a connection.'

'You think she might have done this?'

'I don't know what to think,' said Francis. 'It's like nothing we've ever come across.'

Rose continued to peel back the shroud from the body and what they saw next came as even more of a shock.

Every inch of the woman's skin had been tattooed in dull black ink. There were numbers, symbols, writing and hieroglyphs running every which way across her body – a flaming heart, a star, a flower, a headless chicken, a pentagram, writing, mathematical equations and tribal markings. Egyptian hieroglyphs and scarabs. Some took up large areas of skin, some were absolutely tiny. And between them all, twisted a multitude of sinuous, writhing snakes.

At Francis's gesture, Rose and Rory gently lifted the body and turned her over, to reveal even more of the same.

'What the hell does all this mean?' said Rory.

'I suspect,' said Rose, 'these are the clues you're going to have to solve if you want to find out who she is.'

'And just as importantly,' added Francis, 'who did this to her.'

Rose took a series of photos of them from every angle. Then she pointed to a long slit in the side of the body. It had been crudely stitched up, and Rose snipped through the sutures to reopen it.

'The embalmer would have removed the internal organs via this cut,' she said, 'and then packed them into the Canopic jars.'

She eased the sides of the slit gently open and shone a light inside. The cavity was filled with tiny, linen-wrapped packages. The sickly smell of myrrh and herbs mingled with a whiff of decaying flesh. It wasn't as bad as most bodies smelled, but it still had Francis wrinkling his nose.

'I'm going outside for a smoke,' announced Rory.

Francis could have done with the same, but he was desperate to catch Rose on her own. He waited for the door to close behind Rory before he spoke in a low voice.

'Rose, have you made any headway on that partial footprint at the Mullins's house yet?'

Rose looked up from the cadaver with a frown.

'Matching boot prints isn't my job, Francis. The CSIs are checking it out.'

'But have you heard anything from them?'

'No. They'll report back to Rory with whatever they find.'

'Give 'em a ring for me? See if they've got anything?'

'You're working on this off the books, aren't you?'

'Hardly. I just want to be updated with what's happening. That's all.'

Rose turned her attention back to the mummy. She clearly didn't believe him.

'You'll do it?' He knew he was pushing his luck.

'I'm not going out on a limb for you, Francis. But if I hear anything, you'll be the first to know.'

13

Friday, 3 November 2017

Alex

Alex had seen a dead body before. More than one, in fact. But did that make it any easier? And this time it would be his father. Not a stranger. The prospect of having to go through a formal identification process filled him with dread. In his mind's eye, he pictured his father's body, laid out on a slab of cold marble. But whatever he saw, he was well aware the reality would be different. Much worse than anything he could imagine.

He was sitting in the morgue car park, in the passenger seat of Liv's car. She was sitting next to him, silently waiting for him to say he was ready to go in.

How could you ever be ready for this?

Surely it shouldn't be his job? There were plenty of other people who knew Thierry. But it had to be a blood relative or spouse, didn't it? Marni was being held for his murder. The whereabouts of Paul were unknown. Which left his son.

Alex put a hand on the car door-latch.

'D'you want me to come in with you?' said Liv.

Alex didn't answer. He didn't want Liv to see him cry – and even that thought triggered a swelling in his throat and a prickling behind his eyes. He shook his head and got out of the car abruptly. Leaning against the closed passenger door, he took several deep breaths. He heard Liv's door open and the crunch of her feet on the gravel.

'Are you sure?'

He turned round to look at her over the roof of the car.

'Jesus, Liv. Leave it, would you?'

Her eyes widened. 'I'm only trying to help.'

'You can't help. My father's dead and my mother's been accused of murder. There's nothing you can do.'

'But once she explains what happened . . .'

'They won't fucking believe her. They'll just twist what she says and twist the evidence.'

'What does she say?'

'That Paul was there. My uncle.'

'But . . . didn't Thierry say he was sure that Paul was dead? He told me that because they were identical twins, he knew.'

'He was wrong.'

When Liv didn't speak, Alex smacked a fist down on the roof of the car. 'You don't believe her either, do you?'

He walked away, towards the doors of the mortuary, where he knew he was going to have to confront the painful reality of his father's death. Behind him, he heard Liv getting back into the car. He silently hoped that she wouldn't be there waiting for him when he came out.

He was shown into a small room with a glass window. On the other side of the glass, once they'd opened the heavy blue curtain, he could see his father's body lying on a hospital-style trolley, covered by a white sheet. The man who'd shown him in appeared and drew back the sheet as far as Thierry's collarbones.

Alex's breath caught sharply in his throat.

It really was his father. There had been a small flicker of hope, deep in his chest, that when they uncovered the corpse, he would see his uncle Paul lying there instead. Even if that meant his father had killed his own brother. It would have been better that way round. But now the small flame was extinguished – it was as if a gallon of icy water had been thrown over him. There was his father, dead, laid out in front of him like a piece of meat on a butcher's slab. His skin was sallow, almost grey, and his eyes were closed. But it didn't look like he was sleeping.

Then, in a torrent of hurt and anger, Alex realised he couldn't even remember when he'd last seen his father asleep, so how the hell would he know if that was what he looked like or not. He was thinking stupidly to avoid the real issue. His father was dead. If he'd been asleep, he would never have lain like that, ramrod-straight with his arms at his side. Thierry was a man who sprawled and took up space, who like to spread himself out, one leg on the coffee table or hanging over the end of the sofa, an arm crooked behind his head, pillows and cushions piled high behind him. He would never have lain flat and straight like that.

Alex was overcome with the need to give him one last hug.

When the man wouldn't let him into the room with his father's body, Alex smashed the dividing window with his fist. Shards of glass scattered across the floor. Some even landed on the white sheet covering Thierry's body. Alex's right knuckles were bleeding from half a dozen small cuts, and one larger one. He didn't care. He stood in the middle of the room, sobbing loudly, letting the blood drip to the floor and onto his shoes.

The man came running round from the other side, and the sound of breaking glass brought Rose Lewis out of her lab. He'd met her before, and he allowed her to guide him up to her office, where she removed the splinters of glass from his hand with a pair of tweezers. It hurt like hell, but not as much as not being able to properly say goodbye to his father.

He glared at her.

As she wrapped gauze and a bandage around his hand, she finally spoke.

'Francis Sullivan doesn't believe your mother did it.'

'Of course she didn't.'

'He's suggested that your uncle was at the scene – at least that's what your mother told him.'

'If that's what she said, then it's true.'

'Do you know where your uncle is?'

Alex shook his head. 'If I did, I'd go and fucking kill him.'

Rose glanced up from her work.

'Alex, if you see or hear from your uncle, for God's sake tell Francis. Don't do anything stupid.'

His eyes met hers.

'Please, Alex. I mean it.'

'Okay. Okay, I'll tell Sullivan if I see him.'

He'd always been a good liar.

14

Friday, 3 November 2017

Francis

Why was it so quiet? Francis looked up from the report he was writing and noticed that the door to his office was shut. As a general rule, he kept it open so he could lend half an ear to what was going on outside it in the incident room. He thought for a moment. Rory had come in to see him just after lunch ... and had shut the door when he went out? Francis looked at his watch. Just gone half past two on a Friday afternoon. Had Rory nipped out for a sharpener at the Mucky Duck? Surely not.

Francis rose from his desk, opened the door and stood in the doorway. The larger room was quiet, but most heads were accounted for.

'Where's Rory?' he said, looking towards Angie, who was typing frantically at her desk.

'Gone next door for the arraignment,' she said, without looking up. She was referring to the magistrates' court, which stood adjacent to the police station on the corner of Edward Street and John Street.

'Whose arraignment?'

This time she did look up – and the expression on her face told him she'd put her foot in her mouth.

She shrugged.

'Angie?' He started walking towards her desk.

'Marni Mullins.' She almost ducked as she said it.

'What the hell? Since when?'

'He charged her this morning.'

'But there's evidence that there was someone else there!'

Angie looked at him blankly.

Francis pulled out his phone as he headed down the stairs.

'Rose, did you tell Rory about that other footprint?'

'I'm waiting for a match on the sole, so we know what size the shoe . . .'

'For fuck's sake. He's charged her.'

'But . . .'

He disconnected the call. As he stormed out of the front door of the station onto John Street, he practically knocked over Alex Mullins who was coming in. His face was grey and there were dark rings under each eye. Francis noticed that one of his hands was bandaged.

'I need to see my mother.'

'Alex . . .' What could he say? The kid's mother was about to be remanded, which would see her moved from the station cells to the nearest women's prison – Bronzefield in Middlesex. 'Come with me.'

Alex gave him a suspicious look but fell into step with him.

'What happened to your hand?'

'Nothing. It was an accident.' It wasn't an explanation, but it didn't seem right to question him further.

They turned the corner of the street, then Francis veered left to go up the steps to the ugly glass-and-concrete court building. When Alex understood where they were going, he tugged on Francis's arm.

'What's going on?'

'Your mother's been brought here for her arraignment.'

Alex looked momentarily blank.

'She's being charged with murder, Alex.'

'What the hell? No way.'

'I'm afraid so.'

'You bastard, Sullivan!'

'Not my doing, Alex. I promise you.'

Alex glared at him.

As they came to the security desk, Francis flashed his pass and was let through. He waited at the other side while Alex was walked through the scanner and patted down. Francis scanned the foyer and the stairs, on the lookout for Rory.

'What does it mean?' said Alex, still angry as he joined him.

'It's nothing, just a formality. The charges against her will be read out in court so that a trial date can be set.'

'A trial date? You think she did it?'

'Actually, I don't. But like I said before, it's not my case, Alex.'

He spotted Rory coming out of the men's toilet. Rory's eyes widened as he clocked his superior waiting for him.

'Boss . . . what you doing here?'

'More to the point, what are you doing here?'

Rory glanced at his watch. 'Marni Mullins is due in court in five.' He looked Alex up and down. The boy glared back at him.

'Why wasn't I informed that you were charging her?' said Francis.

'I cleared it with the DCI,' said Rory, puffing his chest a little.

'You do realise there's evidence of someone else being present at the time of Thierry's death?' He felt awkward discussing it in front of Alex, but he couldn't believe what Mackay had done.

'It meant nothing,' said Rory. 'There was an army of CSIs in and out of that kitchen. You can be sure it belonged to one of them. I'm in charge of this case, and all the evidence points towards Marni Mullins being guilty.'

Alex took a step towards him. He was taller than Rory, and he leaned forward on the balls of his feet. 'She didn't do it.'

'That's for the court to decide,' said Rory. 'But here's the thing.

Her prints are on the knife that killed your father. She has previous form. It was the second time in a matter of days that we were called out because of a fight at her house. And, she as good as admitted doing it.' He didn't appear threatened by Alex looming over him – but then they were just feet away from the court security guards.

Alex was shaking.

Francis was as angry as Alex and almost having as hard a time keeping it under control. He put a hand on Alex's forearm.

'I've got to go,' said Rory. Unrepentant.

He disappeared into the bowels of the building. Francis checked the court schedules on the noticeboard at the back of the foyer.

'Court Three,' he said. 'Are you sure you want to be here for this? It's just a formality.'

'Is my mum in there on her own?' said Alex.

'Her lawyer will be there too.'

Alex covered his face with his hands. 'Yes.'

They went up the stairs and through a door that was labelled Court Three. The public gallery was empty, and though below them there were a number of men in suits conferring in front of the bench where the judge would sit, there was no sign of Marni Mullins. Rory appeared and joined the men. Francis recognised one of them as a solicitor from the Crown Prosecution Service.

'What's happening?' said Alex.

'She'll be brought out in a minute.'

As they waited, a few more people arrived in the court, though no one else came to the public gallery. Francis sat stewing. Rory Mackay. Always ready to see someone's guilt, always ready to throw away the key.

Ten minutes passed, but finally they all rose as the magistrate came in. She was a tall, slim woman in her late forties, blond hair scraped back in a chignon, and a stern expression on her face. There were some whispered consultations up at the bench and then the day's business got under way. Marni's arraignment was first on the roster. The clerk of the court called for her to be brought in.

It was a day and a half since Francis had dropped Marni off at the end of Great College Street, but there was a marked difference in the woman he saw in front of him. How could she have lost so much weight in just thirty-six hours? Her complexion was dull, and her whole body was shaking violently. She gripped the front of the dock to steady herself, but the policewoman standing with her also kept a hand on her back. Marni's eyes skittered around the court without settling on anything or anyone, making Francis wonder what sort of state she was in.

'Mum!'

'Shhhh,' hissed Francis.

The clerk of the court stood in front of her and cleared his throat.

'Marni Mullins, you have been charged with the murder of Thierry Mullins on Tuesday, 31st October 2017. How do you plead?'

Francis glanced at Alex as he listened to the words read out loud. The boy's face was twisted with pain. He stared at his mother, waiting for her to proclaim her innocence.

Not guilty. He mouthed the words he wanted to hear.

Francis willed her to say it, but Marni simply stared at the clerk as if he'd spoken to her in a foreign language.

Next to him, Alex was clenching and unclenching his fists in his lap.

With a look of concern on his face, the clerk repeated the question.

Alex stood up. 'She's not guilty. She didn't do it.'

The magistrate's head snapped up and all eyes in the courtroom were upon him. Rory Mackay scowled and shook his head, furious at the unauthorised interruption. Francis turned to Alex, a finger on his lips to tell him to be quiet.

'No,' he said, though not as loudly. 'She's innocent.'

'Quiet!' The magistrate spoke deliberately and firmly. 'Another word and I'll have you removed from the court.'

'But she shouldn't be here,' said Alex.

Jayne Douglas twisted in her chair and glared at him. Marni was staring up at her son as if she'd just woken from a trance.

Francis tugged at Alex's arm, and whispered in his ear. 'We should leave.'

Alex shook his head, but he sat down again. The magistrate gave him a final admonishing look, then nodded at the clerk to continue with the arraignment.

'Marni Mullins, you have been charged with the murder of Thierry Mullins on Tuesday, 31st October 2017. How do you plead?'

This time Marni answered. 'Not guilty.' Her voice rang with powerful conviction throughout the court.

Francis stood up and left the public gallery with undisguised disgust and making no effort to quieten his footfall on the wooden floor. It was a bloody travesty.

'Can I see her now?' Alex asked, catching up with Francis in the corridor.

Francis didn't answer. He jogged down the stairs and around a corner, coming to a stop outside a door marked Court Three.

He waited and a minute later Rory Mackay emerged from the court.

'You've made a massive mistake, Rory.'

'What will happen to her now?' said Alex, not giving the sergeant time to respond.

'She's been remanded in custody to await trial.'

'What about bail?'

'It's a murder charge – no bail.' Rory sounded almost smug.

He'd always resented Marni Mullins, ever since Francis had brought her in to help on the Tattoo Thief case.

'She won't be able to cope with prison,' said Francis.

'Not my problem.'

Francis had had enough. He pulled his arm back and threw a punch, catching Rory with a glancing blow on the side of his chin. It was enough to knock the shorter man back against the wall.

'Fuck!' said Rory, staggering in an attempt to keep his balance, one hand flying to his chin.

Francis stood his ground, rubbing the knuckles of his right hand.

'This is exactly why Bradshaw handed the case to me,' said the sergeant. 'When it comes to Marni Mullins, you can't keep your feelings under control.'

15

Saturday, 4 November 2017

Gavin

Francis came into the incident room looking like someone had pissed on his chips. Rory scarpered away from the whiteboard to his desk in the far corner. Francis glared in his direction, and Gavin wondered what was eating the pair of them now. They were worse than a couple of teenage girls who had fallen out over a crush.

Francis went across to the whiteboard, brandishing a Manila envelope.

'Listen up,' he said, addressing the whole team, 'a quick up-date on the Booth Museum mummy.'

Gavin paused the CCTV footage he was watching and spun his chair round. Francis was Blu Tacking a series of colour images up on the incident board. Gavin stared at them – they showed parts of a wizened, desiccated female body. Wisps of blond hair framed the face, but he had no idea if the woman had been beautiful in life. She certainly wasn't now.

Mummified, she looked a hundred years old, and with all the moisture wicked from her body, her discoloured face reminded him of pictures of concentration-camp victims. The other images were close-ups of various areas of the cadaver – bony limbs, protruding ribs, breasts like empty flaps, claw-like hands and feet. Gavin was shocked to realise that nearly every inch of her leather-like skin was tattooed. She must have spent hundreds of hours and thousands of pounds in tattoo parlours at some point in her life.

The rest of the team were staring open-mouthed as well.

'My god,' said Angie. 'Do we have any idea who she was?'

Francis cleared his throat. 'We can say with some certainty that this is definitely not Alicia Russell – the timing simply isn't right. But more than that – no, we've got nothing yet.'

'How long has she been dead?' said Kyle Hollins, getting up to take a closer look at the images.

'According to Rose, it takes approximately forty days to mummify a body,' said Francis. 'So more than forty days. Rose is working on pinning it down more accurately, as it could be considerably longer. And for the record, no, we don't know the cause of death yet either. Rose will be carrying out a PM on the body tomorrow.'

'Those tattoos should make her easy enough to identify,' said Gavin. 'I'll get onto the missing persons unit and run a search for them.'

'Good. I'll email the images to you,' said Francis.

'Do you know how tall she was?' said Gavin.

Rory, having ventured out from behind his desk, pulled his notebook out of his jacket pocket. 'Five three, or thereabouts. Rose is forwarding dental X-rays to us as well, so you can use those too.'

Francis Sullivan was staring at the board again, almost oblivious to the bustle going on in the room around him.

'What are you thinking, boss?' said Gavin.

Francis rubbed his chin with his hand. 'Just this.' He took a step closer to the images. Gavin went and stood next to him. 'They all look the same, don't they?'

Gavin looked at them. As far as he could see, they were all different. Writing, numbers, symbols, pictures. 'How do you mean?'

'Look,' said Francis, 'they're all the same colour.'

'Black? Most tattoos are.'

'The same black. The same intensity. The lines are of uniform thickness. There are none that are faded or blurred with age.'

'What are you getting at?' said Rory, stepping in for a closer look.

'Right, I'm no expert,' said Francis, 'but it looks to me as if these were all done by the same person, and at round about the same time.'

'And?' said Gavin.

'Doesn't it strike you as odd? Most people get one tattoo at first, and then add another and gradually build a collection. This woman is covered in them, but you can't see a progression in the age or style of the tattoos.'

'I see what you mean,' said Gavin. 'But I don't see what that's telling us.'

Francis continued to stare at the images for a few more seconds.

'Maybe they were all done at the same time?' he said. 'I don't know.' He turned back to the team. 'Kyle, get a list of local women who've been missing more than forty days, then match them for age and height. Angie, carry on digging into Alicia Russell's past. Rory, can you prepare a press conference to appeal for information as to Alicia's whereabouts? Gavin, log all the tattoos the mummy has and get an update from Rose on any new information.'

He disappeared into his office.

Gavin carried on looking at the words and symbols. Could they have some meaning? Presumably they did have to the woman who'd got them tattooed all over her body. But did they have any relevance to her death?

He spent the next hour going through the same pictures on his computer once Francis had emailed them to him. The body had more than forty tattoos in total, and Gavin listed each one, describing what it was, in preparation to send the details across to missing persons. He had height and hair colour – and looking closely he could see the woman had dark roots, so it was clear she wasn't a natural blonde. What he didn't have was eye colour or age.

He called Rose.

'Any idea how old she was?' he said, after explaining what he was doing.

'Not young,' said Rose. 'Her lungs suggest a history of smoking, a fatty liver indicates she was a drinker and didn't take care with her diet. In the X-rays, some of her joints showed the first signs of osteoarthritis, so I would think she was maybe in her late fifties or early sixties. I should be able to narrow it down tomorrow when I do the PM.'

'Thanks, that's good. What about her fingerprints?'

'I'll get them over to you. And the DNA results for matching.'

'Brilliant.'

Gavin put down the phone and added the information about the woman's age to his notes. When he looked up, Francis was standing by his desk.

'One more thing,' he said. 'Can you and Kyle get the images circulated to all the tattoo shops in town. Someone must have done these tattoos, over a relatively short period, and if we can find whoever did them, we can probably find out who she is.'

'Yes, sir. What about issuing them to *The Argus*? Someone's bound to come forward.'

Sullivan frowned. 'Don't talk to anyone on that rag, Gavin.'

'But it seems . . .'

From across the row of desks, Rory caught his eye, then ran his index finger across the base of his throat. Gavin stopped talking abruptly.

'Thank you, Rory,' said Francis, acidly – it obviously hadn't escaped his notice. He turned back to Gavin. 'Look, we've had some run-ins with *The Argus* in the past. I want to keep a tight rein on exactly what information we give them about this case. They can be a bit fast and loose with the facts.'

'Sorry, sir.'

'No worries. Just get on and see if you can get a match with missing persons. Someone close to her must have reported that she'd disappeared.'

Francis slipped back into his office, and Rory came around to lean on the side of Gavin's desk.

'Don't mention *The Argus*,' he said. 'The boss had a punch-up with its star reporter because someone was leaking information to him.'

'Someone?'

'Don't ask. You really don't want to get involved.'

He filled in the enquiry form for the missing persons unit and started compiling a list of the tattoo shops in Brighton and Hove – to begin with.

Someone had to find out who the Booth Museum mummy was, and perhaps this was his chance to prove himself.

16

Saturday, 4 November 2017

Francis

Francis sat at the kitchen table. Robin sat opposite him. The supper plates had been cleared, and between them there was an open bottle of whisky, but only one glass. Spread around it were the twenty-three separate images that catalogued the mummified woman's forty-four tattoos.

'Why did she have so many?' asked Robin.

'Next question.'

'What's their significance?'

'Next question.'

'Do they have anything to do with why she was mummified?'

'Next question.'

'So you're as clueless as I am?' Robin laughed. 'Has a crime actually been committed?'

'That's a good question.'

'Well?'

Francis took a slug of the whisky and poured more into his glass, ignoring his sister's disapproving look.

'Certainly, it seems to be an unregistered death – that's a criminal offence.'

'Not a very serious one.'

'Serious enough. Preventing a lawful and decent burial is a crime, and so is exposing a dead body in a public place, so putting it in the museum might be considered a crime, though technically the body wasn't exposed.'

'Murder?'

'Rose hasn't established the cause of death yet.'

Francis was studying the photos, checking them against the list Gavin had made. The largest number of them were Egyptian – a mixture of hieroglyphs, gods, people, birds and animals. A lot of the tattoos were writing – words, phrases, quotations, some that Francis recognised from Shakespeare and famous poets, and others that he didn't. They weren't all in English. He spotted Latin, French, Italian and other languages among them. There were also a substantial number in foreign characters – Chinese, Japanese, Cyrillic, Greek, Arabic, Hebrew – and others in scripts that he didn't know but suspected were from India and South East Asia. And twisting sinuously and malevolently between them all there was a multitude of snakes, forked tongues darting, eyes shining. Francis could practically see them slithering, hear them hiss.

'What are these?' said Robin.

She was holding up two pictures that featured similar intricate tattoos made up of lines of ornate oriental script and geometric squiggles. Francis studied them. He'd seen tattoos like them before, when he'd been working on the Tattoo Thief case.

'They're Thai tattoos called Sak Yant. Sacred designs, hand poked by Buddhist monks,' he said. 'They bring luck and protection to the wearer.'

'But you thought these tattoos were all done by the same person – not a Buddhist monk?'

'I can't be sure. But the tattooist could have copied the Sak Yant designs.'

They continued sifting through the pictures. There were religious symbols from all the world's major religions, as well as superstitious markings and symbols associated with witchcraft and devil worship. There was even a swastika.

'If there's supposed to be a message in here, it's lost on me,' said Robin. 'There's just too much. You can't see the wood for the trees.'

She was right. There was hardly a square inch of skin that wasn't tattooed.

'A hidden message?' Francis shrugged. 'Without having some context, we don't know what we're looking for, or looking at. After all, the tattoos might have nothing to do with her death or mummification at all. Maybe it's the story of her life, a biography of sorts.'

'Then they must help in finding out who she is. Not many people are tattooed to this extent.'

Francis reached for the whisky bottle but then withdrew his hand, thinking better of it. They were getting along and Robin was as animated as he'd seen her for weeks. She'd taken a hard knock, discovering earlier in the summer that the man she was seeing had not only committed suicide, but that he'd been a serial killer as well. On top of the death of their mother, just a few weeks before, that had taken a heavy toll. Francis had promised himself that he'd make time to spend with her, and sitting here at the kitchen table checking out these tattoos reminded him of when they would do jigsaw puzzles together as children.

Robin noticed his restraint.

'Shall I make us both some tea?' she said.

'I'll do it,' said Francis quickly, pushing back his chair.

She shook her head, smiling at him. 'Fran, it's fine. I can manage to make a pot of tea.'

Francis carried on studying the images.

When Robin spoke next, she had her back to him, spooning leaves into the teapot.

'I miss her, Fran. More than I can say.' Her shoulders were slumped.

'I know. I miss her too.'

'This was her favourite teapot.'

'She'd be happy that we're using it.' Francis wanted to keep the mood light. 'But she'd still be moaning about the way it dripped.'

'Will you come to church with me on Sunday?' she asked.

'I . . . I don't know. I'm not finding it helpful at the moment.'

The back of Robin's head nodded, and Francis heard her sniff. He went back to poring over the photos. He wasn't very good at dealing with his own grief, and he certainly didn't know how to assuage Robin's.

He studied an image of the woman's left thigh. There was a pair of glasses, an anchor, a piece of Arabic script, a tiny drawing of a minotaur, a biomechanical design, a mathematical equation, a third eye symbol in a triangle, the zodiac symbol for cancer, something written in what Francis thought to be ancient runes, and a snake. All jumbled together, practically overlapping. The skin looked hard and dry, and the mummification process appeared to have skewed the shape of some of the tattoos. The pictures were wonky and distorted and the scripts no longer followed straight lines. Or perhaps they'd been like that anyway. There was really no way of knowing.

Francis pushed the pictures to one side. Staring at them would tell him nothing about the woman and why she'd had them done. All he could hope was that a heavily tattooed woman had been reported missing and that the tattoos would lead to her identification.

The doorbell rang. He got up.

'You expecting someone?' said Robin.

'I asked Rose to drop by at some point – I wanted to talk to her out of the office. Might be her.'

He went down the hall to the front door, staring at the figure silhouetted in the frosted-glass panel. He opened it.

'Hello, Rose!' He glanced at his watch. It was well after eight.

'I know, I'm sorry,' she said, rolling her eyes. 'I was working late and I found something. I couldn't wait till Monday morning to tell you.'

'Come in,' he said. 'Tell me what?' He ushered her down the hall.

'Hi,' said Robin, as they came into the kitchen. 'I've just made tea. Would you like some?'

'I'd love some,' said Rose.

Francis remembered his manners. 'Robin, this is Rose Lewis, pathologist. Rose, this is my sister Robin.'

'We've met,' said Rose. 'A few times – visiting you in the hospital.'

Francis couldn't remember an encounter. 'I'll take your word for it.'

Robin brought the tea to the table and they sat down.

Rose picked up a couple of the photos. 'Made any sense of these?'

'No,' said Francis. 'Just looks like a random obsession.'

Rose put them down. 'I've got something.'

Francis waited. Rose Lewis, mistress of the dramatic pause. 'And?' he said, unable to stand it a second longer.

'A partial finger mark.'

'From where? I thought everything around the body had already been double-checked.'

'It's tiny, but maybe enough to get an ID. It was on one of the linen bandages wrapping the body.'

'Surely you can't get a print off fabric?' said Robin.

'Not usually,' said Rose. 'But this fabric was sealed with resin. The finger pad that made it seems to have been covered in tiny particles of natron and they stuck in the resin along the lines of the ridges.'

'What's natron?' said Robin.

'It's a type of naturally occurring salt – a mixture of sodium carbonate decahydrate, sodium bicarbonate, sodium chloride and sodium sulphate. The ancient Egyptians used it for mummifying bodies. They found it in dry lake beds and employed it for a multitude of things as well as mummification.'

'But wait,' said Francis. 'How did whoever did this get hold of natron?'

'I suspect they made it,' said Rose. 'If you know the formula, you can mix it up pretty easily, though you need a huge quantity of it to mummify a full human body. Anyway, that's what we found in the Canopic jars with the organs – and traces of it inside and outside the cadaver. And in this finger mark.'

Robin poured the tea and a couple of minutes were taken up with passing milk and sugar around the table.

'I'll go and watch TV,' said Robin. She left the kitchen.

Once they were alone, Francis said, 'You really think it could be good enough to get a match?'

'I've sent it off to be checked. We'll have to wait and see.'

'Could it actually be a print from the body?' said Francis. 'If the bandage brushed against the victim's hand?'

'It's quite likely,' said Rose. 'In other words, don't hold your breath. It might be nothing. Anyway, what did you want to talk to me about?'

Francis was relieved Rose had waited for Robin to leave before asking this.

'Marni. You know Rory charged her?'

'I know. I'm sorry – but the CPS obviously agree with him that there's enough evidence.'

'That partial footprint throws doubt on the case.'

'I'm sure her defence will make use of it.'

'Whose bloody side are you on, Rose?'

'Sides? We're picking sides? Forget it, Francis. I gather the evidence so we can find the truth. I'm on nobody's side. I hope you're not either.'

84

Francis sank his head into his hands. 'She didn't do it, Rose. I'm sure of it. But I'm not allowed anywhere near the case.'

'For obvious reasons,' said Rose, getting up to leave.

Once she'd gone, Francis reached for the whisky bottle again. Tea wasn't really cutting it.

17

Sunday, 5 November 2017

Gavin

The wind was always ferocious at the top of Peacehaven Cliffs and as the afternoon sky darkened, it seemed to blow harder still. Gavin pushed into it as he strode up the slope towards where he could see the abandoned car. The body was somewhere beyond that. It was raining now, horizontal sheets of it gusting in from the sea – tiny pellets of water that stung his cheeks and made him blink. Angie was somewhere behind him, sheltering in the lee of his body if she had any sense.

They'd listened to the recording of the 999 call at least three times before they'd been able to work out what the hysterical woman had been saying, but once they worked out it was Peacehaven, it had only taken them minutes to find the car she had mentioned.

'She was in a state,' Angie had said, as Gavin had switched off the engine. 'What the hell would anyone be doing up here on a day like this?'

'Probably going to top herself,' Gavin had said, struggling awkwardly into his cagoule before venturing out of the car. Peacehaven Cliffs were almost as notorious a suicide spot as Beachy Head, a few miles to the east.

Instead, she'd apparently stumbled across a dead body and had done her civic duty. So Angie and Gavin had been dragged away from their Sunday afternoons.

The car was a red Golf, parked a few feet back from the edge of the cliff, facing out to sea. Gavin glanced at the number plate. It was several years old and didn't appear well looked after. The rain running off it was making tracks in a coating of dust and dirt. He took a quick picture of the rear plate and emailed it in for a trace.

'Didn't Alicia Russell drive a red Golf?' said Angie, coming level with him.

Gavin nodded. 'She did.'

He glanced in through the car windows. Nothing of particular interest – newspapers on the back seat, shoes, a discarded coffee cup.

'If it's hers, we'd better get the CSIs up here pronto,' said Angie.

'I think they'll be more interested in the body,' said Gavin.

They left the car and carried on towards the cliff edge.

He saw it almost immediately.

'Jesus Christ.'

The woman on the phone had said nothing about this. Perhaps because she'd been almost too hysterical to talk. Or maybe she didn't have the words to describe it. She'd simply said there was a dead body.

A naked woman was spread-eagled on her back, her hands and feet tied to short wooden stakes that had been driven into the mossy grass. In the failing light, her pale skin carried the translucent pall of death, her eyes open and unseeing, staring up at the sky. But Gavin couldn't unsee the most notable feature about the corpse. Her gut had been slit wide open. The ground around her was soaked with blood, glinting red on every blade of grass, even as the driving rain diluted it and rinsed it away.

'Fuck,' said Angie.

'Jack the Ripper,' said Gavin. His voice sounded shaky.

'What?' said Angie.

'It's what he did. Cut them open, ripped them apart.'

They stood staring down at the woman. Tendrils of wet hair blew across her face, obscuring her features.

'Do you think it's her?' said Angie.

'Alicia?'

Angie nodded.

'Could certainly be her car, so it might be.'

They turned away. It wasn't a sight to be endured.

'No wonder that caller was in a state,' said Gavin.

'Right, let's call it in,' said Angie. 'We need a full team of CSIs and the boss will want Rose Lewis on this one for sure. Take some pictures to show exactly how we found her.' She pulled a pair of latex gloves out of her jacket pocket. 'I'm going to check the car – see if there's any sign of her clothes, or the knife he used.'

'He?'

'He or she, but . . .' Angie shrugged and held up her hands. It didn't look like a woman's work.

Gavin made the call back to John Street and then set about blocking off the clifftop path in both directions with crime-scene tape. He put up a cordon all around the car and the body. There wasn't much to tie the tape to, but he spotted a wooden post a bit further along, on the left-hand side of the path. It wouldn't entirely close off access, but it would have to do for now until they could rig up something more effective. Given that it would be dark within the hour, he didn't think there'd be many people out walking up here anyway. Using another couple of posts and a few bushes, he was able to cordon off an area surrounding the vehicle and by the time he'd finished, Angie had examined the interior of the car.

'What about the caravan park?' he said. The lane leading from the main road up to the edge of the cliff skirted along the side of a large static caravan site.

'Won't be many people there at this time of year,' said Angie. 'But can you organise some uniforms to come up and door-knock it, just in case anyone saw anything?'

'Will do. Found anything here?'

Angie pointed into the open boot.

'Women's clothes, soiled.'

Leaning into the boot, Gavin became aware of the smell of excrement. He hated to think what the woman must have been through.

'This has got to have something to do with that mummy in the museum surely?'

'The timing suggests that,' said Angie. 'But what's the link? Did she put the mummy in the museum?'

'Bloody weird, the whole thing,' said Gavin.

'Right, we'd best leave it to the CSIs,' said Angie.

'You're right. Let's go and wait in the car for Rose.'

Over the course of the next hour, the deserted clifftop was transformed into a hive of activity. The CSIs arrived and set up battery-powered floodlights around the car. They erected a large white tent over the dead woman. Because of the wind, it had to be anchored into the ground with pegs and guy ropes. The heavy rain meant that any evidence could have been washed away already, so they worked as quickly as they could.

Rose arrived and examined the body in situ. She took photos and temperature readings. Angie brought up a picture of Alicia Russell on her phone and they both compared it with the dead woman's face.

'It's her,' said Angie, showing the photo to Gavin. 'We'll obviously have to have the body formally identified, but you can call the station and get the search for her stood down.'

Crime-scene investigators dusted the interior of the car for prints and placed all of the litter from the footwell and the stuff from the back seat into evidence bags for further examination. Gavin watched two of them inspecting the boot. After they'd taken photographs, they put each item of clothing into a separate evidence bag, along with a crumpled travel blanket and some empty plastic carrier bags. Rose came over.

'We think she might have been held in here before she died,' said one of the investigators. 'There's evidence of human soil on the clothes and on the blanket.'

Rose peered into the space, Angie looking over her shoulder.

'No sign of a weapon anywhere?' said Angie.

'No,' said the CSI.

They straightened up and Angie looked at Rose. 'Is that what killed her, that wound in her stomach? Or was she already dead when that was done?'

'Too early to say,' said Rose. 'There's no other obvious cause of death. But you know well enough, you'll have to wait for the PM to be sure.'

Angie nodded. She was soaked through and Gavin could see that her teeth were chattering.

'Need anything else from us?' said Gavin to Rose.

She shook her head.

'Right,' he said. 'Let's go.'

As they drove back to the station, the image of the murdered woman materialised in front of him every time he stopped at traffic lights, every time he waited at a junction.

It was a sight he was never going to forget.

18

Monday, 6 November 2017

Gavin

Nathan Cox stared at them, wide-eyed and open-mouthed. Gavin could almost see words forming but none issued forth. He waited for Cox's response without interrupting.

Finally, the man pulled himself together, although when he spoke it was more a high-pitched squeak than a word.

'Dead?'

'Her body was found up at the top of Peacehaven Cliffs, along with her car. Our pathologist thinks she'd been dead at least twenty-four hours before she was discovered, maybe longer.'

'My god.' Nathan's hand went to his mouth. 'How awful. How did she . . . ?'

Gavin didn't want to share the details with Nathan Cox, so he changed the subject.

'Could you round up all your staff in here as they arrive? We'll tell them what's happened, and then we'll need to talk to everyone about when they last saw her and what they might know about her death.'

'Of course.'

'It might be better if you didn't open the museum until we've spoken to everyone,' said Angie.

'It's only me and Martina working here today.'

'Just the two of you?' said Angie.

'Alicia would have been in as well. But Mondays are quiet – it's a small museum.'

Gavin stepped forward. 'Martina's Alicia's niece, isn't she?'

Nathan Cox nodded.

Gavin turned to Angie. 'We haven't found any closer family members to contact, so she won't have any idea that her aunt is dead.'

Angie rubbed her face with her hands. 'I forgot there was a family connection. I'd better tell her on her own in that case. Mr Cox, I would assume, if I were you, that Martina will need to take the rest of the day off. We might need to take her to the morgue to officially identify the body.'

Nathan Cox had turned quite pale. 'I suppose I'm in charge here now – for the meantime at least.' His voice faltered and realising what was about to happen, Gavin quickly guided him to a chair.

'Put your head between your knees,' said Gavin. 'I'll fetch you a glass of water.'

As he left the small staff-room where they'd been talking, he heard footsteps out in the corridor.

'Oh, what's going on?' A young woman was coming towards him. He guessed it was Alicia Russell's niece.

'Come in here, please,' said Gavin.

He led Martina Russell into the room. If she was surprised to see the police back at the museum so quickly, she was even more surprised to see Nathan Cox cradling his head between his knees.

'Nathan? Are you okay?'

'The water,' said Angie to Gavin, and he returned to his mission. 'You might want to sit down,' she continued, addressing the girl.

'Why?' said Martina Russell. 'Has something else happened?'

When Gavin returned, Nathan had regained some of his

colour and was sitting up straighter. He handed him a cup of lukewarm tap water.

'Can you give us a moment?' said Angie to Nathan.

He nodded. 'I'll wait outside.'

'What's going on?' said Martina, as her colleague left the room.

'When did you last hear from your aunt?' said Angie to the girl.

'Like I told you before – last Monday. Tuesday was her day off and then it was on Wednesday that she didn't show up for work. I've been trying to call her since then, but she hasn't answered her phone.'

Angie took a deep breath. Every police officer hated breaking this particular piece of news to family members. It was truly the worst part of the job. Gavin wondered whether he should step in and do it, but it was probably better coming from Angie.

'She's dead, Martina. Alicia's dead. Her body was found yesterday afternoon at the top of Peacehaven Cliffs.'

Martina Russell gasped. 'Dead? How?'

'Martina, why don't you sit down?' Angie tried to guide her towards a chair, but Martina flinched and pulled away.

'No. I won't sit down.'

'I'll get Nathan,' said Gavin. He went to the door and called Nathan Cox back in.

But Martina was less than pleased to see him. She stood directly in front of him – eye to eye, as they were the same height. 'You're pleased about this, aren't you?'

'Don't be ridiculous, Martina. It's a huge shock.'

'But you'll get her job now, won't you?'

Nathan took a deep breath, and stepped backwards.

Gavin didn't do anything. He was happy to let the drama unfold.

'That's a horrible thing to say.' Nathan looked genuinely upset, but Martina narrowed her eyes.

'You never liked her. Don't go crying crocodile tears now.'

Nathan looked over at Angie and Gavin, as if to ask for help, but Martina carried on talking frantically. 'She always said you resented her, that you tried to control her, manipulate her. Pushing to get your way over every little decision. Did you drive her to this?' She ran out of steam.

'Drive her to what, Martina?' said Gavin.

'To kill herself.'

'She's upset. She doesn't know what she's saying,' said Nathan.

Martina dropped onto one of the chairs and started to cry.

'Nathan?' said Gavin. He cocked his head towards the door.

He led Cox a few feet up the corridor so they would be out of earshot. 'What was all that about?'

Nathan glanced up at the ceiling, as if weighing up how he was going to answer.

'It's true. I did have a difficult relationship with Alicia. But that's because she was a bitch. She marched into the job and changed the way we did things, the way we'd been doing things for years.'

'Change isn't always bad,' prompted Gavin.

'She had no idea what she was doing.' Nathan's voice was sharp. Then he backtracked. 'But don't think for one minute that I wanted her dead. All I wanted was for her to listen to me.'

'About what?'

'Things like when she employed Martina. There were a couple of way better-qualified candidates. People who actually knew about birds and wildlife. Martina sits behind the reception desk like a pudding, reading romance novels on her mobile phone. She doesn't involve herself with the visitors beyond the bare minimum.'

Everyday office politics. It didn't seem likely to Gavin that they were the reason why Alicia Russell had turned up disembowelled at the top of Peacehaven Cliffs. But could Nathan Cox have had something to do with the mummy appearing in the museum? He suspected that the mummy was linked to Alicia's death – but he had no idea how.

'Nathan, I'm going to need an account of all your movements from the time Alicia Russell was last seen at work, last Monday, up until yesterday afternoon when her body was discovered.'

'What?' Nathan Cox exploded. 'You think she was murdered? And that I had something to do with it?'

'I need to be able to rule you, and other members of staff, out of being in any way involved,' said Gavin calmly.

Nathan frowned. 'I suppose so. But I'm right, aren't I? She was murdered.'

'The cause of death has yet to be determined,' said Gavin. 'I'm just doing my job, asking questions. Perhaps you could come down to the police station later on today to make your statement?'

'If I must.'

'By the way, Nathan – did Alicia ever mention having any enemies to you?'

Nathan's eyebrows went up and he wrinkled his nose. 'Enemies?'

'Or any unwanted male attention?'

'No.'

'You're sure?'

Nathan shrugged. 'It wasn't the sort of thing she would discuss with me. Maybe you should talk to Martina.'

'Okay. Thank you.'

He went back into the staff-room. Martina was crying softly. Angie, who had an arm around the girl's shoulder, shot Gavin a pleading look as he came through the door.

'Martina, is there someone we can call to come and take you home?' said Gavin.

The girl looked at him with red-rimmed eyes. 'My aunt was the only family I had.'

'You should probably take the rest of the day off, then.'

Martina's expression changed. 'I won't be coming back to work here after today. How can I? They all hate me, and they all hated my aunt.' She picked up her bag and turned to Gavin. 'You said something about going up to the morgue to identify her body? Shall we go now?'

'Sure,' said Gavin.

He escorted her out of the room. There was something he didn't quite like about Martina, but he couldn't put his finger on it.

19

Francis

Francis was beginning to wonder whether he should set up his office in the morgue. Another day, another body – this time Alicia Russell would be on Rose's table. But he needed to know what had killed her, and whether she'd been alive or dead when she'd been pinned to the ground and eviscerated. He needed to know absolutely anything Rose could tell him about her death – where and when and how, if not why.

Had she been kept in the boot of her car for long? Had she been killed where they found her? Did she have any other injuries? Was there anything else that could have killed her first? Death by disembowelment didn't bear thinking about.

Rose had already started the post-mortem by the time he'd donned a white coat and applied the ever-necessary VapoRub to his top lip.

Rose laughed at him. 'I can't believe, after all the autopsies you've watched, you're still rubbing that stuff under your nose.'

'And I can't believe you're not.'

Rose took an exaggeratedly deep breath. 'Ah, but I love the smell of putrescence in the morning.' She grinned at him. 'Actually, the smells are important. They tell me a lot about a dead body – what stage of decomposition it's reached, certain illnesses give off certain smells . . .'

'And what does the smell of Alicia Russell tell you?'

'Not a lot so far. She smells just I would expect, given that her guts have been exposed to the atmosphere for a day or two.'

Rose finished taking a series of photographs of the dead body and dictated various measurements into her phone.

'We're certain this is Alicia Russell?' said Francis.

'Definitely,' said Rose. 'Photographic match. Gavin's bringing in her niece to do the official ID later, but it's just a formality. No doubt about it, I'm afraid.'

'Right. We need to work out a timeline for whatever happened to her. She was last seen at her office on Monday afternoon. Tuesday was her scheduled day off.'

'Then she was discovered dead in her car yesterday afternoon. Five and a half days unaccounted for. Have you found anyone who saw her or spoke to her between those two points?'

'Nothing so far. I've got uniforms knocking on neighbours' doors, but neither next-door neighbour had seen her in the past few days, and the people who live opposite her appear to be away. No one in the street has reported anything untoward. When do you think she died?'

'Judging by the temperature of the body and the progression of rigor when she was found, I think she'd been dead for at least twenty-four hours. Rigor was beginning to recede, but it was freezing cold up on the clifftop, so progress would have been slower than if the body had been indoors.'

'You're assuming death occurred on Saturday at some point?'

Rose nodded. 'Or even Friday night, possibly.'

She was bent over the cadaver, gingerly folding back the flaps of skin over the great gaping wound in the body's stomach and trying to align their edges.

Francis got out his phone. 'Rory, can you get the team to check CCTV for any traces of Alicia Russell's car? See if you can pick it up when she left work on Monday evening. Then check the roads near the museum on Tuesday night, when the mummy was put in there. After that, we're looking out for it driving in the direction of Peacehaven Cliffs – probably late on Friday or on Saturday some time.'

He turned back to Rose. 'Did she die where she was staked out or was she placed there after death?'

Rose thought for a moment. 'As far as I can tell – at the moment – this cut is the cause of death. There's no other obvious cause, though that might change when I open her up fully and we get the bloods back. But given that, if she died from this wound, there would have been a lot of blood, and if she'd been killed elsewhere and transported in her car afterwards, I would have expected to see, and smell, blood in the car.'

'She could have been placed in a bag maybe?'

'Possibly. But no sign of one. There's no significant amount of blood on her clothes.' Rose led him across to a side bench, where the clothes that had been found in the boot of the car were laid out.

Francis looked at them. They were torn, ripped in places, or cut. But the white blouse wasn't bloodstained.

'They were cut off her?' he said.

'I think so,' said Rose. 'The back of her jacket and skirt are grassy and mud-stained. I've sent samples for analysis, and I believe they'll match the grass and mud at the top of the cliff. It looks like she was staked to the ground fully dressed. Then her clothes were cut off her and then she was eviscerated.'

'So alive when it happened?'

'Probably – but I don't know if she was conscious. She might have been drugged. We'll have to wait to get the blood test results back.'

'What about lividity?' said Francis.

'Visible on her back and buttocks, and calves – she was lying on her back when she died, or placed on her back very soon afterwards.'

'Which fits with what you just said.'

Rose nodded.

'Any sign that she struggled against the cords around her wrists and ankles?'

They went back to Alicia's body.

'Look here,' said Rose. She pointed to one of Alicia's wrists. 'There's some chafing and rubbing – she pulled against the restraint. Same on the other wrist. Not so much on the ankles.'

'Can we infer anything from that?'

'Possibly that she was tied by the wrists first. Then the ankles. And then he killed her. So she had longer struggling against the wrist bindings.'

'And what she was tied with? That tell us anything?'

Rose shrugged. 'I've sent the pieces of the cord to the lab. They should be able to pin down the manufacturer, and they'll go over them for fibres and hairs.'

Francis went back to the clothing. 'She soiled herself.'

'Probably loss of bladder and bowel control due to fear. There's no trauma to suggest she was knocked out, but she might have passed out through a combination of low blood pressure, fear, a lack of food, dehydration, not getting enough oxygen – if she was held for all the time she appeared to be missing. I'll know more when I get her blood test results back.'

'Could she have been drugged?'

'It's totally possible – again, we'll have to wait for the blood results. I want to take a look inside her now.'

Francis watched as Rose deferentially investigated the wound across Alicia Russell's stomach. He didn't enjoy autopsies, but it was part of the job.

'This was done with an extremely sharp knife,' she commented. 'Better that than a blunt one, from Alicia's point of view. Her intestines are mostly intact, but the viscera that holds them in position has been torn. Like the killer wrenched them to one side.' She frowned at what she was seeing, then sponged away blood with a length of blue paper towel.

Francis felt saliva flooding his mouth. He was going to be sick. 'I need a smoke,' he said.

'Go ahead,' said Rose, without looking up.

He went outside and steadied himself with deep breaths. It always astounded him how Rose could do her job with such an air of relaxed cheerfulness. Studying cadavers, cutting through flesh, sinew and bone, confronting the worst of what man did to man – or more often, to woman. He'd asked her about it in the pub once or twice and she told him she built a shell, an emotional carapace. She didn't let the dark side of her work into her core. He also knew that every few weeks, she'd take off hiking with her husband, leaving their son with his grandparents. Stomping across the moors or along the cliffs somewhere was cleansing. A form of therapy, by which she could erase the residue left inside her by each day spent working on cadavers.

He made a couple of calls, speaking to Rory about how the team were getting on with the inquiries into Alicia Russell's last known movements, the door-to-door inquiries in her street, and interviews with the other members of staff at the Booth Museum. The detectives and a secondment of uniform officers were working flat out, but nothing of particular interest had come to light so far.

He stubbed out his cigarette and went back inside, hoping that Rose had finished delving around inside Alicia's guts.

'You need to see this,' said Rose, as soon as Francis slipped back into the pathology lab.

The stench of an open bowel hung in the air and wrapped itself around Francis's face. He tried his best not to breathe it in as he approached the table. Rose gave him a look.

'Carry on like that and you'll turn blue.'

Francis grimaced. 'What have you found?'

Rose had most of Alicia's intestines in a steel bowl on her dissection trolley.

'Look here,' she said, indicating the empty cavity of the woman's abdomen.

Francis didn't have clue what he was supposed to be looking at.

'Yes?'

'Something's missing, do you see?'

Francis looked, then he glanced back at the bowl on the side. He looked again. Then it hit him and he recoiled from the body.

'Where's her liver?'

'Not here, that's for sure,' said Rose. 'Someone's taken it.'

Francis considered the possibilities. 'Not pecked out by gulls?'

'No. There are some marks on her intestines of bird activity, but the liver's been cut out with a blade.'

'To sell to someone? For a transplant?'

Rose stared at him. 'The body's been butchered. There's nothing surgical about this work.'

'Does that matter? If they got all of the liver?'

Rose sighed. 'Organ stealing is big money. The organ has to be in perfect condition for the transplant to work. It's done in hospitals – private hospitals in places where questions aren't asked. Not out in the open by someone with minimal surgical skills.'

'Cannibalism?'

'Hannibal Lecter alive and well in Brighton? Doubtful.'

Francis rubbed his temples. He felt the start of a migraine coming on.

Rose pulled a white rubber sheet up over the body.

'One thing before you go, Francis.'

'Yes?'

'The partial footprint at Great College Street. It wasn't a

match for Gavin Albright's shoe, or for any of the paramedics. It wasn't made by anyone I've got listed as being present at the crime scene. It doesn't match Marni's shoes, or Thierry's, or any of the first responders.'

'So there was someone else there – after Thierry sustained the fatal injury?'

'Yes.'

Paul Mullins?

'Marni said it was her brother-in-law, Thierry's twin.'

Rose shrugged. 'What about her son? Could she be saying that to cover for Alex?'

It wasn't something Francis wanted to consider.

'It's reasonable doubt, Rose,' he said. 'Someone else was there. Can you get the CSIs to go over the whole ground floor and the garden again, looking for trace evidence of a third person? If it was Paul, his DNA will be identical to Thierry's, so that won't help. We'll need fingerprint evidence to prove he was there. What about from the knife?'

'There's a full set of Marni's, in blood, on the handle. Someone pulled the knife out of Thierry's chest, and the way these marks are smudged suggests she was doing just that.'

'Anyone else's?' said Francis.

'Smudges, partials – I could give it another look.'

'Yes, please do. And see if any of them match Paul Mullins's prints – I'll get a set sent over to you.'

'Don't get your hopes up, Francis. Marni's handling of the knife was extensive and would certainly have distorted and even destroyed any underlying prints. But, yes, I'll check again.'

'Rory's trying to railroad this case, but I'm very far from certain that Marni did this. She loved Thierry.'

Rose gave him a look. 'You know that doesn't mean a thing when it comes to domestic violence.'

20

Monday, 6 November 2017

Marni

For years Marni had had nightmares about being back in prison. Only now she didn't know if she was awake or dreaming.

She counted the bricks in the wall. It was a way of calming herself down. She never made it from one end of the cell to the other without losing count, but that wasn't the point. It was a monotonous task and it slowed down her breathing, dulled her senses.

She wasn't dreaming. And each time she realised it, panic spiked in her chest, robbing her of breath and of focus.

Her mind was groggy. She felt like she'd been drugged. She slept a lot, hardly aware of whether it was day or night, despite the small, high window opposite the door. Meals were brought to her, then taken away uneaten. A doctor had been in to check her blood sugar and to give her insulin. She thought this had happened more than once, but she couldn't be sure.

How long had she been here?

Why was she here?

Thierry!

The memory of what had happened roared in like a juggernaut and her body flinched as if she'd been slammed against the wall.

'No . . . no . . .'

They thought she did it.

She banged on the back of the door until her fists were bloody. A woman guard, middle-aged and exhausted, came to see what the noise was about.

Marni tried to explain.

'This is a mistake. They've got it wrong and I shouldn't be here.'

The woman's face took on a sneer.

'They all say that, love. Just keep the bloody noise down.'

'But I didn't do it. Paul Mullins killed my husband.'

'Tell 'em when you go to court. Nothing I can do.'

'I need to see DI Sullivan.'

The guard slammed the door and left Marni alone.

Hours passed. Marni sat on the bed, shivering, trying to keep her mind blank, but feeling angrier and angrier. Why would no one believe her? Where was Sullivan?

'Visitor,' said a voice through the hatch in the door.

It was a different guard, a man. He escorted her down long, cold corridors of grey brick, unlocking doors, then relocking them once they were through. He nodded at other guards they passed, but didn't say a word to Marni.

'Who is it?' she said.

He shrugged. Why should he care?

He brought her to the visitor centre and showed her into a large room that looked like a community hall – there were low tables and soft plastic chairs, as well as a play area for children in one corner. Marni had expected a cubicle with a glass window between her and her visitor, like she'd seen in films, but this was much more relaxed. She looked around the room.

'Alex!'

Her son stood up and rushed towards her, arms open wide.

'Sit down,' barked the guard who'd brought her in.

Alex faltered but didn't go back to his seat.

'Mum.'

She stepped forward and hugged him. He was real. He was solid. He smelled familiar.

'Sit down, both of you,' said the guard, his voice firm.

Prisoners and visitors already seated at tables were looking round at them. A woman Marni recognised from her cell block frowned at her and bobbed her head. Marni got the message.

'Come on, Alex. Do what the man says.'

'Fuck the man,' said Alex under his breath.

But they found a table as far away from the guard station as possible and sat down. Marni leaned forward and gripped Alex's hands.

'It's so good to see you,' she said.

'It's not good to see you – not in here, not like this. It's wrong.'

'I know.'

'You didn't do it, Mum. I know that, but nobody will fucking listen to me.' Alex's eyes flashed with anger and he spoke through gritted teeth.

'DI Sullivan believes me,' said Marni.

'Sure. But what's he doing about it? Why hasn't he got you out?'

Marni sighed. She felt as angry as Alex, but she didn't want to show it. He was already dealing with Thierry's death. She didn't want him worrying about her.

'Listen, babe, they'll find some evidence that will show Paul did it.'

'They won't. Why would they bother looking when they've already got someone in jail for it?'

'It's just remand, until the trial.'

Alex slammed a fist on the table. 'You don't get it, do you, Mum? No one's coming to your rescue. They're going to let you rot in here.' His face darkened and crumpled.

The guard came towards them.

'You need to calm down, mate, or you'll be out.'

'I'm sorry,' said Marni. She touched Alex's hand again but he pulled it away furiously.

The guard stayed where he was, frowning at Alex.

'What did you do to your hand?' said Marni, wanting to change the subject. One of his fists was bandaged.

Alex didn't answer her and the guard didn't move.

'Leave us alone,' Alex said quietly, looking up at the man.

'What did you say?'

'I said, leave us alone.' His voice was louder now.

The woman from Marni's cell block looked around, shaking her head.

'Right, visiting time's up for you two,' said the guard. He looked at Marni. 'You, stay seated.' Then he stepped forward and beckoned Alex with his hand. 'You, time to leave.'

Alex stood up, but his stance showed that he was going nowhere.

'You can't do this. I'm allowed an hour with my mother.'

'Not if you can't behave.'

'Alex . . .' said Marni. He'd always had a temper, and it had always got the better of him. But it couldn't happen here and now. She started to stand up.

'Sit down!'

A woman guard, alerted by the raised voices, was approaching from across the room.

'Come on, sunshine,' she said to Alex, deliberately smiling to diffuse the tension. 'Let's get you out of here.'

Alex turned to the new voice, his scowl darker than ever. Then he glanced back at Marni.

'Mum?'

Marni shook her head. 'Come back tomorrow, babe,' she said.

At that, any semblance of self-restraint gave way. Alex kicked out at the table, sending it spinning in the direction of the male guard.

'She didn't do it,' he shouted. 'She didn't bloody do it.'

The female guard lunged for him, but he was too quick. He set off across the room towards the exit and finally did what they wanted him to do. He left.

Marni watched him go, her eyes pricking with tears. But she didn't want to cry in front of the two guards.

'He'll be lucky if he gets back in,' said the male guard, straightening up the table.

Marni put her head in her hands. Thierry would never have behaved like that. Sure, he had a temper, but he could keep it under control when he needed to. Alex was different. He got into fights at the drop of a hat. How many times had she been called in by his school because he'd punched some other kid for calling him names? And since then – there had been black eyes and split knuckles with no explanation. Screaming arguments with Liv. Slamming doors at home.

He was out of control.

Violent.

More like Paul. And it terrified her.

21

Tuesday, 7 November 2017

Francis

'Francis Sullivan! Long time no talk.' One of his least-favourite voices – it felt like an assault.

'What do you want, Fitz?' It was Tom Fitz of *The Argus*, a man Francis would happily never talk to again.

'I know I'm the last person on the planet you want to talk to.' The guy was a mind reader. 'But I'm about to write a story, and I think it would be a professional courtesy to let you know first.'

'It had better not be about me.' This was going to be some kind of wind-up, and a big waste of his time. Perhaps he should hang up.

'If I said the words "Canopic jar", would you be interested?'

Good thing he hadn't hung up. 'Go on.'

'Someone – I don't know who – has sent me a Canopic jar. Like those ones your lot found in the museum last week.'

Fitz had written a double-page spread on the discovery of the mummy. God knows how he'd found out about it, but once he had he was all over Nathan Cox like a rash – and Cox had spilled every last detail.

'Right, don't open it. Don't touch it. And don't write about it. Are you at your office?'

'Yes, but ...'

'Wait there for us.' Now he hung up. 'Rory? Come on.'

They drove to *The Argus* office in stony silence. Francis didn't bother to fill Rory in, and Rory didn't ask what was going on. Charging Marni Mullins had fractured the fragile working relationship he'd hoped to build between them, and Francis was in no hurry to fix it. Rory still hadn't got over the fact that he remained a sergeant, and that a younger man had been promoted over him. It seemed like it was one step forward, two steps back at the moment. He called Rose from the car.

'Will you be at the lab later?' he said. 'Someone has sent Fitz a Canopic jar.'

'And?' said Rose. 'He's just printed a massive story about the mummy and the possibility of an Egyptian cult in Brighton. I'm surprised he's only received one.'

Speculation about Kemetism, the modern practice of the ancient Egyptian religion, had formed the backbone of Fitz's piece.

'You're right. It might be a copycat. But it might not. So can we bring it over for you to take a look at?'

'Sure.'

As soon as Francis laid eyes on the jar on Tom's desk, he knew it wasn't a copycat or prankster. The vessel was identical to the Canopic jars that had been left in the museum with the mummy. This one had a carved human head for a lid.

'You've opened this, haven't you?' said Francis, sniffing the air. He could smell herbs, natron and something putrid.

Fitz looked sheepish. 'I took a look before I called you,' he admitted. 'I didn't think it would have anything in it.'

'And?'

'It does. It's full of salt. I didn't look further because of the stink.'

'When did it arrive?' said Rory. He had his notebook and pencil out.

'I've been away for the last couple of days,' said Fitz. 'But I think it was delivered on Saturday. Is that right, Graham?'

He turned to look at another man who was at work a couple of desks away.

'Yup. Saturday.'

'Who delivered it?' said Rory to the man.

'I don't know. A courier, I suppose.'

'Did you sign for it?'

'No.'

'Who was it addressed to?'

'No one. But Tom wrote the article on the Egyptian mummy, so it made sense to leave it for him.'

Saturday. Now it was Tuesday. Three days wasted because Fitz had been off.

'It came with this,' said Fitz. He was holding up a small roll of cream-coloured parchment. 'It was tied to the jar.'

Clearly, he'd untied it and opened the scroll.

Francis pulled on latex gloves and took it from him. 'You've still got what it was tied with?'

Fitz glanced towards the bin by the side of his desk.

Rory pulled on gloves and took an evidence bag out of his pocket.

'There,' said Fitz, pointing into the bin with a pencil.

While Rory retrieved the evidence from the bin, Francis unfurled the scroll. It was similar to the one that had been left in the museum. It had the same hieroglyphs in the centre of the square of paper, but underneath them there was some writing.

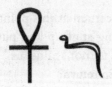

Apophis, the Great Serpent is coming.
Ra will fall.
The sun will set.

Francis studied it. The hieroglyphs and the writing had been executed using the same pen. The lines of the handwriting sloped slightly towards the right. The writing was uneven, and untidy.

'Does this mean anything to you, Fitz?'

The reporter shook his head.

'I don't suppose it's worth asking you to keep this out of the paper?' Fitz had never been co-operative when it came to holding back critical details.

'He sent it to me,' said Fitz. 'I don't see why I should.'

'Not specifically to you,' said Rory.

'To the paper. He clearly wants us to write about it.'

'Doesn't mean you should, though, does it?'

'Rory!' said Francis. An argument with Fitz would get them nowhere. There were plenty of other details about the mummy that Fitz had no way of knowing, and if the killer was going to communicate with a reporter, they needed to keep him on side. 'Write your story then, Fitz. But work with us this time – if you receive anything else like this, call us. And don't open things or touch things ... these could be critical pieces of evidence in a murder case.'

'Murder?' said Fitz. 'Is that what that mummy was all about? Was there a body inside it, Sullivan?'

Shit.

'Listen – nothing's certain at this point. So don't fuck up my investigation by making stuff up and putting it in your paper. Like I said, work with us, not against us.'

'And what do I get in return?'

'That warm, fuzzy feeling that comes from knowing you've done the right thing,' said Rory.

'Anything I can confirm, you'll hear it first,' said Francis.

'Deal,' said Fitz. 'Now, what can you give me on the Peacehaven Cliffs body?'

Rose prised the lid off the jar. The air was filled by the stench of rotting meat. Both Rory and Francis took a step back. They watched, repulsed, as she used a narrow steel spatula to gently ease the contents out of the jar onto a stainless-steel tray. At first, white crystals – natron, as they now knew. Then the crystals became dark. Rust-coloured. Globules of . . . leathery meat, crusted with bloodstained natron. Francis looked away, feeling sick. If it was what he suspected, they'd found Alicia Russell's missing liver.

And it had been sitting on Tom Fitz's desk for the last three days.

22

Tuesday, 7 November 2017

Francis

Francis stood in front of the whiteboard in the incident room. He had two dead women on his hands. Both murdered. He had no idea still how the mummified woman had died, or even who she was. But Alicia Russell was another matter. Saying she'd been eviscerated seemed something of an understatement. What had happened to her seemed like a form of ritualistic torture. That the killings were linked, he had no doubt. The Booth Museum connected them, even though they didn't yet know the identity of the mummified body.

The team were assembling behind him, and he could sense the buzz of energy in the room. Another killing meant another victim. But their clients weren't just the dead. They served every potential victim. When they caught a killer, they were saving somebody's life and that was just as powerful a driving force as the need to seek justice for those they were too late to help.

Rory came in and the undercurrent of excited whispering stopped. The sergeant still commanded more respect with the long-serving members of the team, and Francis wondered if he could do something on this case to improve his standing with the old guard. Probably not, given that he had a superior and a subordinate who had turned undermining him into a joint enterprise.

The murder board was filling up with pictures. There was the mummy, still wrapped, and then all the separate images of her tattoos. There was Alicia Russell in a corporate head-and-shoulders shot, and also spread-eagled, naked and bloody, on the clifftop. There were pictures of the other staff members at the museum. Were they potential killers?

At the other end of the board, divided from the Booth Museum case by a thick black line, an image of Thierry Mullins scowled straight at the camera. It had been taken a couple of years before by a police photographer when he'd been pulled in under suspicion of drug dealing. Beneath it, there was a similar photo of Marni, taken on her arrival at the station the previous Tuesday. Francis avoided looking at them, the one of Marni in particular.

'Boss?' It was Angie. 'Everyone's here.'

'Sure,' said Francis. 'Let's get started.'

He turned to face the room. Kyle was still chuntering to the crime researcher sitting next to him, but Gavin was facing the front, all ears.

'We've got our work cut out for us,' said Francis. 'Two apparent murders that are linked to the Booth Museum. Alicia Russell's body was discovered at the top of Peacehaven Cliffs on Sunday. Her liver had been removed. The killer packed it into a Canopic jar and delivered it to the offices of *The Argus* late on Saturday.'

'So why didn't they call us then?' said Kyle.

'Tom Fitz was covering the Booth Museum story and he was away for the weekend. One of his colleagues left it on his desk.'

There was a collective groan as this piece of information was digested.

'Gavin, can you go back to *The Argus* and try and pin them down on time of delivery and any other details. If the killer's sending messages to them, we need them on our side. I want you to act as liaison with them so they come to you first if he contacts them again.'

'On it,' said Gavin.

'The jar came with a piece of parchment attached – the same as the parchment we found at the museum, same hieroglyphs, but also with a message in English.' He pointed at a photo of the scroll on the board.

'Sir?' said Kyle.

'Yes.'

'Information back from forensics. The scroll from the Booth has been identified as being a piece of papyrus.'

'You can still get that?' said Angie.

'Apparently so,' said Kyle. 'On the internet. Ten ninety-nine for thirty-two sheets. CSI are digging into the source of it for us.'

'Good work, Kyle. Get them to check whether the two messages are on the same material. Angie, anything new on Alicia Russell's last movements?'

'Yes, boss. A woman who lives diagonally opposite saw her putting her bins out last Tuesday morning.'

'She's sure about this?'

'We've checked – Tuesday is bin day in that street, and the woman said she was in a blue sweat top, leggings and trainers. The clothes she described were on a chair in Alicia's bedroom.'

'What time was that?'

'She wasn't totally sure – sometime after she got out of bed at seven thirty, but before the bin lorry came, which was usually at about eight thirty.'

'Okay, that's the last sighting of Alicia Russell to date,' said Francis. He wrote the time and place up on the whiteboard. 'We need to pin down exactly what happened between then and her death, which we presume to have been at some time on Saturday.' Then he pointed to the image of the mummified woman. 'It's too early to have had any DNA test results back from the mummified cadaver, but we're looking for a heavily tattooed middle-aged woman, who must have been missing for at least a month and a half, if not considerably longer.'

'Gavin, how many possibles have you got on the mis-per list?' said Rory.

Gavin had been tasked with identifying missing women who fitted the information they had on the mummy.

'Taking it back to women who've been missing for up to a year, and who disappeared from Surrey, Sussex or Hampshire, there's nudging three hundred,' said Gavin. 'I've ruled out a few as too young or too old – but of course, she could have been missing longer, or from further afield. I haven't started on hair colour yet. It's too easy for people to change their hair colour when they go missing, so I don't see that as reliable.'

'What about DNA?' said Rory.

Gavin pursed his lips in a rueful expression. 'We don't have DNA samples for most of the missing women on the list.'

'Seriously?' said Angie.

Gavin shook his head. 'It's a fact. There's no central database of DNA of people reported missing. There needs to be, but there isn't.'

'Needle in the proverbial,' muttered Kyle.

'Well, keep at it,' said Francis. 'Rule out those that you can. Talk to Rose about the cadaver's natural hair colour, check the missing list for any tattoos like the ones on our body, and get Rose to take an X-ray of her teeth as well. Start looking at their dental records. Use anything you can to rule people out.'

'What about an appeal to the public?' said Angie.

Francis crinkled his nose. 'We don't have much to give them. I'm not releasing a picture of the cadaver – the mummification process has distorted the facial features too much to be of any use for identification purposes – and I'm not convinced the woman had the tattoos before she went missing.'

'And if she's been missing a month and a half at least, anyone close would have reported it by now,' added Gavin.

Francis pointed at the pictures of the two dead women. 'The big question is: were these two women killed by the same person?'

'Same MO?' said Kyle.

Francis shook his head. 'We don't know how the mummy died. There's a chance that it could have been accidental, but given that we've got a mummified corpse and a presumably unregistered death, I think it's a fair assumption that she was murdered.'

'There are similarities, aren't there?' said Angie. 'Organs removed, Canopic jars – can't see that there would be two killers in the area doing that at the same time.'

Francis nodded. 'One issue is how the killer gained access to the Booth Museum to set up his Egyptian tableau – there were no signs that he broke in, so either he had keys or someone let him in. It's probably fair to assume that person was Alicia Russell. Was she simply his victim or was she more than that? Angie, can you look into who had keys for the museum, and where, in particular, Alicia's keys are.'

'Yes, boss.'

'Her car showed evidence of her having been kept in the boot for some time, which means the killer presumably drove it up to Peacehaven. CSI is combing the car for forensics, but we've got nothing concrete yet. It's critical that we trace the vehicle's movements over the period since she was last seen emptying her bins on Tuesday until her body was discovered on Sunday. Now, you've all got more than enough to keep you busy, so let's get to it.'

Francis left the incident room humming as the team digested the new information. He made his way up the stairs to Bradshaw's office feeling unspeakably weary. A session with the chief would suck out all his enthusiasm for the job, and all the belief he had that he could get the cases solved. But he'd promised an update and it was better than having Bradshaw at the team meeting.

Furthermore, this made the perfect opportunity to brief Bradshaw on the cases away from the rest of the team.

DCI Martin Bradshaw had the corner office two floors above the incident room. The door was open when Francis arrived, so he gave a courtesy knock and waited on the threshold.

The chief beckoned him inside with a wave of his hand. His face, although jowly, bore the perennial tan of a man who aspired to spend more time on the golf course than behind his desk.

'Sit down, Sullivan.'

This was new. Francis couldn't ever remember being invited to sit in Bradshaw's office. He generally liked to keep his minions standing while he lectured them on their shortcomings.

'Thank you, sir.' Francis took one of the two hard wooden chairs that stood in front of the desk.

'I want to have a little chat, Sullivan,' said Bradshaw, eyeing him across an empty blotter. 'But get me up to date on your case first, please.'

'Certainly, sir.' What was the little chat going to be about? Momentarily distracted, Francis launched into the details of the investigation so far. He slipped a small nugget of information into his narrative that he'd purposefully kept back from the rest of the team. A not entirely accurate snippet.

'The mummified woman had a small clay figure called a shabti in each hand.'

'What's that?'

'The ancient Egyptians buried their dead with figures that could act as servants for them in the afterlife.'

'Interesting. Where do you think they came from?'

Francis shrugged. 'They're pretty crude. The killer could have made them. We're having all the artefacts and linen strips analysed to find out where they might be from and what they're made of.'

No interruptions so far. No sharp rebukes for doing things wrong or for not having identified a suspect yet. The chief was on his best behaviour. Was he ill?

'Right, you need to keep at it. The identity of the dead woman is critical and somewhere, in that whole Egyptian display, your killer must have left a trace of himself.'

'That, and finding out the meaning of all those tattoos.'

'Don't waste your time looking at those. Not until you know for sure they're something to do with why she was trussed up like that.'

'Fair enough, sir.'

He went on to update Bradshaw on Alicia Russell's murder. Bradshaw took notes but didn't ask any questions.

'And what about the Mullins case? How's Rory getting on with preparing that for the CPS?' The way he said it, slowly drawing out each word, put Francis instantly on his guard.

'Rose has found an unidentified partial footprint in the blood on the kitchen floor. Whoever it was went out by the back door and into the garden.'

'Probably one of the crime-scene team,' said Bradshaw.

'They've all been ruled out. Everyone who we know was at the scene has been ruled out. This is an unidentified individual who was present at some point after Thierry Mullins was stabbed.'

Bradshaw considered the implications in silence.

'It means the defence will be able to argue reasonable doubt,' said Francis, joining the dots for him.

'And what do you think? Would you say there's some doubt that Marni Mullins did it?'

'Yes, I would, sir. In my opinion, Sergeant Mackay jumped the gun by having Mullins charged and arraigned. Marni Mullins claims that Thierry's twin brother, Paul, is responsible.'

'Paul Mullins? She's just trying to shift the blame. But she's got form for stabbing and the knife's covered in her prints.'

Bradshaw stared at Francis. It was a look of utter disdain. He drew in a heavy breath.

'Listen, Sullivan. Like I said, I wanted a chat with you. You're an intelligent officer. You've got lots of potential. But I'm seeing a pattern starting to develop here. Every case.'

'Sorry, sir. You've lost me.' Francis could guess what was coming, but that didn't mean he was going to make it easy for Bradshaw.

'You've been working for me for over a year now, and in several high-profile cases you've been . . .'

'Yes?'

'You get too personally involved. You need to maintain a professional distance from the people you're investigating.'

'If you're suggesting there's anything other than a professional relationship between myself and Marni Mullins, you'd be very wrong.' It was true. There was nothing going on between them now. 'She came on board during the Tattoo Thief case, and her help and later her evidence were critical in securing Sam Kirby's conviction.'

'For manslaughter.' Like a dog, worrying at a wound, rather than letting it heal. It seemed like he was never going to forgive Francis that verdict. It should have been murder, rather than manslaughter due to diminished responsibility. 'I understood you were friends with the woman.'

The emphasis he put on the word 'friends' made Francis wince. Anger made him tighten his diaphragm and sit up straighter in his chair.

'The woman – Marni Mullins – saved my life.'

'So now you feel you owe her, so you're trying to get her off a murder charge.'

'No, sir. I owe her nothing. I'm doing for her what I'd do for anyone in the same circumstances. I'm making sure we take full account of all the evidence, not just the evidence that suits the narrative certain team members want to build.'

He'd claimed the moral high ground, and Bradshaw was going to find it tough to argue against that.

'You're a witness in this case. Don't sabotage it, Sullivan.'

As if.

'No, sir.' He pushed back his chair and stood up.

'You know Mackay was in the running for the DI job when you joined the team, don't you?'

'He might have been in the running, but let me remind you, sir. I got the job.'

'Mistakes happen.'

'It wasn't.'

They locked eyes.

'That remains to be seen.'

23

Wednesday, 8 November 2017

Rory

Rory, Gavin and Angie stared at the names on the screen. They'd created an Excel document which listed missing women and matched them against things they knew about the mummified cadaver. They had precious little information to go on – her height, her natural hair colour. Only a few of the sets of details being held on the missing women included dental records. This had allowed them to rule a few people out. The mummified ca-daver had several amalgam fillings in her back teeth and none of the dental records they did have access to showed a match.

The tattoos might prove useful if they'd identified someone on their list who had the same tattoos, but there was no one with anything remotely similar. They had been useful in ruling out a couple of women on the mis-per list who had different tattoos. There had been a young woman, too young probably, who they'd dismissed as she had a *Finding Nemo* tattoo on one ankle, and a few butterfly and flower tattoos had resulted in their owners being struck off the list of possibles.

'We've got a choice,' said Rory. 'We can assume she had all those tattoos after she went missing, that whoever mummified her was also responsible for tattooing her, or – if we think she had those tattoos already – we can widen the search area and check the mis-per lists for the whole of the UK.'

'And if that doesn't throw up anyone, what then? Europe? The world?' said Angie. 'I still think we should issue pictures of the tattoos to the press. Someone is bound to recognise them.'

'Not if they were the work of the killer,' said Gavin. 'What about a two-pronged approach? We widen the list to check primarily for anyone with the tattoos, but at the same time drill down into this list,' he pointed at the screen, 'on the assumption that the tattoos were done after she went missing.'

Angie grimaced. 'You really think that could be it? Someone held her long enough to do all those tattoos, then killed her and mummified her? Why would someone do that?'

Gavin shrugged.

'That works. Gavin, can you get onto Missing Persons for a wider list?'

'On it, boss.'

Gavin went back to his own desk, leaving Rory and Angie studying the list of women who'd gone missing in the local area. It was a simple process of elimination to delete women who were the wrong height, although Rose had suggested they allow a greater margin of error than usual, given that the desiccation of the body would have made the mummified woman appear shorter than she probably was when alive.

They weeded out a few women on the basis of distinguishing scars. Another handful were ruled out on the basis of ethnicity. Although the mummification process had darkened the woman's skin, Rose had confirmed that she was Caucasian.

Rory went outside for a quick smoke, while Angie collated the remaining possible identities into a list. He thought about the case for a moment, then stubbed out the cigarette half done. He'd been vaping perfectly happily for months, so why the backslide? The stress of the job was getting to him – and he was letting it.

He went back upstairs, stopping off to grab some coffee on the way.

'How many have we got?' Rory asked, putting down a couple of mugs next to Angie's keyboard. He sat down and studied the screen.

'There are still seventeen on the list that could be her.'

'Any specifically from Brighton?'

'Eight of them.'

'Let's look at those eight first. Have we got photos?'

Angie nodded. 'But they vary in quality, and the mummy's face is . . . weird.'

She opened her desk drawer and pulled out an image of the dead woman. The dry, leathery skin was pulled taut across the bones of the face, making the nose appear hooked and the cheeks sunken. Her eyes were closed, but without the bulge of eyeballs behind the lids, they seemed unnaturally hollow. The cheekbones were sharp ridges above the concave planes of the face, the lips pulled back over stark teeth. There was no way of knowing precisely what the woman had looked like in life, but now she looked skeletal, like someone who had been starved.

'Gives me the creeps,' said Rory.

'And she won't decay now,' said Angie, sounding slightly awed. 'She'll be like that forever if she's kept dry.'

They laid out the photos of the eight women on the desk to compare them with the mummy.

Rory jabbed a finger at one of them. 'This isn't her. The nose is too long and the chin's more pointed.'

Angie looked at it and nodded slowly. 'I think you're right.' She put the image to one side.

It was hard to see any similarities between the mummy's face and the other women. Their pictures had been taken before they went missing, while they were still alive. They were smiling or laughing, looking at the camera. Their cheeks were full and their eyes bright.

'Shows how much of our bodies are made of water,' said Angie.

'Like biltong,' said Rory.

Angie pulled a face. 'What about that one?' she said, pointing at a picture of a laughing middle-aged woman. The quality was poor and the colours grainy. She was sitting in a pub, in the midst of a group of people, ranks of empty glasses lined up in front of them.

'Hard to say. Certainly not enough to assume they're the same woman.'

They stared at them in silence for a bit longer.

'Glad you're back, Angie,' said Rory, surprising himself as it seemed to come out of nowhere.

'Thanks.' She didn't look round at him.

'How are you doing?' He lowered his voice so the rest of the room wouldn't hear. 'You must miss Tony?'

'A lot.'

'Things going okay with Gavin?'

Angie nodded. 'He's a nice guy, easy to get on with. He seems pretty keen on the job, unlike others I could mention.' She cast a meaningful look in Kyle Hollins's direction. He had something of a reputation for taking shortcuts where he could.

'He's not so bad,' said Rory. 'But I think the DI made a good call bringing Gavin on board. Any of those women got tattoos?'

Angie scrolled through the information about them on screen. 'None of them mention tattoos specifically.'

Rory sighed. It was the mundane reality of police work that they would spend hours collating and comparing information and find nothing to move them forward in the case. The lack of progress was depressing. And his mood wasn't helped by the fact that his own boss was currently trying to undermine all the progress he'd made on putting the Mullins case to bed.

'Kyle, found any sign of Alicia Russell's car yet?'

Hollins had been spooling through the footage of the major routes through Brighton and out towards Peacehaven to try to find out when the red Golf had been driven up there – and who was behind the wheel at the time.

'Nothing so far, sarge.' His eyes looked glassy.

'Take a break,' said Rory. It was too easy to miss what you were looking for when your concentration wandered. 'It's time for coffee.'

The whole team seemed to sigh with relief in unison.

Rory relaxed in front of his computer, scanning the BBC news site while he sipped his drink. More crap about Brexit that he couldn't be bothered to read. He switched across to *The Argus* website and sat up sharply.

New killer, new terror

Egyptian nutter embalms second victim
and sends us sick message

Tom Fitz. This was his idea of working with them? He read the whole story. Tom had some details about Alicia Russell's death that he was sure they'd never released to the public. The discovery of her cut-away clothes in the boot of her car? The length of time she'd been missing? Of course, the bulk of the story focused on the receipt by *The Argus* of the Canopic jar. He'd taken photos of it before the police had taken it away. And of the papyrus scroll. So now that message was out in the open. He framed it as being a personal message to him, which it certainly wasn't, and finished his article with a chilling challenge to the so-called Embalmer.

If you want to talk to me, let's arrange a meeting.

Bloody idiot!

He raced into Francis's office but the boss wasn't there. Nobody seemed to know where he was. And this wasn't the day to go AWOL.

24

Wednesday, 8 November 2017

Marni

Marni felt terrible.

As she was on remand, she was perfectly within her rights to wear her own clothes – but the clothes she'd been arrested in had been covered in Thierry's blood. No one had brought her any clean clothes, and now she found herself wearing the standard prison issue of a blue sweatshirt and grey sweatpants. They were worn and baggy, and smelled dirty before she'd even put them on, let alone now, five days later. Her hair was greasy, and her skin felt dry and flaky. She'd hardly eaten since she'd been brought here and her belly was concave and taut, not an ideal situation for someone who was diabetic.

She didn't know who to expect when she was taken out to the visitor centre, but it certainly hadn't been Francis Sullivan. Seeing him in a freshly pressed suit and pristine white shirt made her feel even more wretched.

'What are you doing here?' She didn't bother to greet him properly. 'I thought you weren't allowed on the case.'

She dropped into the chair opposite him to avoid any closer contact. Once the woman prison officer who'd delivered her had moved away, she allowed her eyes to meet his.

'Marni, how are you?'

'You're seriously asking me that?'

'Okay, not the right question. Do you need anything?'

'I need someone to believe what I've been saying.'

'So tell me.'

'I loved Thierry. I would never have hurt him.' She could see disbelief in Francis's eyes. 'Okay, sure, we had our arguments, but I wouldn't have killed him, for God's sake.' Anger rose in her gullet like bile.

'Then tell me what happened. Give me something I can use to get you out of here.'

Marni rubbed her eyes and took a deep breath. 'It was Paul. Like I already told you.'

'What was he doing at the house?'

'I don't know. He was there when I got back, after you dropped me off . . . ' She stopped abruptly. *What the hell had Paul been doing there?*

'Do you think he was actually coming after you? That he wanted to finish what he started last summer?'

Marni glanced down at the livid scar on her hand – a result of a confrontation with Paul when he first appeared in Brighton earlier in the year.

'I don't understand him,' she said. 'He thinks he wants one thing, but seems to actually want something else. He's totally messed up.'

Francis poured water from a plastic jug into a cardboard cup and held it out to her. She grasped at it but didn't get a proper grip. The cup rolled across the table, water flooding to its edge and onto the floor. Francis pushed his chair back to avoid getting soaked, but she sat where she was, uncaring about the deluge soaking through the grey marl tracksuit bottoms she was wearing.

'I don't think I'm ready to talk about it,' she said. 'You should go.'

Francis shook his head. 'I'm not going anywhere, Marni. If you're not ready to tell me what happened that evening, then let's start with a bit of background. Tell me about Paul. Why did he come back to Brighton? What did he want?'

Marni sat up in her chair, arching her back and folding her arms behind her head. 'Paul wants Alex,' she said simply. 'He's always believed he's Alex's father.'

'Is he?'

'It's complicated.'

'Why don't you go back to the beginning?'

'It's a long story. I'm tired.' Too tired to dredge through the past that she thought she'd left behind.

Francis put out a hand to capture one of hers. 'Help me to help you, Marni.'

It had been a long time since Marni had told anybody about what had started all those years ago in France. Only maybe it had ended now – with Thierry's death. She shook her head. It wasn't over yet. Not while Paul was still alive and breathing.

Francis was watching her, waiting for her to speak, but her mouth was dry. She refilled the cardboard cup and drank some water. She could do this. She had to do it for Alex's sake – Paul was still out there, alive and breathing. Still dangerous.

'The summer when I was seventeen, my sister Sarah suggested going to France for a couple of months. Of course I agreed. It wasn't going to be a holiday. We couldn't afford that. But we thought we'd be able to find casual work, waitressing or whatever.'

'What year was it?' said Francis.

'1998. It had been a rubbish summer so far and all we wanted was some sun. Someone told Sarah the south of France was always hot, so that's where we headed. We took the train to Marseille and ended up finding jobs in Aix-en-Provence – about twenty miles north. We called it Aix at first,' she said, pronouncing the X hard. 'The locals laughed at us, but we didn't care. We were working in a bistro on the Place Jeanne d'Arc, probably the worst waitresses ever. The owner was a greasy little toad called Eric, with a big belly and a bald head. Always shouting at us in an accent we couldn't understand. We kept out of his way as much as possible. We were young and he couldn't keep his hands to himself.'

'Where did you stay?'

'We shared a room, two floors above the restaurant. It was tiny and it was so hot, but we had to barricade the door with a chair to keep the bastard out.'

'Is that where you met Thierry?'

The memories of that long, hot summer dissipated and the drab grey visiting room came back into focus.

'Paul. I met Paul first,' she said, her lip curling. She hated even saying his name. 'He used to come into the café every morning for coffee before he started work.'

'Tell me about him.'

'I was instantly attracted to him. He was older than the boys I knew at home – in his mid-twenties, beyond my realm of experience.' She drank some more water. 'I thought he was attracted to Sarah at first, but he wasn't. It was just his way of building up my trust.'

What if she'd never met him, if he'd used a different café?

'We went out a few times. I was very infatuated with him. He had money and he paid for everything. He would hang around the bistro every evening until I finished work and then we'd go drinking in a tiny bar a couple of streets away. He was very possessive, jealous from the start and I liked it. I didn't know any better.'

'What did Paul do?'

'He and Thierry had set up a little tattoo shop on the edge of town. It was the only place they could afford to pay the rent. But tattoos were starting to take off, and they were both good. That's why Paul had the cash to take me out.'

She waited, expecting Francis to ask more questions, but he sat in silence, seeming quite content to let her tell the story at her own pace.

'Sarah went home at the end of the summer, but I stayed on, on my own. I asked Paul if he would tattoo me. Before meeting him, I'd hardly come across tattoos. Paul was covered in the most amazing black and grey tattoos. I was fascinated by them and I wanted one of my own, so I went to the tattoo studio. That's when I met Thierry. That's when the trouble started.'

She paused.

'What happened?'

'At that point, I had no idea that Paul had a twin.' Marni shifted in her chair. 'Paul came in and found me talking to Thierry. He totally lost the plot, accusing Thierry of trying to make a move on me. Nothing could have been further from the truth, but Paul was furious.'

'What did Thierry do?'

'He just laughed. I could see that Paul was scared of him. Later, he told me never to talk to Thierry again – or he'd make me regret it.'

'He threatened you?'

'I should have realised then. But I had no experience with men. I thought it just proved how much he loved me.'

Francis looked shocked.

'There's more. I was stupid. I asked Thierry to tattoo me. That night, Paul beat me up.'

'Can you show me Thierry's tattoo?'

Marni pulled up the sleeve of her sweatshirt to expose a dense, dark tattoo – the figure of a male angel, head bowed and hooded, with a flaming sword in one hand and a feather in the other. He wore the breast plate and leather skirt of a Roman centurion.

'You've seen it before.'

Francis nodded, but was still transfixed.

Marni shivered and pushed her sleeve back down. 'That's when I should have left.'

25

Marni

'Time's nearly up.'

It was the woman guard who'd brought Marni to the visitor centre. She stared down at them in a way that was anything but friendly.

Francis dug into his trouser pocket and pulled out his warrant card. She looked at it and nodded. 'Okay.'

Francis went to the vending machine and fetched two cups of coffee.

Marni cleared her throat. Telling the story was making her hoarse. She wanted to finish.

'To cut a long story short, I fell in love with Thierry and moved in with him. He was kinder to me than Paul was, and we had a much better connection, instantly – physically and mentally. Thierry was more mature and I didn't feel like I was constantly walking on eggshells because of his ego. Paul couldn't handle it. He wouldn't leave me alone. He followed me to work and watched me from outside the bistro, leaning against a lamp-post across the road.'

'Weren't you frightened of him?'

'No. He was scared of Thierry. That was my protection. When I was still with Paul, he'd tattooed me one night, while I was drunk. I didn't even realise what was happening, but when

Thierry found out, he beat Paul senseless. That's when I left Paul for Thierry.'

'What was the tattoo?'

'A garland of roses, just underneath my left breast. I had it lasered away when I came back to England.' But there was still a white scar, a constant reminder. 'Paul wouldn't leave me alone.'

'Did he threaten you?'

Marni shook her head. 'He never even spoke to me. But his presence was a constant threat. He would push past me, knocking into me with his shoulder, or he'd follow me. Not surreptitiously, but actually walking half a pace behind me. If I stopped for anything, to cross a road, whatever, he'd bump into me.' Her hands were shaking in her lap. 'I ignored him as much as possible, but it started to wear me down. I began to be afraid of him.'

'What did Thierry do?'

'I didn't tell him. There was already enough bad blood between them, and I was scared Thierry would kill him.'

'So what happened?'

'It went on for months. I couldn't bear it so I decided to put a stop to it. Paul still lived at home with their mother. I went to her house one afternoon to confront him. It was the worst decision of my life. I was going to have it out with him, tell him to lay off.'

Francis shook his head – he could probably guess what was coming. He'd heard the bare bones of the story before.

'That was when he raped me. His mother was out, and he pushed me back onto her kitchen table and forced himself on me.'

'For the love of God, Marni . . .'

She remembered Paul answering the door, bare-chested, in tight jeans. She remembered going into his mother's kitchen – the smell of cabbage and stale coffee. There were breadcrumbs on the table, a half-eaten French stick lying on the counter. She remembered the gingham curtains that hung at the kitchen window, a little too short, fluttering in the draught.

She'd looked around and realised they were alone.

'Where's your mother?' she'd said.

Paul had shut the front door and leaned back against it. 'You didn't come here to see her, did you?'

Marni re-experienced the sensation of fear that had flooded through her.

She remembered the sound of buttons ringing on the floor tiles as Paul ripped open her shirt. The hiss of lace fabric being rent, his hands on her bra. The scratch of his nails on her stomach as he tugged off her jeans. The sharp edge of the kitchen table cutting across her buttocks. The breadcrumbs like grit under her bare back.

A fly buzzed lazily around the ceiling light.

Outside, a car horn blared angrily.

She remembered the pressure of Paul's hand across her mouth, the salt taste of his skin. She remembered him grunting as he struggled to undo his flies while pinning her to the table with his body weight. She remembered watching a bead of sweat forming on his forehead – and how it felt as it landed on her cheek. She remembered trying to scream, then trying to bite his hand.

But she didn't remember the moment of penetration. At least her mind had been kind enough to black that out.

'Breathe,' said Francis. 'Put your head between your knees.'

Marni snapped back to the present with relief. She'd relived what Paul did to her too many times, but she never became numb to the effect of it. He'd raped her – because she'd chosen his brother over him.

'When he finished,' she said, the words coming slowly, 'he threw me down onto the floor. Then he went upstairs. I heard him taking a shower.'

'Is that when you stabbed him?' said Francis.

'No,' said Marni. 'I ran away. I was still scared of him then. But later I got angry. I couldn't tell Thierry what had happened, but it was there, like an invisible wall between us. He knew there was something wrong. I refused to talk to him, and we had our first row. That was when I knew I needed to take revenge for what Paul had done to me. That's when I stabbed him.'

It was a knife from Thierry's kitchen. Not a huge chopping blade, just a slim paring knife. She'd wanted to maim rather than kill. She'd waited outside Paul's new tattoo shop in the dark, her hand shaking.

Paul had finally emerged. Marni had waited for a few seconds. She didn't have to do this. She could turn and go back to Thierry's flat. It would be warm. They'd drink some wine, make love, listen to music while they smoked in bed.

But she had to do it.

He'd taken a short cut through an alley – he was going back to his mother's house.

She'd hurried after him, her trainers making no sound on the wet cobbles. She'd gained on him. As long as he didn't look round . . .

He had looked round, but only when it was too late.

The blade had sunk into his side without much resistance.

'With no thought of the consequences?'

What a typical Frank Sullivan question. Like he'd never done anything without careful planning in his life. He'd certainly never have let anger or a hunger for vengeance get the better of him. Marni stifled a sob and bit down on her knuckle. Francis reached out and touched her knee, but quickly withdrew his hand. Physical contact wasn't allowed between prisoners and visitors.

'The police broke down Thierry's door at dawn the next morning. Paul had been found and taken to hospital and, of course, he told them it was me. The police came for me and I ended up being charged with attempted murder. They kept me in prison until the trial.'

'That would be normal for such a serious crime.'

'I was a kid.'

'You told them he'd raped you?'

'Of course. But it was too late. They just shrugged that Gallic shrug, and said I should have reported it when it happened. If there'd been any evidence ... well, things might have been different.'

'Why didn't you report it?'

So even Francis wasn't above victim blaming. She stared at him, challenging him to tell her it was all her own fault. But his expression was sympathetic.

'I wanted to pretend it had never happened. I wanted to protect Thierry from the unpleasant truth that his brother was a rapist. And then I found out I was pregnant, and I didn't know who the father was. It could have been either of them.'

'Would you have terminated if you'd known for certain it was Paul's?'

'Probably not. I don't know. But there was no way of ever knowing which one of them was the father. Even a DNA test wouldn't help – they're identical twins.' She'd slipped back into talking about Thierry in the present tense, but she didn't correct herself.

'You were carrying twins, right?'

'I didn't learn that until they gave me a scan in the prison, just before the trial. It was a shock. But I couldn't even start to process it until the trial was out of the way. I stood in that dock, sick with fear, and I couldn't understand a word the lawyers or the magistrates said. They were all men, old men. I knew they'd find me guilty. *Coupable.*'

'Did Thierry know that Paul could have been the father?'

'Of course. He knew by then that Paul had raped me. But

he stood by me – he always stood by me. I was sent to Les Baumettes, in Marseille. France's most violent prison. I was a foreigner there and I'd stabbed a Frenchman. No one wanted to be my friend. I was attacked by a group of women in the showers. I lost one of my babies.'

They came at her while she was still under the jet of water, and shoved her around until she was unsteady on her feet. They were fully dressed, wearing heavy trainers. One of them stamped down her shin, onto the bridge of her foot. With a yelp of pain, Marni lost her balance and fell onto the tiled floor. One of the others kicked her in the stomach and then the breasts. Another kicked her back.

'Allez,' said a voice from the shower-room doorway. 'Le garde.'

They'd disappeared as quickly as they'd come, leaving Marni gasping in agony on the cold, white tiles. The shower was still running and when someone found her, fifteen minutes later, the water rushing down the drain was red with Marni's blood.

'The weird thing was, the day before the attack I'd got a letter from Paul.'

'Surely he wasn't allowed to write to you?'

'He'd put that it was from Thierry on the outside of the envelope, but I knew both their handwriting. He said he hoped that nothing bad would happen to my babies.'

Francis's head snapped up. 'A threat? Did you show anyone the letter?'

Marni shook her head. 'It was with my stuff, back in my cell. And when my things were brought to me at the medical unit, it had gone.'

26

Wednesday, 8 November 2017

Francis

As she told her story, Marni's voice had grown huskier and by the time she finished, Francis was having to strain his ears to hear her. When she fell silent, he picked up his coffee cup – but there was nothing left in it. Marni's had remained untouched throughout. She looked grey with exhaustion and he doubted she even had the energy to raise a cup to her lips.

'Were the women who attacked you ever prosecuted?'

'No.'

'Did you see them again?'

Marni shook her head. 'I spent the rest of my sentence in the medical unit, and by the time Alex was born, I'd served my time – though there was still a suspended sentence. Thierry and I moved to England straight away. We didn't want our child anywhere near Paul.'

'How did Thierry feel, knowing that Alex could have been Paul's son?'

'I know it was hard for him, but he chose to accept Alex as his.'

'Did you ever hear from Paul once you were over here?'

'Not for years. Nothing until he turned up here last summer, wanting to claim Alex as his own.'

Francis was silent. He knew that Paul had been in prison for another rape in the intervening period, and that there'd been a run-in between him, Marni and Thierry when he'd shown up in Brighton. Francis had questioned both Thierry and Marni at the time, but they were convinced he'd gone back to France. If he was back here now, it seemed not only possible, but likely, that he and Thierry had got into a fight.

Why wouldn't Rory give any credence to Marni's assertion that Paul had done it?

'Do you need a break, or do you want to tell me what happened last week?'

Francis hadn't thought it would be possible for Marni to turn any paler, but she did, and her hands shook uncontrollably in her lap. He felt torn. As her friend, he wanted to do nothing more than sweep her into his arms and give her the hug she so desperately needed. But he was here as a police officer and he was determined not to behave in a way that could be deemed unprofessional.

'Marni.' He spoke softly, putting a hand out to touch her shoulder. 'I'm so sorry for your loss. Thierry was a good man at heart.'

She wrinkled her nose and pursed her lips in an effort, he thought, to stop herself crying.

'God knows, he wasn't the easiest man to be married to.' She sniffed and rubbed a sleeve across her nose. 'But he didn't deserve what he got – a damaged wife. Our marriage was broken before it had even started.'

'I'm sure he loved you.'

'That's not always enough.'

Francis hadn't even experienced that. Her answer made him feel unqualified and inadequate.

'I need more coffee, and I'm getting you some more food.'

As he turned away, Francis took a deep breath. She'd been through so much that he hardly wanted to push her to relive this latest trauma. But if he was going to get to the bottom of what had happened to Thierry, he needed to know every last detail that she could give him.

He went to the vending machine and bought a chocolate bar for Marni. He didn't believe she'd eaten a decent meal since she'd been arrested, and she would be no good to him if she passed out. Then he turned to the coffee machine. Someone should report them for breaching the Trade Descriptions Act, he thought to himself, as he watched the watery brown stream of liquid being dispensed into a cardboard cup.

When he got back to where they were sitting, Marni had drawn her feet up under herself on the chair. Her arms were folded along the top of the chair back, and her head rested on her arms. Francis thought she was asleep. He didn't say anything, but put the two coffees and the chocolate down on the table.

Marni raised her head and he realised then that she hadn't been asleep. She'd been crying.

'Do you want me to come back tomorrow?'

She shook her head. 'I'll tell you now.'

'What was Thierry doing at the house? I thought he'd moved out.' He wanted to ease her gently into her story.

'He had moved out. But he still had stuff there, and I'd asked him to come and pick it up while I was out.'.

Francis pushed the chocolate bar towards her, but she ignored it.

'When I got home, I saw that the front door was open. Not wide open, but just like someone had pushed it shut and the latch hadn't caught. I thought it was Thierry being careless on his way out.'

'But it wasn't?'

'No. As soon as I came in, I heard a racket from the kitchen. Noises of fighting. Thierry's things were still in the hall and the kitchen door was shut. I thought maybe it was Alex, but when I called to him, it was Thierry who answered. He yelled at me to get out.'

'Did you hear anyone else?'

'Not when I was in the hall. I went into the kitchen and they were there, fighting on the floor.'

'Who was fighting?'

'Thierry and Paul. It was dark and there were no lights on. As I ran towards them, I saw that one of them had a knife.'

'Which one?'

'I don't know. It was dark. One of them ran for the back door, leaving the other lying on the floor – I couldn't tell which was which. When I went to the one on the floor, I realised it was Thierry. He'd been stabbed.' Marni stopped talking, overcome. She put a hand to her mouth and jerked in the chair as a huge sob racked her body.

Francis waited, silent.

'I pulled the knife out. I thought I was doing the right thing, but he died . . . ' She was crying uncontrollably now. He could hardly imagine how terrible it must have been. She'd been with Thierry, on and off, for nearly twenty years.

This time Francis didn't care about whether it was professional or not. He pulled his chair close enough to hers so that he could lean over and pull her into his arms. Her head came to rest on his shoulder and he rubbed her back. Now she was finally telling her story, it seemed as if all of her grief was spilling out of her at once. Her tears soaked through Francis's jacket, then his shirt, until he could feel them on his skin. It was the shoulder on which she'd tattooed the black outline of an octopus – it seemed so long ago now. Their relationship had changed so much since then.

'Marni?'

She raised her head from his shoulder to look up at him. Her lashes were clumped with tears, her cheeks wet.

'Marni, are you absolutely, one hundred per cent certain that it was Paul that you saw running out of the back door that evening?'

Marni stiffened in his arms as anger flashed across her face.

'I have to ask.'

She slumped back against him. 'Of course. Yes, it was definitely Paul.' She gasped back a sob. 'He must have come to the house looking for me. Or more likely, Alex.'

He held her tighter.

'I promise you, Marni. I'll find him and I'll make him pay for this. And I will get you out of here. Believe in me.'

But deep inside himself, a small voice whispered.

Are you making promises you can't deliver?

27

The Embalmer

Kemetism. Derived from the Egyptian *kmt*, being the native name of Ancient Egypt, also known as **Neterism** (from nṯr, the Coptic ⲚⲞⲨⲦⲈ *noute*, meaning 'deity'), or **Egyptian Neopaganism,** is the contemporary revival of Ancient Egyptian religion. A *Kemetic* is one who follows Kemetism.

The man says a prayer. Its purpose is to summon the Great Serpent within his breast. To prepare him to do the god's bidding. To prepare himself for immortality.

It's time for another sacrifice.

On the seafront, marking the point where Brighton ends and Hove begins, there's a statue. It's made of bronze, but the years have weathered it to a blueish-green. It's an angel, balancing on a globe, supported on the tails of four dolphins. The angel of peace. In her left hand, she holds an orb. In her right hand, an olive branch. She's stood here for more than a hundred years, a memorial to Edward VII, who died in 1910. Three steps climb to the base of the pedestal, and it's surrounded by a postage stamp of grass.

This is where the man waits for his intended victim. He sent his quarry a message, the sort of cryptic invitation that the fool would respond to. And he's proved right – there's the man now, walking towards him, the only person in sight on the deserted promenade. Because even Brighton's busiest stretch is empty in the small hours . . .

'Hey there.'

The victim looks his way.

'You remember me don't you, Luke?'

Coming closer, Luke peers at him. It's still dark, though.

'I've changed a lot,' the man says, by way of explanation. And it's true. He has changed a lot. Beyond recognition, one might say.

'I don't know you,' says Luke.

'But you do.'

The man doesn't care that his victim doesn't remember him. Their shared past was a long time ago. And all that matters is the sacrifice.

A moment later, Luke's lying on his side on the grass at the base of the statue. He's winded, his hands on his guts, his spine curled protectively. He coughs, fighting for breath. His eyes are wide with fear, and maybe shock, the whites showing brightly in the moonlight.

The man stares down at him and listens to his whimper. A wide-legged stance, crossed arms resting on his chest.

'Please . . .'

It's pathetic. There's a plaque at the base of the plinth. The man reads out what it says. 'In Deo Fidemus. *Faith in God. Do you have faith in God, Luke?' His tone is one of cruel amusement. He doesn't say to which god he's referring. He hisses, enjoying the sense of power that's building within him.*

He puts his foot on Luke's neck, because he's not interested in hearing Luke's reply to his question. Then he steps back and stares up at the statue. There's no blindfold on the angel. Her bronze eyes are open. A silent witness. An angel of vengeance, perhaps. For it is vengeance that has determined Luke's fate.

'You still don't remember me, do you?' says the man.

Luke stares up at him. 'I tell you, I don't know you.'

Luke knew the previous version of him. Before the tattoos. Before the piercings. Before the brands. Before the cuts. Before he transformed himself into a god. The man doubts that Luke could put two and two together and work out who he was.

'It doesn't matter. I'm not doing this for you.'

The man takes aim to kick Luke in the mouth. He thinks better of it. There'll be enough pain in a few minutes' time. The headlights of a car show up further down the front. He moves to put the plinth of the statue between him and the car. He's not worried about Luke, who's lying flat in the shadows. As the car passes, he moves around the pedestal to avoid being seen. He should get on with the sacrifice.

The man's wearing a battered parka, and from an inside pocket he pulls out a couple of cable ties. He rolls Luke over onto his front and grabs one of his arms. He secures a cable tie around the wrist. Not too tight – it's not his intention to stop the blood flow – but tight enough that Luke won't be able to wriggle his hand free. He takes the other cable tie and threads it under the first. Then he positions Luke's other wrist so he can secure it with the second tie. DIY handcuffs in a couple of moments.

He manhandles Luke up the three steps at the base of the plinth and puts him in a sitting position. Luke is as limp as a ragdoll. Fear has paralysed him, stolen his anger – the only things that move are his eyes, whites flashing in terror. The man brushes Luke's hair back from his forehead and makes a soothing sound, as if calming a child.

'You were a cruel boy,' says the man. 'And now it's caught up with you.'

Luke's mouth opens as if he's about to speak, but the man shoves a balled-up rag into it before any words are formed. It gives him immense satisfaction to silence him. Once and for all. Luke stares up at him, and finally the man sees a glimmer of recognition in his eyes.

'Yes, now you know who I am, don't you?'

Luke and he had been best friends at primary school. But when they changed schools, Luke had found new friends. Boys who could play football and ride bikes and tell jokes. Boys who taught him to be cruel and who laughed at others' expense. Wanting to be like them,

Luke had laughed louder than them. Had become more cruel. And who better to be cruel to than the little boy who had once been his friend?

Luke starts to struggle desperately, throwing himself onto his side in an attempt to roll down the steps. He makes loud guttural noises at the back of his throat.

'Shut it!' The man kicks him in the ribs, hard enough to wind him again.

Luke is struggling for breath, unable to pant through the rag in his mouth.

The man props him up again, laughing softly as he notices the sheen of tears on Luke's cheeks.

'You used to call me the cry baby. You're the cry baby now.'

Incanting the name of his god, the man releases a knife from its sheath. A shining blade that will assuage years of humiliation. A balm for all that pain.

Luke's bladder releases, soaking through his trousers in seconds, a cloud of warm steam rising around them.

His last living act.

It's the man's turn to laugh. At long last.

'You know my name now, don't you?'

He bends down and sets his blade to work.

28

Thursday, 9 November 2017

Francis

'Who were you talking to at this hour?' said Robin, coming into the kitchen in her dressing gown.

Francis closed his laptop and unplugged it from the charger. He'd been hoping she wouldn't be up quite yet. It was only just after seven.

'My brother,' he said.

'Your brother?' Robin's eyebrows shot up.

'Kit,' said Francis, pouring himself a second cup of coffee.

'Yes, I know you mean Kit. But it just surprises me to hear you referring to him as your brother.'

'Well, he is. He's our brother.'

Robin's face took on a sour expression. She'd never forgiven their father for leaving. Or for marrying again. And his arrival at their mother's funeral a few months earlier with a small child in tow hadn't sat well with her at all. Realising that their father now had a new, young family had come as a shock to both of them.

'How long has this been going on?'

She had an unerring capacity for making him feel like a naughty schoolboy, caught raiding the biscuit tin.

He shrugged. 'I want to get to know him.'

She sat down opposite him with a glass of juice.

'I don't see why. We're never going to have a relationship with him. He's only four years old and he's a stranger as far as I'm concerned.'

'I don't think he should be. Apart from Dad, he's our closest living relative.'

Francis felt a surge of relief when his phone rang.

'I'd better take this.' He got up and went to stand by the back door, where the signal was better.

'There's been another one.' He recognised Tom Fitz's voice.

'Another what?'

'One of those jars.'

'Don't touch it – I'm on my way.' He disconnected the call. 'I've gotta go,' he said to Robin.

She rolled her eyes. Francis was only too conscious that somehow his work always sent him a lifeline when he was getting into a tricky conversation with his sister.

Tom was waiting for him by the office's outer door. Without saying anything, he pointed to the front step. Francis looked down and saw another of the rough clay jars. This one's top was shaped like a baboon's head. Peering more closely at it, Francis could see that it had a small papyrus scroll attached to it, the same as the other ones.

'That's where you found it? You haven't moved it yet, have you?'

'Haven't touched it.'

Francis got out his phone and took a couple of pictures of it in situ. Then he called Rose.

Within twenty minutes the area was cordoned off, and Rose Lewis had arrived to take custody of the jar. She drew Francis to one side.

'You know, I've been reading up on these. There are four jars, four head shapes.'

'Right.'

'The last one had a human head. That represents Imsety, the god of the south. That jar always contains the liver. This one,' she pointed at the jar, 'is a baboon head. That's Hapi, the god of the north. The baboon-headed jar is always used for the lungs.'

Francis felt his stomach churn. 'You think that this jar contains a pair of lungs?'

'We'll find out when I get it back to the lab.'

'What are the other two jars?'

'One is the jackal-headed Duamutef, god of the east, used for the stomach, and the other is Qebehsenuef, god of the west. That one has a falcon head and is used for the intestines.'

Another thought struck Francis. 'Alicia Russell's body wasn't missing its lungs, was it? Or any of the other parts.'

Rose shook her head. Her expression was grim. 'Just her liver.'

'So if there are lungs in here, they belong to someone else. Open it now, Rose – I need to know if we should be looking for another body.'

Rose pulled on a pair of latex gloves and placed the jar on top of a large plastic evidence bag.

Tom Fitz came over to watch the procedure. Francis glanced round at him.

'Fitz, whatever we find in here stays out of your paper. At least for the moment, yeah?'

The reporter was looking pale. It was always his intention to plant himself right in the middle of the stories he reported on, but now he was involved in the random appearance of body parts, he didn't seem quite so cocksure.

He nodded at Francis, biting his bottom lip nervously.

Rose clutched the jar and slowly twisted its top until it came loose. She put the jar down on the plastic bag and gently lifted the lid. The familiar smell of herbs, spices and rotting flesh rose to Francis's nostrils.

Using a fine steel spatula from her kit bag, Rose eased out

the top layer of natron. She hooked some dark red tissue from beneath it and examined it more closely.

'Yup, that's lung tissue.' She twisted it slightly to catch the light. 'And it's from the lungs of a smoker – there are traces of tar inside the air sacs.'

She poked the tissue back into the jar and replaced the lid.

'It's definitely not from Alicia's body – you're sure of that?'

Rose nodded. 'I'm certain. Her lungs were intact and she wasn't a smoker.'

'Shit,' said Francis.

'What?' said Tom.

'Somewhere, soon, we're going to discover another body, this one missing its lungs. The third body. Three bodies means we've got a serial killer on our hands.'

Rose stood up. She'd placed the Canopic jar inside the evidence bag, and was holding a smaller one into which she'd scooped the natron that she'd dug out.

'What about this?' she said to Francis. She held out the small papyrus roll to him.

Quickly pulling on a pair of gloves, Francis took it from her. He undid the raffia and unrolled the stiff parchment. He immediately recognised the hieroglyphs – the snake and the ankh symbol – but there was more writing underneath them this time. He read it out loud, his voice faltering slightly as he grasped what he was saying.

A message for Frank: I'm coming for you.
But you can breathe easy until my next delivery.

'Jesus,' said Tom. 'What the hell's that all about?'

Francis's head was spinning. He knew the message was for him. But nobody had called him Frank since he was at school. Nobody apart from Marni. Suddenly this whole thing had taken on a personal dimension.

Rose grasped the top of his arm. 'You okay? You look like you've seen a ghost.'

Francis looked up. 'I'm fine,' he stammered.

'It's a challenge,' said Tom. 'The killer's taunting us. Not only do we need to work out who he is, but we need to work out who this Frank is.'

'I need to call this in,' said Francis. He dialled the duty sergeant at John Street.

'I was just going to call you,' said the sergeant.

'Why?' A sense of dread made Francis shiver.

'Report of a body, down by Hove Lawns. Sounds pretty nasty . . . you'll probably want to get down there. Meantime, what can I do for you, sir?'

'Nothing. I'm on my way. Call Albright and Burton, get them out there too.' He disconnected. 'Come on, Rose. We've got another.'

29

Thursday, 9 November 2017

Gavin

Harry Albright-Singh cracked eggs into the pan and stepped back just in time to avoid a splash of oil. The whites sizzled and bubbled up. Gavin watched him. His hands, specifically. He loved Harry's hands – long, slim fingers that made quick, dextrous movements. Harry prodded the edges of the eggs with a wooden spatula, checking that they weren't sticking to the pan.

'You're whistling,' said Gavin.

'And?'

'Not a tune. Just whistling.'

'I'm happy.'

As if the words had tempted fate, Gavin's phone buzzed on the kitchen table. Gavin saw Harry frown slightly as he took the call.

'Got a body.'

'Yeah ... where?' Gavin walked over to the patio doors and looked out on the garden as he listened to the duty sergeant. The leaves needed raking.

'The statue of the angel. It's at the Brighton end of the Hove Lawns.'

'Okay – I'll be there in five.' He dropped the phone on the table. 'Can you stick one of those eggs in a roll?'

'Sure.' No more whistling.

'Sorry, mate.' Gavin shrugged – he wasn't supposed to be working today. It was Harry's day off and they'd had plans. Shopping for Gavin's birthday present, maybe lunch somewhere in town, a film. 'I'll let you know as soon as I know how long I'll be. It's a body.'

Harry grimaced. He didn't really like to hear the details of Gavin's work. He tore off a piece of kitchen paper, folded it around the fried egg roll and held it out.

'Thanks, babe. I'll make it up to you. Promise.'

The Hove Lawns stretched west along the seafront for nearly a mile from the boundary between Brighton and Hove. Gavin knew the statue of the angel. It was only a few minutes' walk from the small terraced house he shared with Harry, but he took his car so he'd be able to drive to the station afterwards.

He pulled up and parked on a yellow line at exactly the same time as a black BMW Z4. It tucked in behind his Audi, and Rose Lewis emerged onto the pavement a fraction after him, followed by the boss from her passenger seat. They crossed the road together, exchanging hellos.

'Nice car,' said Gavin. He wasn't jealous. Not one little bit.

Angie Burton was waiting for them on the paved area at the edge of the Lawns, watching as a couple of uniforms extended crime-scene tape to cut off the pavement on either side. She came towards them and after a cursory nod, began to explain what was going on.

'The station got a call just after seven. A man on his way to work, about six thirty, spotted someone sitting on the steps at the bottom of the angel statue. He thought the guy was asleep, but as he got closer, he saw the blood and realised he was dead.'

'The witness made that assessment for himself?' said Francis.

'There's an awful lot of blood.' Angie looked a little bilious.

'He immediately called an ambulance. The paramedics arrived at seven, and confirmed the death.'

Gavin looked round. There was no sign of an ambulance now.

'I took their details and let them go,' said Angie. 'They've got more important things to do than hang around with a cadaver.'

'Show us the body,' said Rose.

Angie led them around to the far side of the statue, and Gavin saw him. A man, sitting on the top of the three steps that surrounded the plinth. If he'd been alive, he would have been looking out to sea. The statue was far enough from the main road along the front that the drivers of passing traffic wouldn't have spotted him, though if he'd been on the road side of the plinth, he would have been more obvious to them.

Gavin did a quick visual assessment. Thirty-ish, tall, the early indications of weight gain – a softening of the face that had probably once been angular and handsome. Short blond hair, recently cut. Despite the pallor of death, the sort of tan that, in November, suggested foreign travel or regular sunbeds. It made his skin look yellow now. His eyes were open. But most striking of all – his torso was drenched with blood. His clothes had been cut away from his body and as far as Gavin could see through the gore, he'd been slashed open along a horizontal line just where his ribcage ended. Blood had soaked through his clothing. The steps he was propped on were red with it, and it glistened darkly in the grass at the base of the plinth. Gavin looked away quickly but the ferrous smell hanging in the air stopped him from clearing the image from his mind.

'He's not a rough sleeper,' said Francis. 'Look, that's a smart suit, and his shoes are polished.' He bent closer to the body and pointed at the man's wrist. He was wearing a chunky gold watch that looked expensive. 'It's not a mugging.'

'No,' said Angie. 'That was my first assumption, but it doesn't seem to be the case.'

'What can you tell us, Rose?' said Francis.

'Hmmm.' Rose stepped up closer to the body, pulling a pair of latex gloves from her pocket and putting them on. She leant in close to study the man's gaping wound. 'Yup,' she breathed, gently pressing her index finger upwards into the cut.

'What?' said Francis, peering in over her shoulder.

'His lungs have been removed,' she said. 'I'll check for a match in the lab, but chances are we've found our victim.'

Gavin wondered what she was talking about.

'*The Argus* received a Canopic jar containing lung tissue earlier this morning,' said Francis, bringing Gavin and Angie up to speed.

Rose straightened up. 'I would guess we're looking at the same killer as Alicia Russell. The cut's in a different position, but that's just because he was harvesting different organs. I need to take pictures in situ.'

As Rose sorted out her camera, Francis put on latex gloves and checked the pockets of the man's bloody suit jacket. He pulled out a black wallet and rifled through it.

'Money's still here,' he said. 'Ah.' He pulled out a driving licence. 'Luke Bridges.'

'Call that in to the station,' said Angie to Gavin. 'See if he's been reported missing.'

'Got an address for him,' said Francis, holding up a small rectangle of pink plastic. 'Adelaide Crescent. That's not far away. Rose, can you take charge here?'

'Sure. Let's all step back now. I need to suit up before doing more – and I'll get the CSIs organised.'

'Gavin, get back to the station and take a look at the CCTV. See if you can work out when he arrived here and what happened – if the cameras picked it up.'

'We might be a bit far back from the road, but I'll see what there is.'

'Rose, early guess at a time of death?'

'Making an initial estimate from the early onset of rigor – I'd say he died sometime between one a.m. and four a.m. this morning. I should be able to tighten that up a bit once I've taken his core temperature, but that's basically your window.'

'Right, Angie, let's go and check out the dead man's address.'

30

Thursday, 9 November 2017

Francis

Luke Bridges' wallet had more secrets to divulge.

'We've got a business card, too,' Francis said. 'Apparently he's the sales director of a company called Falmer Racing Bikes. Based up at the Sussex Innovation Centre on the university campus.'

Gavin let out whistle. 'I know them – amazing bikes.'

'You've got a motorcycle?' said Angie.

Gavin laughed and shook his head. 'Bicycles, and I'd give my eye teeth to have a Falmer.'

'Why don't you just get one then?' said Francis.

'Yeah, north of six grand apiece. That'd go down well with Harry.'

'Gavin, head back to the station and open a book on this one. As well as checking the CCTV, look for any parallels or connections with the Russell case. Angie, we'll go and check out the home address – Adelaide Crescent in Hove.'

Gavin headed back to his car.

'That's just off the front, isn't it?' said Angie, falling into step with Francis as he walked away in the opposite direction.

'Yes, only a little bit further along,' said Francis. 'Look, we don't know yet if he's married or not. You might need to play the Family Liaison role. Feeling up to it?'

Angie pulled a face – Francis knew it wasn't her favourite part of the job, and she was still in a vulnerable place. Although she was back at work, some days he didn't feel that she was entirely present. It was going to take a long time for the old Angie to fully reappear.

'I'll be okay – as long as we can call in a proper FLO if he does have a family.'

'Thanks,' said Francis. 'I want to move as fast as possible on this. It looks like it's linked to Russell and the mummified woman. It's critical that we find the link between the victims – It's the only way we'll be able to pinpoint the killer.'

Angie shuddered and stared out towards the sea. 'Whoever it is, he seems pretty fucked up.'

'Which means he'll do it again. And again . . .'

She turned back to face him. 'What if there's no link?' said Angie. 'Bridges lives close enough to the murder site that he could have simply been in the wrong place at the wrong time. Maybe it was an opportunistic killing.'

They turned off the seafront into Adelaide Crescent, a horseshoe-shaped curve with a small, elegant park in the middle. To the north of this was the long rectangle of Palmeira Square. Both were lined with grand, sweeping terraces of smart Georgian houses – white stucco, wrought-iron railings and Juliet balconies in volume.

'Posh round here, isn't it?' said Angie. 'He must have been doing all right in the bike business.'

Francis shrugged. 'Or family money.' A small bike start-up was hardly likely to have paid for a flat in this part of town.

Angie gave a dry laugh. 'Yes, I forgot some people have that.'

Was it a little dig? Francis couldn't be quite sure – but he knew his own reputation in the department for being a 'posh boy'.

The imposing front door had a selection of doorbells. Angie pressed one of them with her index finger.

A woman's voice answered. 'Yes?'

'Police,' said Angie. 'Could we come up and talk to you for a moment, please?'

'About what?' The woman sounded indignant.

'This is Luke Bridges flat?'

'He lives here, yes.'

'We'll need to come upstairs.'

There was an electronic buzzing and Francis leant against the heavy door. Above them, he heard the sound of another door opening. There was a staircase directly in front of them, so he led the way up. On the first-floor landing, a blonde woman stood in the doorway of a flat. She was on the unhealthy side of thin, but she sported a deep tan. She looked them up and down expectantly.

'Are you Mrs Bridges?' said Angie.

The woman shook her head, a puzzled look on her face. 'No. We're not married – we live together. Don't say the bastard's still married?'

'No, no,' said Angie quickly. 'We didn't know if he was married or not.'

'D'you want to come in then?' The woman turned away and retreated into the flat.

Francis exchanged a look with Angie as they followed her inside.

She called him a bastard. To people she didn't know, to the police. That was interesting.

The woman took them into a large living room, with three floor-to-ceiling windows which overlooked the square at the front. Francis's feet sank into the pale carpet as he took in the modern artwork on the walls and the angular modern furniture. The woman took up position by the fireplace and faced them.

'What's 'e done then? You lot don't drop in to pass the time of day.'

'What's your name?' said Angie.

'Steph. Steph Carter.' Her eyebrows were raised.

There was a photo on the mantelpiece showing a couple. It was of Steph Carter and Luke Bridges. They were somewhere on a hilltop, both holding expensive-looking mountain bikes. Maybe that was why she was so thin.

'You might want to sit down, Steph,' said Francis.

'No ...' Steph shook her head, as Angie took one of her arms and guided her to a sofa on one side of the fireplace. 'Please don't tell me ...' She had guessed what they were going to say.

'I'm afraid a body has been found and we have reason to believe that it's Luke Bridges,' said Francis. His tone was gentle but it couldn't in any way lessen the impact of the news.

Steph dropped onto the cushions like a stone, her face crumpling.

'Could you have made a mistake?' Her voice sounded like a little girl.

Francis shook his head. 'I'm sorry. When did you last see him?'

'He went out last night. I didn't wait up.' She stopped talking, overcome by emotion.

Angie sat next to her, slipping an arm around her shoulders. 'It's all right. Take your time.'

Steph sniffed and pressed the back of her forearm against the bottom of her nose. 'He wasn't here when I woke up.'

'Where did you think he was?'

'Still out. At a club ... or gone home with someone.' The crying overtook her again.

'Some water, boss? And tissues.'

'Of course,' said Francis.

It was his cue to take a surreptitious look around the flat, while Angie tried to glean what she could from Steph Carter. Beyond the living room, he found a kitchen and a small study – practically a box room. There was a large double bedroom with an en suite, the bed unmade and clothes left untidily over the backs of chairs. He made his way quietly back to the study. The desk was for the most part tidy, apart from a wire in-tray piled high with papers and documents. He leafed through the top few. Bank statements for personal accounts, sales reports for the bike company, utility bills, a membership renewal for a health club … He wouldn't find anything here in the space of a minute or two, so he went back to the kitchen to fetch the water. There would be time enough. The team would go through the flat with a fine-tooth comb, and through every other aspect of Luke Bridges' life, until they'd found out what linked him to Alicia Russell and the museum, and who had killed him. It had sounded like there was an ex-wife – that would need looking into.

He took a glass of water and a box of tissues into the living room. Angie was on the phone.

'It would be good if you could come and be with her,' she was saying. 'We wouldn't want to leave her on her own.'

Steph Carter took the water gratefully and drank half the glass.

'Can you tell me a little bit about Luke?' he said. 'Who his friends were. Where he would have gone last night.'

'He had a gang of mates, cycling friends, but I don't think he was out with them last night. Mostly they weren't the clubbing types. He had other friends he saw when he went clubbing. Women, some of them.' Her face twisted into a sneer.

'You wondered before if he was still married? Presumably he's got an ex-wife?'

'Sandra. He wouldn't have been with her. She ran off with another bloke. He was a mess when I met him. Couldn't forgive her. The bloke used to be one of his cycling buddies – but they don't see each other any more for obvious reasons.'

'Do you know his name?'

'Kevin. I don't know his second name but Luke will …' And

then she realised what she'd said and burst into tears.

'This Kevin. Would you call him an enemy of Luke's?' Francis wanted to press on and get as much information out of Steph before she could start to dwell on what had happened and re-frame everything she said to fit with her own imagined version of events. Not that this murder looked like a fight between love rivals – not with the Canopic jars and the other bodies.

Steph took a moment to consider the question. 'Well, I'm pretty sure they wouldn't give each other the time of day, but why would Kevin want to kill him? He'd already got the girl. And Luke had moved on anyway. We've been together three years now.'

'Anything else you can think of?'

'I was going to leave him,' she said, looking up apologetically. 'I told him so last week. I was fed up with the way he treated me.'

'How did he treat you?' said Angie.

'Seeing other women, sleeping around.'

'You suspect this or you know for sure?'

'I confronted him,' she said. 'Last week. I accused him and he didn't deny it. That's when I said I was leaving him.'

'How did he take it?'

Steph grimaced. 'Not good.' Then her face screwed up again. 'He didn't top himself, did he?'

'I don't think so. We'll know more after the post-mortem.'

This really wasn't the conversation to have now. Francis looked to Angie for assistance as she lowered her phone from her ear.

'Steph's sister is coming over,' said Angie. 'I can stay here until she arrives, if you need to be getting on.'

Francis beckoned her over to the window, leaving Steph dis-solving on the sofa.

'Will you be able to take them to the morgue to do the formal ID?' he asked.

'Sure.'

'Let's get it done then. We need to get moving on this case. I'll head back to the station if you're okay here. Find out what you can about the ex-wife, her new partner, and also about any business associates he has.'

'Will do, boss.'

It was a long walk back to the station, but it gave Francis the time to think things through. He thought mostly about Marni. He called Rose.

'Get any other prints off the knife yet?'

'No. Just Marni's.'

'And the footprint?'

'Nothing else there.'

'Damn!'

'She could plead self-defence, Francis. They'd broken up. Thierry was in the house.' She paused. 'He had quite a track record with the police – he was a violent man.'

'No chance,' he said, shocking himself with the strength of his anger. 'He dealt drugs and he got into fights, but he was never violent towards women. There's not a single complaint against him from Marni, or any other woman. She shouldn't need to plead guilty to something she didn't do.' He stopped, realising he was almost shouting.

Rose gave him a couple of seconds. 'Okay.'

'The evidence you found of the other footprint . . .'

'It's not enough to get her off, I'm sure of it. The circumstances suggesting it was her are too persuasive.'

'There was someone else there.'

'But there's nothing to suggest it was Paul Mullins. It's more likely to be a CSI whose shoeprint we missed.'

'So what the hell am I going to do to help her?'

'This really matters to you, doesn't it?'

'I want to see justice done.'

'It's more than that, Francis, isn't it?'

'So help me.'

'What about the CCTV footage?'

'The cameras don't cover Great College Street.'

'And Abbey Road? If there was someone there that we don't know about, I think he took off through the back gardens. They lead out onto Abbey Road, from where he could have run off in the opposite direction to Great College Street.'

Francis slapped his palm to his forehead.

'You okay?'

'You're brilliant, Rose. You know that?'

He started to run, dialling Kyle Hollins as he did.

'Kyle? You in the station? Get me the CCTV footage for Abbey Road on the night of Thierry Mullins's murder. We just might have missed something.'

He hoped to God Rose was right.

31

Friday, 10 November 2017

Gavin

'Here we are – Science Park Square,' said Gavin, pulling into a parking place. 'Got a ring to it, hasn't it?'

'No unnecessary imagination squandered on that name,' said Angie with a smile.

They got out of the car and looked round. The anodyne modern office buildings could be a business park anywhere, Gavin thought to himself. They were at the University of Sussex, and it was about as far removed from dreaming spires as one could imagine. It was, however, where Falmer Racing Bikes were based, working as a start-up business out of the Sussex Innovation Centre. Gavin and Angie had phoned ahead and snagged an appointment with the company's MD, Roger Hazelton.

'You saw the girlfriend yesterday?' asked Gavin, as they stood waiting in the reception area of the red-brick office blocks that surrounded the square.

'Yes. Didn't get much from her.'

'Mr Hazelton will see you now,' said the receptionist. Her bored expression told Gavin that she wasn't impressed with the fact that they were police.

They followed her through a door on the right-hand side of her desk, then down a corridor.

'In there,' she said, pointing to a pair of grey double doors at the end. She turned and went back the way she'd come, leaving them to see themselves in.

Gavin pushed open one of the doors, just as a man stretched out his hand to pull one open on the other side.

'Come in,' he said. 'I'm Roger Hazelton.' He was about the same age as Luke Bridges had been, and he sported the same dark tan – and in keeping with his business, he was dressed in Lycra cycling kit, emblazoned with the Falmer Racing Bikes logo. 'Sorry,' he said, glancing down at what he was wearing, 'just cycled in.'

'I'm Detective Constable Albright,' said Gavin. 'This is DC Burton.'

Hazelton ushered them into a cavernous room that seemed part office, part bicycle repair shop. There were bits of machinery and work benches, and everywhere parts of bikes – wheels, handlebars, gear mechanisms. On the far side of the space, a middle-aged man was working a piece of metal on a grinding machine. It didn't look very cutting edge as far as Gavin was concerned. Hazelton led them to an area near the full-length windows where there was a sofa and a coffee table.

'I take it you're here about Luke?' he said, indicating that they should sit.

'You've heard?' said Angie.

He nodded. 'I can't believe it. Steph phoned me yesterday and said he was dead. What happened to him? I couldn't get much sense out of her.' He pulled up a spare metal chair and planted it opposite them.

Gavin and Angie had discussed what they were going to say with Francis before coming out. Gavin hadn't been quite sure whether they should make it public yet that Luke Bridges had been murdered, the assumption being that if they told his work colleagues it would be fully out in the public domain. Angie had argued that they should be honest about what had happened. After all, the sort of questions they would need to ask would make it quite clear that his death hadn't been due to natural causes. 'Ask what you need to,' Francis had said, 'but then don't confirm or deny anything they might suppose as a result.'

'Mr Hazelton, when did you last see or speak to Luke Bridges?' Gavin took the lead with the questions, as agreed.

'Wait.' Hazelton frowned. 'You haven't told me what happened to him yet.'

'He was found sitting at the base of the Angel of Peace statue by Hove Lawns early on Saturday morning,' said Angie.

'But how did he die?'

'We're not at liberty to discuss that at this point,' said Gavin. 'Can you tell me when you last had contact with him?'

'Yes . . . of course.' Hazelton thought for a moment. 'I last saw him at work on Friday. I left early and he was still here.'

'What time was that?'

Hazelton shrugged. 'Half past three? Maybe a bit later.'

'Did you speak to him at any point after that?'

'No.' Hazelton looked from one to the other of them. 'Why are you asking these questions? Was there something suspicious about his death?'

'Was Mr Hazelton depressed or upset in your opinion?' said Angie.

'You think he killed himself?' He shook his head. 'No, he wasn't the type to do something like that.'

'Had he argued with anyone in the last few days?'

'Not that I know of. I mean, things weren't great with Steph, but I'm sure they were working it out.'

'Steph said she'd told him she was going to leave him.' Gavin watched Hazelton's expression closely as he imparted this. He didn't look surprised – but then his hooded eyes hadn't given away much emotion at all during the course of the questions. He

168

seemed a little cold in face of the fact that his business partner had just been discovered dead.

'She might have been. His personal life was a mess.'

'In what way?' said Gavin.

Hazelton shrugged. 'Always some drama going on between Steph and the ex. He would wind them up about something, then watch the fallout.'

'We understand he had an ex-wife as well?'

'Where are these questions leading?' His eyes narrowed.

'Do you have contact details for her?' said Angie. 'We need to inform her of what's happened.'

'Can't you get her number off his phone?'

The sound of the grinding machine in the background stopped, making Gavin suddenly aware of how noisy it had been.

'Mr Hazelton, do you know if Luke had any money problems or if he'd fallen out with friends, family or business associates?'

A glimmer of understanding crossed Hazelton's face. The question told him that the police thought his colleague had been murdered. But he shook his head.

'No. Luke was a good guy. Everyone liked him. Our business is doing fine. It's not always easy, running a small company like this – but we're moving ahead. Great things in the future.'

Gavin felt that Hazelton was parroting a well-rehearsed speech about his company – the sort of thing he would say to his bank manager or investors. He wondered how true it was.

'Thank you,' he said. 'So you don't know of any enemies that he might have had?'

'No,' said Hazelton firmly.

'Have you ever heard Luke mention someone called Alicia Russell?'

'What? No.' He glanced at his watch. 'Look, I've got an important meeting in a little while, and I need to get out of this kit.' He stood up and stared pointedly at the door.

'Thank you, Mr Hazelton.' Gavin fished out a card. 'If you think of anything that might be at all relevant, please give either of us a call on this number.'

Hazelton took the card but barely glanced at it.

'We'll see ourselves out,' said Angie. She obviously wasn't impressed with Roger Hazelton.

'Jerk,' she hissed, once they were through the double doors. 'He told us precisely nothing – a big waste of time.'

'Seems like he was more interested in his business than his partner.'

Gavin turned as he heard the door opening behind them. The man who'd been using the grinding machine came out, closing the door deliberately. He was older, with scruffy grey hair and a beard that was in need of trimming. He was dressed in oil-stained overalls, and his mechanic's hands were grimy.

'Excuse me?' He sounded uncertain.

'Yes?' said Gavin.

'I couldn't help overhearing . . .' He glanced nervously back at the door. 'I don't want to talk out of turn . . .'

Angie stepped forward, almost into his personal space. It meant he'd be able to say whatever he needed to say more quietly.

'Look, it sounds like you think Luke was murdered?'

Angie gave an almost imperceptible nod. Gavin realised it was the best way to keep the man talking.

'I was here on Friday afternoon. They had a row.'

'Who had a row?'

'Luke and Roger. A real humdinger – I thought they were going to come to blows.'

'Do you know what they were arguing about?'

The man shrugged. 'The company's not doing as well as Roger would have everyone believe. Luke wants to invest more money in marketing. He thinks . . . thought that we should reduce the quality of some of the components we use to pay for it. Roger wasn't having any of it.'

'What's your name?' said Gavin.

'Graham Pringle. I'm chief engineer. I design the bikes.'

'So what did you think of Luke's plan?' said Angie.

'Terrible. Going down the road of making cheaper bikes would put us in competition with manufacturers in Eastern Europe and China. I would have resigned if Roger had agreed to it. But Luke was impatient. He wants – wanted money and he wanted success, without having to put in the graft.' He looked towards the doors again. 'I'd better go.'

'Thank you for talking to us,' said Angie.

Gavin gave him a card and he disappeared.

'What do you make of that, then?' said Gavin, as they made their way back to the car.

'Interesting,' said Angie. 'But if the business partner did it, what are his links to Alicia Russell and the museum? Something's just not adding up.'

'You're right. But maybe Bridges' ex-wife can shed some light on it.'

'Maybe. Looks like we'll have to have his phone hacked. After all, we have those people, don't we?'

'Or we could just resort to dead man's finger,' said Gavin with a grin.

32

Francis

'Tell me more about Luke Bridges, Rose. Did he die in situ?' He heard her shuffling papers at the other end of the line.

'Nothing so far to suggest he didn't. Grass and dirt on the soles of his shoes visually match the small area of grass around the base of the statue, suggesting at some point he was upright there. I also found a small clipping of opaque plastic, consistent with a cable tie. On inspecting his wrists, there are signs of chafing, so I think at some point they were secured.'

'But not when he was found?'

'No.'

'What else? Cause of death – is that definite?'

'Of course, I'm not going to say it's definite until I've completed the PM. But, yes, ninety-nine per cent sure that the wound killed him. His lungs were ripped out, and there's nothing to suggest he was already dead when that happened.'

'Any other injuries?'

'A couple of abrasions on his knuckles, a slight bruise on one knee. He could have been in a scuffle, but not a major fight or beating-up. Nothing else obvious from my initial examination of the body. He's got a couple of scars, but they're old and not of significant size.'

As Rose spoke, Francis brought up the news section of *The*

Argus's website on his PC. He wanted to check that Fitz was keeping his side of the bargain by not spilling everything they knew about the murders so far. It was all pop-ups and adverts, until a sensationalistic headline and a picture of Tutankhamun leapt out at him: Whose mummy is this?

'Damn!'

'I'm sorry?' Rose sounded more than put out.

'Not you, Rose. That bastard Fitz. Listen to what he's published: "*The Argus* was once again at the centre of the Egyptian murder mystery that's baffling the police investigation squad led by DI Francis Sullivan. This creepy embalmer has so far left a mummified body in the Booth Museum, and is thought to be responsible for two further disembowelled corpses. *The Argus* has been the recipient of a pair of ghoulish Egyptian burial jars containing organs from the dead bodies, and secret messages addressed to an unknown person are quickly turning this into Brighton's most terrifying mystery ..." This is bullshit. Sorry, Rose – gotta go.'

The story went on, embroidering the role of the newspaper in the case, hinting that they alone could solve it – the promise of an ongoing drama and plenty of excitement to come.

He glanced at the byline. It was written by Fitz.

At the bottom of the page there were links to the story so far – Fitz's take on the discovery of the mummy and an exclusive interview with Nathan Cox. He could see quite clearly that most of the details had been supplied by Cox, to which Fitz had added a liberal dash of lurid speculation. But further down the page, there were the details of what the police had found when they'd unwrapped the mummy, which in Fitz's prose sounded like nothing more than the unwrapping of a particularly special birthday present. And there – the critical detail – in each of the dead woman's hands they had found tiny carved shabti, ancient figurines buried with the dead to act as their servants in the afterlife.

'Rory?' he yelled from his doorway.

Rory was at his desk in the incident room, typing at high speed with two fingers.

'Boss?'

'Got a moment?'

'Sure.' He typed a last few words, then came across to Francis's office. Francis nodded at him to close the door when he came in.

'You seen today's *Argus*?' Francis said, as Rory sat down opposite him.

Rory shook his head. Francis twisted his monitor round so Rory could see the screen. The sergeant skimmed the pages quickly.

'Same old shit from Fitz – he's ramping up the heat, making people jump at their own shadow.'

Francis nodded in agreement. 'Playing his favourite tune – what have the police done to catch the killer? If you read some of the comments, you'd think we were the bad guys.'

'He probably puts his mates up to leaving half those comments.'

'Maybe, but not for much longer.'

'What d'you mean?'

'Look – he says the body was found with a shabti in each hand.' Francis pointed at a paragraph of Fitz's piece.

'I don't remember that.' Rory looked puzzled.

'So you didn't tell him.'

'Of course not.'

'I know. I told one person. One person only.' He paused. 'And they told Fitz.'

Realisation dawned across Rory's features and he started to nod. 'You think it's Bradshaw?'

'I know it's Bradshaw.'

'But it could have been Rose. Or one of her lab technicians. They must have all known what she found when she unwrapped the body.'

'You're right. They did. They knew the truth – that the woman was found with a shabti in one hand and an ankh in the other.'

'Of course, I remember the ankh.'

'Exactly. It's the symbol for the Egyptian word for life – and it's one of the hieroglyphs he uses on the papyrus messages. But that's not the point. The fact is, I fed Bradshaw inaccurate information and now it's turned up on *The Argus*'s website. I've got him, Rory.'

Rory's eyebrows shot up.

'Got him? What the hell are you planning, boss?'

Francis leaned back in his chair and studied his deputy. Rory looked nervous. He'd always been Bradshaw's man. He was frowning as he stared back at Francis.

For Francis, this was the moment to draw the line. 'You're either with me or against me, Rory. In this and in everything.'

Rory shook his head. 'You know the chief is scared of you, of what you represent. He's old school. You kids come in here and think you can run the show. He's not ready for that.'

'It doesn't excuse what he's done – it's plain wrong.'

'You're making this personal.'

'He made it personal first. He's done all he can to obstruct me. He's tried to take me down. Now I'm going to take him down.'

Rory let out a low whistle.

'You can run to him, Rory. You can tell him what's about to happen. But if you do, you'll go down with him.'

'Jesus, boss, you're not pulling your punches.'

Francis felt a head of steam building up inside, ready to burst, but he also needed to be mindful of alienating Rory. Going up against the two of them together would be mad.

He leaned forward on the desk, resting his weight on his elbows. 'Rory, I respect you and the years of experience you've got on me. I think we work well together – and we could work even better together.' He paused, gauging Rory's reaction. 'I know you wanted this job, and I know I should have been more sensitive to that.'

'For fuck's sake, boss . . .'

'So?'

'So what?'

'Are you with me moving forward? I'm only going to ask you this once. Ever.'

Rory closed his eyes and pinched the bridge of his nose. Francis waited, wondering what thoughts were running through Rory's head. It was a high-risk strategy and he wondered if he was making a mistake, pushing his number two in this way.

But the chief was a duplicitous shit who couldn't be trusted. A red line had been set down and it was up to Rory to decide which side of that line he stood on. He couldn't straddle it any longer, playing them off against each other to his own advantage.

'Boss?'

'Yes?'

'I'm with you. Let's bring him down.'

33

Saturday, 11 November 2017

Gavin

Thank God it was Saturday. The week had been full on. Something had gone down the previous day between Rory and the boss, and Gavin hadn't been able to work out if they'd had an argument or a pow-wow. Whatever it was, they hadn't been in the mood for sharing. He'd kept his head down and got on with his assigned tasks – the morgue was getting crowded and he was desperate to find something that would give them a breakthrough.

That was why he was in the office, rather than still home in bed with Harry. He scanned the morning's emails, quickly moving most of them to his admin folder. He couldn't be bothered to read the latest directives on which form he should fill in to claim expenses or changes he needed to be aware of in the benefits-in-kind tax rules for personal mileage in his unmarked car. Nothing that couldn't be dealt with later.

That meant he could get on with looking into something, or rather someone, more interesting. Roger Hazelton.

When he'd first suggested taking a closer look at Hazelton, Rory and Angie had been sceptical. Despite Graham Pringle's assertion that Hazelton and Bridges had argued, it seemed a long shot that the result would have been murder. But Gavin had pushed for it. He hadn't liked what he'd seen at Science

Park Square. Hazelton had looked distinctively shifty when answering a couple of the questions they'd put to him. There was something – not to put too fine a point on it – sleazy about the man, and from what he'd seen of Bridges' lifestyle compared to the tiny business start-up . . . it called for some further scrutiny, that was all.

Sullivan had agreed with him and suggested digging into Hazelton's alibis for the times of death of Luke Bridges and Alicia Russell. He organised for Hazelton to be brought to the station by a couple of uniforms. Nothing like the pageantry of a formal request for interview to make a subject twitchy.

He'd been right. Hazelton paced the interview room, his arms folded firmly across his chest and a deep scowl on his features. Gavin watched him through the two-way glass for a few minutes as he and Angie worked out what to ask him. A couple of times Hazelton came up to the mirror, cupped both hands against it and stared through – but Gavin knew he wouldn't be able to see even the faintest shadow.

'Please take a seat, Mr Hazelton,' he said, as he entered the room.

Roger Hazelton ignored the instruction and glared at him. 'What exactly is the meaning of this? I answered all your questions yesterday.'

'Yes, you were very helpful, thank you. But we've just got a few more points to cover, so we thought it would be easier if you came in.'

'Easier for who?'

'Sit down, please. Let's make this as quick as we can.'

Angie came through the open door with a plastic jug of water and three paper cups. She put them down on the table and then went back to close the door.

Roger Hazelton sat down reluctantly. 'Ask away. I've got nothing to hide.'

A textbook response to being put in the glare of the spotlight.

'Thank you, Mr Hazelton,' Angie said.

Gavin poured a cup of water for each of them, watching Hazelton carefully as he did. A vein at Hazelton's left temple pulsed and fluttered, showing his nerves.

'Perhaps you could start by telling us where you were between midday on Friday, the third of November, and midnight on Saturday, the fourth of November.' The window of time for Alicia Russell's murder.

Hazelton frowned. 'I'm sorry,' he said, 'but what's all this about? I thought you were investigating Luke's death on Friday night.'

'Saturday morning,' corrected Gavin.

'We are,' said Angie. 'However, I'd like to know where you were on the third and fourth of November.'

'I've no idea – I'll need to check my calendar. What days of the week were they?'

'Friday and Saturday, like I said,' said Angie, calmly. Hazelton was getting rattled.

He dug into his trouser pocket and produced a sleek, black iPhone. He opened the screen using fingerprint recognition, and quickly clicked through to his calendar.

'I thought so,' he muttered. 'I was out that evening. With an old school friend.'

'Name?' said Gavin.

He paused a fraction too long. 'Sarah Bateman.'

'You were at a mixed school?'

'There's nothing odd about that,' said Hazelton.

'No, of course not,' said Gavin. 'I just thought from your accent that maybe you went to an all-boys school.'

'There were girls in the sixth form.'

Angie gave Gavin a look, but Gavin made a mental note to ask where he'd gone to school.

'Are you married, Mr Hazelton?' said Angie.

'Yes.' The answer was clipped. He wanted to close down this line of enquiry.

'What's your wife's name?' said Gavin.

'Dawn.'

'Was she with you that evening?' said Angie, tone even.

'No. She doesn't know Sarah Bateman.'

'I see,' said Gavin. 'What school were you and Miss Bateman at together.'

'Mrs Bateman,' said Hazelton. 'Brighton College.'

'You know we can check this information,' said Angie.

'Yes, I'm sure you can,' said Hazelton. 'Sarah and I have been friends on and off for years. That evening, we had dinner at Malmaison, down near the Marina. I had a room booked there for the night. And if possible, I'd rather you didn't mention this to my wife.'

'Of course,' said Angie. 'I understand. Perhaps, if you could give me Mrs Bateman's phone number, she could corroborate what you've told us.'

'I still don't understand why you're asking about that date in particular,' said Hazelton, phone number not forthcoming.

'Did you know Alicia Russell?' said Gavin, attempting to catch him off balance. Angie gave him an approving glance.

'You already asked me that yesterday,' said Hazelton.

'You remember the name from then? Or is it a name you're already familiar with?'

'I don't know her.'

'So if I look through your list of contacts, I won't find her name? Or her number?'

'No.'

'Would you mind showing me your contacts list at the letter R?'

'I want access to a lawyer.'

And that was that. Roger Hazelton called his lawyer, who hurried to his side, and advised him to answer every subsequent question the same.

'No comment.'

'No comment.'

'No comment.'

34

Saturday, 11 November 2017

Francis

The train had been packed, but the tube was even more crowded. There was a stink of wet wool, damp overcoats and stale cigarette smoke, and some woman had been particularly heavy-handed with a very cheap perfume. Francis breathed through his mouth as he felt elbows and backpacks pressing against him with each bump and sway of the carriage. A visit to London always made him appreciate Brighton more.

It was still raining when he emerged at Holborn, and he cursed himself for not having the foresight to bring an umbrella. However, the walk wasn't far enough to warrant a taxi, so he dug his hands into his coat pockets, put his head down and strode off as fast as he could along the busy pavement. He was adept at dodging the meandering tourists – that, after all, was one problem Brighton and London had in common.

By the time he arrived at the British Museum, his hair was plastered to his head and dripping down the back of his collar. He jogged up the steps and ducked behind one of the huge pillars, where he raked his hair straight with his hands. It would have to do.

'I've got a ten o'clock appointment with Professor Grieg,' he told the woman behind the reception desk.

'Department?' she said.

'Egyptology.'

She made a brief call to announce him, then put down her phone. 'He'll meet you by the Rosetta Stone. Go through the Great Court and take the left-hand exit into Room 4. You won't miss it.'

It only took him two minutes to reach the Rosetta Stone, but it was ten minutes before anyone appeared who wasn't obviously sightseeing. While he waited, he studied the huge black slab of stone – granodiorite, apparently – and the extraordinary ancient inscriptions carved into it. Hieroglyphs, Demotic script and Ancient Greek versions of the same text, which had made it the key to unlocking the meaning of the ancient Egyptian pictograms.

'I'm Professor Grieg,' said a voice behind him, making Francis turn around.

If he'd been expecting an Indiana Jones character, he'd been way off the mark. No Fedora, no whip, no matinee idol looks.

In fact, the man who greeted him with a firm handshake and introduced himself as Professor Matt Grieg in a pronounced American accent was approximately the same age as Francis. But that's where the similarity between them ended. While Francis was, as usual, in a dark blue suit with a sober tie, Grieg was in selvedge denim, a T-shirt and a battered pair of Doc Martens.

'DI Francis Sullivan. Good to meet you.'

'You're admiring the stone, I see.'

'What does it say?'

'It's a decree, establishing the divine cult of King Ptolemy the fifth. But you didn't come all this way to talk ancient history, did you?' Grieg blinked a couple of times as he made eye contact.

Francis shook his head. 'I'd like your opinion on a case I'm working on at the moment.'

'What sort of case?'

'Murder. So far, we've got the mummified body of a woman, and two disembowelled corpses. Organs were removed and delivered in Canopic jars to the offices of our local newspaper.'

'When you say mummified . . . ?'

'Organs removed, brain removed, dried out with natron and then wrapped in linen and resin.'

'Do you have any idea of the time period or provenance of the mummy?'

'My pathologist is finding it difficult to pinpoint the approximate date of death – she hasn't had to assess mummified bodies before now – but clearly longer ago than forty days.'

Grieg's eyes widened. 'You're shitting me. I thought you meant you'd found an ancient mummy.'

'Not at all,' said Francis. 'Someone's done this relatively recently.'

'Then I'm not sure how I can help you.'

As they spoke, they'd wandered down the long gallery in which the Rosetta Stone was housed. They passed huge stone statues of pharaohs, carvings of Egyptian gods and marble busts of kings and queens. Despite showing the ravages of time – chipped noses, broken-off chins, missing arms – they were still awe-inspiring.

Francis tore his gaze away from a pair of winged Assyrian lions to refocus on the conversation.

'The mummified woman was tattooed all over her body. A lot of them are hieroglyphs. And the Canopic jars came with scrolls attached, again featuring hieroglyphs. I wonder if you would look at them for us.'

'Of course,' said Grieg. 'Let's go to my office.'

They went up the vast stone staircase at the end of the gallery, and Grieg led Francis into the Egyptian Collection. The rooms were smaller, with lower ceilings, than the galleries below, but by no means less impressive. They passed through a room that was crammed with ancient mummies, their stained and dirty bandages far more in keeping with Francis's expectations than the pristine mummy from the Booth Museum. It was all he could do not to linger and press his face up to the glass cases as he would have done when he was a child.

But Grieg hardly seemed to notice them, and wove his way swiftly between them until he came to a locked door. He opened it with a passkey and ushered Francis into a small, neat office with a couple of desks. Framed posters for special exhibitions adorned the walls, apart from one which was taken up by a large bookshelf crammed with books on Egyptology and ancient history.

'Grab a seat,' said Grieg, 'and let's see what you got.'

'These.' Francis placed his leather document holder on the desk, unzipped it and pulled out a series of photographs of the Booth Museum mummy, before and after unwrapping, and images of the papyrus messages. He passed them across to Matt Grieg. There was a sharp intake of breath as the professor considered what he was seeing.

'Wow – tell me more.'

'It was discovered – or more accurately, it was deposited – in one of Brighton's museums. We have no idea who put it there or why they're doing this.'

'Yes, I saw a headline in the paper about it – just assumed it was some kind of joke,' said Grieg. 'Are you treating it as a suspicious death?'

'We're not sure yet of the precise cause of death,' said Francis, carefully avoiding a specific answer. 'But whether she was murdered or not, it certainly qualifies as an illegal disposal of a body.'

'And you think her tattoos have some kind of significance?'

Francis shrugged. 'At the moment I'm completely in the dark as to who the woman is and why this was done to her. Anything you can tell me will broaden my knowledge.'

'I understand.' Grieg picked up the sheaf of images. He

studied them for a few minutes, leafing backwards and forwards through the pile.

'Quite a mash-up,' he said, pulling a couple of the tattoo images to the front. 'I can only really comment on the Egyptian motifs.'

'That's what I need help with,' said Francis. 'The other tattoos seem straightforward enough, but I'm wondering if there's some sort of hidden meaning in the Egyptian symbols.'

Grieg pointed at the first picture. 'These snake tattoos … they're rendered in the style of Apophis, the Egyptian snake god. He was the enemy of the sun god Ra, and he promoted chaos, darkness, earthquakes, storms. A bringer of death.'

Francis looked at the sinewy, sweeping curves of the snake, and at the black patterns marked out along its back.

Grieg traced the outline of the snake with his finger. 'Look, these other tattoos virtually fit within the snake's curves. This one' – he pointed at a small group of hieroglyphs – 'means heart.'

Francis studied it. 'What about this?' On the other side of the snake's body there was a series of three lozenge shapes with tall stems.

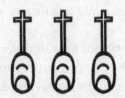

'Beauty,' said Grieg. He picked up another of the photos. 'Look here – this one means to beat.'

'And this means book ...'

' ... and the verb to teach.'

Francis annotated the photos as they went through the hieroglyphs one by one.

On their own, none of them made any sense as a message or seemed to be particularly tied to any of the other tattoos, hieroglyph or not. But they were words with resonance. Heart ... beauty ... teach ... mother ... blood ... wrongdoing ... woman ... bird ... to beat ... fool ... secret ... Could there be some sort of story here? Something that could be built into a picture of the woman's life?

'Can you discern any greater meaning from them?' he asked Grieg.

The expert's eyes widened. 'How do you mean?'

'I don't know – do they link to or suggest any particular Egyptian story or character?'

Grieg picked up the pile of images and leafed through them again, shaking his head. 'No, they don't suggest any of the familiar tropes that you might find in temples or tombs. But the hieroglyphs we see on antiquities tend to relate to kings and queens, telling their life stories. They're not just jumbles of random words.' He paused, gazing at the last picture. 'Maybe you need to look at them in combination with the non-hieroglyph tattoos. I don't know. I don't think I can really help you very much.'

'Okay. What about the papyrus messages?'

Grieg studied the images of the ankh and the snake.

'The snake's easy,' he said. 'That's Apophis, the Great Serpent and enemy of Ra, the Sun God. The bringer of chaos.'

'That would certainly make sense,' said Francis.

'And the Ankh is the symbol of life. The pharaohs used it to represent their power to reincarnate themselves in the afterlife. It's a sign that is also used to illustrate the power to bestow life.'

'And if you can bestow life, you can take it away.'

Grieg raised his eyebrows. 'The bringer of chaos who takes away life – that's your man, certainly.'

'The local rag seems to have christened him the Embalmer.'

Grieg gave a wry smile. 'The Embalmer? Perfect.' He picked up the most recent of the messages and read the English writing out loud. '*You can breathe easy until my next delivery*. He's making it personal. My expertise only extends to the ancient world, DI Sullivan, but I would say you need to take this as a direct threat.' He paused and stared Francis directly in the eye. 'Whoever this message is addressing is likely to be the Embalmer's next victim.'

35

Saturday, 11 November 2017

Francis

Booth mummy: you won't guess probable cause of death.
Rose.

Francis reread the text, then took a taxi directly from the station to the mortuary. Rose had a knack for tantalising messages, and there was no way he was waiting until tomorrow to find out what she'd discovered. He paid the cabby quickly, telling him to keep the change, and rushed through the vestibule into the morgue. Rose was bent over a microscope, singing along to The Humming Chorus from *Madame Butterfly* which she had on at full volume.

Francis tapped her on the shoulder and she jumped.

'Jesus, Francis! Don't creep up on people.'

'I didn't creep. I even said hello when I came through the door.'

Rose looked sheepish and turned down the volume.

'Good set of pipes, though,' added Francis, and then enjoyed watching Rose's cheeks take on a subtle flush.

'Right.' Rose was all business. She went over to the bank of stainless-steel drawers where the bodies were kept and pulled open one that was labelled 'Booth Museum mummy'.

Seeing the diminished, leathery body of the unidentified woman brought an unexpected surge of pity to Francis's chest.

In trying to solve the riddles tattooed on her body, it had been too easy to forget the person she must have once been, especially as they still knew absolutely nothing about her life.

'The problem with doing a post-mortem on a mummified body is that the mummification process means the organs have already been removed. In particular, the brain is disposed of, and although we've got her liver, lungs, stomach and intestines in the Canopic jars, they're all significantly denatured by the desiccation process.'

'But you said on the phone you'd found out the cause of death.'

'I have.' She pointed to a long slit on the left-hand side of the woman's torso. 'The lungs, liver, stomach and guts were removed via this cut and packed into the burial jars, with natron to dry them out. The challenge is to work out which changes in the body were due to the mummification process and which came about as a result of whatever killed her.'

She shut the drawer and opened the one below it. The four Canopic jars that had been discovered with the body stood in a line on its steel base. Slipping on a pair of latex gloves, she picked up one of them and motioned for Francis to follow her over to her work bench.

'This jar contains the woman's lungs. They were quite literally squashed inside here and the salt they were packed in has completely dried them out. In other words, they're damaged almost beyond recognition.'

She carefully drew out a lump of reddish-brown organic matter and placed it in a stainless-steel dish. Francis wouldn't have even recognised it as human tissue. A musty smell invaded his nostrils, but behind it there was just the faintest trace of something incense-like. He wrinkled his nose.

'Dried flesh and myrrh,' said Rose. 'An irresistible combination.'

'Preferable to the usual smells in here.'

'I didn't think these were going to tell me anything.' She prodded them with a pair of tweezers. 'They're really a mess. But I took a closer look.' She used the tweezers to show him an area that she'd sliced into. 'I cut a cross section and studied it under the microscope. Of course, the tissue showed changes at a cellular level. The natron draws out the moisture by osmosis – it creates a hypertonic environment and the cells dry out. This causes them to shrivel like raisins.'

She put down the bowl and led him across to the microscope. 'Look here.'

Francis looked down the eyepiece and adjusted the focus knob. A rust-coloured blur became sharp.

'You're looking at a section of lung tissue. It doesn't compare to normal lung tissue remotely.'

Francis had to take her word for it as he had no idea what normal lung tissue would look like under the microscope.

'So in fact,' said Rose, 'it didn't really tell me anything about the cause of death at all.'

Francis raised his head from the microscope and frowned at her. 'So what did?'

She took the slide out from under the objective lens and replaced it with another one.

'This.'

Francis looked down the microscope and refocused again until a thick, black thread materialised in the viewfinder.

'What is it?'

'It came from inside her left lung. It's a piece of pubic hair.'

'So she swallowed a hair? What does that tell you?'

'Two things. Firstly, she didn't swallow it. If she had, it would be in her stomach. Secondly, if you breathe in a fragment of hair or dirt, it doesn't generally reach your lungs. It will catch in your nose or make you cough. For that piece of hair to have reached as far as one of the secondary bronchi, which is where I found it, she must have inhaled water. In other words, she drowned. Or was drowned by someone else.'

'And you think the latter?'

Rose shrugged. 'How many grown adults fall into bathtubs and drown?'

'Drunks?'

'If she fell asleep in the tub, the moment she took in any water she would have woken up and coughed it out. And even if she was drugged or drunk, and drowned accidentally, it means someone discovered the body and then decided to mummify it, rather than call an ambulance. Sounds a little far-fetched, don't you think?'

'They wanted a body to mummify, so they drowned her.' Francis completed Rose's implication. 'In her own bathtub?'

It was a rhetorical question. Rose replaced the lung tissue into its jar and put it away in the drawer.

'Clearly, I'll have the hair checked for DNA to see if it's one of her own, or if it's someone else's. What were you doing in London?'

Francis explained and fetched the images from his document folder. 'Got time to take a look?'

Rose checked her watch. It was after five. 'Ten minutes. Then I need to pick up Laurie from the childminder.' Laurie was Rose's son. Seven years old, going on thirty-five.

Francis spread the images out on the workbench, arranging them in relation to where they were positioned on the body.

'Matt Grieg suggested that the tattoos might be in groupings around the different snake tattoos.'

Rose studied them. 'Do these markings on the snake mean anything?'

'Grieg didn't say they did. But he translated the hieroglyphs for me.'

'Blood,' said Rose, pointing at one of the annotated groupings of Egyptian symbols. 'And secret. They both go with this snake.'

'But to teach and to beat are definitely aligned with this snake. So maybe each snake is telling us a separate story.'

'Beauty, love, heart – these hieroglyphs go with this snake.'

'And look, so do these other tattoos.' Francis pointed to a traditional pin-up girl tattoo and a deep orange chrysanthemum. It reminded him of Marni's beautiful signature chrysanthemum tattoos, though this one wasn't nearly as detailed as hers.

'The killer's story? His life story perhaps?' said Rose. She gathered up the pictures and thrust them at Francis.

'Look, I've got to go.'

'There's just one thing I don't get,' said Francis, putting the images back in his case. 'She got the whole treatment – fully mummified – but Russell and Bridges were just disembowelled and then left. No mummification. No tattooing.'

'Timing?'

'A month and a half of waiting for the first body to mummify,' said Francis. 'But after that he couldn't wait?' He shook his head. 'There's something different about her, something significant.'

Rose shrugged. 'She's the first.'

'Like a trigger? Something triggered him to kill her, and now he's on a spree? He can't stop himself and he can't slow down, so he can't do the same amount of work on these victims.'

'He'll carry on until he reaches the end. Whatever that might be.' Their eyes locked. 'Frank. It's the short form of Francis, isn't it?'

Francis nodded.

Rose continued to hold his eyes. 'He knows you, Francis, doesn't he? So here's the question – do you know him?'

Francis wished he knew the answer.

36

Sunday, 12 November 2017

Alex

Her Majesty's Prison Bronzefield looked nothing like what Alex expected. No heavy stone walls, no guard towers, no huge iron-studded wooden gates. From the outside, the front entrance looked more like a Travelodge hotel built in an area where no one would want to come and stay.

Liv had driven him there, and said she'd wait in the car. As he walked from the car park up to the prison entrance, his heart was pounding. He was scared that, after his last visit, they might not let him see his mother. And he was worried about how she was coping. There was no way she should be in prison.

Francis Sullivan might believe his mother was innocent but he was doing fuck all to get her out, or to find Paul. Because he wasn't officially on the case? What a lot of bullshit. More like he was spending all his time and energy running around after this mummy killer from the museum. Alex felt sick at heart and he knew it was going to be hard to see his mum still in prison, and how distressing she must be finding it. He was so desperate to see her, he felt like he wanted to cry – the same gut-churning feelings that had engulfed him when he was dropped off at primary school for the first few weeks. At least because she was on remand rather than convicted, he'd be able to visit every day if he wanted. He wondered if Liv would lend him her car so he could come up here as often as possible.

Behind the high wall that surrounded the prison, he could see the pale grey roofs of a cluster of modern, two-storey buildings. He headed across the road to the entrance – a sign pointed out the Visitors Centre Reception and, taking a deep breath to calm himself down, he pulled open the door.

Once inside, he again followed the instructions to place his mobile phone, cigarettes and lighter, and any metal or glass items into a locker. Through the half-hour of waiting, ID checks and searches, his hands shook and his voice betrayed him with a tremor, but he was finally shown into the visiting area by a solid woman in an unflattering uniform and heavy, black-rimmed glasses.

'You got an hour,' she said, and left him sitting at a small table. The furniture was bolted to the floor.

Ten minutes passed and nothing happened. He looked around the visiting area. A young girl in prison uniform sat opposite an older woman, her mother presumably. The girl was crying and the woman was holding her hand, looking equally distressed. A couple were whispering frantically, their voices rising as the conversation turned into an argument. No one looked happy to be there.

Finally, a door at the opposite end of the room opened and a similarly dressed warder ushered Marni in. She looked around the room, wide-eyed and nervous, as if she didn't know who she was looking for. When her eyes lighted on Alex, she let out a sharp cry and ran towards him.

'No running,' snapped the woman who'd brought her in. 'No hugging, no physical contact.'

But she was too late and Alex stood up to receive his mother's embrace.

'Mum!'

'Alex!'

'Break it up, you two.'

Marni clung to him tighter as the warder hurried towards them.

'It's okay, Mum,' said Alex. 'Let's sit down.'

The warder put a hand on Marni's shoulder and the last thing Alex wanted was to risk being chucked out again before he'd had a chance to speak to her.

As they took their places on opposite sides of the table, Alex was able to assess the changes that the short time in prison had made in his mother. She'd lost weight, and the remnants of last summer's tan had given way to grey prison pallor. But more disturbing, the light had gone from her eyes and as she stared at him across the Formica, he wasn't even sure that she was focusing properly.

'Are you okay, Mum?'

'I am now that I've seen you.'

He managed a glimmer of a smile, despite the grinding anxiety in his gut.

'Francis Sullivan called me. He believes you didn't do it, Mum. He's going to do all he can to prove that it was Paul.'

Marni sighed. 'I know – he came to see me a couple of days ago. But Paul's clever. He won't get caught.' She sounded utterly defeated.

'He doesn't need to be caught. They just need to find some evidence against him.'

'They would have found it by now, if there was any.'

She was probably right, but for her sake and his own, he couldn't give up hope.

'We'll get you out.' He wasn't sure who he meant by 'we'. Him and Francis? A man he hated.

He glanced across at the warder. She was leaning on the wall near the door, scanning the room. He supposed she was watching in case any of the visitors tried to pass across contraband items. He reached out to take his mother's hand – and was shocked by how cold her skin was.

'Mum, I hate that you're in here. I know how hard it is for you.'

Marni didn't speak, but squeezed his hand.

'I'll try and come as often as I can.'

'I'd like that.' Marni's words were clipped. She was biting back the urge to cry.

They didn't have much else to talk about, but Alex stayed for his full hour until the warder came across to take Marni back to her cell. Now it didn't matter if he hugged her – they could tell him to leave if they wanted.

He'd be back. He'd keep his promises to her – to visit her often and to find a way of getting her out.

Alex stared down at the text message in disbelief.

> Let me explain what happened.
> It wasn't how you think.

How the hell did Paul know what he thought anyway? And what was there to explain? If Paul thought that having killed Thierry, he could simply step into his brother's shoes . . .

Another text came through.

> You need me more than ever now.
> We're family.

He tossed his phone down onto the coffee table in front of him.

'What is it?' said Liv, looking up from her own screen.

'A message from Paul, saying he wants to explain.'

Liv's eyes widened. 'From your uncle? So he's admitting he was there?'

'Of course he was there. You can't think for a minute that Mum did it? Jesus, Liv.'

'No. No, never in a million years. But the police are convinced that she did it – enough to have her in prison.'

'On remand.'

'Sure, but in their eyes she's guilty.'

And in everyone else's too, so it seemed. Alex hated the thought that there were people who assumed she'd done it, just on the basis that she'd been arrested for it. He knew she was innocent – and it would be easy to say that that was all that mattered. But it wasn't. He had to find a way to prove it hadn't been her. And that meant showing that it was Paul.

'Are you going to see him?'

'He's not my father and I hate him. But maybe I should hear what he's got to say.'

Liv looked astounded at his words. 'Alex, he probably killed your father. Now he wants to explain. For god's sake . . . You can't take his word for anything. How do you know he doesn't want to finish the job by killing you too? The man's dangerous.'

'But he might tell me the truth about what happened. It could be a way of exonerating Mum.'

'And what if he did? He'll never admit being there to the police.'

Alex felt drained. Seeing his mother crushed and defeated in the stark surroundings of the prison had shocked him. Everything had seemed so bleak. He felt as if he couldn't face Paul, but maybe he had to.

'I hate the idea of you meeting him.'

'Leave it, Liv. I need to work out how to handle this.'

Liv sighed loudly, making her exasperation with him quite clear. 'If you feel you've got to see him, why don't you record what he says and take it to the police?'

Alex shrugged. He'd thought of that, but dismissed it. 'He won't say anything – it'll just be bluster and crap.'

'It doesn't matter. There's a chance he'll slip up. Let something out. Even if it's a tiny chance, it's worth doing.'

'Maybe.'

'It's probably the only way.'

'I'm scared, Liv.'

'Why? You think he'll pull a knife on you?'

'No. I'm scared that I am actually his son. And that I'll pull a knife on him.'

But it was settled. He picked up his phone and sent Paul a text.

37

Francis

Francis stared across his kitchen table at Alex and Liv for a full minute before he remembered to shut his mouth.

'You're out of your tiny minds.'

'No, we're not,' said Alex. 'You know she's innocent. We're going to prove it.'

'Paul Mullins is already on the run for GBH for attacking your mother last summer, and now there's the distinct possibility that he murdered your father. The police are never going to sanction a secret meeting between you and him. It's way too dangerous. Sergeant Mackay will flat out refuse.'

'Which is why I came to you.'

'My hands are tied. I'm a witness in this case, which means I can't be operational.'

'So my mother gets to stay in prison? You know what it's doing to her.'

'I know, and I want her out of there as much as you do. But you've got to let Mackay handle this.'

'He's done a great job so far,' said Liv, scowling. 'If your lot had actually managed to catch Paul after he beat up Marni last summer, Thierry would probably still be alive.'

'Jesus, Liv!' said Alex.

The accusation cut Francis like a knife. They'd had an APW

out for Paul Mullins for months but Thierry's brother had gone to ground most effectively. With no sign of him anywhere, Francis had assumed he'd gone back to France. Apparently not.

'If he's been in touch with you, the best thing you can do is let us have the details. We'll be able to trace the mobile phone he's using, and that should give us a location for him.'

'If I don't agree to the meeting, he'll smell a rat and go to ground,' said Alex.

'And he'll probably ditch that phone anyway,' said Liv. 'He wasn't born yesterday.'

They had a point.

'Let me see his messages,' said Francis.

Alex accessed the thread and held up his phone for Francis to see. But he kept a tight grip on it – he clearly didn't trust Francis enough to hand it over.

P: Let me explain what happened. It wasn't how you think.
P: You need me more than ever now. We're family.
   A: Yeah, like they say, you don't get to choose your family.
P: You're not giving me a chance, Alex.
                  A: What do you expect?
                  A: I think you killed my father.
P: No, I wasn't even there . . .
P: You know it was your mother . . .
P: Meet me and we can talk about it.

'The last message arrived just over an hour ago,' said Alex. 'I haven't answered it yet.'

As soon as Francis looked up from the screen, Alex thrust the phone back into his jeans pocket.

'You should let me have that,' said Francis. 'We need to track him down and question him.'

'You need to bloody arrest him,' hissed Liv.

Alex frowned at both of them. 'I want to meet him,' he said. 'I could get a confession out of him.'

Francis shook his head. 'No way.'

'But, don't you see? I'm the only person who can do this. He won't talk to anyone else.'

Francis considered his words. It was true that Alex was probably the only person Paul would agree to meet, and definitely the only one he might – just – tell the truth to.

'Like I said, you'd be mad to try this. You can't meet him on your own. What about if I set up a meeting for you with Rory? See what he thinks?'

Liv and Alex exchanged glances.

'No way,' said Alex. 'He's the one who put my mother in jail. There's no way he'll help me get her out. And if you won't help either, I'll do it alone.'

Francis grimaced. 'My advice to you is not to try this. But if you won't take that advice, let me give you some other help.'

'Like what? Can you get hold of a wire for me to wear?'

Francis sighed, and rubbed his eyes. 'We're not in a bloody TV show, Alex. But you should be able to record any meeting on your phone. Better still, why don't you let me come with you?'

'No. He won't talk if you're there. If I can get him to confess and bring back a recording, it'll be enough to get my mother off the hook. After that, I'll give you the phone, I'll tell you where he is, anything. But I need to get that evidence first.'

'So it's more important for you to get your mother off than it is to catch the man who killed your father?'

'Of course it is.' Anger flared in Alex's eyes and Liv quickly put a hand on his forearm. 'I'm not saying I don't care what happens to Paul. I want him to rot in prison for the rest of his life for what he's done – to my mother and my father. But getting Mum out of prison is more important.'

Francis stared at his hands on the table in front of him. What could go wrong? Everything. He had every reason to believe that Paul Mullins was a violent psychopath. Alex hated him, and believed that he'd killed Thierry. Was there any chance that the two of them could sit down and have a rational conversation about this? Not in a million years.

But . . .

He needed to find Paul. He needed to get Marni out of prison and the right man in there. And after months of searching, they were no nearer to apprehending Paul Mullins than they had been when he'd first appeared in Brighton the previous summer. If Alex wouldn't co-operate with them, they could still follow him to the meeting and pick Paul up.

'This is not in any way sanctioned by the police, but if I can't stop you doing it, let's plan it properly.'

Alex's face lit up with relief.

'You can record it on your phone – we'll hide a tiny mic in your clothes. And I'll get hold of a stab vest for you.'

'You really think he needs one?' said Liv.

'Of course he does. Paul Mullins might be your uncle. He might want to be your father. But he's also a very violent man.'

Alex shook his head.

'I'll wear recording gear. I'm not wearing a stab vest – and I don't want you and your boys anywhere nearby. This has to go down my way.'

'At least wear the vest?'

'He's not going to stab me. He wants me to be his loving son.'

'And when he realises he's not going to get that? How do you think he'll react?'

'Come on,' said Liv. 'He's a mad man and you can't trust him, Alex.'

'Fine. I'll wear a stab vest. I'll record what he says and I'll let you have the recording. If he admits to stabbing my father, you can get my mother out, right?'

'Of course,' said Francis. *If the confession was convincing enough.*

'Okay. I'll set up a meeting.' Alex got up from the table and Liv followed suit.

'Let me know when and where,' said Francis, showing them to the door.

If this went wrong . . .

He went back into the kitchen and poured himself a large whisky. But not too large to drink it down in one. Then he called Rory.

'Sergeant, can I suggest you put eyes on Alex Mullins – and don't let him out of your bloody sight.'

38

The Embalmer

Apophis (/ˈæpəfɪs/; Ancient Greek: Ἄποφις) is the name of the ancient Egyptian god who represented chaos (*ı̓zft* in Egyptian). He was the sworn enemy of the sun god, Ra, who was his brother, and of light and Ma'at (order/truth). He appears in ancient Egyptian art as a giant serpent.

There's a seagull. It wheels and swoops above the pier, drawn by the smell of chips and doughnut fat. The sky darkens as it shrieks to its mate, but the sound is drowned out by the fairground rides – pulsing disco music and screeching girls, clashing discordantly from the Turbo Coaster, the Air Race and the Waltzers. The bird dives and snatches up a fragment of hot-dog bun, thrilled with the night's work so far. The summer tourists are long gone, but the pier's still the best place for easy pickings.

There are people on the pier, laughing and shouting to one another, just like the gulls. Flashing coloured lights make their complexions green, orange, red, and their eyes bright. Pints of beer and candy floss. And more trips to the toilet because it's cold out there, above the dark water.

There's a woman. Sitting on a wooden bench, all on her own. Pulling her neat coat around narrow ribs. She's checking her mobile obsessively. Nothing odd about that, these days. She's sheltered from the wind, but this side of the pier is quiet and there aren't many people here. She shivers.

The Embalmer watches her from the shadows.

His summons worked – and now she's waiting for him to appear. His heart flutters like a teenager going on a date. A date that's long overdue. He walks silently down the pier towards her. He glances from side to side, but all the deckchairs are empty at this time. He tugs the zip on his jacket up, high under his chin. The quilted hood hides his hair and his facial features. Nondescript. That's the look he's aiming for. No one will notice him.

Except, perhaps, the woman on the bench. But even she won't recognise him. He's changed a lot.

He stops in front of her.

'Hello, Ada.'

She doesn't smile. 'You're Josh?'

There's something about her tone. Disdain? She's looking him up and down.

'Yes.' It's not his name, but it's the name he used to reel her in on the dating app.

She starts to stand up. 'Shall we get a drink? At the Horatio?'

He sits down. She hovers for a moment between sitting and standing.

'Let's talk for a bit,' he says.

She sits back down. Perches, right on the edge of the bench.

'You don't remember me, do you?' he says.

She looks shocked.

'You look just the same,' he says. 'Though maybe a bit older. Of course a bit older.'

She blinks.

'It's nice that you came,' he says. Conversationally.

She's still mute.

He begins to suspect that she regrets coming. He casts around for something to say or do to make her feel more comfortable.

'You have nice skin,' he says. 'You always did.'

'You have nice eyes,' he says. Because she does.

She slides along the bench a little. Away from him.

He slides along the bench a little. Closer to her.

She turns her head to look at him.

'I don't know who you are,' she blurts. 'You are Josh, aren't you? From UrbanSingles? You don't look at all like your profile picture.'

'I am.' He smiles at her.

'Then why are you acting like we've met before?' She sounds unnerved. That's not a bad thing.

'Because we have, Ada.'

'I don't remember you.'

'That's a shame,' he says. 'You see, I remember you very well indeed. I remember what you said to me. How you treated me.'

She peers at him, blinking. She's trying not to cry, he thinks.

'How you humiliated me.'

She makes a move to stand up again.

'Sit down.' The sharpness of his voice makes her jump.

She does what he tells her to, and that makes him happy. He relaxes again. Things are going well.

He smiles at her. He still feels very attracted to her and this was something he wasn't expecting. He's spent so long hating her he assumed he'd be repulsed when he saw her again in the flesh.

In the flesh. He savours the thought.

She doesn't smile back at him. She pulls that face he's seen so many times before. Like she's sucking on lemons.

No matter. No matter at all. Not this time.

'You promised me a date. Do you remember?'

This time she shakes her head vehemently.

'But you dumped me. You never showed up.'

The heat of the humiliation floods through him, making him angry. He's played with her – a cat with a mouse. But now it's time for the sacrifice.

'Walk with me.' There's an edge of steel to his voice, and his hand closes like a vice on her arm.

She pulls away, terrified, but he doesn't let go. He pulls her in close to his body and shuffles a few feet with her. When she tries to scream, he clamps his other hand across her mouth. He pushes her down into a narrow space – the back of one of the rides. She manages to cry out, but it's drowned by disco music and the screams of the girls who are having fun.

He leans over her and unbuttons her coat.

He unbuttons her blouse.

She struggles but he slaps her.

He pushes down the waistband of her skirt.

It's dark, but he knows well enough what he's after. He glances around to check for the jar that he placed here earlier in the day. Its jackal head seems to smile at him in the gloom. He draws a knife from inside his jacket and tests the blade. He knows it's sharp enough, but he loves to feel its sting on the pad of his thumb.

She lets out a sharp cry as he makes the first cut, but the wind snatches it away.

It takes him less than a minute, and the job is done.

Apophis will be pleased with his progress.

Frank Sullivan won't.

39

Sunday, 12 November 2017

Francis

A text buzzed in just as Francis switched out his bedside light. It was nearly midnight – and that could mean only one thing. He squinted at the phone in the darkness. It was Rory – it appeared he'd already called twice while Francis had been in the bathroom.

Woman's body found on pier.

His chest tightened. Please, not another. He threw on the clothes he'd just taken off and galloped down the stairs. He heard his sister's bedroom door opening as he ducked into the kitchen for his car keys.

'It's just work,' he called up to her, leaving the house without waiting for her answer.

The traffic was light and it only took him three minutes to reach the Palace Pier. Rory and Gavin were waiting for him at the entrance. The metal gates spanning the front were shut, apart from a single narrow opening to one side. Rory stood leaning on the gate post, tired-eyed and crumpled after a long day. Gavin, however, was more awake, sporting jeans tight enough to make one's eyes water and an even tighter white T-shirt that showed off his enviable pecs. Francis's eyebrows went up before he had time to stop them.

'Yeah, I know,' said Gavin. 'I was out clubbing.'

'Seriously?' said Rory. 'Rather you than me.'

'You should come along one night. You've probably got some old-timer moves worth seeing.'

Francis smiled. If he was taking the piss out of Rory, Gavin was definitely part of the team.

'Okay, lead the way,' he said to Rory. 'The sooner we take a look, the sooner Twinkle Toes can get back to the dance floor.'

As they walked the length of the pier, Rory brought him up to speed on the situation.

'The pier closes its gates at ten p.m., so just before that, the staff do a sweep to check there are no more punters hanging around.'

'Is that an issue?' said Francis.

'Apparently,' said Gavin. 'Sometimes they find drunks passed out on benches, or teenagers who think it would be fun to have the run of the place after closing.'

'And tonight they found a body?'

Rory resumed his report. 'Most of the staff leave just after ten, the catering staff a little later when they've finished clearing up, and then the manager finally locks up.'

'Security guards?' said Francis.

'Not at night, but there are CCTV cameras at various points.'

They were walking past the large central pavilion of the Palm Court. Francis was reasonably familiar with the set-up, having spent enough of his teenage years hanging around on the pier. There was a bar and a restaurant, as well as a fish and chip outlet, with several areas of outdoor seating.

'Where's the body?'

Rory pointed. 'Up ahead, near the end. She was discovered by one of the cooks at Horatio's, on his way off the pier.'

Horatio's Bar was a facsimile of a traditional pub, down at the far end of the pier among the fairground rides.

'Any suggestion of the cause?'

Rory stopped and looked round at him. 'Didn't I say on the phone? Disembowelled.'

'Shit. Another.' Francis felt his stomach lurch. 'What can you tell me about her?'

'She's well-dressed,' said Gavin. 'Still got her handbag. Certainly doesn't look like she was robbed.'

They were walking down the right-hand side of the boardwalk, but Rory swerved through a gap in the wooden shelter that ran down the centre to bring them out on the other side. Francis saw a flash of blue-and-white crime-scene tape ahead of them, and beyond it a number of figures in uniform and white scene-of-crime suits.

'You've spoken to the manager about keeping the pier shut tomorrow?'

'Yes,' said Gavin. 'He's not happy, but tough.'

'The guy who found her threw up by the body. Then he went to his boss, who called for an ambulance in case there was anything they could do. One of the paramedics confirmed that she was dead. Quite cold – dead for some time, maybe an hour or two.'

'Is he still around, the bloke who found her?'

'Yes. I've got a uniform taking his statement.'

'Okay – keep him here until I've had a chance to talk to him. Any ID on the body?'

'Yes. She had an iPhone and a purse in her handbag – credit cards and cash. And the bag and the purse look expensive.'

'Who was she?'

'Ada Carmichael. Driving licence in her purse, and the photo on it matches the body.'

They reached the crime-scene tape and Gavin held it up so Rory and Francis could duck underneath it.

Ada Carmichael might have been an attractive woman, but death had robbed her, bestowing on her instead a face of infinite sorrow and fatigue. The harsh glare of the CSI's LED lamps revealed every contour, every wrinkle, every blemish on her grey skin. Black hair, neatly cut in a bob, but now mussed up, strands sticking to her cheek. She was sprawled against the railing of the pier, just by the side of the ghost train. Her eyes were open, and if she could see, she'd be staring out across the flat, gunmetal sea to the slate-black horizon.

Like the previous bodies, she'd been eviscerated and now lay in a congealing puddle of her own blood.

Francis felt a splutter of rain against his cheek and felt thoroughly depressed.

'You've called Rose?' he said.

Rory nodded.

Alicia Russell. Luke Bridges. And now Ada Carmichael. What did they have in common? What linked them to the mummy in the morgue?

Francis turned away from the body.

'I could do with a coffee,' he said. He had a feeling he'd be up for a few more hours yet.

Gavin went down to Horatio's to see what he could rustle up.

The staff who hadn't already left by the time the body was discovered were being held in the Palm Court, further up the pier, but everyone who'd worked there that evening would need to be questioned. Someone must have seen the woman coming onto the pier, and someone must have seen the killer coming onto or leaving the pier.

If only they had some idea of whom they were looking for.

Rose arrived, but even her cheery greeting didn't make him feel any better.

'Oh, this is just great for a Sunday night,' she said, rolling her eyes.

Francis hovered at her shoulder as she assessed Ada Carmichael's body.

'How long do you think she's been out here?'

Rose gave him a look over her shoulder. 'Give a girl a chance. Go and do something useful and I'll talk to you when I've finished.'

Something useful. He headed off to Horatio's.

The chef who'd discovered Ada Carmichael's body was a young man called Lowell Anderson. He was taller than he appeared comfortable with, all knees and elbows, shoulders rounding to minimise his height. When he spoke, although his English was fluent, he had a strong Sudanese accent.

'It was an odd thing that I came across her,' he said. 'Most evenings I walk down the other side – I don't know why. But tonight, I picked this side and there she was.' His hands were shaking, so he pressed them down on his thighs.

'What did you do when you saw her?' said Francis.

'I just saw the blood. It's dark there, so at first it looked black, but closer up I could smell it. I realised she was dead and I threw up. I'm sorry.'

'Don't worry,' said Francis. 'Did you call the ambulance?'

'No, I ran to my boss and he did that when I told him I thought there was a dead woman behind the ghost train.' He nodded in the direction of the manager, who was sitting at another table, talking frantically into his mobile.

Francis knew he'd have all this in the statement that had already been taken, but sometimes witnesses remembered additional details.

He went back to see how Rose was getting on. She'd shifted Ada Carmichael into a black body bag and was just doing up the zip.

'She's been dead for at least a couple of hours.'

'It's the same as Luke Bridges and Alicia Russell, isn't it?'

'Her stomach's missing.'

'And that was definitely the cause of death?'

'Probably, but I won't know for sure until I do the PM.'

That meant another Canopic jar would be on its way. He dialled Tom Fitz's number.

'Where are you?' said Fitz, before Francis had a chance to speak.

'On the Palace Pier.'

'I'm coming to you.' Fitz disconnected, and although Francis tried him again, he didn't pick up.

He turned back to Rose.

'Have the CSIs picked up any useful evidence?'

'Hot dog wrappers. Sweet papers. A broken hair clip.' Rose shook her head. 'No bloody knife. I really can't help you.'

Rose started packing up her kit, and Francis stood staring out to sea for a few minutes. This killer, the Embalmer, as Fitz had christened him, had to be stopped. But he felt clueless. They hadn't made any progress at all.

Raised voices beyond the crime-scene tape caught Francis's attention.

A man was shoving past the uniformed officer and running towards them. Francis recognised the way he moved. He was clutching something bulbous to his chest.

'No way, Tom. You can't be here.'

'I need to speak to Francis Sullivan.'

Francis stepped forward to block Fitz from seeing the body, but the reporter deftly side-stepped him. As he did, Francis saw that he was carrying a Canopic jar with the head of a jackal.

Rose straightened up, and Tom Fitz bent down to stare into the body bag.

'Jesus Christ!' He staggered back and bumped into the corner of the ghost train's wooden structure, dropping the Canopic jar. It shattered on the boardwalk, spewing out a mess of bloody natron and stinking entrails.

'Come on, Tom, come away,' said Francis.

'No . . . oh my god.' Fitz's hand was clutching at his collar. 'It's Ada.' He shook his head. 'It can't be.' His voice cracked with emotion.

'You know her?' said Francis.

Fitz was looking unsteady on his feet. Rose took his arm and guided him to sink down onto the nearest bench.

'It's Ada Carmichael,' he said. 'My stepsister.'

40

Monday, 13 November 2017

Alex

Alex Mullins had spotted the police tail as soon as he left the flat. It didn't bother him – he was perfectly confident in his ability to give Rory Mackay's boys the slip. He knew cut-throughs and alleyways, pubs with back doors and garden walls he could climb over. It didn't take long to shake them off.

Once he was sure there was no one on his tail, Alex doubled back through the Lanes and came down to the front. He jogged across the road towards the pier entrance, then hurried on past it to Madeira Drive. He dropped down onto the beach, figuring that any cop car going along the drive wouldn't spot him if he kept in close in the shadow of the promenade. He checked his watch. He had time, even though walking on the shingle slowed him down.

A couple of hundred yards along and the road had levelled with the beach, so he cut further down to the water's edge, angling his body out towards the sea, so he wouldn't be facing the road. He could walk faster here on the compacted sand. He would be early for the meeting, but he'd allowed extra time to lose his police accompaniment – and he just felt that it would give him a slight advantage to be the first to arrive. He wanted to see which direction Paul would come from.

Madeira Drive brought back memories. He and his dad had

watched the Brighton speed trials here every year – cars and bikes with souped-up engines and custom paint jobs roaring along the straight. Across the road, the pale turquoise and white wrought iron arches that lined the length of the drive reminded him of childhood afternoons on the beach. He'd tried to count the arches once, but after losing count three-quarters of the way along, he couldn't be bothered to walk all the way back to the beginning. He passed the crazy golf and the playground, both closed at this time of year.

Black Rock was in sight, and beyond it the marina. This was where he'd agreed to meet Paul. It was dusk and there was virtually no one on the beach, apart from a lone woman, throwing a stick into the sea for her dog – a monstrous beast that rushed in and out of the water, barking with the sheer joy of being alive.

Then he spotted Paul, leaning on the rail of the Black Rock car park, also watching the woman with her dog.

His breath caught in his throat.

He needed a cool head. Francis had come to see him with a stab vest, and had again tried to persuade him not to go ahead with the meeting. The vest was now lying unused on his bedroom floor. He'd gone as far as to try it on, but it looked bulky, even under his quilted jacket and, anyway, he didn't think for a minute Paul would try to stab him. This whole exercise was all about Paul's claim to be his father.

Alex grimaced at the thought. Never in a million years would he accept that as true. Even if it couldn't be proved one way or the other with DNA testing, he believed – no, he knew – that Thierry had been his father.

As he walked up the sand and got closer, the shared resemblance between Paul and his father hit Alex like a battering ram against the chest. He coughed a little too loudly, and the crack of sound made Paul look in his direction.

'Alex! *Bien*, I thought you wouldn't come.'

Alex shook his head, hardly trusting himself to talk. As he went around the end of the railing and up to the car park, he surreptitiously checked that his phone was set to record and put it in the breast pocket of his jacket. He wondered if it would pick up the hammering of his heart. He stopped next to Paul and gripped the rail to stop his hand from shaking. This was the man who had killed his father. This was why his mother was languishing in that filthy prison, with its stink of cabbage and disinfectant. And here he was meeting up with the bastard. Anger churned through him and he fought to get his feelings under control so it wouldn't show in his body language.

Paul reached into a plastic bag by his feet and offered Alex a can of beer. It made Alex realise he wasn't the only one who was nervous. He took the beer, making eye contact with the pretender, but remained silent. He was going to wait and see what Paul had to say for himself. Paul fidgeted, opening his own can and taking a long draught. Then he lowered the drink and stared at Alex. It was the uncomfortable kind of silence that made Alex want to scratch himself. He took a small sip of his beer.

'You know your mother is the worst kind of bitch, Alex. She took my child from me and now she's taken my brother.'

Alex wondered if Paul had already been drinking.

I've never been your child.

He wanted to say it, desperately, but he restrained himself.

'Tell me what happened, Paul. You were there, weren't you, when my father died?'

'Sure, I was there. Your mother went mad. She tried to kill me, and she ended up killing Thierry instead. The man she claimed she loved.'

'You're saying it was an accident?'

Paul shook his head. '*Non.* No. It was no accident. Thierry was defending me and she got more and more angry. Thierry stood in front of me, so she couldn't get to me. So then, she stabbed him with the knife.'

'Which knife?'

'I don't know. A knife she had in the kitchen. Marni always has a knife. That's her problem.' Paul's hand went unconsciously to his gut – to the place where Marni had stabbed him twenty years ago.

Alex made eye contact again, daring Paul to look away first. He did.

'I don't believe my mother killed my father.'

'He wasn't your father.'

Alex's stomach muscles tightened and he gripped the metal railing harder, oblivious to the cold.

'I don't believe my mother killed Thierry. I think you did it.'

Was an accusation the best way to get Paul to confess, or had that been a mistake?

Paul shrugged. 'She told you that. She's a liar.'

'Why didn't you stay and help him? You could have saved his life.'

'No, I couldn't.'

'You could have told the police exactly what happened.'

'It would have been my word against hers.'

'But running away hardly makes you look innocent.'

Paul stooped down and pulled another can of beer from the bag. He snapped the tin open and drank from it noisily, then coughed loudly. When he was able to speak, he held out one hand, palm up. 'What can I say to make you believe me? I understand – you don't want your mother to go to prison. But I won't go to prison for her.'

It wouldn't be for her. Alex was well aware of his mother's volatile temper, but not in a million years would she have stabbed his dad. Her problem was that she loved him too much, not that she hated him. He took another sip of his beer, playing for time, unsure how to proceed. All he wanted to do was smash Paul in the face.

'Why are you still here in Brighton? In England even?' he said finally. 'The police are looking for you.'

'I'm here because you're here . . .'

'I don't want you here.'

Alex had had enough. Paul had admitted to being there when Thierry was stabbed. Wasn't that enough to throw doubt on the charge against Marni? He looked around and saw a litter bin a few feet away. He went and dropped his hardly drunk beer into it.

Paul watched him through narrowed eyes.

'I know you did it,' said Alex, turning to face him again. 'And I'll do everything I possibly can to make you pay for it.'

A muscle in Paul's jaw twitched and his face turned darker as blood rushed to his cheeks. He lowered his brows and spoke through gritted teeth.

'Thierry had it coming to him. But I swear to you, Alex, it was in self-defence. He attacked me first.'

It sounded like a confession.

No longer able to contain himself, Alex drew back his arm and then threw the punch of a lifetime.

But Paul had years of experience fighting in the prison court-yard. He anticipated Alex's move and blocked it with his forearm.

'*Merde!*'

'Fuck you!'

Alex took another swing at him and this time landed his knuckles with an almighty crack on Paul's left eyebrow. Paul staggered back and caught hold of the railing for support. Alex stepped forward and brought his knee up into Paul's groin. With a yelp of pain, Paul dropped to the tarmac. There was a frenzy of barking and the monster dog ran up to them.

Alex ignored it and turned on his heel, leaving Paul to fend off the mutt's attentions. Then he was hit by a moment of blind panic – the phone – how could he have been so stupid? But it was still there, in his pocket. He climbed up onto Marine Parade, waiting until he was out of sight of the car park, then pulled it out.

Please, God, let it have picked up what Paul said.

'. . . but I swear to you, Alex, it was in self-defence.'

It was muffled, but Alex could just make out the words.

Got him!

41

Monday, 13 November 2017

Francis

Francis lit a cigarette and despised himself for it. The habit had crept up on him, from being a crutch during moments of stress to being a crutch, period. This was his fourth today, though at gone eight o'clock, he felt certain it would be his last. He stood out on the front doorstep, the door a couple of inches ajar behind him. He couldn't afford to close it properly – Robin would be bound to hear his key in the lock and he couldn't stomach another lecture. Even if she had his best interests at heart.

He saw the killer's latest message in his mind's eye.

Here's a question for you, Frank.
Will you find me before I find you?
It's a tricky one, isn't it?
But let's take a look at the facts.
You don't know who I am.
But I know where you live . . .

The threat was clear enough, but Francis wasn't afraid. If the killer came after him, it might be their best chance of catching him. A skein of smoke twisted over his shoulder and was sucked into the house. Francis sighed, hoping it wouldn't reach as far as the living room.

The sound of footsteps on the pathway beyond the front gate made him jump. Maybe he was more nervous than he cared to admit. The hinges of the gate creaked and Francis took a step forward, every muscle tensing.

'DI Sullivan?'

Francis exhaled – he knew the voice. Alex Mullins came through the stone arch towards him. What could he want at this hour?

'I got it. I've got it recorded. He definitely did it.'

As Alex came closer, Francis could see a sheen of sweat on his brow. He was panting, as if he'd run there from somewhere.

'Slow down, Alex.' He stubbed out his cigarette in the stone planter by the door and kept the butt to put in the bin. 'You've seen Paul?'

Alex nodded.

Francis sighed as he led the boy inside. 'Why didn't you tell me you were going to meet him?'

'It happened really quickly. I didn't have time.'

'You're not a very good liar, Alex.'

Alex shrugged as they reached the kitchen. 'Come on, Francis, you know as well as I do that your lot would have blundered in and ruined it. This was the only way I was going to get anything useful.'

After binning the cigarette end, Francis took a glass out of a cupboard and filled it with water from the cold tap. He handed it to Alex, who drank it greedily. They sat down at the kitchen table.

'Everything okay?' Robin appeared in the doorway.

'It's fine,' said Francis, impatient to find out what Alex had got. But Robin didn't leave.

'This is Alex Mullins,' Francis added by way of explanation.

Alex nodded at Robin, then turned his attention back to his phone.

'Work,' said Francis to her, curtly.

'Right,' said Robin. She sounded put out, but she left them to it.

'Listen,' said Alex.

He played back a recording on his phone. Not every word was clear, but Francis could hear two men talking. One was definitely Alex, while the other one had a French accent. He held up a hand and Alex pressed pause.

'That's definitely Paul?'

'Yes,' said Alex.

'Where did you record this?'

'At Black Rock car park, at the end of Madeira Drive.'

'You met him there on your own?'

'Yes.'

'You deliberately did what I asked you not to.'

'I got the confession.'

Alex pressed play and the recording continued. The two argued and Paul denied any involvement, but then he admitted that he'd been there.

'This is good.'

But then the recording became muffled. The voices were indistinct. Francis looked at Alex.

'You got into a fight with him, didn't you?'

'What would you have done if someone had just admitted killing your father?'

'He might have had a knife.'

'I'm fine.' He rewound a few seconds and Francis leaned forward, listening intently.

'Thierry had it coming to him. But I swear to you, Alex, it was in self-defence. He attacked me first.'

Alex pressed stop. 'There. That's it. He confessed.'

Would a jury see it that way? Was the recording clear enough for the meaning to be unequivocal?

'That's brilliant, Alex. But you still should have let us know what was going on. We could have picked him up as he left the car park, and by now he'd be in custody.'

Alex shook his head. 'He wasn't born yesterday. He would smell a rat and I would have risked not getting anything.'

He put the phone back in his pocket, but Francis held out a hand.

'I'll need that.'

Alex looked up, surprised. 'Seriously? Can't I just send you the recording?'

'No. And I need you to come in and tell Sergeant Mackay exactly what happened.'

It took some doing, but by eleven the next morning Francis had managed to convene Alex, Marni's lawyer Jayne Douglas and Rory in a meeting room at John Street. There was an uneasy silence as they settled round the table.

Rory, in particular, looked nonplussed by the turn of events. 'What's going on, Sullivan?'

Francis cleared his throat. 'Last night, Alex came to me with a recording of Paul Mullins confessing to Thierry's murder.'

'What the hell?' exploded Rory.

Jayne Douglas's eyebrows shot up, but she didn't speak.

'It throws fresh light on the case, and may constitute cause to drop the charges against Marni Mullins,' said Francis.

'May?' said Alex. 'You need to let her go right now.'

Rory gave him a cold stare. 'That will be up to the CPS.'

'The Crown Prosecution Service,' said Jayne Douglas, for

Alex's benefit. 'They make the decisions about whether to go ahead with or drop charges.'

'Then we should be seeing them, not Sergeant Mackay,' said Alex. His temper was rising.

Francis placed a hand over his for a second. 'This is the first step, Alex. Sergeant Mackay's in charge of the case. He'll need to present the new evidence.'

Alex snatched back his hand and glowered from one policeman to the other.

'Can we hear the recording, please?' said Jayne Douglas.

'Of course.' Francis had made copies of it and returned Alex's phone to him. He opened his laptop and located the confession. He explained when and how it had been made and how it had come into his possession. Then he clicked on 'play'.

The table fell silent as they listened to the recording of Alex's conversation with Paul Mullins. Jayne Douglas gasped as it came to the end.

'See?' said Alex. 'My mother's innocent.'

Rory looked furious.

'Thank you,' said Jayne Douglas. 'You'll forward a copy of that to me?'

'Yes,' said Francis.

Rory's eyes narrowed. Francis knew he was overstepping the mark. As a key witness, he wasn't supposed to be involved, and here he was, shooting down Rory's case in flames. He hoped it hadn't blown their fragile truce.

Jayne Douglas looked at Rory. 'You'll get this across to the CPS today, Sergeant Mackay?'

'I'll want to have it analysed by a forensic audio analyst first. We need to know what we're listening to.'

'I think it's perfectly clear what we're listening to,' said Douglas. 'The man on this recording quite clearly admits to killing Thierry Mullins in self-defence. If you don't get it across to the

CPS office pronto, I will. There's no excuse for Marni Mullins to remain in custody for this crime.'

'Miss Douglas, the police need to be satisfied that this is a genuine recording before we decide what to do with it. We'll also need a statement from Alex about exactly how this recording was secured. It might not be admissible in court.' Rory locked eyes with Francis.

Francis went out on a limb. 'I understand that Kyle Hollins has been checking the CCTV for Abbey Road on the night of Thierry Mullins's murder. Is that correct, Sergeant Mackay?'

Rory glared at him. 'Someone going up or down Abbey Road proves nothing.'

'Not on its own,' said Francis. 'But taken together with this confession, the figure Hollins saw *running* along Abbey Road could be significant.'

Rory scowled but said nothing.

'I'll be pushing for a speedy release,' said Jayne Douglas. She stood up. 'Alex, we're done here.'

Alex frowned at Francis. Clearly, he'd been expecting decisive action and was disappointed he wasn't getting it. But he followed the lawyer out of the room, leaving Francis and Rory alone. Francis could feel the tension like a coiled spring between them.

Rory opened his mouth to speak.

'Don't,' said Francis.

'You put him up to that meeting, didn't you?'

'Absolutely not. That would make it inadmissible in court. When he suggested doing it, I went out of my way to persuade him not to.'

Rory gave him a look that spoke volumes.

'This is out of order, boss, and you know it. And that Abbey Road stuff – you're meddling in my case.'

'Rory, you know solving a murder isn't about just getting any

227

old conviction. It's about getting the right conviction. Alex Mullins has walked in here with evidence that throws huge doubt on your charge against his mother.'

'If you were involved in any way with how that evidence was gathered, it won't stand up in court. Paul Mullins's defence will claim entrapment.'

'You can let me worry about that. I told Alex not to do it in front of another witness. This recording will stand up in court. It's the real deal, Rory.'

Rory's lip curled with disgust. 'Can I respectfully remind you, sir, that as a witness you can't be a part of this investigation?'

'All I've done is pass on the evidence, Mackay. But can I respectfully remind you that I'm still your superior officer. If I feel you're dragging your heels over this, I'll have no compunction about stepping in and talking to the CPS myself. Do you understand, Sergeant?'

'But I need to verify the recording first . . .'

'What you need to do is get Marni Mullins out of Bronzefield and then concentrate all your efforts on finding the actual killer. Paul Mullins.'

42

Rory

It was all going in the wrong direction.

Rory sat at his desk, ruminating. At the end of the previous week, they'd had one murder suspect banged up, and three other murders to solve. Now the CPS was looking likely to set their prime suspect free, and they had another dead body on their hands. What had the boss been bloody thinking by insisting the charges get dropped immediately? They could continue to hold Marni Mullins on remand while they investigated Paul Mullins. After all, what proof did they have of the veracity of this so-called confession? He knew all too well that relying on this type of evidence for a case could massively backfire. But the boss had a crush on Marni Mullins – that much was clear – and now he was thinking with his dick, instead of putting his colleagues and the case first.

And as for the other bodies piling up in the morgue? With most cases it often seemed darkest before the dawn, but currently they were flying blind. He stared down at his jotter, where he'd listed the main points of the Booth Museum case so far.

Mummified body, organs removed and placed in Canopic jars – unidentified through dental records, DNA or missing persons reports.

Alicia Russell – museum manager, disembowelled at the top of Peacehaven Cliffs.

229

Luke Bridges – disembowelled at the base of the Angel of Peace statue. No discernible links to Alicia Russell or the museum.

Ada Carmichael – disembowelled and left on the Pier. Links to Bridges or Russell?

Canopic jars containing removed body parts sent to Tom Fitz at The Argus.

Rory had a feeling that if they could find a link between Ada and one of the others, it might give them a hint about the killer, or at least some suggestion of how or why he was choosing his victims. But as more and more bodies piled up, the less they seemed to have in common. Apart from all living in Brighton. And now tension was rising across the city.

KILLER ON THE LOOSE screamed that morning's *Argus* headline.

The local radio station was broadcasting extended news bulletins featuring vox pops with frightened women who wouldn't let their teenagers out and indignant middle-aged men who thought they knew how to solve things better than the police.

And as for those weird messages written on papyrus? The boss seemed to think they were addressed to him, but Rory really wasn't so sure.

He got up and went over to Angie's desk.

'What've you got?'

Angie was examining CCTV footage from the pier to work out when Ada Carmichael had arrived there and to see who was on the pier at the same time as her.

'The coverage's a bit patchy, to say the least.' She pointed to a diagram of the pier she'd printed out. 'There are cameras here, at the main entrance gates, which means everyone who comes onto the pier is caught, both when they arrive and when they leave. That's good. But further down the pier, there are a couple of cameras at the entrance to the amusement arcade and then nothing until you reach the food court right down the end where the rides are.'

'What about where the body was found?'

'That's not covered.'

Hardly surprising. Every two-bit pickpocket knew to look out for CCTV these days, so a killer who'd so far managed to rack up three dead bodies without leaving any significant evidence was sure to have checked out where the cameras were.

'Have you got an arrival time for her yet?'

'Yes.' Angie pulled up a section of footage on her monitor. 'Look here.' She pressed play and the grainy image started to move in fast motion – a stream of people coming on and off the pier. Not as many as there would have been if they were looking at July or August, but it worked to their advantage. Trying to spot someone in a dense crowd was virtually impossible, but this made it easier to pick out individuals and see what they were wearing.

After twenty seconds Angie paused the footage. 'This is her.'

A woman in a dark coat came through the gates. She had the same dark bob as Ada Carmichael and the same-shaped handbag. The images jumped a couple of seconds at a time. Outside the gate, she was looking around. Her expression looked concerned as she came through the gate and onto the pier, and as she passed out of shot, she was studying the screen of her mobile.

'Who's she looking for?' said Rory. It seemed quite clear to him that that was what she was doing.

'That's what I thought,' said Angie. 'She definitely looks like she's expecting to meet someone there.'

'What about the other cameras? Where does she go? Who does she see?'

'There's one frame of her going down past the amusement arcade. She's walking down the west side of the boardwalk to-wards the rides at the end.'

'Still looking for whoever it was?'

'I don't know,' said Angie. 'She doesn't show up at all on the footage from the food-court cameras, so it doesn't look like she went that far. But you can cross from one side of the pier to the other quite easily. Although the wooden shelter with the benches runs virtually the whole length of the pier, there are plenty of gaps in it.'

Rory studied the still Angie had brought up. Ada Carmichael, on her own, walking past the amusement arcade. Her expression, as far as he could make it out, looked serious, anxious even. Was she meeting someone she didn't like, or was maybe nervous of? Or just looking for someone she'd never met? Knowing what happened to her not long after the image was captured gave the picture an air of tragedy. The knowledge that Ada Carmichael was Fitz's stepsister made it seem more personal, somehow, even though he didn't know her.

'And what about people coming and going at around the same time?'

'Ada arrives on the pier at approximately 8.30. The gates closed at ten, apart from the small gate at the side, which the staff use to leave after the pier's closed.'

'And there's no other way to leave, apart from the main gates that are covered by the camera?'

'Short of taking a dip in the sea? No.'

'So, someone comes in either before or after she arrived, but definitely leaves after her death.'

'I've tried to work out the shortest time span possible,' said Angie. 'Ada arrived at 8.30, and we see her passing the amusement arcade at 8.36. It would have taken her, say, another five minutes to walk down to the end of the pier where she was found – so she arrived there at the earliest at 8.41. But she might have dawdled or wandered further down and back again before she met up with whoever she was meeting. We just can't tell.'

'But the killer can arrive at any time before her,' said Rory. 'And given we don't know if she had to wait for him, he could have arrived some considerable time after her. Could she have stopped for a drink somewhere without the cameras picking it up? She might have met him in one of the bars.'

Angie frowned. 'If she'd gone into the food court, the cameras by its entrance would have picked her up. Likewise, if she'd gone into Horatio's, the food-court cameras would have tracked her ... But she might have stopped in the Palm Court, or at Victoria's Bar at the back of it.'

'Kyle's interviewing all the staff that were on duty on Friday. Maybe one of them saw her or served her a drink. In the meantime, when's the earliest the killer could have left?'

'Right, say she arrived at the end at 8.41 – that's the earliest we can put her there. If the killer was there already, how long would he need? The minimum possible time?'

'Not long ... If he just grabbed her and went at her with the knife – just a few minutes?'

'I don't know,' said Angie. She glanced across at the photos on the whiteboard. 'We should check with Rose, but it must take some time to disembowel a person, and take out a particular organ. I think he must have immobilised her, and removed some of her clothing to get the right spot.'

'But there were people on the pier. What if she screamed?'

'Not that many at that time of night. They were right behind one of the noisiest rides. And maybe he gagged her – that would add to the time it would take. Again, we'd better check with Rose for any signs of gagging, like fibres or abrasions.'

'So how much time shall we allow?'

They looked at each other. How long was a piece of string? And what did the killer look like anyway? They could sift through the footage of everyone who went on and off the pier, and maybe if they put out an appeal for witnesses, they'd be able to identify and rule some of them out. But it would take time, and it didn't seem, to Rory, like it would get the results they needed.

'Keep at it, Angie, and let me know if you find anything.'

He went back to his desk. He needed to work out a strategy for hunting down Paul Mullins. So far, the team had worked bloody hard on both cases and it seemed like they'd achieved absolutely nothing.

It was time to take action. Something that would show the brass they'd made a mistake when they'd put Francis bloody Sullivan ahead of him.

But what?

43

Francis

Francis stared down at the museum mummy's twisted body, wondering if he would ever decipher the history that someone had mapped onto her skin with black tattoo ink. He had sketched the outline of her, back and front, and now he was dividing the tattoos up into regions, as they each seemed to be associated with one of the twisting snakes that entwined her limbs and torsos. The Embalmer's sick puzzle, imprinted on a dead woman? If so, it was a game he didn't want to play but, if he had to, one which he was determined to win.

He had numbered the snakes, one to five, wondering what each represented. A chapter in the woman's life? A period of time in the artist's life? He was certain each one of them was telling a story. And how did they fit with the papyrus messages?

He slid the steel drawer shut with a clang. Rose was upstairs in her office, but Francis was waiting downstairs. Tom Fitz was coming in to identify Ada Carmichael's body, although they had no doubt that it was her. It was a formality that had to be done, and Francis would take the opportunity to ask him a little more about Ada's life. He wanted to know who her friends were and whether she'd been dating anyone. And they needed access to her phone. Maybe it could shed some light on what she was doing on the pier, on her own, on a Sunday evening in November.

He heard the slamming of the double outer doors. Before he reached it, the inner door opened and Tom Fitz stepped into the lab. Fatigue showed in the web of lines around his eyes. Usually the picture of robust good health, the reporter looked as if he hadn't slept for several days.

'Tom, I'm sorry for your loss. I'll fetch Rose.'

He took the stairs two at a time up to Rose's office. A thought skittered into his mind that he instantly hated himself for – now, for once, Tom Fitz wouldn't be making capital out of other people's grief. He scowled, pushing open the office door.

'What is it?' Rose frowned in response to his expression.

'Tom Fitz is downstairs to identify Ada Carmichael.'

'Oh no, poor Tom.'

Rose swept past him onto the small landing and headed down the stairs. By the time he got to the bottom, she was embracing Fitz.

'I'm so sorry, Tom,' he heard her saying. Tom's reply was muffled.

Francis's memory stirred. Rory had once hinted at something between Rose and Tom Fitz. Long before Rose was married. Francis had ignored it at the time, but there was a level of intimacy here he hadn't expected.

'I'll show you her now,' said Rose.

Ada Carmichael's body had been prepared and placed in the small viewing room at the back of the mortuary. Rose had conducted her autopsy and done her best to close up the gaping wound in Ada's stomach. Of course, Tom wouldn't see that. Once he was ready, Rose would simply draw back the covering sheet to reveal the dead woman's face. But even that would be hard enough for Tom, thought Francis. Tough crime reporter maybe, but no one was immune to the distress of seeing a family member laid out dead in the morgue.

Francis waited outside in the lobby. He didn't need to witness the other man's pain to know what he must be going through.

Ten minutes later, Tom emerged, looking, if anything, even more depleted than before he went in. His cheeks were damp with brushed-away tears.

'I'll buy you a drink, mate,' said Francis.

Tom nodded, and followed him outside.

Francis carried the two pints of IPA to the small table Tom Fitz had selected at the rear of The Gladstone. It was the nearest pub to the morgue, and Francis had been here on numerous occasions with Rose and Rory. It could be noisy in the evenings, particularly when they had live bands, but on a winter's afternoon, it was quiet. The bar was practically empty.

He sat down and watched as Fitz took a long drink from his glass. He hadn't spoken as they'd walked down the lane to the pub, and Francis had respected his silence. For once, he was about to turn the table on Fitz and be the one asking the questions, but he wanted to give him time to gather himself after what must have been a harrowing experience.

Fitz wiped his mouth on the back of his hand.

'You've got to catch the bastard who did this, Sullivan.'

'You know I'll do everything I can,' he replied. 'I need to ask you a few questions about her.'

'Fire away.'

'You were obviously close . . .' It wasn't so much a question as a prompt.

'We were. My mother and Ada's father got married when we were both eight years old. I hated her at first – I hated all girls at that age. And she hated me. It took a good couple of years before we could even stand the sight of each other.'

'Were you both only children?'

'No.' Fitz shook his head. 'I've got a younger brother. She had a much older sister. Then our parents had a couple of kids together. One of those huge, sprawling families. But Ada and I were the same age, and we went to the same school, so we were pretty much thrown together. It killed me when people at school found out she was my stepsister. She was a goody-goody.'

'But you got on as adults?'

'Yes. Things changed when we were in our teens. Another divorce to live through. Her father drank. My mother was chaotic. Her older sister had left home. We were both looking out for the younger kids.'

'And now? What did she do for a living?' Francis sipped his beer, noting that Fitz had nearly reached the bottom of the glass.

'She was in HR. She worked for a software company. Not very glamorous or exciting, but she seemed happy enough.'

'Boyfriends?'

'I'll get another drink,' said Fitz.

Avoiding the question?

'Just a half,' said Francis. He wasn't even halfway through his first pint, but he wanted to keep Fitz talking.

'Boyfriends,' said Fitz, sitting down a couple of minutes later. 'Yes, but not many. No one at the moment, as far as I knew.'

'And would you?'

'Know? Probably. We kept in touch. I go – went – round to hers for Sunday supper often enough. She generally told me if she was dating someone.'

'What about past boyfriends?'

'She was seeing someone last year for a while ... Roger somebody. It just petered out. You looking at a boyfriend for this?'

'Roger Hazelton?'

Fitz sprung to attention. 'Could be. Have you got something on someone called that?'

Francis shrugged. 'Listen, Tom, this being your sister puts you in a different position than if you were simply reporting on the story. You have a right to know things that I wouldn't necessarily tell you as a reporter.'

'I get that.' Fitz sounded irritated. 'And maybe some of my reporting on the story makes me partly responsible.' The irritation turned to dejection. 'She was a good kid, Francis. She didn't deserve this. I'll do whatever you need me to do to nail who did this.'

'Hazelton was Luke Bridges' business partner. Apparently, they'd argued. But I don't think it means much – he has an alibi for the night Alicia Russell died, and the motives wouldn't add up.'

'But you'll double-check?'

'We will. We've got Ada's phone and we'll follow up on anyone she's had contact with.'

'Okay.'

'Meantime, this doesn't go in the paper.'

'Of course not. I'm not going to write about my sister's private life.'

'What about that burial jar? When did that arrive at your office?'

'I was working late. When I left, I found it by the office front door – it was locked at that time of night. I brought it straight to you.'

If only he'd left it in situ for them to photograph. Instead, Rose had had to scrabble around the pier on her hands and knees picking up the pieces.

'Have you got a security camera trained on your office door by any chance?'

Tom let out a harsh bark of laughter. 'Are you joking? We run that place on a shoestring.' Then his expression turned serious. 'Bradshaw told me. The guy took her stomach . . . ' His voice cracked and he took refuge in his pint.

Bradshaw.

'I need to be able to trust you, Tom, if you're going to help me.'

'This is family. It's personal.'

It had been personal for all the other families of the victims that he'd so irresponsibly written about in the past. But now wasn't the moment to remind him.

Instead, Francis took the plunge.

'We have reason to believe that the messages the killer's sending are directed at me. Frank is a diminutive of Francis. It's what I was known as at school.'

Fitz took a mouthful of beer and thought for a moment. 'So he knows you? Or just targeting you as the officer in charge?'

Francis shrugged. 'He hasn't given up anything yet that shows a personal link, even though he claims there's one.' He changed the subject. 'On the pier's CCTV, it looked like Ada was looking around for someone, like she was going to meet a friend. Any thoughts?'

'Nothing comes to mind – but I didn't know all her friends, or people she could have known through work. Have you asked her flatmate, Cally?'

'Angie Burton's going to talk to Cally later today, and like I said, we're going through her phone. We need access to her laptop, as well.'

'Okay. Let me work with you on this one, Sullivan.'

'On one condition.'

'What's that?'

'If you need information, you come to me. No more talking to Bradshaw behind my back.'

'I don't know what you're talking about.'

'I think you do. I've read things in *The Argus* that could only have come from Bradshaw.'

Fitz shifted his gaze away, but didn't say anything.

'He feeds you all the information you want. You've got something on him, haven't you?'

Fitz gave the slightest of nods.

Francis took a long drink from his fresh beer to hide the rush of excitement that was coursing through him.

'We'll find this killer, Tom. Then you and I will sit down together and figure out how things are going to work between us in the future.'

Bradshaw wasn't going to like it. But he could sod off.

44

Marni

The night terrors still came.

Knowing that she was likely to be released didn't make Marni's last few days in Bronzefield any easier. As she lay in bed, the memories crowded in – that horrifying feeling of blood and life leaching out of her on a cold prison floor. Tobacco-stained teeth in a mouth that gaped with laughter. The worn patina of the black leather boot that had slammed her in the belly. Sharp, physical pain that blunted her mind and eviscerated her heart.

Every morning she woke up confused, sleep-deprived, and wrung out, struggling with the most basic tasks. Hands shaking too much to apply toothpaste to toothbrush. Too clumsy for a hot cup of tea.

How long had she been here?

But this morning, they woke her early and, in a haze of sleep and anxiety, she gathered her few belongings and followed the warder through the silent prison to the discharge area. They patted her down and gave her no privacy as she changed out of her prison kit back into the clothes she'd been wearing for her court appearance. They were crumpled and smelled musty. They hadn't been cleaned during the time she'd been inside – just bundled into a bag with her other possessions.

As the charges had been dropped, she was ejected without the usual plethora of licence conditions and parole appointments. She stumbled out through a small door and blinked at the bright white of the sky. The air was fresh and didn't stink of prison. She looked around. She'd been given money and told to get a bus, but she didn't even know where the bus stop was. She'd got her mobile back, but the battery was flat. Anyway, who would she call? Last time she'd left a prison, Thierry had been there for her. For her and Alex. The memory stopped her in her tracks.

A dark saloon car was waiting, engine idling, just beyond the red-and-white traffic barriers. The front passenger door opened and Alex appeared behind it.

'Mum!'

'Alex!'

Marni couldn't help herself and broke into a run, arms outstretched. He came round the door and seconds later she felt herself being swept into his embrace, and he seemed taller, broader, stronger. She didn't want to cry, but she did. She took a deep breath, fighting back against the tide of emotion that threatened to overwhelm her.

'Mum, thank God you're out. Are you okay?'

Marni leaned back so she could look at him. 'Now I've seen you, I'm fine.'

Jayne Douglas emerged from the driver's side of the car.

'Marni, how are you?'

'I'll be better once we're away from here,' said Marni.

Alex opened the back passenger door and they both slid onto the beige leather of the back seat – and into a different world. Marni sighed and took a final look at Bronzefield as the lawyer turned the car around.

'You must be relieved to be out,' said Jayne.

Marni shook her head. 'I don't know . . . Relieved, of course. But I'm so angry. I shouldn't have been in there in the first place. They just didn't listen to me.'

Alex reached out and took her hand.

'Francis believed in you, but the rest of his team were against him. They couldn't look beyond the end of their noses to see what was going on.'

It hardly compensated for what she'd been through – how could Francis Sullivan have let her languish in a cell for so long?

Jayne turned out of the prison access road in the direction of the M25.

'What happens now?' said Marni.

'What do you mean?'

'Do I have to go back to court?'

Jayne Douglas glanced across at her, then back at the road. 'No. Of course not. The charges have been dropped – that means it's over.'

'Why did they suddenly drop them?'

'Because of Alex's evidence.'

'What evidence? There can't be anything short of a confession from Paul that would finally make them believe my version of events.'

'That's exactly what he gave them.'

Marni twisted in her seat to face her son. 'What? How did you . . . ?'

'I confronted Paul and taped the conversation.'

With a sharp intake of breath, Marni was thrown right back to the moment she'd walked into her kitchen to find Paul and Thierry in the centre of a growing pool of blood.

'Please God, tell me you didn't really do that. Did Francis Sullivan put you up to this?'

'It was my idea,' said Alex. 'Sullivan was against it.'

'The police had nothing to do with it,' said Jayne. 'Thankfully, because if they had, it wouldn't be admissible in court and you'd probably still be inside.'

Marni bit on her lower lip. She'd rather suffer a thousand years in prison than lose Alex.

For the rest of the journey, she just held Alex's hand, lost in a troubled world of her own, while Jayne took a number of calls and Alex rested his head on her shoulder. Finally, when they arrived back in Brighton, Alex sat up straight and leaned forward.

'Can you drop me here?' he said, as they drove down Old Steine, before turning into St James's Street.

'You're not coming home?' said Marni.

'I'll come by later, I promise.'

'I'd be happier if you would come home for a while . . . with Paul still out there.'

'I'll be fine, Mum.'

Then he was gone, leaving Marni feeling unsettled and wondering when she'd next see him.

Jayne restarted the car and took Marni to Great College Street.

'Have you got house keys?' she asked, as Marni reached for the door release.

'Yes. Thank you for coming for me, and for bringing Alex.'

'Will you be all right now?'

Marni smiled, hiding the trepidation she felt. 'Of course. Alex said he'll come round later.'

'Okay. Let me know if you need anything.'

Marni got out of the car. Jayne Douglas didn't mean *anything*. She meant if you've got any legal issues . . . Marni unzipped her bag and dug around for her keys. Despite what she'd said, she felt far from fine. The last time she'd been in the house she'd been clutching Thierry's dead – dying – body. She'd been soiled by his blood. She'd been dragged out, kicking and screaming, by a giant of a policeman. And that was the last she'd seen of her husband. She wondered where his body was – in the morgue, of course. In a cold steel drawer, waiting until the police decided that his loved ones could send him on his way. Bastards.

Her eyes filmed over with tears, but it didn't matter. She could have unlocked her front door with her eyes shut.

As she stepped inside, she sniffed. Something pungent hung in the cold air, the stink of something rotten. The house was completely silent. No barking as Pepper ran to greet her – Alex had taken him to Liv's. She dropped her bag on the table in the hall and went towards the kitchen, partly thinking about putting the heating on, while at same time wondering about the smell.

It grew stronger as she pushed open the kitchen door, sharp and acrid, catching in the back of her throat.

She immediately realised what it was. Thierry's blood. Black and sticky, smeared by the footprints of the police as they'd dragged her away. It didn't seem real, but she knew what had happened here. She gasped, then ran across to the sink, vomit flooding her mouth before she got there. There wasn't much to come up – she'd hardly eaten in prison – but she stood bent over the stainless-steel bowl, retching until she had no more to give. The sight of Thierry's lifeblood so carelessly spilled on the tiled floor that he himself had laid . . . She hadn't expected it. It wasn't that she'd assumed someone would have cleaned it up. It was that she hadn't thought about it at all.

And now it confronted her, the repulsive gore pulling her right back into the moment. Thierry slipping from consciousness. Paul nearly skidding in the blood, as he couldn't get away fast enough. The horror of realisation. All of it, all over again. She couldn't breathe, and as her legs shook, she gripped the strip of countertop along the front of the sink.

Water.

She opened the tap, pushing the lever to the cold side, and splashed her face. She drank from her cupped hands. After a minute, she turned off the tap and stood in front of the sink, eyes closed, breathing deeply, not wanting to turn around and confront her new reality. Gradually, her heart stopped pounding and she opened her eyes.

She needed to see Alex, and to talk to him. But she couldn't have him come here and see this. She looked around the kitchen. As well as the blood on the floor, every doorknob and cupboard handle had a silver dusting of fingerprint powder. The police had been thorough in their job, but they'd left a mess.

Taking a deep breath, she went out to the hall and dug her phone from her bag. She brought it back to the kitchen and put it on the charger, then rolled up her sleeves. Bucket. Mop. Bleach. Scrubbing brush. Cloth. Cleaning liquid.

An hour later, when the doorbell rang, she was on her hands and knees, blinking away tears as she tried to scrub her dead husband's blood out of the grouting. Still wearing rubber gloves, she answered the door, not caring how dishevelled or tear-stained she might appear.

'Marni!'

Francis Sullivan stood on the threshold and, other than Alex, she realised he was just about the only person she could bear to see right now. She stepped back to let him in without speaking, and as he hugged her, she felt herself go rigid. She wasn't really sure she was even ready to see him. Obviously sensing her hesitation, he stepped back quickly.

'How are you?' he said, as he followed her into the kitchen. He looked around, taking in the cleaning paraphernalia and the bucket of pink-tinged water.

'Oh god, did no one arrange to have this cleaned up?'

The tight grip in which Marni managed to hold herself collapsed. She felt her bottom lip tremble and the tears came again, unbidden. She wanted to be strong but the sympathy in Francis's voice had undone her. He stepped forward and took the scrubbing brush from her hand.

'Let me. You sit down.'

It was the last thing she'd ever imagined seeing – Francis Sullivan on his hands and knees, scrubbing her kitchen floor in his suit. He concentrated on the task in hand, giving her time to pull herself together. She stared up at the ceiling, taking deep, slow breaths until the urge to cry had passed.

After a few minutes, Francis sat back on his haunches and looked across at her.

'You know, of course, that we've got a confession from Paul.'

She nodded.

'I've redoubled our efforts to find him, but we've got no idea where he is. Can you think of anywhere that he could be hiding?'

'The hostel where he stayed before?'

'We've checked that, and the manager knows to get in touch with us if he turns up. But I don't think he'll go back there.'

Marni couldn't think of anywhere else. 'Do you really think he's still in the city?'

Francis shrugged. 'He was here on Thursday, when he met Alex. He might have left since then, but I get the feeling he can't stay away.'

Marni shivered, even though the heating had kicked in and the kitchen wasn't cold any more.

Francis stood up and poured the bucket of bloody water down the sink. It was an almost unbearable act for Marni to watch. She wasn't sure she could have managed it herself. Was it really so great to be out of Bronzefield and back in her own home?

'Have you seen Alex yet?' said Francis, as he finished putting away the cleaning materials.

'Briefly. He's coming back later.'

'Listen, Marni . . .' His eyes searched hers, and though she was tempted to look away, she held his gaze. 'I'm not really happy about you being here on your own. Do you think you can get Alex to stay for a while? Just until we've got some idea of where Paul is?'

'I don't want Alex here if there's any chance of Paul turning up. I don't want him anywhere near the man who killed his father.'

Francis digested her words. 'Fair enough. But you're a threat to Paul. You're the one eyewitness who can place him here when Thierry was stabbed. That puts you in danger.'

'I'm not scared of Paul.'

'You should be.'

Marni shrugged.

'I want to give you police protection.'

'No.'

'Marni . . .'

'No. Look, thanks for your help, but I need to phone Alex now.'

Marni felt like a bitch as she hustled Francis out. But she needed time alone so she could start to grieve for her husband. As the door closed behind him, she sank to the floor and finally let the pain of losing Thierry wash through her.

45

Wednesday, 15 November 2017

Francis

Francis left Great College Street kicking himself. He should have given Alex a heads-up to get some cleaners into the property. He could hardly bear to think of what it must have been like for Marni to come back into her house alone and find the whole stinking crime scene in all its gory glory. She was so vulnerable and so alone. He decided to have a quiet word with Alex and suggest that he stayed with his mother, regardless of her views on the matter. Paul Mullins was clearly a psychopath and it seemed unlikely that he would let matters rest.

As he got out of his car in the police-station car park, he saw Rory standing outside the heavy double back doors, smoking a cigarette. So much for all that smugness over vaping when Rory had given up smoking during the summer – he'd lasted all of a few months. Francis lit one of his own and went across to his sergeant.

'All right, Rory?'

'Not particularly. Just heard that the CPS have released Mullins.'

'I know. I've just been to check that she got home okay. Bloody CSI hadn't sent any cleaners in – she was scrubbing her husband's blood off the floor when I arrived.'

Rory rolled his eyes. He was clearly still furious about the taped confession. They'd listened to it over and over again up in the incident room. 'No jury's going to convict Paul Mullins on that – it's ambiguous at best.'

'Works both ways though,' Francis had replied. 'No jury will convict Marni after hearing it – it's more than enough to raise reasonable doubt.' Bradshaw had been equally unimpressed and now the pressure was on Rory to bring in Paul and secure a conviction – or else.

'Oh, and more bad news . . .'

'What?' said Francis.

'Hazelton's date with Sarah Bateman stands up as an alibi. She vouched for him, he produced a receipt from Malmaison for the date of Alicia's death, and one of the waiters recognised a picture of him.'

Francis shrugged. He'd never thought Hazelton had been in the frame for Alicia Russell's killing anyway, so checking his alibi was just a formality. They were looking for some sort of lunatic, and Hazelton just didn't have it in him.

'So we're back at square one,' he said. 'And now we've got another body to contend with as well.'

They stubbed out their cigarettes and went upstairs to the office.

'Tell me what you know about Ada Carmichael,' said Francis, addressing the members of the team who were present.

'According to her driving licence, she's thirty years old,' said Gavin. 'She lived on Stanley Street, near Queen's Park.'

'And the flatmate?' said Francis. 'I take it no one had called her in missing on Friday night?'

'Shared a house with a girlfriend,' said Kyle, 'but she was away for the weekend. Angie's gone to interview her this morning, so we should get some more details about her personal life.'

'Got anywhere with her phone yet, Gavin?'

Gavin shook his head. 'It's got touch ID, so no luck so far.

Got a guy coming over from forensics with an extraction gizmo – he'll be able to crack it wide open.'

'Excellent. Let me know if you find anything relevant.'

'Of course.'

'Kyle, how's it going with the statements from the pier staff?'

'All done, sir. But nothing useful between the lot of them.'

Francis had suspected this would be the case. The CCTV was more useful, but all the staff were busy working and none of them had noticed anything around the time Ada was on the pier.

'Also, where are we with the list of missing women? Been able to exclude most of them?'

Kyle picked up a sheaf of paper from his desk. 'We've just got two left on the list – a Lynne Mazur and a Denise Drysdale. Lynne Mazur's been missing for nearly two years. Last seen leaving a pub in Portslade, a Saturday night, near closing time. No sightings. No leads. I spoke with the officer on her case – they reckon that she probably hitched a lift with the wrong bloke.' He shrugged. 'Doesn't really add up for our case.'

'And the other?'

'Denise Drysdale. Claimed to be an actress. Known to have done exotic dancing. Didn't show up for work. She's got family in Spain, so might just have decided a life of sunshine was preferable.'

'When was this?'

'Five, six months ago.'

'Doesn't sound very promising either. Well, keep at it, Kyle. Maybe widen your search parameters.' He glanced up at the clock on the incident-room wall. It was gone six. 'Okay, call it a day. Let's hope we hit some leads tomorrow.'

The team started packing up and Francis headed back down to his car. He was a man on a mission.

*

'Since when did you do DIY?' Robin came into the kitchen and put a bag of groceries down on the kitchen counter.

'Let me help you with that,' said Francis, putting down the drill he was wielding.

'It's fine. I can manage to put the shopping away, Fran.' She sounded tetchy, like she always did when anyone reminded her of her limitations. 'But what are you doing?'

'Fitting new window locks,' said Francis, turning back to his task.

'But . . . we already had window locks. What was wrong with them?'

'They were ancient. These ones will be more secure.'

Robin looked into the bag from the DIY store on the kitchen table.

'You're doing the whole house?'

'Yup,' said Francis, lining up the parts of a lock on the frame of one of the kitchen's two sash windows.

Robin put away the shopping in silence, while Francis drilled. When he stopped drilling, she spoke again.

'Why this, all of a sudden?'

'No reason. But now you're living here, I just thought it was worth making sure we're totally secure.'

She looked at him with raised eyebrows. 'Not very convincing. What aren't you telling me?'

'Nothing. It's like I said – the old window locks were ancient. Anyone could bust through them.'

'But no one ever has.'

She was clearly suspicious, but the last thing Francis wanted to do was worry her by telling her about the messages from the Embalmer. 'Look, if you don't want to feel safer in your bed, I'll put the old locks back on,' he said, with a grin.

'No, no. Just wondered, that's all. Is it something to do with your work?'

'Jesus, Robin. No. It's just something that was long overdue.'

'Fine.' Now she was affronted. 'I'm going to watch television.' She left the kitchen.

Francis got on with what he was doing.

Maybe he should tell her? But, on balance, he decided not to. She already hated his work. No point in giving her another reason to moan about it. However, he was more worried than he was prepared to let on. There had been something menacing about the Embalmer's last note, and the hint of a connection between them. He'd missed something . . . something that linked him to the man with the knife – but what could it be?

46

Marni

Marni lay back in the bath and closed her eyes. It seemed like a luxury after the foul-smelling prison showers that brought back so many bad memories. Rose-scented bubble bath that Alex had given her for Christmas the year before, rather than a floor slick with soap scum and scattered with other women's pubic hairs. Physically, it felt good, but it didn't make her feel any better in herself.

Even though he'd already moved out, everything in the house reminded her of the times she and Thierry were together. She experienced sudden sharp pangs of grief when she looked round to see an armchair they'd argued over the colour of, or the sketch of her lying naked on their bed that now hung on the bedroom wall. These catastrophic moments were interspersed with periods during which she felt tired – beyond belief – and despondent. Surely life didn't have any more to throw at her? She certainly had nothing left to respond with.

The water was cold, so she pulled out the plug and wrapped herself in a towel. She sat on the edge of the bath, listening to the water drain away down the plughole. Listening to the beating of the rain on the bathroom window. Then she started shivering and realised where she was, and that she needed to go and put something on and have something to eat.

She moved through the house like a somnambulist.

In the bedroom, she threw the towel across the end of the bed. She caught sight of her body in the mirror. Skinny. Pale. Bruised. She didn't remember how she'd bruised herself – one on her thigh, one on the other shin – but the prison cell had been all hard surfaces and jutting edges. She lay down on the bed and cried. This wasn't how her life was meant to have turned out.

She wondered if there was wine down in the kitchen, but even that didn't goad her into action. She didn't want alcohol.

There was a noise downstairs. She got off the bed and went out onto the landing.

'Pepper?'

Silence.

She remembered — the dog wasn't at home. He was still over at Liv's flat. Fear gripped her and she ran back to the bedroom to snatch up her robe. She was breathing fast as adrenalin flooded her body.

'Who's there?' she shouted.

She picked up the heavy metal torch that stood next to her bedside table. She walked slowly, still barefoot, to the top of the stairs, where she paused to listen.

Nothing. The house seemed quiet.

What had she heard? She replayed the sound in her mind, but she couldn't place it. She tiptoed down the first few steps, straining her ears. All was quiet. The hall was dark – the light from the upstairs landing only lit up the top half of the stairs. She retraced her steps back to the landing and switched on the hall light. And then she realised what the noise had been – a batch of junk-food flyers lay on the floor by the front door. It had been the flap of the letter box.

'Fuck!'

How could she have been so stupid? She breathed a heavy sigh of relief, went downstairs and scooped up the leaflets to put them in the bin. In the kitchen, she took a sliced loaf out of the freezer and put a piece in the toaster. She needed to normalise things. She couldn't go on with this constant rollercoaster ride, and she needed to look after herself. She checked her blood sugar levels and made a note for herself to call the pharmacy the next day and sort out her prescriptions. She called Alex and left him a message, asking him to bring Pepper back, then she took her plate of toast through to the living room. She wasn't ready yet to spend time in the kitchen, and she wondered if she ever would be. Maybe she should think about moving house. She wondered where else she could go. She'd always lived in Brighton, but now . . . she wasn't so sure. Every street, every pub, all her local haunts – they were all saturated with memories of Thierry. Perhaps it was time for a change.

Pepper's excited barking outside the front door drew her out of her reverie.

'Alex!'

'Mum, I should have brought him earlier.'

'It's fine.'

Pepper jumped up at her, pushing at Alex's legs to insert himself between them. Marni squatted down to greet him, and the house felt a little more like home again with the dog's presence.

'My good dog, that's my boy.' Pepper slobbered over her face and for once she didn't care. He felt warm and sturdy, and his stubby tail wagged his whole hindquarters from side to side.

They went through to the kitchen, and she noticed Alex looking around.

'I'm not drinking,' she said quickly. 'I'm really going to look after myself.'

'That wasn't what I was looking for.' He frowned. 'This is where it happened, isn't it?'

Marni looked away with a sharp intake of breath. She nodded.

'I want to kill him, Mum.'

'I know.' She could hardly speak.

'I came this close.' He held up his thumb and forefinger, a scant inch between them.

Marni could hear cold, hard fury in her son's voice. He was so like his father.

But she didn't even know who his father was. Paul or Thierry?

'Promise me you won't see him again? What you did to get the confession was brave, but he's a dangerous man.'

'I can't promise that, Mum. I need to get him.' *Was that his father talking?*

'He needs to go to prison. Leave it to the police.'

'Come on, that wanker Sullivan couldn't bring in a shoplifting granny.'

He was wrong. Francis Sullivan knew how to do his job perfectly well when he wasn't hamstrung from above, but she was too tired to argue about it.

'I can't lose you too, Alex,' she said.

He stepped forward to hug her again. 'You won't, Mum. I promise you. Just call me whenever you need me, and I'll come round straight away.'

Marni hugged him back and Pepper danced wildly round them, barking excitedly.

'Here,' he said, disengaging, 'let me cook something for you.' He went over to the freezer and started pulling things out. 'Prawns, salmon ... fish pie?'

'That would be heaven.'

'You know I'm here for you, Mum. Really.'

But could she rely on Alex? Or would he turn out to be like his father? Unreliable, feckless, womanising ... if his father was Thierry. Or something far darker, if his genes had been given to him by Paul. And how would she ever know which? She pushed the thoughts out of her mind and went to help him prepare the food.

47

Thursday, 16 November 2017

Marni

For a Thursday evening, the tapas bar was quiet. Marni looked round and remembered the first time she'd come here with Francis. She was sitting at the same table. He'd hardly touched his wine, and had even seemed a little scared of her back then. He'd changed a lot over the eighteen months or so that she'd known him. She'd seen him sink a bottle of whisky and she'd tattooed an octopus on his shoulder – or at least she'd started to, never finishing the job as things had gone sour between them.

Now? He was older and wiser. He'd had a tough start as a DI, with two horrendous serial killers and the death of his mother in a short space of time. He bore the scars of what he'd been through, and she liked him all the more for it.

'Penny for them?' said Francis, dropping into the chair opposite. He helped himself to a glass of wine from the bottle she'd ordered for them. Yes, how he'd changed.

'Just deciding what to eat,' she said.

'Good. You've lost weight.'

'And it's your business?'

Francis grinned at her. 'Sorry. Of course it's not. But at least you're answering back and not letting me get away with it.'

She took a deep breath. She didn't feel ready to flirt with him, but it was reassuring to see him. They pondered the menu, and ordered a selection of dishes and a basket of bread.

Francis looked more serious. 'Have you seen Alex?'

Marni nodded. 'He came with Jayne to collect me, and brought Pepper home later.'

'Is he staying with you?'

'No, he's back at Liv's. I don't want one of these boomerang kids that keeps coming back home, and I'm quite big enough to look after myself.'

Francis wrinkled his nose, but bit his tongue until after the waiter who brought the bread was out of earshot.

'I don't think you should be on your own, not with Paul still on the loose.'

'I'm not on my own. I've got Pepper.'

'The world's best guard dog? Yeah, let's see how that works out.' Francis smiled. Pepper was one of his biggest fans.

'I've got a guy coming next week to instal a burglar alarm. Alex insisted on it.'

'Problem with alarms,' said Francis, tearing a bit of bread in half, 'is that your neighbours will sit indoors, cursing the noise it makes, and not bother to come to your aid. Unless you have it connected to a monitoring service.'

'It won't even go off,' said Marni.

'How can you be so sure? What if Paul comes back?'

Marni fingered the blade of the knife by the side of her plate.

Francis snatched it away. 'No, Marni! That is not the answer. Jesus, you'll just end up back in jail again. Or worse.'

The waiter arrived with a tortilla and a pungent dish of garlic prawns.

'Everything okay?' he asked, in a strong Spanish accent, concern knitting his brows.

Francis put down the knife. Marni smiled at him.

'This looks delicious,' she said.

Francis poured them both some more wine and they ate in silence for a few minutes.

'Marni, I don't want to see you get hurt.'

'That ship sailed a long time ago.'

'More hurt. Hurt again.' Francis stabbed a slice of fiery orange chorizo with his fork. 'Paul is a dangerous man, you know that. You're on your own.'

Marni shrugged. 'What are you suggesting I do?'

'Go and stay somewhere else. At least, until he's been caught or we know he's out of the country.'

'No.'

'What about staying at your sister's? Or with Liv and Alex?'

'No. My sister will be all, "I told you so." And Liv and Alex . . . it's pretty new. I don't want to cramp their style.'

Francis's eyebrows shot up. 'They're dating? But aren't they first cousins?'

'Liv was adopted. Sarah couldn't have her own.'

'How's Alex doing?'

It was a question Marni had been asking herself. She shrugged. 'On the surface, he seems okay, but he's always been good at hiding his feelings.' She took a mouthful of wine and stared down at the glass in her hand. 'His childhood was . . . chaotic. Thierry and I broke up and got together again maybe half a dozen times, and each time he thought it was for good. It's damaged him, and we were to blame.'

'He's got the resilience of youth. He's tough.'

'No. He's not.' The assumption made her angry. Sure, he'd looked tough when he'd had his dreadlocks and his fuck-you attitude. But it had all been an act. A face he put on for the outside world. 'You don't know him, Francis. And your dealings with him have always been . . .' She struggled to find the right word. 'Combative.'

'Fair enough.'

'Now his father's dead. I was in prison. I think Liv's been really worried about him.'

'I think he's been just as worried about you.'

'You spoke to him?'

'When you were in Bronzefield. Listen, Marni, I know I mis-judged him at first, but I think he's okay. You've done a good job with him, despite the circumstances.'

Francis Sullivan didn't know the half of it and he was being patronising. She concentrated on peeling a prawn. She wasn't going to thank him for his concern about her son.

Francis carried on eating as well, and there was silence for a few minutes.

'More wine?'

'Sure,' said Marni.

Francis attracted the waiter's attention and ordered another bottle.

Marni thought of Thierry, and felt suddenly upset. Even though she and Thierry had broken up – again – months ago, it felt strange to be sharing wine with Francis. The waiter brought a fresh bottle of Rioja over to their table and Francis tasted it, giving the waiter a curt nod. Thierry would have spent longer considering the wine. He might have discussed it with the waiter, asked about where it came from and what grapes were used. Francis and Thierry were so different.

When the waiter had gone, Francis filled up her glass.

'Marni ... ' He paused and took a deep breath. 'I've got a proposal for you.'

She waited.

'Well, it's not a proposal.'

'It either is or it isn't.'

'It's nothing like that. I just think it would be a good idea if you ... if you maybe came and stayed at my house for a bit.' He looked terrified. 'Just till this business with Paul is sorted out. Just in the spare room. My sister's living with me, too.'

It all tumbled out in a rush. How long had he been hatching this little plan?

'Is this why you asked me out?'

'God, no. I just wanted to see how you were, check you were okay. I only just thought of this as an option when you said you couldn't stay with Sarah or Alex.'

'You want me to move in with you, Frank?'

'Just come and stay for a bit. You'll be safer.'

His hand snaked out and grasped hers. It was comforting.

Marni couldn't deny to herself that the idea sounded tempting. She'd been unnerved too many times already by perfectly explicable noises. And it was true, Pepper wouldn't be any help as a guard dog. Besides which, being around people would do her some good. Stop her sinking into depression and drinking too much.

'Yes, okay.' She raised her glass to her lips to curb the impulse to immediately say no.

'You'll come?'

She nodded.

Relief flooded Francis's features as he smiled.

'I didn't think you'd agree to it.'

'It's not much fun being on my own at the moment.'

'It's pretty quiet at my house.'

'That's fine by me.' She scraped up some garlic mayonnaise with a corner of bread. 'What about your sister? Will she mind?'

'Of course not,' said Francis. 'She'll be fine.'

Marni had only met Robin Sullivan briefly, but Francis had talked about her. From things he'd said, she wasn't so sure Robin would be overjoyed at her presence in their father's house.

'Okay.' *Would it be?*

Francis raised his glass. 'Cheers. I'll come round tomorrow and help you bring your stuff over.'

And then he leaned forward across the table and kissed her. It was just a peck, as brief as a kiss could be. But it unleashed a wave of confusion that shocked her to the core.

48

Friday, 17 November 2017

Gavin

The boss was in his office, sulking. Seemed like the investigation into the Booth Museum mummy was making no progress whatsoever. Rose had apparently discovered some tiny grooves – called parturition pits – in the woman's pelvis bone that indicated she'd given birth to a child.

It wasn't welcome information to the investigation.

'As of now, we've been through the list of women missing in Brighton and Sussex and eliminated those of the wrong age, wrong height and so on,' Francis had said to the team. 'We've got two left – Denise Drysdale and Lynne Mazur – and this doesn't help.'

'Why? They've both got children?' said Angie.

'No. Neither of them do. Which means we've got to rule both of them out. According to Rose, there's no doubt that the mummified woman had a vaginal birth. We're going to have to widen the search.'

Now Rory and Kyle had been tasked with opening out the investigation of missing women to cover the whole of the UK, but even the boss had admitted they were grasping at straws. Not that he would say it out loud, but this wasn't quite how Gavin had pictured it when he signed up to become a detective. He'd had his baptism of fire on the Poison Ink

Killer case, and now he was stuck behind a desk.

Still, you couldn't be out chasing someone if you didn't know who you needed to chase.

At least his ten o'clock appointment held the promise of something more interesting.

In fact, Jim Harper was early, which Gavin decided to take as a good omen. He was the force's specialist in forensic extraction – in other words, the go-to man when an investigation needed to access the data on a suspect or victim's mobile phone. The boss had asked him to liaise with Harper over extracting information from Ada Carmichael's mobile. Gavin opened his desk drawer and pulled out a plastic evidence bag as a PC showed Harper into the incident room.

'Jim Harper? I'm Gavin Albright. We spoke on the phone.' He held out a hand.

'Good to meet you,' said the other man. He was short and stocky, and his grasp was firm.

Gavin grabbed the chair from Kyle's desk – he was out with Angie speaking to Ada Carmichael's co-workers. Once they were both sitting down, Gavin shook the iPhone that had been found in Ada's handbag out onto the desk.

'This is it,' he said. 'Victim's phone – recovered from her handbag on the Palace Pier on Friday night. We're interested in calls and text messages leading up to that point. From the CCTV on the pier, it appeared that she was looking for someone. We need to know who she was meeting.'

'Fine,' said Harper. 'I can get the data for you, no problem. It'll be up to you to go through it all.'

He lifted his briefcase from the floor onto his lap and unzipped it. Gavin watched him pull out a small hand-held gadget that looked more than anything like an early Game Boy.

'What's that?'

'The Universal Forensic Extraction Device – UFED,' said

Harper. 'This baby'll crack that phone right open.'

'What if it's got Touch ID?'

'It bypasses all of the average mobile phone's security measures. I'll be able to access her contacts list, call history, social media, SMS messages, browser history . . . basically I'll be giving you back-door access to her entire life.'

'Is that legal?'

Harper shrugged. 'Currently, it's a bit of a grey area . . . Yes, it's legal, but probably just because the law hasn't caught up with it yet. Anyway, we're sanctioned to use it at the moment.' Gavin decided it might be better not to probe further. If something on Ada's phone could give them a lead on the killer, he'd take it.

Harper picked up the iPhone and flipped it out of its leather cover. He quickly checked the exact model and then switched on his UFED. Gavin watched, fascinated. Mobile phone technology had made a huge difference to people's lives, but it was easy to see how it made them vulnerable. What if gadgets like this got into the hands of the wrong people? He glanced at Harper, who was attaching the iPhone to the UFED with a short cable. Were they, the police, even the right people? He had to believe they were, or he couldn't do the job. And in this case, it was easy – Ada Carmichael had been murdered and they were going to find out who did it.

'Okay,' said Harper. He picked up the UFED and tapped a few keys. The screen of the iPhone lit up. 'That's it – we're off.' He put the device and the phone down on Gavin's desk, side by side.

'How long will it take?'

'A few minutes. How about a coffee?'

Ten minutes later, Harper disconnected the phone from the UFED and then reconnected the extraction device to his laptop. He booted up the computer and selected an icon from the desktop – Cellebrite.

'What's that?' said Gavin.

'Cellebrite are the manufacturers of the data extractor. They also make the software that analyses it.'

The screen opened up.

Virtual Analyzer – Powered by Cellebrite

Harper clicked on a few more menu items and they were in. A white screen headed *Extraction Summary*, with a series of menu buttons. *Chats. Contacts. Passwords. Searched items. User accounts. Web bookmarks. Emails. Device events.* Next to each of these was a number – Gavin assumed this related to how many items were in each heading.

'My god,' he said, 'you've got everything.'

'Pretty much,' said Harper, with a grin. 'What do you want to look at?'

'Contacts,' said Gavin, with no hesitation. 'Can we get the list printed out?'

'Sure can.'

In a matter of moments, Gavin was holding a printed list of all the contacts on Ada Carmichael's phone. Names, numbers, email addresses, even street addresses.

'Perfect,' said Gavin. He'd go through it in detail after Harper left.

'Next?'

'Personal email account.'

Harper opened up Ada Carmichael's inbox. Gavin had a momentary twinge – it was like reading somebody else's diary. But Ada Carmichael was dead and they had good enough reason to be rifling through her virtual existence. Gavin scanned the screen – Ada's inbox had more than two hundred emails in it, about half of them not even opened. A lot of these seemed to be from Amazon, eBay and ASOS, plus a scattering of other online retailers and advertisers. The curse of modern life.

More interesting were the ones that had been opened. He

spotted Tom Fitz's name a couple of times, and a few other names he already had listed as friends or relatives. They opened a few that had arrived during the day before Ada made her ill-fated visit to the pier. There was one from her flatmate, forwarding a utility bill for Ada to see. One from her stepmother, concerning the arrangements for a Sunday lunch some weeks in the future. That wouldn't be happening now. Advice that a package from Etsy had been shipped, and more advice about when it would be delivered. But nothing about arrangements for that evening.

'It's going to take some time to go through all these. Can you transfer them to my computer?'

'Easy,' said Harper. It only took him a couple of minutes to set up a new folder on Gavin's desktop, and then to transfer all of Ada's data from the device. 'That's the lot, so you'll be able to go through it all at your leisure. But what d'you want to look at next?'

'Chats,' said Gavin. It was the most likely way she'd made the arrangements for her night out.

'Messages? WhatsApp? Facebook Messenger? UrbanSingles?'

'Start with Messages. Then the dating app.'

There were messages from her older sister, work colleagues, her flatmate, friends, both male and female. Ada sent and received a lot of texts, but none of them mentioned Sunday evening or the pier.

'WhatsApp?'

'Not so much activity here,' said Harper.

There were just a few incoming messages from Tom Fitz – it seemed it was his favoured communication tool, rather than hers.

'Let's take a look at UrbanSingles,' said Gavin. 'Could it have been a date gone wrong?'

'If the guy didn't like her, he could have just left. Killing her seems a bit extreme.'

Gavin allowed himself a half-smile. Gallows humour didn't

mean they didn't care what had happened to Ada.

Harper opened up the dating app and they studied the screen. It only took Gavin seconds to realise what they were looking at.

'Got him!' he said under his breath.

Ada Carmichael had swiped right, fixed a date and got herself killed. It was there in black and white – a series of escalating messages between her and a man calling himself Josh that culminated in the arrangement of a date on the Palace Pier on Sunday evening.

'Josh?' said Harper. 'You think that's him?'

'If you're going to use a fake name, use a popular name. Makes perfect sense. He probably claims his surname is Smith.'

'Sure. Anyway, looks like you've got him. You can just work back from his UrbanSingles account.'

The profile picture showed an average-looking man, probably in his thirties, but there was no reason to think that this was actually the man who went to meet Ada on the pier.

'He probably set it up using a fake name, a fake picture and a VPN,' said Gavin. 'If this was premeditated – and given the links to the other killings, I'd say it was – he'll have at least done that much to cover his tracks.'

'No worries. Give me a few hours and I'll get back to you.'

'Great.'

Jim Harper packed up his kit and took his leave, while Gavin printed out the exchange between Ada Carmichael and the mysterious Josh.

He knocked on the door of Francis's office and pushed it open.

'Boss, you need to see this. It could lead us to the killer.'

49

Francis

The name might have been fake, but the address that went with it probably wasn't. Jim Harper had been as good as his word. Within twenty-four hours he'd come back to them with information. The name the man had used was Josh Roberts – and it was almost certainly false. But having the address where he'd been logged onto the internet when he arranged his date with Ada Carmichael was a huge step forward.

'It's a flat, boss,' said Gavin, bursting into his office. 'A maisonette, in fact, in Lodsworth Close.'

'Where's that?'

'Part of a housing estate, up the north end of Whitehawk. The Swanborough flats.'

Francis nodded. 'Right, I know where you are now.'

Gavin hardly let him finish the sentence. 'And, believe it or not, the registered tenant is one Denise Drysdale.'

'The woman from the missing persons list?'

Gavin nodded. 'One and the same.'

'Get the team together – we're going up there.'

Half an hour later, Francis, Rory and Gavin were heading out through Brighton towards Whitehawk. Kyle and Angie were following in a second car. Francis had secured a search warrant for the property. They hadn't been able to get an arrest warrant for Josh Roberts as it was clear from the dating profile that this was a fictitious name.

'What else did you find out, Gavin?' said Francis as he steered them along Eastern Road through Kemptown.

'Denise Drysdale has apparently been the tenant there for the last eighteen years. No one else lives there, according to the electoral register.'

'Or no one who bothers to vote,' said Rory.

'She's claiming single person discount on her council tax,' said Gavin.

'How old is she?' said Francis.

'Fifty-six.'

'Josh Roberts used the address to set up his UrbanSingles account. He might be her boyfriend, a relative or even a lodger,' said Francis. 'Whoever's in there, I want them brought in for questioning, and the whole place searched. What we really want is the phone or computer that Roberts used to set up his dating profile – if we get that, we'll find out who he is and his real name.'

'Then we'll arrest him?' said Gavin.

'Of course,' said Rory.

'Not so fast,' said Francis. 'We still have to establish that Ada met up with the guy she was messaging with, and furthermore that he was then the person who killed her. What if he didn't show up for the date and our killer was opportunistic?'

'You don't really believe that's the case, do you, boss?' said Rory.

'No, not given the link with Denise Drysdale, but we need to do things right. No technical errors that can fuck up the case later, if it gets to court.'

Rory directed him to take a left off Wilson Avenue onto Swanborough Drive. Francis checked in his rearview mirror that Angie had taken the turn. He was familiar with the Whitehawk area – it was one of Brighton's poorest wards, though on the outskirts of the city, so it didn't have an edgy, urban vibe. Behind the Swanborough blocks of flats there were allotments and a community orchard, and beyond that more open land that was sometimes used by travellers.

They parked outside one of the lower blocks in the development, just four floors, rather than the eight that some of the buildings had. Angie pulled up beside them, and once everyone was out of the cars, Gavin pressed the buzzer for Denise Drysdale's first-floor flat.

They waited in expectant silence.

There was no answer.

A woman came out of the entrance hall and stared at them with an expression that told Francis she knew exactly who they were.

'We're looking for Denise Drysdale,' he said. 'Do you know if she's around?'

The woman eyed him suspiciously. 'Haven't seen her in months.'

'Do you know where she is?'

'Nah, not a clue. Probably visiting her sister on the Costa del Crime.' She looked as if she was about to say more but then thought better of it, clamping her mouth shut. It was the sister, they'd found out, who'd reported her missing.

'Thank you,' said Francis, his tone dismissive.

The woman took a few steps from the front door into the parking area, then turned around and stood staring at them. Waiting to see what they would do next.

Francis wasn't wild about having an audience, so he turned his back on the woman.

'We've got a search warrant,' he said. 'We're going in.'

'Do you want me to fetch the enforcer?' said Gavin. He was referring to the steel battering ram they'd brought in the boot of Francis's car.

'Let's take a look first.' Francis lowered his voice. 'I'd rather our friend went on her way, before we show that off.'

Rory was still holding the front door open from when the woman had emerged, so they all filed inside.

'She ain't there,' the woman shouted after them.

It was true. There was no answer when they knocked on the front door of the first-floor flat. After ascertaining that the nosy neighbour had disappeared, Gavin brought the battering ram up. The others stood back as he swung it hard against the lock. The door burst open on the second impact and Francis led them inside.

Denise Drysdale's flat looked ordinary enough at first glance, but it smelled strange. A mixture of uncleaned hamster cage and rotting vegetation. Rory crossed the living room and threw open the window.

'Smells like something died in here,' he said.

'You're not wrong,' said Gavin, wrinkling up his nose.

'Look for evidence of where Denise Drysdale might be, and also for information on any male associates she has – husband or partner, other male relative such as son or brother . . .'

They spread out around the flat. It had two bedrooms, a living room, a kitchen and a bathroom. Angie went into the main bedroom.

'Hasn't been dusted for weeks,' she said. 'Doesn't seem like anyone's been living here for several months.'

'Mouldy cheese and rotten lettuce in the fridge,' said Gavin.

Francis went into the second bedroom.

And stopped in the doorway. His eyes widened and his jaw went slack. It took him a moment to appreciate what he was seeing, but only a moment.

'Shit! Here's the source of the smell,' he called out to them.

The double bed had been pushed up against one wall, partially blocking the built-in wardrobe doors. Along the opposite wall, at right angles to the window, there were four glass tanks. Large glass tanks. Each of them was occupied by a single, enormous snake. Francis felt his heart leap into his throat.

Angie, Rory and Gavin crowded the doorway – Francis hadn't got very far into the room and he wasn't going further.

'Christ,' said Rory.

Gavin had blanched and taken a step backwards.

'What the fuck are they?' said Angie.

'Snakes,' said Rory.

'Thank you, yes, well done,' said Angie, her sarcasm breaking the tension that had gripped the room. 'I mean, what kind of snakes? Poisonous, or the ones that crush you?'

Nobody knew.

The room was hot and dry

'The radiator's on,' said Angie. She'd pushed past Francis and gone further into the room. She peered at the coiled snakes through the glass sides of the tanks.

'Are the tops of the tanks secure?' said Rory from the doorway.

'Are they even alive?' said Gavin. There was hope in his voice for a negative answer.

Angie jumped back. 'Yes. One of their tongues just flicked out.'

They were huge – thick ropes of muscle sheathed in shining brown and gold scales. The diamond patterns on their backs were intricate and beautiful – and they reminded Francis of one thing. The patterns on the snake tattoos that curled across the body of the mummified woman.

This couldn't be a coincidence.

'Right, let's not take any chances,' said Francis. 'Out of here, Angie, and call the RSPCA to come and collect these. Gavin, Rory, search the rest of the flat. I'll door-knock the neighbours.'

In the corner tank, one of the snakes opened an eye and made a harsh, guttural hissing sound.

50

Francis

Francis almost bumped into the woman they'd spoken to on their way in. She was loitering in the entrance hall, neck craned to see what was going on up the stairs, logging every little detail no doubt for spilling in the pub later.

'What's your name?' he said to her.

She turned with a start. 'What's goin' on?'

'I asked you your name.'

'I live in the building. I got a right to know.'

Francis stepped forward, and pulled out his warrant card. 'Name?'

'Melba. Melba Black.'

'Which flat do you live in?'

'This one.' She cocked her head over her shoulder to indicate the front door of the ground-floor flat just behind them.

'How long have you lived here?'

Melba screwed up her face in thought. 'Moved in when Suz was three ... she's sixteen now.' She sounded surprised by the passing of the years.

'So that would be thirteen years,' said Francis.

She nodded. It was clear to him that she was simply agreeing for the sake of it, rather than having done the maths.

'And Denise Drysdale has been your upstairs neighbour for all of that time?'

275

'Yes. Not that I know her really. She keeps herself to herself. A bit hoity-toity with the likes of me and mine.'

'Is there a Mr Drysdale?'

Melba let out a short, sharp bark of laughter. 'Never. There's been men . . . sometimes. Not for very long. She can't keep 'em.'

'Why's that?'

Melba shrugged. 'You ever met her?'

'No.'

'She's . . . she's nervy. Twitchy. I think it gets on a bloke's tits, when a woman's like that.'

'Did you ever hear her arguing with anyone in her flat?'

Melba shook her head. 'Her flat's not right above mine – it's on the other side.'

'Any recent boyfriends?'

'No.' She paused. 'Apart from . . . I think she might have had someone a couple of months back, for a bit. But I'm not sure he was her boyfriend. He seemed quite a lot younger. Only saw him a couple of times, actually. Could have just been a tradesman.'

'Can you describe him?'

'Not really. Just a guy in a hoody and a baseball cap.'

This wasn't much help.

'One last thing. Did Denise have any tattoos?'

'Never saw one. Doubt it very much – she was a bit, you know . . . a bit too straight-laced for anything like a tattoo.'

Francis let her go and went back up the stairs pensively. If Denise Drysdale and the mummified woman were one and the same, she certainly had tattoos now. He wondered how quickly Rose could make the match. A DNA test would take forever, but if they could find a reference in the flat to a dentist she used, dental X-rays might be the quickest way of confirming the mummy's identity.

'Here, boss – you need to see this.' It was Rory, emerging from Denise Drysdale's kitchen, looking a bit green.

'What have you got?' said Francis, still thinking about the mummified woman as he followed Rory through the kitchen door.

'Look.'

Rory held open the door of a small upright freezer. It was crammed with bulging polythene bags. Francis bent down and squinted at them.

'Rats,' said Rory. 'Dead rats. And there are some in the bottom drawer of the fridge.'

Francis felt his stomach churning. 'For the snakes?'

'Presume so,' said Rory, closing the freezer door.

A scream from the landing made them forget about the rats.

'Angie?'

'Shit! Shit!' Angie nearly knocked Francis over as she headed at a run towards the front door. Gavin barrelled through right behind her.

'What?' said Francis.

He wished he hadn't asked. He wished he hadn't even come to this bloody flat. A deep-throated purring sound came from somewhere behind him – it wasn't so much a hiss as a soft growl. In front of him, across the bedroom, the glass lid of one of the tanks had been knocked crooked.

'Don't move, boss,' said Rory.

Francis ignored the advice and turned round. A snake that was bigger than anything he'd ever imagined was gliding effortlessly along the corridor towards him. Rory cowered in the kitchen doorway as it slithered past. He stepped back and slammed the door shut, leaving Francis on his own with the creature.

'Thanks, Rory.' The words came out as an unintelligible squeak.

Two round gold eyes with vertical black slits for pupils stared up at him malevolently. When had the thing last been fed? A forked tongue tasted the air, accompanied by a prolonged hiss. Francis's blood turned to iced water. Every hair on his body stood up. His chest tightened in the grip of fear, just when he needed extra oxygen. The snake was between him and the front door. If he retreated, it would be into the bedroom, where there were three more such creatures – and what if they got out of their tanks?

The boa was just a long tube of brute muscle.

'You'll be okay,' shouted Rory from behind the kitchen door. 'They don't eat humans.'

Francis didn't speak. Even though the snake was directing an icy stare at him already, it felt somehow wrong to draw added attention to himself.

In his pocket, his phone began to ring.

The snake opened its jaws wide and snarled.

Francis drew his mobile out of his pocket in a slow, fluid movement. He glanced down at the screen. It showed Angie's name. He raised it to his ear.

She still sounded out of breath and terrified. 'The RSPCA … on their way. They said … don't touch it. Move away from it slowly … no sudden movements.'

Easy for them to say. They weren't facing down a bloody giant snake in a small space.

His heart hammered against his chest. The creature was inching closer, sniffing him with its fluttering, forked tongue.

Bugger the advice.

He took a deep breath, and put one foot behind him to push off with. Then he leapt as far and as high as he possibly could from a standing start. He launched himself over the snake's head and down the hallway at a gallop. But his trailing foot landed on the snake's back, grinding down its side onto the floor. The snake's head whipped round and its sickening rasp sounded louder and angrier than ever. Francis fought to keep his balance, pushing his body forward to give himself some momentum.

At the same moment, the kitchen door opened a crack and

Rory tossed the body of a dead rat at the snake's head. It bounced off the opposite wall and fell at the snake's side as the kitchen door slammed shut. Momentarily distracted, the snake sniffed at the corpse. By the time it looked up again, Francis had the front door open and was vanishing through it.

He'd never slammed a door so hard and so fast in all his life. Then he slumped forward onto his hands and knees, panting loudly on the landing floor.

'You okay, boss?' said Angie, coming across to him. She hardly sounded much better herself.

He nodded without speaking.

'What about Rory?'

Francis finally allowed himself a sigh of relief. 'He'll be fine. As long as snakes can't open doors.'

51

Saturday, 18 November 2017

Francis

Thankfully, this particular snake couldn't open doors. In fact, it was far more interested in the dead rat that Rory had thrown at it than the human visitors to its habitat. Two officers from the RSPCA arrived with a special snare, which they quickly looped over the drowsy creature's head and had it back in its tank within minutes. Then, one by one, they transferred the boas into travel containers and took them down to their van.

'You were lucky,' said one of the snake wranglers. 'They were well fed – all of them had probably eaten within the last week.'

'The last week?' said Gavin. 'You're joking?'

'No,' said the man, 'they only eat once a fortnight or so.' He got into his van and gave them a cheery wave as they drove off.

The team could breathe again.

Back at the incident room, they started going through a couple of bags of papers, documents and ephemera they'd removed from Denise Drysdale's flat once the snakes were out of the way.

'Right,' said Francis, feeling a lot calmer now he was back in control. 'I want you to look for anything that points to an identity for the younger man coming and going from Denise's flat. We're also looking for something that might tell us who her dentist was. And anything at all that gives us her movements in recent weeks. We still don't know precisely when the mummified woman died, so check for appointments and receipts that will give us the latest dates that Denise was going about life as normal. Hopefully, we'll be able to tie the two together.'

He went into his office and opened the desk drawer. There was a half-bottle of whisky pushed to the back. He'd had a fright and he was still a little jittery. He pulled the bottle out and unscrewed the cap. But when he smelled the liquor, it didn't feel right to be drinking in the office, so he put the top back on and put it away. He could have a drink later, when he got home and could tell Robin all about it.

There was a knock on the door.

'Boss?' Gavin came in. 'Take a look at this.' He held out a rectangular slip of paper, printed as a form in blue ink. 'It's a pay slip. For a Euan Drysdale.'

'From where?'

'The Brighton Dome.' The theatre complex that stood behind the Pavilion.

'Current?'

Gavin squinted at the piece of paper. 'No. It's from 2016.' He handed it to Francis.

Francis scanned the document for information, but there wasn't much to see. Euan Drysdale was paid hourly at a rate that seemed less than the minimum wage.

'Okay, let's go down there and ask some questions.'

Half an hour later they found themselves in the theatre manager's office.

'Yes, I know Euan.' His voice sounded weary, giving Francis the impression that he didn't like the employee very much.

'Is he working for you now?' said Francis.

'On and off. He does props for our productions. Comes in when we need something.'

'Can you tell us about him?'

'Not much to tell. I don't really know him, beyond his work.

Which is adequate. Bit of a weird guy, I suppose.'

'In what way?' said Gavin.

'Quiet. Slips in and out without saying hello to anyone. Works odd hours.'

'Where exactly does he work?' said Francis.

'He's got a workshop under the stage of the Studio Theatre,' said the manager.

'Mind if we take a look at it?' said Francis.

The manager stood up and turned to a key board behind his desk. He plucked a set of keys and held them out. 'Drysdale has got his own keys, so he comes and goes as he pleases.'

They followed the man's directions to a low, black-painted door by the side of the stage in the complex's smaller theatre. Francis tried the keys and unlocked it. There was a short corridor, then another door, that opened with the second key on the ring. It opened into a pitch-black space. Francis felt the wall to the side of the door until he found a switch.

The low-ceilinged room which was flooded with light seemed strangely familiar to Francis, and in an instant he realised why.

'Tutankhamun's tomb,' he muttered, taking a step forward.

'I was about to say the same,' said Gavin at his shoulder.

Every space was cluttered with a messy tumble of objects and artefacts, many of which looked like they could have come straight out of an Egyptian burial chamber. A shrine to an Egyptian deity dominated the entire space. On a low plinth that stood along the back wall, there was an almost life-size statue of a figure. A man, in the classic Egyptian pose with one leg extended in front of the other as if he was walking. His body was black and he wore a simple pleated skirt that was painted gold. He had a gold headdress, similar in shape to that worn by Tutankhamun, crested at the front by the head of a rearing cobra.

'Christ,' whispered Gavin.

Around the figure was an array of smaller figures, other Egyptian gods and animals, and positioned at either end of the plinth was a pair of brass incense burners, their bases black with sooty remnants of whatever had been burnt in them. Along the front of the shrine stood a row of familiar-looking Canopic jars.

Francis had no doubt what he was looking at.

'Wait a minute. Look at this.' Gavin was pointing at a poster pinned up on the wall to the left of the door they'd just come through. It was for a performance in the main concert hall of Verdi's opera *Aida*, set in ancient Egypt.

'These are just props,' he said.

'I don't think so,' said Francis. 'Look at those jars – they're the same as the ones being delivered to Tom Fitz.'

He circled the room, taking in every detail. Underneath his feet, something crunched on the concrete floor. He knelt down and inspected it closely. There was something grainy and crystalline. He licked his forefinger and pressed it onto some of the grains. When he held it up, there were several white crystals clinging to it.

'Crack?' said Gavin.

Francis sniffed his finger, but there wasn't much of a smell.

'Or natron?' He brushed the crystals off against the leg of his suit and carried on looking around.

'Gavin, can you get hold of Rose? We need her and a crime-scene team.'

'What crime?' said Gavin.

'I have a feeling this might have been where the body was mummified.'

Gavin went upstairs to get a phone signal, and returned a couple of minutes later. 'She was already in her car, so she'll be here in five.'

'Excellent.'

Francis pulled a pair of latex gloves out of his pocket and bent down to examine the Canopic jars in front of the shrine. They were all empty. In a corner, two stuffed birds lay on the floor, one with a broken wing, the other one missing its beak. Francis recognised them – they were the sea eagles that had been in the large glass case in the Booth Museum. Along one wall was a workbench, on which he found remnants of the materials used for making the jars – traces of clay and plaster, spatters of coloured paint. But although he examined the work surface closely, he could find no sign of blood on it. Underneath the counter was a row of three cupboards. As he pulled open one of the cupboard doors, Rose arrived.

She bent down next to him to examine the contents of the cupboard.

'This,' she said, 'is a natron factory.'

Francis looked to where she was pointing. On the bottom shelf were a number of plastic buckets, a large jam-making pan and, leaning into the corner, a twenty-five-kilo sack of salt. The plastic top was crumpled over – the bag was less than half full. The next cupboard under the counter had narrow shelves. On the bottom shelf were a couple of packages of sodium carbonate and sodium bicarbonate.

'How did he make it?' said Gavin.

Rose tilted the edge of the jam pan, so they could see the inside. It was crusted with crystalline white deposits.

'It's pretty easy. You boil up a mixture of salt, sodium carbonate and sodium bicarbonate and let it dry.' She put a gloved hand into one the buckets and brought out a handful of what appeared to be lumpy salt. 'This is it, the finished product. I suspect I'll get a match between this and the natron in the Booth Museum Canopic jars. And look here.'

She pointed to the third cupboard. 'White linen. Looks the same as our mummy wrappings.'

'Okay, thanks, Rose,' said Francis. 'Gavin, get every item in here catalogued, with photos, and ask the CSIs to check all of it for finger marks and traces of DNA.'

'Yes, boss.'

'And we need to move fast, Gavin. This guy's an active killer.'

Francis continued inspecting the items in the room. On the wall opposite the workbench, there was an alcove. A black curtain hung across the opening. He went across the room and drew back the heavy velvet drapery. Crammed into the tiny space was a huge sarcophagus. Francis could see that it wasn't stone, like the genuine ones he'd seen at the British Museum. He rapped on the lid with his knuckles. It sounded hollow and plasticky, as if it had been moulded out of some sort of resin.

'That's probably from the opera,' said Gavin.

Francis would have believed him happily if he hadn't seen one thing. On the lid there was a painting of a long-dead Egyptian king – arms crossed over his chest, holding the crook and flail that were the symbols of his authority. His gold striped head-dress was crowned with a serpent, and the shroud in which he was wrapped was painted in gold and studded with coloured glass. A narrow panel ran down the centre of the figure, decorated with a string of hieroglyphs. Francis studied them carefully, looking for the familiar snake symbol. He had no idea what they meant – maybe the name of the king?

The top of the sarcophagus rose up at the end to accommodate the figure's feet. Here there was another gold panel, but the writing was in Roman lettering.

Francis stared at it, blinked, and stared at it again. He thought he'd misread it.

But he hadn't.

Rose came up beside him and read the words out loud.

'Frank Sullivan.'

He was staring down at his own sarcophagus.

52

Francis

It seemed strange to have Marni sleeping under the same roof as him. She guarded her independence so carefully that he'd never expected her to come and stay. Clearly recent events had taken their toll on her, and she wasn't as robust as she might have been. Francis wondered what Alex thought of his mother taking refuge at a policeman's house.

Of course, he'd forgotten about Pepper.

The dog's barking in the kitchen had woken him up at six a.m. He'd lain in bed listening to it for a few minutes, waiting for Marni to come downstairs to let the dog out. But then he realised – she was another floor up from him, and if she was still asleep, it probably wouldn't wake her. He dragged himself out of bed, pulled on a robe and headed downstairs.

He heard Robin's bedroom door opening on the landing above him.

'What's going on, Fran? Sounds like there's a dog in the house.'

Damn! He'd wanted to get the chance to talk to Robin before she was confronted by their visitors, but he and Marni had come in late the previous evening and Robin had already gone to bed.

He went into the kitchen and Pepper jumped up at him, over-joyed as ever to see a human, and even more so because it was his best-friend-elect, Francis Sullivan.

'Shush,' said Francis, trying to push Pepper down and steer him towards the back door.

'Francis!' Robin followed him into the room. 'Whose dog is that?'

Hearing a new voice, Pepper rushed across to where Robin was standing. Eyes wide with horror, Robin took a step back into the hall. She'd always been nervous around dogs, and Pepper threatened to knock her over with his exuberance.

'Pepper!' Francis lunged forward and grabbed him by the collar.

Robin glared at him. 'Whose is it?'

'Marni Mullins's.'

'What's it doing here?'

'It's staying with us for a while.'

'I thought you said she was out of prison.'

'She is.' He knew he was being obtuse. Putting off the inevitable.

'So?'

'She's staying with us too.'

Robin's eyebrows shot up. She didn't need to say what she was thinking.

'It's not like that, Robin. She's up in the playroom.' The spare bedroom under the eaves still carried its childhood epithet.

He opened the back door and ushered the dog out into the tiny courtyard behind the house with a gentle nudge of his toe. Pepper went grudgingly, obviously far more interested in what was going on in the kitchen. Robin sat down at the kitchen table, resting her elbows on its scarred pine surface.

'Why does she need to stay here?' Robin's tone was hostile.

Just as she said it, Marni appeared, bleary-eyed, muss-haired, in the kitchen doorway. She was wearing a tight T-shirt that clung, clammily, to her body, and a pair of pyjama shorts. She couldn't have looked more different to Robin, who despite still being in her dressing gown, had not a hair out of place.

'I thought I heard Pepper barking,' said Marni.

Pepper bounded back into the kitchen, leaving wet footprints across the clean floor. Marni bent down to gather up the dog, kissing him on the nose.

Robin rolled her eyes.

'Marni, this is my sister, Robin,' said Francis. He was thoroughly on the back foot and felt like he was losing control of the situation rapidly.

'It's all right,' said Marni. 'We can go. We don't need to stay here.'

'Of course you do – for all the reasons we discussed the other night. I don't want you alone in your house. You'd be a sitting duck.'

Chastened, Marni sat down at the kitchen table across from Robin. They eyed each other suspiciously. Francis put on coffee, thinking longingly of when he'd had the house all to himself.

Despite the fact that it was Sunday, he took refuge in the office, reviewing everything they'd uncovered the previous day. The sarcophagus. With his name on it. It wasn't hard to conclude that he was now a target. For some reason the so-called Embalmer – presumably Euan Drysdale – wanted him dead. But who was Euan Drysdale? He felt sure he'd never heard that name before and, apart from the payslip from the Dome, they couldn't find any information on a man of that name living in the local area.

Certain facts just didn't add up. Denise Drysdale, the missing woman, had no children. So what was her relationship to Euan Drysdale? They'd spoken to Denise's sister and she'd made no mention of any other relatives. The mummified woman couldn't be Denise Drysdale, because that woman had had a child.

He called Rose. Her husband answered the phone, immediately grumpy on hearing Francis's voice.

'No, I'm not coming in,' said Rose. 'It's Sunday. You can have five minutes on the phone.'

'Tell me what you got from Drysdale's flat?'

'I've sent hair samples from the plughole in the bathroom and from a brush we found in the master bedroom for testing against hair from the mummy's head,' she said. 'But they'll take a while to come back. We'll also compare the natron and the linen wrappings from the Dome with those on the mummy. I feel fairly confident we'll get a match.'

'If it's not her,' said Francis, 'it could mean that he's mummified more than one person.'

'Let's just wait for the test results.'

She changed her mind and met him down at the morgue half an hour later.

Francis opened his document case. 'I've got a photo of Denise Drysdale from her missing persons file. I'm pretty sure that's the mummified woman.'

He handed it to Rose and she studied it, before handing it back to him.

'Let's take a look.'

Rose opened the drawer that contained the mummified remains. Francis held up the picture. Despite the dark, desiccated skin, the sunken cheeks and the hollowed-out eyes, there was enough of a resemblance for him to feel certain they were the same woman. The hair was the same, and the shape of the nose similar – though the mummy's nose appeared sharper for having lost its fleshiness.

'What do you think?' he said to Rose.

'It's her,' she said. 'The DNA checks will confirm it, but this is definitely Denise Drysdale.'

At last, they had the identity. Now the mummy became a real person to Francis. He could start to find out about her life and, with any luck, track down her killer.

'But . . . the giving birth thing?' It didn't make sense.

'What?' said Rose.

'You said the mummy had given birth. In Denise's file it says she was childless.'

'Where did that information come from?'

'Her sister.'

'Well, she would know.'

'Could you have been wrong about the scars on her pelvis?'

'No – the mummy definitely gave birth at some point. And if the DNA matches, it means so did Denise Drysdale. Looks like you've got another mystery on your hands to solve – the vanishing baby.'

It seemed certain that the tattoos that covered Denise Drysdale's mummified body were not something she'd had in life. There were no signs of them in any of the selection of holiday snaps and party photos that he found in her missing person's file, and if anything these pictures showed him that Melba Black had been right in her assessment – Denise Drysdale definitely didn't look the type to cover her body with ink.

If that was the case, and the killer had done the tattoos just before or just after killing her, perhaps they would tell him more about the killer than about her. After wolfing down a supermarket sandwich for his lunch, Francis laid out the photos of the tattoos on his desk. What message or messages did they contain? He studied them. The Egyptian shrine underneath the Studio Theatre stage had featured the snake god, Apophis, prominently. The Great Serpent, enemy of the sun. The tattoos seemed grouped around further snake representations. Did the Embalmer see himself as the snake? Or was the snake his enemy . . . which would make him the sun? None of it seemed to make much sense.

He needed to decipher the killer's message.

There were six snakes in all. One on each leg, one on each arm, one on her back and one on her front. And each snake had a multitude of other, smaller tattoos clustered around it.

In other words, six stories.

Francis grabbed the notepad from his desk drawer and picked up a pencil. He numbered each of the snakes in the relevant photo, and then started listing the tattoos.

Snake 1 – left arm

hieroglyphs for beauty, heart, companion and love

old school love heart, dagger dripping blood, Medusa's head, Irish Claddagh, rose

Snake 2 – right arm

hieroglyph for snake, warrior and coffin

scales of justice, crucifix, Japanese oni demon, cricket stumps, eight ball, ACAB

Snake 3 – torso, front

hieroglyphs for blood, abandon, ancestor and secret

shamrock, a scroll containing the word mother, Celtic triquetra, bunch of lilies

Snake 4 – torso, back

hieroglyphs for brother, fool, fear and friend

winged eyeball, bicycle, Icarus, tarot card for death, a pair of clasped fists, three dots

Snake 5 – left leg

hieroglyphs for teach, to beat and book

a pair of glasses, anchor, minotaur, biomechanical

Snake 6 – right leg

hieroglyphs for woman, bird and wrongdoing

fox, eagle in flight, sugar skull, runes, papal mitre

Making a list didn't really help him any more than sitting and staring at the images. Anything he could glean from them, stories he could make up to fit the pictures, were nothing more than speculation. A million miles from solid evidence. This wasn't going to be the solution.

He gathered up the prints and headed for home.

When he arrived, Robin was in the living room, watching a drama box set, and he had a vague feeling that he should go and join her to be sociable. But . . . he wasn't sure he could face it. The case was preying on his mind, and he had no reason to think that the killer wouldn't strike again. He had no idea how much time they had, but the clock was undoubtedly ticking – and the killer appeared to have singled him out as a target.

Why?

He couldn't get it out of his mind – the sight of his own name painted on the wooden sarcophagus.

'What are those?'

He hadn't heard Marni coming into the kitchen behind him. She was barefoot and her untidy plait made her look as if she'd just got out of bed.

'Tattoos.'

'Well, yes. That much I know.'

'They're pictures of the mummified body left in the Booth Museum.'

Marni flicked through them. 'It's not great work, is it?'

'We think they might have been done after the woman was dead.'

'That makes sense – they haven't healed.'

'Marni . . .'

'No, don't even ask it. I wouldn't have a clue who might have done them. Some scratcher – they're definitely not professional.'

'I wasn't going to ask that. I just wondered if any of them had any particular meanings. Something that might lead us to the killer.'

Marni sat down opposite him at the table.

'Like a secret code that'll give you his name and address?'

She was right. The question was ridiculous.

'Let's go outside for a smoke,' he said.

'Why not?'

Pepper stirred from the cushion he was lying on in the corner as they went towards the back door. He padded after them into the back yard.

Francis offered Marni a cigarette and lit it for her, then lit his own. He took a deep drag, then exhaled.

'Do you remember when . . .' started Marni.

'My first cigarette, and I nearly choked.'

They both laughed.

'Now look at you.'

'I blame you, Mullins.'

'You can fuck right off,' she said good-naturedly.

She stubbed out her cigarette in the flower pot of sand by the back door. Francis hadn't finished his yet.

'I think it's time for me to leave,' she said, turning suddenly serious.

'What? You've only been here a day.'

'No, I mean leave Brighton.'

'Why?' Francis could hear a slight edge of panic in his voice. He pulled hard on his cigarette.

'This place was me and Thierry together. It's not right, being here without him.'

'But Alex is here. Your whole life is here.'

Marni turned to look at him. 'Alex wants to study graphic design up in London. And what have I got here? Just a rented tattoo studio. I can tattoo anywhere.'

'How's your hand?' he asked. He wanted to change the subject. 'Are you able to work yet?'

Marni looked down at the angry red scar – the result of her clash with Paul the previous summer.

'It's getting there. I can draw, but it gets achy if I work too long.'

'And you can still tattoo?'

She nodded.

'Maybe … maybe while you're staying, you could finish my tattoo?'

'Maybe …'

53

Gavin

'Did Denise Drysdale have a baby or not? According to Rose, the mummy did. We're almost certain that the mummy is Denise Drysdale. But according to her sister, she never had a child. Does Euan Drysdale exist or not? Apart from the payslip we found in Denise Drysdale's flat, we can't find any other record of him. Someone called Euan Drysdale worked making props for the Dome, but there are no council records for him, and he was paid in cash, so no bank details.'

The boss seemed to have a steady supply of questions without answers at the Monday morning briefing. Gavin jotted them down as Francis spoke, and the list was getting longer.

'Could Euan Drysdale be the mummy's missing baby?' he continued. 'It's safe to assume he was the killer. The stuff we found at the Dome might just be circumstantial evidence, which we need to tie to the killer using DNA, but it all hangs together – the natron, the linen, the Canopic jars, the shrine to the snake god, the sea eagles from the Booth Museum.'

'And the sarcophagus with your name on it,' said Rory, his voice lowered. 'Reckon he's got you in his sights, boss.'

Angie glared at him. 'He's just taunting us, that's all.'

Francis shrugged. 'You're probably right, Angie. Everything

he does is over-theatrical. Attention seeking. He wants the fame and glory of being a successful killer.'

'Talking of fame and glory,' said Rory, 'how much of this are we sharing with Fitz?'

'Nothing so far,' said Francis, 'and as little as possible after that. Okay – assignments. Angie, could you liaise with the CSIs to see what they've come up with from the Dome materials and the stuff taken from Denise Drysdale's flat?'

'Yes, on it.'

'Kyle, go down to the Dome and interview any members of staff that worked with Drysdale. Get a record of when he was working there and when he wasn't. And ask how they came to employ him, yeah? And Gavin, follow up on Denise Drysdale. Something isn't right. Maybe talk to her sister again.'

Back at his desk, Gavin started digging into Denise Drysdale's past. He set up a Skype call with her sister – a woman called Marsha Cotton, who lived in Malaga. She was in fact only Denise's half-sister. She was considerably younger than Denise, who'd left home while Marsha was still a kid. They hadn't been close, keeping in touch sporadically with Christmas cards and occasionally seeing each other if Denise went to Spain on holiday.

'I hadn't heard anything from her in months,' Marsha said when Gavin asked her when she'd last seen her sister. 'I tried calling, I sent her a postcard telling her to ring me. My oldest got married in the summer, and I wanted to invite Denise to the wedding. Eventually, I reported her missing, just because I hoped the police would find her more easily than I could. But they drew a blank.'

She also filled Gavin in a bit on Denise's life. 'She was a model when she was younger. Not well known. A few TV ads, some catalogue work back in the day when Littlewoods was a thing. Enough to eke a living from until the work dried up in her late thirties. Since then, life hasn't been so kind to her. She never married, never had a job she really loved.'

'Did she have a child?' Gavin had asked.

'No. Never.' Marsha was unequivocal. 'I'd know if me own sister had a kid, wouldn't I?'

So Denise Drysdale had given birth but never had a child. Schrodinger's baby. Gavin was left with two possibilities. Either the child had been stillborn or Denise had given her baby away – and had never told her sister either way. But even a stillbirth should have been registered.

He went online and searched the register of births – they'd got the information that she was childless from the missing person report filed by her sister, and at that time there had been no reason to question it. But now it was worth a look. He checked against mother's name, starting from the year when Denise turned sixteen – if she'd got pregnant any younger than that he didn't think she would have been able to hide it effectively from her family. The first few years drew a blank, but then in the records for 1987 he found Denise's name. A birth had been registered – a boy, who would now be thirty years old, if he was still alive. There was no father's name on the record, and the child had been called William Denis Drysdale.

'Got it, boss,' he shouted triumphantly, as Francis appeared in the doorway of the incident room. 'Denise Drysdale gave birth to a son in 1987 – William Drysdale.'

'So where is he now?' said Francis, coming over to Gavin's desk and looking at the screen over his shoulder.

'About to check death or adoption,' said Gavin.

'Good work. Let me know what you find.'

William Dennis Drysdale wasn't dead. But a quick Google check of his full name brought up nothing. The boy had apparently disappeared, and this suggested to Gavin that adoption was probably the answer – his new parents would undoubtedly have changed his name to one of their own choice. This presented a problem. The adoption records would show the names of the new parents, and the name of the child they adopted. The new name. Not necessarily the old name. But they would also show the child's date of birth.

He keyed the information into the search form. The baby had been born in Brighton, so he took a guess that Brighton would have been the local authority under whose jurisdiction the adoption took place. Of course, he was searching in the opposite direction to most people – usually it was a search by adopted individuals to discover their birth family. The way the search form was set out reflected this, assuming that the post-adoption information was known, while the pre-adoption details were to be the subject of the search.

He wondered if William Drysdale, or whatever he was now known as, had ever searched for his birth mother.

He needed help with this. He set up an appointment to speak with a woman in the council's adoption team for advice on how to find the information he needed.

Angie came over to his desk.

'I couldn't do it,' said Angie.

'What?'

'Give up a kid. Just goes against nature.'

'I don't imagine it was an easy decision for her,' said Gavin. 'I wonder if he knew he was adopted . . . if he ever tried to find her.'

'You would, wouldn't you?'

'And if he found her, would he feel that the abandonment was a good enough reason to kill her?'

It seemed that he had.

Chapter 54

Monday, 20 November 2017

Marni

She would never see Thierry again.

Next to that, going back to work seemed pointless. Life seemed pointless.

Marni was having a hard time processing all that had happened – that Thierry was gone, her time in prison, the long shadow that Paul still cast over everything. Not to mention the fact that he could still be here in Brighton. She just had to hope that he had fled – back to France, or anywhere rather than here. And she was worried about Alex. Her relationship with him had been tenuous at best before all this had happened, and now he seemed to have retreated further into himself. If he and Paul crossed paths again, she didn't dare speculate what might happen. She couldn't go back to the house where Thierry had bled to death in front of her very eyes, but neither could she spend all her time at Francis's house under the unwavering gaze of his disapproving sister. She hated being there while he was out at work. The studio became her refuge.

She definitely wasn't ready to accept bookings though, so she switched off her phone and lost herself in the process of drawing. She wanted to design a tattoo that would honour Thierry and what he'd meant to her. She'd never stopped loving him, even when they were divorced and through all the time they'd been apart. That they'd broken up again just a couple of months before his death didn't make it any less devastating to her.

As she sketched, the scar between her thumb and forefinger started to throb. It was the damage from the last time she'd seen Paul. He'd left a scar on her body and a scar on her heart. But she'd done as much to him, hadn't she? How she wished things could have been different. If only she'd met Thierry before she'd met Paul. If only it had been Paul who was injured in the fight rather than Thierry.

What if?

If only . . .

A tear fell onto the wreath she was drawing and she viciously scribbled over the centre of the sketch. It wasn't the right thing to remember him by. She screwed up the piece of paper and tossed it across the floor. Pepper lunged forward to chase it, then turned up his nose at it when he realised it was just a ball of paper rather than something he could eat.

Outside it was getting dark. She didn't want to be alone. She would go back to Wykeham Terrace and wait for Francis to get home from work.

Her car was parked in the small yard at the back of the studio.

'Come on, Pepper.' She clipped a lead onto him and grabbed her bag.

Although she shared parking with the shops on either side, her red Suzuki Swift was the only car out here. The deux chevaux she'd driven for the last fifteen years had finally died, and she was still getting used to the new car. It seemed all mod cons to her, even though the model she'd bought was already several years old.

'In you get,' she said to Pepper, opening the passenger door.

'Marni.'

She recognised the voice before he stepped out of the shadows, and her heart froze.

She tried to scream, but Paul had a hand over her mouth before any sound had issued forth. She wanted to bite him, but the flat of his palm was crushed against her lips and she couldn't even get her mouth open. She tried to fight him off using the car keys as a weapon but only succeeded in dropping them. As they struggled, Pepper started to bark, jumping up at Paul and snapping at his arms.

He kicked the dog to one side, making Marni struggle even harder. Pepper yelped, and slunk away round the back of the car. With his hand still across her mouth, Paul jolted Marni's head back, smacking it against the roof of the car. Disorientated, Marni staggered against the passenger-side door, powerless as Paul pushed her backwards into the seat.

'If you scream, if you make a noise, you'll never see Alex again. *Tu comprends?*'

Marni struggled to nod her head.

Paul slammed the door shut. Marni watched, horror struck, as he hunted under the car for the keys. She grabbed the door catch and shoved the door open with all her might, hoping to strike him on the head as he bent low on the ground. But his reactions were too fast – he heard the click of it opening and thrust up an arm to protect himself. He slammed the door back hard. Marni yelped with frustration as she heard the lock mechanism click into place. He stood by the window, holding up her car keys – his mouth curling into a cruel grin. In the sodium glare from the nearby streetlight, his teeth flashed gold and Marni felt sick.

How could she have been so stupid, not to have looked around carefully before she came out to the car?

Maybe she had a chance. Moving slowly so Paul wouldn't notice what she was doing as he came around to the driver's side of the car, Marni felt for her phone in the pocket of her sweat top. It was there. She didn't dare pull it out in case he saw the light from the screen. But she needed to call Francis, let him know what was happening. She arched her wrist to widen the pocket opening and glanced down. The movement caused the phone screen to light up, casting the interior of the car in a faint blue glow.

The driver's door opened, and Paul lunged into the car. He grabbed her arm and wrenched her hand out of her pocket. She left the phone behind but, slippery as an eel, he let go of her wrist, pushed his hand into her pocket and retrieved the phone. He dropped it onto the driver's seat, struck a blow to the side of her head and snatched it up again.

'*Putain!*'

He straightened up, out of the car.

Dazed, Marni watched as he went to the front of the bonnet. He bent down and when he straightened up the phone was no longer in his hand.

Shit!

He got back in and started the engine. David Bowie music flooded the car. 'Aladdin Sane'.

'You stupid bitch,' he said.

He leaned across her and Marni cowered in the seat – but he was just reaching for her seat belt.

'What do you want with me?'

Paul slammed the car into gear and reversed out of the small yard. Marni heard the crunch as the front wheel went over her mobile. Damn it! How could she have been so stupid? If she'd kept the phone on her, at least if anyone realised she was missing they would have been able to use it to triangulate where she was. But not now. As the car hesitated at the pavement while Paul checked for other vehicles, Marni saw Pepper, skulking in the corner of the yard. And as they backed onto the road and then drove away, she heard him barking.

'For god's sake, Paul. I can't just leave Pepper like that.'

'Fuck the dog. Someone will find him.'

'He can get out onto the road. He'll get run over.' Marni's fear had been completely subsumed by her anger and her concern for her pet. 'Stop the car now.'

She tried the handle of the passenger door. They weren't moving that fast. She could throw herself out onto the road. She'd probably be fine.

'Don't even think about it.' Paul's hand slammed onto the button that locked the car doors.

'Fuck you!'

She grabbed at his arm on the steering wheel and yanked it. The car veered into the path of oncoming traffic, but Paul was strong enough to shake her off and swerve out of the way of a large black BMW with just inches to spare. Car horns blared and Paul accelerated, swearing loudly in French. He took a sharp left turn into a quiet residential street and pulled over.

Marni tried the door again but of course it was still locked. She knew what was coming and braced herself.

Paul hit her again. This time she blacked out before she even felt the pain.

55

Monday, 20 November 2017

Francis

' . . . so, as you can see, we've made significant progress.'

Did that sound convincing?

Francis finished his summary and stood waiting for Bradshaw to respond. It was clear from the chief's restlessness and frowning during the update that he didn't agree.

'How many killers are currently terrorising my city?'

His city.

'One, sir. Well, strictly speaking two – but Paul Mullins only really poses a danger to Marni and Alex Mullins,' – which was bad enough – 'not to the city in general.'

'He is, however, a convicted rapist, isn't he?' Bradshaw was referring to a charge for which Paul had served eight years in prison in France.

'We're doing everything we can to locate him.'

'Which isn't very much, is it?'

'Sir, we've circulated his image widely. We've had a five-minute slot on *Crimewatch*. We've canvassed all the hostels and fleapits in Brighton and Hove where he might hang out. I've had uniform PCs constantly looking for him in pubs and bars on their beats.'

'But no sign of him?'

'No, sir. Given that he's wanted for murder, I think there's a very good chance that he's fled back to France.'

'You've had all exit points alerted?'

'Yes, sir. But he came into the country without showing up on our radar, so I suspect he's travelling with a false passport.'

'Interpol onto it?'

'Yes, sir.'

Bradshaw bristled and shifted in his chair. 'And remind me of your progress in the other case. You've got no bloody clue when it comes to suspects, have you?'

'In fact, we have, sir. We've finally got an ID on the museum mummy. We believe she had a son, who was given up for adoption, who might be the killer.'

'Might be. Four dead bodies and counting, Sullivan.'

Francis felt himself flushing. He hadn't wanted to talk about the ID of the Embalmer. The trail had gone cold as to Euan Drysdale's real identity. But beyond that, it was looking like he wasn't getting anywhere.

'We're trying to trace what happened to the child. And we know that the killer worked at the Brighton Dome under an assumed name, so we're working that angle too.'

Bradshaw pounced on it. 'If you've got a name, what are you waiting for? Get him in here and put him under pressure.'

'That's our intention when we locate him.'

'For fuck's sake. Can't you ever find anybody?'

Francis took a step towards Bradshaw's desk. He'd had enough. 'Sir, the team is stretched to its limits here. I need more manpower and more resources. If you would lift the overtime ban ...'

Bradshaw stood up. He hated to be looked down on. 'Not a chance, Sullivan.'

'I'm running two major manhunts, sir. People are getting scared to go out of their houses.'

'And I need to make cuts in spending.'

'But you still expect results.'

'Too damn right I do.'

'Sir.'

Francis had to resist the urge to click his heels together and salute as he turned to leave the chief's office.

He stopped at the door.

'Tom Fitz.'

'What about him?' Bradshaw spoke slowly, enunciating every word. His tone was icy.

'What's he got on you?'

'What the hell's that supposed to mean?'

'I think you know what it means.'

Bradshaw came around the desk. He was a big man, broad as well as tall, and he knew how to use his size to intimidate.

'You're skating on thin ice, Sullivan.'

But I'm lighter and faster.

There was no going back from that. It had been a stark declaration of intent that had slipped out of his mouth before he'd even had a chance to think it through.

By the end of the day, Francis was convinced it had been a mistake. Quite possibly the biggest mistake of his career to date. Alienate your boss. Threaten your boss. Not a good idea at the best of times. But when you're demonstrably failing to deliver results?

Shit.

Francis walked up the path and pushed open the gate into Wykeham Terrace. It was late now. Robin would already have eaten. He'd said he'd have a drink with Marni earlier, but she was going to text to confirm what time and he hadn't heard from her. Maybe it was for the best. A personal entanglement with Marni Mullins would be complicated. He didn't need that right now. He needed to focus on his work. What was the link between him and the killer? He couldn't work it out and it was driving him to distraction. Did it mean he was somehow linked with the victims? There was definitely something he wasn't seeing.

'Fran, is that you?'

He'd hardly got his key out of the lock and shut the door behind him.

'Yes.'

'You missed supper.' Robin appeared at the living-room door. 'I can go and heat some up for you if you like.'

Her tone sounded wounded and Francis felt a flash of annoyance. She wasn't his wife or his mother.

'I'll sort myself out. Don't you worry.'

She traipsed behind him into the kitchen.

'You work too hard. It's not good for you.'

Francis dropped the hand that had been reaching for the fridge door and spun round to face her.

'For God's sake, Robin. Four people have been murdered and had their guts stuffed into Canopic jars. Marni's husband is dead, and you think I should be taking life easy?'

He glared at her.

Robin took a step back as if she'd been slapped in the face.

'You really don't have a clue about my work, and what I need to be doing. It's not just you, Robin. Other people are relying on me too.'

'Fine. There's shepherd's pie in the fridge. You can heat it in the microwave.'

'I'll pass, thanks,' muttered Francis, but Robin was already out of the door.

Good. She would only disapprove.

He opened a cupboard and took out a bottle of whisky, then he fetched a glass. He took the stairs two at a time and slammed his bedroom door. He needed time on his own. He needed to think. He needed the burn of the spirit at the back of his throat to bolster him against the rising tide of self-doubt that threatened to overwhelm him.

56

The Embalmer

Isfet or **Asfet** – the ancient Egyptian philosophical concept of chaos and violence, to perform evil. Egyptian mythology pairs Isfet with **Maat** or **Ma'at** (**mꜣ't** /ˈmuʁʃat/) – the ancient Egyptian ideology of truth and balance, encompassing law and order, morality and justice. Maat is responsible for regulating the actions of mortals and the deities who bring chaos. These ideological opposites are in constant and bloody conflict.

There's a Pavilion. A Royal Pavilion.

Outside, it has onion-shaped domes and minarets. Inside, it has gilded dragons and Chinese lanterns. A ravishing oriental fantasia beside the sea. It was built by a prince for the entertainment of the beau monde. The good world.

But there's another world, behind the trompe l'oeils *and beneath the domes. A world of dark passages and abandoned rooms and secret staircases.*

This is the Embalmer's world.

The Embalmer knows his way around the Pavilion. All of it. And he comes here in the small hours, when it's quiet and dark, and the only sound is the whirr of the security cameras sweeping an arc and watching nothing. Because he never steps into their field of vision.

The police may have discovered his workshop under the theatre, but that doesn't matter. He's reached the endgame now and for his finale, this is the chosen venue.

There's a hostage.

A hostage tied to a chair in a dusty room. Gagged. Wondering if life is over. Struggling. Whimpering.

The hostage doesn't know the man who came out of the darkness, or have any idea of what his intentions might be.

Only the Embalmer knows why he's taken this hostage in particular. He needs a juicy piece of bait to reel in his next victim. This hostage might die or this hostage might survive. The Embalmer doesn't really care.

All he cares about is securing the ultimate sacrifice. The person he's wanted to kill so badly, for so long. A jumped-up little shit who thought he was better than everyone else in the class. Best at everything. Always in charge. Such a clever boy. He made everyone else look useless.

This is the one that will buy the Embalmer immortality. After this, people will be afraid to speak his name. Apophis. The Snake God. Back on earth, walking among men after six thousand years forgotten.

All he needs to do is kill his nemesis.

The clever boy.

Who won't look so clever when he's dead.

57

Tuesday, 21 November 2017

Francis

Francis was awake. Just. His eyes seemed glued shut. His head felt as if it had spent the night in a tumble dryer. Why hadn't the alarm gone off? Any attempt at movement was out of the question – he shifted his foot and felt overcome by a wave of nausea.

He opened his eyes to stop his head spinning and the first thing he saw was the empty whisky bottle on the bedside table. The room was too bright, so he pulled his pillow over his face. His tongue was stuck to the roof of his mouth, and he felt hot and cold at the same time.

He dozed for a minute, but the urge to be sick woke him, and he spent the next ten minutes staring down the lavatory bowl, promising, promising, promising to himself that he would never drink whisky again. At least not for a bit.

There was a note on the kitchen table – Robin had gone into Brighton to meet a friend and wouldn't be back until later. Francis looked at his watch. It was gone ten, and he was beyond late for work. He'd need to think up a plausible story. There was no sign of Marni or Pepper. She must have gone over to the studio already. It suited Francis fine. He wasn't ready for small talk and he didn't need people seeing him in this state. He made coffee, filled a pint glass with water and searched the kitchen drawers for Nurofen. Then he sat and waited patiently for recovery to kick in.

It took about half an hour before he felt properly human again, albeit a fragile human. A shower certainly helped, and a slice of toast and marmite settled his stomach.

Yesterday, the case had seemed to be going backwards. Today, he needed to reverse that. It was easy to see why Bradshaw would be frustrated with him, and his response to that – a veiled threat – hadn't necessarily been that clever. The chief was now alerted to the fact that he was suspicious of his relationship with Tom Fitz. He should have kept that particular powder dry.

But what was done, was done. The best thing now was to work to uncover Ada's killer, and perhaps in his gratitude, Fitz would cough up what he needed to know about Bradshaw.

God, how he hated playing politics. He'd much rather just get on with the job.

Gavin was alone in the incident room when Francis arrived at work.

'Where's Rory?' he said, giving no reason for coming in so late.

Gavin looked up from his computer. 'Something about a dental appointment. I think he'll be here later.'

'And Angie?'

'She's taking a day off.'

'Good. She works too hard. What are you working on?'

'Yesterday, I got in touch with the city adoption service. Waiting for them to get back to me. Now checking databases for the name Euan Drysdale, but he's not showing up anywhere.'

Francis went into his office and closed the door. He still felt rough and just the thought of staring at a computer monitor made his head hurt. He leant back in his chair and closed his eyes. His world spun.

No. No way.

Black coffee. He wondered if he could take it through a drip. It helped and he settled down to clearing his inbox. It was time he had a meeting with Tom Fitz, and he needed to formulate a strategy to make sure the team made progress on solving the mummy murders and on locating Paul Mullins.

Twenty minutes later, there was a knock on the door.

'Come in.'

It was Gavin. 'Boss?'

'What?' He didn't mean to sound irritable, but it came out sharper than he meant.

'I feel like we've hit a brick wall with this case. Not sure what to try next.'

'Okay, what do we know about Euan Drysdale? He worked at the Dome, but they seem to know nothing about him. Online searches for him have come up blank, suggesting that's not his real name. Whoever he is, he took over Denise Drysdale's flat and kept his pet snakes there. We don't know if he was living there or not, though there are reports of neighbours having seen him occasionally going in or coming out.'

'We've had the flat under surveillance in case he returned to feed the snakes, but nothing so far.'

'Do we have a photo of him?'

'No.' Gavin shook his head.

'See if the Dome have one, or go through what was retrieved from Denise Drysdale's flat. If we get a picture, we can get Fitz to run it in *The Argus*. Someone must know who he is.'

'Overtime? If we get a picture, Kyle and I could go out this evening and show it round the pubs. Somebody must know him.'

Francis knew Bradshaw would have a fit if he put in even a moderate overtime bill. 'Yes, you and Kyle. Start with the pubs, then head for the clubs as they open.' If Bradshaw wanted results, he was going to have to pay for them.

'I'll talk to Kyle and see if I can track down a picture.'

When Gavin had gone, Francis turned back to his emails.

Finally, he was starting to feel better and wondered if a spot of lunch might be in order.

Lingering over a cheese and ham sandwich from the Verdict Café, he studied Denise Drysdale's tattoos again. He was looking at the one he'd labelled Snake 2, trying to make sense of the smaller graphics scattered around the coils. There were hieroglyphs meaning snake, warrior and coffin, and a scales of justice, a crucifix, a Japanese *oni* demon, cricket stumps, an eight ball, and the initials ACAB. The latter was an old style prison tattoo which stood for All Coppers Are Bastards. Francis knew it used to be a common sight on the knuckles of habitual offenders – but not any more. He couldn't ever remember seeing a criminal sporting it. But put together with the set of scales, and there seemed to be something of a law and order theme. The eight ball and the cricket stumps . . . games and sports.

Snake 4. The bicycle. Luke Bridges worked for a company that made racing bikes. Did any of the other tattoos on Drysdale's back contain anything else that could connect to him? A tarot card for death. Icarus, flying too close to the sun. Clasped fists. Three dots. And the weird winged eyeball? What did any of it mean?

Francis started to research the meanings on the internet. Three dots – it was another prison tattoo, but this one signified *mi vida loca* and was sported by Hispanic gang members in America. My crazy life. Hieroglyphs for brother, fool, friend and fear. Clasped fists meant friendship. A friendship gone wrong?

Who had Luke Bridges been friends with? And who had he fallen out with?

He was about to call Gavin back into his office to discuss the possibility when the desk sergeant – an overweight cop called Byron – appeared in the doorway. He leaned on the doorframe, panting, as if he'd run all the way up the stairs.

'Sir . . . this came . . . addressed to you . . .'

He was holding out a small, white roll of paper. As he stepped forward, Francis recognised it for what it was – a papyrus scroll. He came round the desk and snatched it from Byron.

'When did it arrive?'

'Just now – I knew you'd want it immediately.'

'Who brought it?'

Byron shook his head. 'I was away from the desk for a minute, taking a solicitor down to the cells. When I came back, it was just lying there.'

Of course.

'Right. Thank you. Can you check the CCTV footage covering the desk – when you've found the relevant section, send it to Hollins or Albright.'

Byron heaved a great sigh, then nodded. 'Yes, sir.'

When he was alone, Francis opened the scroll. It was a handwritten note, in the same hand as the previous papyrus scrolls had been.

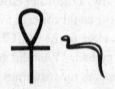

Francis Sullivan,
Indulge me with a moment of your time.
I have something of yours.
A someone, in fact.
Follow my instructions and maybe they'll live.
Maybe not.

There was no sign-off, but above the writing there were two hand-drawn hieroglyphs. The serpent and the ankh. Francis knew who it was from. He read it again, and then again.

But there were no instructions to follow.

58

Tuesday, 21 November 2017

Francis

Rose stared at the message through her magnifying glass, poring over every detail.

'The paper looks the same.'

'Papyrus?' said Francis.

Rose nodded. 'Yes, and I think from the same source. We'll need to compare it with the previous ones.'

'And the writing?'

'Fountain pen.' Rose looked up from the image to meet Francis's gaze full on. 'The handwriting's similar to the other messages, isn't it?'

'Yes. And look at the letter A here and then compare it with this.' He took out a copy of the Snake 2 image from his document case. Snake 2 was the one with the ACAB tattoo.

'One's tattooed, one's written in ink. They look like the same hand,' said Rose, peering from one to the other through her magnifying glass. 'But one letter's not enough for a definite match.'

'It's enough for me not to ignore it or write it off as a joke,' said Francis. Anxiety was unfurling itself in his gut like an alien incursion, and he felt sick.

I have something of yours.

A someone, in fact.

'You think he's taken a hostage?'

'How else can I read it?'

'Who could it be?'

'The implication is that the hostage is someone close to me. I couldn't get Robin on the phone as I drove up here. I'm worried.' That was an understatement.

'Put out a missing person bulletin and keep trying.'

Francis nodded, hardly trusting himself to speak.

'But it doesn't make sense,' said Rose. '*Follow my instructions.* There are no instructions.'

'So I have to wait for another scroll to arrive?'

Francis checked his mobile for what must have been the twentieth time since coming into Rose's office. No message from Robin.

'How easy would it be for someone to get hold of your email address?'

'If he's really holding someone hostage, someone who knows me, then he could have got it off her.'

'You really think he's got Robin?'

'I can't take chances, Rose, I've got to find her. If you come up with anything else on this, let me know straight away. I've put Gavin to work on checking the CCTV footage of the front desk, but it was just left by a guy in a hoody and dark glasses.'

'Call me when you find Robin.'

'Of course.'

Francis ran down the stairs from her office two at a time and slammed out through the double doors at the front of the building. He disregarded the thirty-mile speed limit on his way across town to Wykeham Terrace.

Please God, let me find Robin at home and safe.

But then he remembered – prayers don't work – so he drove even faster.

The house was empty. Robin's note was still on the kitchen

table, where he'd found it earlier. How long would she likely be out for if she was going to meet a friend? There was still no sign of Marni or Pepper either. His footsteps seemed to echo in the hall and thud more loudly than usual on the stairs. Having lived here alone for nearly five years, it suddenly felt strange to be the only person in the house.

He tried both their phones again, and then went up the second flight of stairs to Marni's room. Her bed was made. It seemed a little unusual to him – all the glimpses of Marni's personal life he'd ever had gave the impression of reigning chaos. There was a book lying on the end of the bed, a heavy hardback.

A World Atlas of Tattoos.

And then he remembered staggering noisily up the stairs last night, at some point halfway through his whisky bender. He'd wanted to talk to her. He'd wanted her to stop him drinking any more, and to send him to bed, chastened and sensible.

She hadn't been there, but that book had. In exactly the same spot where it lay now.

The obvious conclusion – that she hadn't slept in her bed last night – hit him like a sledgehammer. Was Marni the hostage the letter was referring to, rather than Robin?

Panicking, he ran down the stairs and back into the kitchen. He dialled both their numbers again. Neither of them answered.

He called Alex.

'When did you last speak to your mother?' he said, without preamble.

'Why?'

'I don't know where she is.'

'Are you her keeper?'

'Don't piss me around, Alex. When did you last talk to her?'

There was a pause at the other end of the line.

'I don't know. Yesterday.'

'Shit. You haven't spoken to her today?'

'No. I called her earlier but she didn't pick up.'

'You don't know if she had plans last night?'

'You're seriously worried, aren't you? What's going on?'

Damn! Francis didn't want to tell Alex about the message – but it was only fair to give him some sort of explanation for his questions.

'Nothing's going on. It just looked like her bed wasn't slept in, and I wondered where she was.' He tried to make his voice sound casual, even though he felt anything but.

Alex wasn't fooled. 'She's a grown woman – you wouldn't be checking up on her. You think something's happened, don't you?'

'No. I don't know.'

'You think it's something to do with Paul?'

'No, I have no reason to think Paul's got anything to do with this. Listen, Alex, it's probably nothing. I'm sorry I worried you. But if you hear from her, let me know, would you?'

There was a grunt and Alex disconnected.

He tried Robin's number again.

He tried Marni's.

He called Gavin. 'Put out an APW on Marni Mullins and Robin Sullivan. They're both missing.'

Which one of them did the Embalmer have?

59

Marni

Paul was sleeping.

Marni watched him sleep. There was nothing to be gained by waking him up, even though she could tell by the quality of light filtering through the net curtains that it was no longer early. The splitting pain in her head that she'd woken up with earlier had now receded to a dull but persistent ache. Her mouth was dry and whatever Paul had used to tie her wrists and ankles was cutting into her flesh. She needed her insulin dose.

But still she didn't want to wake Paul.

She struggled to pull herself up into a sitting position, and looked around. She was slumped in the corner of an L-shaped sofa. The upholstery was pale grey and felt rough against her skin. Paul was sprawled on a matching armchair opposite her. If she half-closed her eyes she could be looking at Thierry. The same body shape, the same head shape, even the same breathing pattern. But with her eyes open, Paul was a completely different person. A strange and, in some way, distorted version of her husband. His hair was more grizzled, his skin more pock-marked, his hands not so long and elegant as Thierry's. He smelled different. And he made her feel different. Her emotional response to Paul had been hostile for so long now – that was never going to change.

There was something weird about the room, too. Windows

on three sides, but no window sills. The floor was carpeted, but it was the type of tight-woven texture used in offices and shops. A slight pitch to the ceiling, with a single, metal beam running down its centre. A galley kitchen at the end of the room – but the cupboards weren't the usual depth. A small table, with four chairs tucked right under.

Wondering exactly where she was, Marni pushed the grey-tinged netting to one side with her forehead. There wasn't much to see. Directly opposite the rain-specked window, at a distance of about fifteen feet, stood a static caravan on a concrete platform, making Marni realise instantly that she was inside a similar structure. She craned her neck to look at the gap between them – a stretch of short mown grass fell away and beyond that, in the distance, the grey amalgamation of sea and sky. Rainclouds looked like a dull smudge on the horizon.

They must be somewhere on the coast outside Brighton. She racked her brains as to where there were static caravan parks, but she couldn't pinpoint anywhere in particular. There were plenty of sites along the south coast, and she had no recollection of how long they'd driven for. The land seemed to fall away – cliffs maybe? That would suggest they were east of the city.

How long had Paul been here? She looked around the interior again. The place didn't look lived in. There was a supermarket carrier bag on one of the kitchen counters, an open packet of biscuits close to it. But other than that? No personal possessions, no clothes or books, or photos. Maybe it was a holiday rental home. She doubted that Paul would be legitimately renting it. Perhaps he'd just broken in. Holiday sites were dead at this time of year, and if he came and went under the cover of darkness, and didn't switch any lights on, he could maybe get away with staying here for a few days without discovery.

But the car. That would be a giveaway that someone was here.

She supposed he must have parked it somewhere nearby, out of sight.

But why had he brought her here? If he wanted rid of her, he could have done that easily enough by now. However, for all his violent ways, she didn't think Paul was a calculated killer. That was his problem – he never calculated anything when it came to the consequences of his actions. Do something on the spur of the moment, think later.

Paul stirred in the chair, and Marni slid down on the sofa so she could pretend to be asleep.

'Marni, *reveille-toi!*'

Marni blinked a few times and made a pretence of looking around. 'Where are we?'

'Never mind that,' said Paul.

Marni levered herself up into a sitting position and swung her legs round to put her feet on the floor.

'I need some water,' she said. 'And I need the toilet.'

'*Merde.*'

But Paul came across to where she sat. He pulled something out of his pocket and she heard a familiar click. A flick knife being opened. He leered at her and flashed the blade in front of her face, making her cower against the back of the sofa.

'Don't try anything, Marni.'

He sliced through the silver duct tape that had been used to secure her wrists and ankles.

She stood up experimentally, wincing as the blood returned to her hands and feet. Paul grasped the top of her arm and steered her towards a tiny bathroom, just beyond the kitchen area. She went inside and tried to pull the door shut, but he thrust a booted foot into the gap.

'*Non.* The door stays open.'

Marni looked at the frosted glass window. Even if she smashed out all the glass, it would be too small for her to escape through.

Paul stood with one foot and one shoulder jamming the door open, but she could see he was looking the other way. She did what she needed to as quickly as she could, then washed her hands.

'Is this water okay to drink?' she said.

'*Je ne sais pas.*'

'Do you have bottled water?'

'*Non.*'

She ran the tap again and scooped up handfuls of water to slake her thirst.

She emerged and Paul walked her back into the living room. When she sat down, he taped up her wrists and ankles again.

'Why am I here, Paul?'

He glared at her. 'Because we need to talk.'

'We've got nothing to talk about.'

'You're wrong. We 'ave everything to talk about.'

'You killed Thierry. I'll never forgive you for that.'

'He would have killed me.' Paul's face crumpled. 'He was my brother. This was your fault. You came between us. But, Marni,' he knelt down in front of her and placed his hands on her knees, 'despite all that has happened, I never stopped loving you.'

Marni shrank back from him. 'This is a strange way to show it.'

'You and Alex.'

Fuck him!

'You barely know Alex. He's not your son.' Marni's whole body tensed with anger. Paul's logic was warped. What made him think she would ever want to have anything to do with him? Whatever his plan was, he hadn't thought it through.

Paul said nothing, but he went to the end of the room and raised the net curtain so he could look out of the window.

'I need my insulin.'

He ignored her.

'Paul, I need my medication. Seriously.'

This time he turned around. 'I'll call Alex,' he said. 'He can bring it.'

Panic tightened Marni's chest. She didn't want Alex anywhere near Paul.

'No. You get it. Leave him out of it.'

'You're scared I'll corrupt him? I'll turn him against you?'

'Do you think if he sees that you're keeping me tied up, he'll be impressed? You killed his father. You can't replace Thierry. Alex will never allow you to do that.'

'Shut up!'

'Because you know I'm right? What is it that you want, Paul? What can you possibly hope to achieve by taking me prisoner?'

She'd hit a nerve. Paul strode across the room, making the flimsy walls of the mobile home shake. Marni braced herself – she knew what was coming, and she wasn't wrong. Paul hit her, the outside of his fist glancing along the bottom of her chin as her head snapped back. Marni gasped, and bent forward to rest her head on her knees. Her eyes watered and it felt as if her jaw had been dislocated. She took deep breaths and tried to focus on the tops of her shoes.

She heard a noise and looked up. Paul was pulling on a light nylon bomber jacket. He picked up her car keys from a shelf in the kitchen area.

'Where are you going?' she said, her voice a whisper.

'Where do you think? To get your bloody medicine.'

'Thank you.' For all his protestations of love for her, it was the first thing he'd done that was remotely decent.

The door slammed behind him before Marni realised her mistake. Her meds were at Wykeham Terrace, but Paul would be going to her own house on Great College Street.

'Paul?' she yelled. 'Paul? Come back.'

She listened for his return. But all she could hear was the wind tearing through the gap between the caravans.

60

Tuesday, 21 November 2017

Alex

Alex felt rattled by Sullivan's call. He didn't think the cop would be prone to old-womanly worry, so he wondered if there had been something left unsaid. He tried Marni's phone for the tenth time and got put straight through to voicemail. He couldn't help but have a bad feeling about it.

'Maybe she didn't want to stay with Francis any more and went back to Great College Street. If you're worried, babe, go home and check on her,' said Liv. 'Perhaps it's just a problem with her phone.'

Alex tried the landline, but he knew Marni barely ever bothered to answer it if it rang – she just assumed it was cold callers as no one used the landline number any more.

'You're right,' said Alex. 'I'll go and see if she's there.'

He took Liv's bike and cycled across to Great College Street. The centre of Brighton was busy with late-afternoon shoppers, and the traffic was thick, but it still only took him ten minutes to get there. He leaned the bike on the front fence and went up the short path to the front door. He opened it and stepped into the hall.

'Mum?' He was greeted with silence. 'Pepper? Here, boy!'

There was no one home and the air smelled stale, as if there hadn't been a window opened in days. He went through to the kitchen and then peered out of the back door in case his mother was in the garden. He ran upstairs and checked her bedroom and the bathroom. She definitely wasn't home, and neither was her bag anywhere in evidence.

He would try the studio.

When he drew a blank there too, Alex started to become really worried. It wasn't like his mother to disappear like this, and not to respond to calls. He hadn't seen her car either – not in the vicinity of the house or at the back of the studio.

Where the hell was she?

He scrolled through his contacts, trying to come up with someone she might be hanging out with. *Dad.* Seeing his father's number was like a punch in the chest, but he couldn't bring himself to delete it from his phone. It was too final an act. He carried on down the list.

Paul.

He still had a number for Paul, from when they'd met at the Black Rock car park. He called the number and held the phone to his ear.

No answer. He wasn't surprised. He didn't think Paul was around. Most likely he was back in France, and he'd certainly have a different mobile by now.

Unsure of what to do, but now incredibly worried, Alex cycled back to her house. If she'd been out somewhere in the car with Pepper, maybe she'd got back by now. She'd laugh at him and tell him how stupid he was to have worried about her.

As he turned the corner into Great College Street, he saw the little red Suzuki pull up outside the house. The driver's door opened. He breathed a sigh of relief and was about to call out her name, when something stopped him. The foot that appeared below the rim of the door was wearing a boot – a man's work boot. He dropped back around the corner, and leaned his bike on the wall of the pale blue house that stood at the junction.

When he peered cautiously around the edge and down Great College Street, he was just in time to see Paul Mullins walking up to the front door. He seemed to be on his own and there was no sign of Marni. So why was he driving her car?

Paul disappeared inside the house. Alex made a snap decision. He walked as quickly as he could down towards the car, pulling out his mobile.

Pick up, damn you!

Francis didn't answer his call, so he left a message.

'I can't find Mum, but Paul has her car. I'm going to investigate.'

He disconnected – there wasn't time to explain what was happening.

Up close to the car he could see there was definitely no one in the passenger seat, and he peered in through the back windows. No sign of Pepper, either. What was Paul doing with the car and what was he doing in the house?

He tried Marni's phone again. Still no answer.

The boot was unlocked and empty – and as he stared down at the tartan dog rug that lined it, he knew what he had to do. He scrambled into the tiny space, curled up, and pulled the door down gently. He didn't want the noise of it slamming to alert Paul inside, and he also didn't want it to fully shut. He would need to be able to get out again. The hatchback door came to rest gently against the lip of the boot, and he was plunged into total darkness. He was lying curled up on his side, his head crushed against the bulge made by the petrol tank, his feet pushing against the other side. It was incredibly uncomfortable and he hoped he wouldn't be cooped up in here for long. But he felt certain that if Paul had Marni's car, he also knew where Marni was. Adrenalin washed through him, and he found himself breathing more quickly. And more noisily. He closed his eyes and tried to calm his breathing. When Paul got back into the car, he'd need to be absolutely silent.

He didn't have to wait long. He heard the front door slam and Paul's footsteps across the pavement. The driver's door opened and the car shifted as it took Paul's weight. Alex bit his lower lip, hardly daring to breathe. But he had to and he quickly realised that short, shallow breaths were the most effective for staying silent. Paul muttered something in French and then started the car.

As they pulled out of the parking space, the boot door rattled slightly against the sill. Shit! Alex prayed that Paul hadn't noticed over the noise of the engine. He moved enough to release a corner of the dog blanket underneath him, and fed some of the fabric into the gap between the door and the sill to act as a buffer. The rattling stopped and he breathed a silent sigh of relief.

Then he had another thought. His phone! Francis could call back at any moment and give the game away. It was difficult to move enough to be able to fish it out of the pocket of his hoody – and when the screen lit up automatically, he had a moment of blind panic that Paul would see the flash of light from the rear of the car. He pressed it to his chest, once again fighting to get his breathing under control. Once the screen had gone dark again, he felt for the button at the side that allowed him to set it to silent. He didn't dare switch it right off – it felt like his only lifeline to the outside world – and he wanted to feel it vibrate if Francis did call him back.

From inside the boot, Paul's driving seemed erratic. He took corners fast and braked abruptly. Alex tried to work out where they were going. It seemed easy enough at first. Paul drove to the end of the road and turned left – that would put them on Abbey Road. They quickly came to a stop, then the car pulled out and turned right. They were going along Eastern Road now, away from the city centre. Paul didn't use the indicators, and sped up and slowed down unevenly. Alex tried to gauge how far along

Eastern Road they were going, but the further they went, the harder it got. A stop for a few minutes suggested traffic lights. After a while, Paul took a sharp left, and shortly after that Alex thought they went around a roundabout.

Now he was lost. He wasn't at all sure how far they'd gone and after several turns and roundabouts, he'd completely lost his sense of direction. He pulled out his phone again – maybe he could use it to check his precise location. But the power was low and, wherever they were, it wasn't picking up a signal.

Where the hell was he being taken? And what would he find when he got there?

61

Marni

Marni was alone in the caravan. But how long she had until Paul returned was anybody's guess. There was a small digital clock on the fascia of the cooker. She had no idea if the time it showed – fifteen twenty-five – was accurate. Certainly, there was that late-afternoon darkness outside the window, but it had been dull and overcast all day. Maybe if she noted how long Paul was gone for, she could work out how far from Brighton they were.

Because that would be useful, right?

Except she wouldn't know how long he'd have spent searching the house for her meds. Or if he'd spent time doing something else. And as the minutes ticked past, she decided it really didn't make any difference how long he was gone for if she didn't use the time to do something useful.

She was slumped in the corner of the sofa. It was uncomfortable, with her arms behind her back. Her ankles were taped up so tightly that one foot crossed over the top of the other, meaning she couldn't stand properly on two feet – so she couldn't jump across the floor to try the door. And if the door was unlocked, she couldn't make good her escape unless she could at least walk or preferably run.

So, the most important thing to do was to get the bloody tape off her arms and legs. She pulled her legs up as tightly as she could and bent her head forward, but there was no way she could catch the edge of the tape in her teeth. She writhed like Houdini, desperately trying to pass her arms under her arse to bring them round to the front – but all she managed was to fall off the edge of the sofa onto the floor, landing on her elbow with a resounding crack.

Her eyes watered with the pain and for a few moments she had to focus on breathing deeply until it receded. She wiped her eyes on the grey upholstery and blinked until she could see clearly again. Somewhere in this godforsaken little dump there had to be an edge sharp enough to cut into the tape. It couldn't be that hard to get through – not like rope or cable ties. It was just bloody duct tape. If she could get a nick in the edge of it, she should be able to rip through it by forcing her wrists or her ankles apart.

She looked around. The kitchen seemed the most likely place for something of use. She started to wriggle, caterpillar style, across the floor. The carpet was harsh and scratchy, with surprisingly poor grip. She felt like she was floundering rather than making much progress. She tried rolling and fared better, until she knocked her head on the side of the kitchen units jutting out into the middle of the room.

'Ouch!'

She lay panting for a moment, then manoeuvred herself around the units into the middle of the galley kitchen. There were a couple of drawers under the worktop and presumably one of them contained cutlery. She just needed to somehow pull herself up and get them open.

She needed to be able to stand.

Wondering how much time she had left until Paul's return, she strained her ankles this way and that against the tape to try to stretch it. She needed enough give in it to allow her to straighten her feet enough to take her weight, and to let her balance. With her arms tied behind her back, this would be tricky. She manipulated her feet until her calf muscles and her Achilles tendons burned, but it seemed to make no difference. The layers of tape that wrapped around her ankle several times seemed to have no give in them at all.

That wasn't going to work.

She looked up at the two drawers. They each had a small wooden knob at the centre. If she could get herself up onto her knees, she might be able to pull each one open using her mouth or her teeth. She rolled onto her side, pulled up her knees, and pushing off from the floor behind her with her fists, she managed to somehow get herself up into a kneeling position. Once she'd caught her breath, she shuffled round to face the two drawers. The knobs were at face height. Up close, they looked somewhat grimy and greasy, and bile rose in Marni's throat at the thought of putting her mouth over them.

She swallowed hard and clamped her teeth onto the first of them. She pulled. There was no movement and she had to let go for fear of breaking her teeth. She tried again to no effect. It was too stiff, even when she clamped her teeth on tightly and leaned back with all her weight. It left a foul taste in her mouth, and she spat on the floor to get rid of it.

Turning her attention to the second one, she shuffled sideways until she was positioned directly in front of it. This one was just as grubby, and had a notch out of it where the wood had split. Grimacing, she bit down hard on the wood and tried again. Nothing. She took a deep breath, absolutely determined. This time, when she pulled back, the drawer edged a sticky couple of millimetres proud of its surrounding. Another attempt and it swung out fast. Leaning back, Marni had no way of stopping herself crashing down, smacking her front teeth on the top of the knob as she let go and hitting the back of her head on the cupboards opposite.

She slumped sideways to the floor, moaning. She could taste blood in her mouth and her left front tooth was like a spear of pain going up into her top jaw.

But above her, the drawer was open, and what's more, she'd heard the distinctive rattle of cutlery as it had crashed out of its housing.

Not caring about the pain at the back of her head, or in her mouth, she struggled back up to a kneeling position and shuffled forward. She could just look over the rim and into the drawer. A pink plastic cutlery tray held spoons, forks, teaspoons and – yes! – knives. They were only table knives, but they had an edge, and that was what she was after.

But how to get one out of the drawer?

She looked at the clock on the cooker. Half an hour had passed. Paul could come back at any moment and she was making such slow progress.

'Help! Is there anybody there?' she shouted as loudly as she could. She doubted she would get a response but at least it was a way to vent her frustration. 'Help!'

She turned back to the knife issue.

Although she could see into the drawer, it was too high for her to reach over it and pick up one of the knives with her teeth. And given the depth of the cutlery tray, she wasn't sure she'd be able to do that anyway. But there had to be a way of getting one of them.

The clock counted off another minute. She was running out of time.

She slammed the drawer back in with one of her shoulders. There had to be something else, something she could use.

There was a cupboard under the sink. She should look there. Almost crying with anger and frustration she shuffled over to it, ignoring the pain in her knees. Another knob to get her teeth around, but the cupboard opened easily enough. She peered into the shadowy interior. Bottles of cleaning products, crusted cloths, a dustpan and brush. Behind them all, right at the back, a small toolbox.

'Yes.'

She had to use her head to sweep the cleaning gear to one side. Then she leaned as far forward into the cupboard as she could and grabbed the end handle of the toolbox with her teeth. She gave it a tug. Pain shot through the left side of her top jaw and she let go. There was blood on the handle. She pursed her lips, pressing them against her teeth to try and blot out the pain. Then she gave it another go. Slowly, she managed to drag the toolbox across the floor of the cupboard. When she got to the edge, she gave it a final, sharp tug and it fell to the floor, spewing open. Tools spilled out around her – screwdrivers, a hammer, a small wrench and what she dreamed of seeing most, a Stanley knife. Now maybe she'd be able to give Paul what he deserved.

It was only when she bent forward to pick it up with her teeth that she heard it.

The sound of an approaching car. And it was getting louder.

62

Francis

Francis listened to the message with disbelief.

He'd been pacing the incident room, shouting instructions to the rest of the team – no chance of anyone getting away early this afternoon – and trying to formulate a foolproof way of finding out where the killer's message had come from and how to find the two missing women – one of which was presumably being held hostage by the killer.

He came off the phone to find that he'd missed a call from Alex. So when a message came in a moment later, he'd listened to it straight away.

And the silly fucker hadn't told him where he was.

Or any of the other details that might just be useful – such as the number plate of the car and what exactly he meant when he said he was going to investigate. But if Paul had Marni, that meant the Booth Museum killer must have Robin. Both scenarios filled him with fear.

'Gavin, Marni Mullins owns a red Suzuki Swift. Get the reg details and get them circulated to traffic and uniform. Paul Mullins is apparently driving it. Put out a public appeal for anyone who sees it to get in touch – but not to approach the driver as he could be dangerous.'

'Yes, boss.'

'Kyle, put GPS traces on their mobiles.'

'Marni and Robin?' said Kyle.

'Yes, and Alex Mullins.'

He called Tom Fitz.

He didn't have time to wonder whether he could trust Fitz now – he'd just have to. And given Tom's more personal involvement on the case, he had a good reason to co-operate.

'Tom, I've got two missing women – Marni Mullins and Robin Sullivan ...'

'Your sister? Jesus, Sullivan ...'

'Can you put out an appeal on *The Argus* website and social media channels. I'll have one of my team send over pictures.'

Angie was listening and nodded at him. 'I'll do it,' she mouthed.

'Details?' said Tom.

Francis filled him in with physical descriptions and last known whereabouts.

'What's going on? Is this to do with Ada's killer?'

'Strictly off the record?'

'Yes. Fine.'

'The killer sent a message saying he's got a hostage. Someone close to me. But that's not for public consumption. We're searching for the women and waiting for his next message – he said he'd issue instructions.'

'Right, I'm on it. Keep me posted, yes?'

'As much as I can.'

As soon as he put down the phone, Gavin burst into his office.

'A traffic patrol car just spotted the red Suzuki – I told them to follow at a distance.'

'Where are they?'

'Heading east on Eastern.'

'Let's go.'

They ran down to the car park and jumped into Gavin's car.

Gavin put on the lights and the siren as he manoeuvred out onto Edward Street.

'Put your foot down,' said Francis, frustrated as Gavin slowed down to the speed of the traffic.

'Sir.' He blasted the siren over and over, until dozy drivers got out of their way. 'Down to the front or continue along Eastern?'

'Let's drop down to the front,' said Francis. 'Less traffic on the way out of town, and fewer traffic lights. We should be able to gain ground on them, and if the Suzuki's heading out of town, it'll drop down onto the A259 at Roedean Road.' He picked up the handpiece attached to the radio. 'This is DI Sullivan. Do you still have the Suzuki in sight?'

'Yes, boss.'

'Can you see who's driving?'

'We're not close, but it's definitely a man, either Asian or black.'

Paul Mullins.

'Okay. We're on Marine Parade heading east. Expect to intercept at the far end of the marina. Let me know immediately if he turns off that route or stops.'

'Will do.'

Francis got out his phone and dialled the incident room. Kyle Hollins picked up.

'Yes, boss?' he said as Francis identified himself.

'Is Rory back?'

'I haven't heard from him.'

'Kyle, I need you to talk to Tom Fitz and to the desk sergeant on duty. If either of them get delivered one of those burial jars or any type of papyrus message, I need to know about it immediately. Got that?'

'Sure. I'll do it now.'

Francis's stomach was churning. Where the hell were these

instructions the Embalmer had promised?

They were going past the marina now.

'Cut the lights and the siren,' said Francis, 'and slow down.'

As they came to the end, the Roedean Road fed in on the left. With perfect timing, Marni's red Swift swerved out onto the main road ahead of them. Francis felt certain it was Paul Mullins behind the wheel.

He grabbed the radio.

'We've picked him up. You hang back but keep following as well.'

'Yes, sir.'

As the coast road led out of the city, Paul Mullins increased his speed. He was going well above the sixty-mile-per-hour limit. Gavin skilfully matched his speed, while staying far enough back not to arouse suspicion. At the Ovingdean roundabout, he let another car in ahead of them, so Paul wouldn't constantly see the same car in his rearview mirror.

The traffic slowed down as they came into the village of Rottingdean. The car between them and the Suzuki turned off onto the High Street. Francis shrunk down in his seat, hoping that Paul wasn't the sort of driver that took note of what was going on behind him.

A text notification drew his attention back to his phone. It was from Kyle. No messages yet. Francis slammed a hand on the dashboard.

'What?' said Gavin, braking sharply, his knuckles white on the steering wheel.

'Sorry. Keep going.' Then he thought of something else, and punched a button on his phone. He got the answerphone. 'Rory, where the hell are you? Not still at the bloody dentist.' He dropped the phone onto his lap.

The Suzuki was two cars ahead now and they were coming out of the village. The road swung back towards the cliff edge, with Saltdean on the left. Paul accelerated again, but one of the cars in between didn't follow suit.

'Come on, come on,' said Gavin. He swung out towards the centre of the road to see it was safe to overtake, but quickly dropped back into their lane. A lorry thundered by in the opposite direction. The distance between them and the Suzuki was widening.

Thankfully, the slow driver turned off. Coming out of Saltdean there was a short stretch of dual carriageway. Gavin gunned the engine and made up ground. There was still one car between them when they came into the thirty-mile-per-hour zone of Peacehaven, but it put them in a comfortable position. Francis breathed a sigh of relief. He'd thought they were going to lose him.

'Where the hell's he going?' said Gavin. 'I keep expecting him to turn off or stop somewhere, but at this rate we'll be in Eastbourne before we know it.'

'And then what?'

Peacehaven was a strung-out village of retirement bungalows and second-hand car dealers. Pedestrians crossed the road and the traffic didn't seem to be in any hurry at all. The red Suzuki sounded its horn at a grocery delivery van that was blocking the carriageway, then pulled round it sharply, only to be blocked again by a taxi dropping off an elderly woman.

They tailed it cautiously, past a Tudor-style Indian restaurant, past a brace of 1930s semi-detached houses, past a primary school ... and then, abruptly, at the end of the village, without indicating his intention, Paul turned off to the right.

Gavin waited in the left-hand carriageway for oncoming traffic to clear.

'I'll follow him, right?'

'Yes,' said Francis hesitantly.

The road that Paul had turned into was nothing more than

a lane, the scrubland on either side interspersed with the occasional bungalow. This is where following him would start to look suspicious. Francis glanced at the satnav on the dashboard. The road they were turning onto was called the Highway. It led past a large holiday park and then wound around via a few large, isolated houses, before returning to civilisation on the outskirts of the next village along the coast, Seahaven. Where the hell was Paul going?

'Stay right back,' said Francis. 'His destination must be somewhere round here.'

The road curved round to the left, and the Suzuki disappeared from sight. Gavin drove up to the curve, then slowed down, nudging his way round until they saw a flash of red ahead of them. They followed at as much of a distance as they dared, past a couple of large houses. The road widened, to allow for parking on either side, and a large green board announced 'Rushey Hill Caravan Park'. Row upon row of static caravans were lined up on a gentle slope of well-manicured grass.

No doubt, at the height of summer, the place would be heaving, but on a cold November afternoon, it took on a sad and deserted appearance.

'I know this place,' said Gavin. 'Had an auntie who used to holiday here when I was a kid – we'd always come across and visit her.'

'It's huge,' said Francis. 'Is it all just holiday rentals or do people live here?'

Gavin shrugged.

Ahead of them, the Suzuki turned off the road onto one of the lanes leading down into the park.

'Stop here,' said Francis.

Gavin pulled the car over just beyond where Paul had disappeared.

'We should follow on foot – looks like he'll be in one of these caravans. Radio the uniforms and tell them we're here, and that they should park up and await further instructions.'

'Right, gov.'

Francis got out of the car and walked back to the top of the lane where they'd last seen the Suzuki.

His phone beeped – it was a text message from Kyle.

Fitz's office has received a scroll. He's on his way there to collect it. Call you in five.

In the distance, between a gap in the caravans, Francis saw a flash of red. The Suzuki came to a stop.

63

Tuesday, 21 November 2017

Alex

Alex felt sick. He had no idea how long they'd been driving – more than half an hour, less than an hour – but he'd had enough. A sudden sharp turn onto a bumpy, tyre-crunching surface made things even worse. He had to brace his legs and shoulders against each side of the boot to stop himself being jumped up and down. An involuntary gasp escaped and for a few long seconds he thought that Paul would slam on the brakes and come around to the boot to investigate.

His phone, still pressed up against his chest, had vibrated several times during the journey. Hopefully it was Francis Sullivan calling him back and not just Liv wanting to know what they were doing for supper.

The car finally ground to a halt. Alex wondered where they were, and listened for Paul getting out. But he didn't. He just sat where he was, in silence. Why? Checking his phone? Or were they lost? Without the noise of the engine to cover his breathing, Alex didn't dare move.

But he listened intently for sounds outside the car. There was no other traffic noise – and he would surely hear it if anything else drove over the rough surface they'd just come across.

He felt like he was suffocating. He desperately wanted to push the boot door up a crack to let in some fresh air, but he didn't dare.

He waited.

Finally, he heard the driver's door open, and then the shift in the car as Paul got out. The door slammed shut, making the unsecured boot rattle.

Shit!

Footsteps crunched on rocky ground, going away from the car.

Alex could breathe again.

Everything was quiet. He raised the door of the boot a couple of inches and manoeuvred so he could prop it open with the toe of one shoe. It gave him enough air to breathe. He raised his head and squinted out of the crack.

All he could see was what looked like the side of a garden shed, painted a chalky, off-white colour. Someone's garage, maybe? It was no help. He pushed the door up higher and looked around. It wasn't a shed. It was a small static caravan and there were lots of them, all the same. Row upon row, stretching away up a gentle slope. He was in a holiday park, somewhere, that was clear enough. But how many of these static caravan sites were there along the coast? Loads, and he needed Sullivan here now. He opened the mapping app on the phone and found his location – just east of Peacehaven.

He quickly typed a message.

Got in the boot of Mum's car. Been driving since last text, now stopped. In a holiday park near Peacehaven.

He pressed send, hoping that he'd given the police enough information. Once his screen showed that the text had been delivered, he opened the boot further, slipped out onto the ground and silently closed it again. After the cramped conditions, every muscle felt stiff, every joint complained.

Which way had Paul gone when he'd left the car?

342

He looked around. He was at the bottom of the slope, at the edge of the caravan park. Beyond the last row, there was an expanse of neatly mown grass, then several metres of scrubland leading to the cliff edge. No fence. No safety signs. The land just seemed to fall away – and beyond it, the sea.

His phone vibrated and he looked at the screen. A reply to his text message.

Stay in the car – we're coming.

'Fuck that!' he muttered. If Paul was holding his mother captive in one of these caravans, he needed to get her out. He couldn't wait for the bloody useless cops to turn up. He'd seen first-hand already how they cocked up rescues. He still had nightmares about being handcuffed to a rusty ladder down in the Brighton sewers.

He listened for a few minutes, looking around, but the place seemed to be completely deserted. There was the odd car, parked between the static caravans, but no sign of people. On the far side of the park, he could see one window with a light on, but that was all. Running at a crouch, he made his way towards the front of the car and looked over the bonnet at the caravan opposite. It had large, panoramic windows across the end facing the sea. The curtains were open, and in the dull light of the late afternoon, the interior looked dark and empty. He crept closer and stared inside. He could see a large room, with a sofa and a table and chairs, stretching back to a small kitchen area. There was no sign of recent habitation.

He turned his attention to the caravan on the other side of the Suzuki. The windows were obscured with net curtains, so he couldn't see in. He skirted onto the grassy area in front of the caravans and walked on silent feet until he was able to duck down right under one of the side windows. He could

343

hear raised voices coming from the inside.

'Why didn't you say your meds were somewhere else?'

'I shouted after you, but you didn't listen.'

'And how could I have got them if they were in a friend's house? What friend?'

'None of your business.'

'Pah! Like I said, we should have called Alex . . .'

'You need to let me go, Paul. You've made your case, but you're wrong. Me and Alex, we'll never be your family.'

There was the sound of a slap and Alex heard his mother cry out. He moved towards the door, desperately looking around for something he could use as a weapon. If Paul dared to lay another finger on his mother, he was going to kill the bastard.

A movement registered in Alex's peripheral vision. At the same time his phone vibrated with a notification. He moved along from the window to make sure he was out of sight, but as he did, his foot slipped noisily on a patch of gravel.

'What was that?' said Paul, inside the caravan.

Alex pressed himself hard against the wall right beneath the window, praying that the sound hadn't blown his cover. He looked towards where he'd seen the movement. Francis Sullivan, another man, and two uniformed officers were running down the slope towards him, darting from one van to the next to keep out of sight as far as possible. Francis was waving at him frantically, gesturing for him to get away from the caravan.

But if he did that, and Paul was looking out of the window, he'd be spotted. He pointed towards the window with his index finger, hoping Sullivan would understand what he was trying to convey.

There was a heavy thud from inside the caravan. His mother screamed. The door sprung open and Paul Mullins burst out.

In his right hand, he was holding a knife.

Alex lunged for him.

344

64

Tuesday, 21 November 2017

Francis

Francis watched the scene unfolding in front of him in slow motion, as he ran towards it as fast as he could.

Paul Mullins saw him and there was a fleeting moment of eye contact, before he was startled by Alex Mullins springing up from beneath the window. Alex shouted something, but the wind whipped it away before Francis could make out the words.

'Paul's got a knife,' yelled Gavin, overtaking Francis on the rough track.

Stones skidded under his feet and his lungs burned.

Where was Marni?

Alex lunged towards Paul, but the older man anticipated his move and danced to one side. He held up the knife, not pointing it at Alex, but more as a deterrent.

Alex stepped towards him.

'You're not my father.'

'I am. Believe me.'

'You killed my father.'

'No.'

'Drop the knife,' yelled Gavin. He was nearly upon them.

Alex lunged again, grabbing for Paul's right hand. But Paul flicked his wrist, turning the blade on Alex, catching him across the forearm. Alex's momentum was still carrying him forward, and with a grunt of pain, he smashed into Paul's chest.

'Alex, get away from him,' yelled Francis. Bloody stupid kid. Paul Mullins had spent years in jail – he knew how to fight.

For a second the two men tussled, but then Paul broke away and started running across the grass to the scrubland at the cliff edge. Alex stumbled over the steps to the caravan door and sprawled onto the gravel.

Gavin ran to him to help him up.

At the same moment, Marni appeared in the doorway. She was on her knees and one side of her face was covered in blood. The other side of it was deathly pale.

'Mum,' cried Alex. 'Help her,' he said, shaking Gavin off.

Gavin went over to her and Francis watched as he picked Marni up and took her back into the interior.

Alex, now on his feet, looked around for Paul, who was running along the top of the cliffs in the direction of Peacehaven.

'She's okay,' yelled Gavin, from inside.

With a look of grim determination, Alex took off after Paul.

Francis had reached the caravan but he couldn't stop. He had to get to Alex before the boy caught up with Paul.

In his jacket pocket, his phone buzzed, but he ignored it and kept running. The grass was spongy underfoot, the surface uneven, and now the day was losing its light, it was hard to see where he was putting his feet.

Ahead of him, Alex stumbled but kept going. He was closing the gap between himself and Paul.

'Alex, wait,' called Francis, his breath coming in great, ripping gasps as he tried to gain ground on both of them.

The three men ran along the cliff edge for what seemed, to Francis, to be forever. His legs were starting to cramp. In truth, it was just a few hundred metres, but Francis had never put so much effort into a sprint.

Alex was younger and fitter than both of them.

He caught up with Paul at a point where the land sloped more steeply to the cliff edge, just on the edge of the village of Peacehaven. There was a fence here, but Francis watched in horror as Paul scrambled over it. Alex took a leap at his back as he went over the wire mesh. They both fell to the other side and rolled, wrestling, on a sloping patch of thrift and bracken.

Francis crashed into the fence, gasping for breath.

He saw the flash of Paul's blade as they twisted. Below them, a series of steps had been cut into the chalk face of the cliff. On either side, the white walls dropped a sheer fifty metres to the concrete undercliff walk below.

'Alex, let go of him!' Francis shouted.

But Alex had one hand firmly clasped around Paul's right wrist, the hand in which he was holding the knife. He was trying to smash it on the ground to make Paul drop the knife, but the undergrowth made it a useless attempt.

Drawing on his last reserves, Francis clambered over the fence. He stood above the two men as they writhed on the ground, looking for an opportunity to grab Paul and pull him off. The moment came. Paul was on top of Alex. Francis dropped to a squat and grabbed both his shoulders. He heaved backwards, but his right foot skidded on wet bracken, shooting away from him. He landed on his back with a thud, and a second later found himself underneath Alex and Paul as they continued to tussle.

'*Lâchez-moi* – get off!'

Francis brought a knee up viciously, hoping he would hit Paul rather than Alex, but intent on breaking the melee apart.

A yelp of pain from the boy told him he'd hit the wrong one. A moment later a blow to his head partially stunned him, and once again he felt the weight of someone else on top of him.

A hand landed across his face and he twisted his head. The hand moved with him. Desperate for air, he bit the side of the palm. There was a taste of salt and dirt before the hand was snatched away. A roar of pain that sounded more like Paul than Alex.

As they struggled, the undertow of gravity pulled them further from the fence. The incline at the top of the cliff was steeper here and the damp vegetation was slippery. Francis stuck out a leg with the intention of using it to lever himself up, but his foot hit nothing.

They'd reached the edge.

In a panic, Francis let go of the arm he was grasping and reached out for a handful of bracken. A hand grabbed at the back of his trousers and caught his belt, pulling him further down. The bracken tore through his hand and he found himself flailing as he tried to gain some purchase on something solid. He kicked with his feet to try and get free from whoever had hold, but they hung on. The front of his belt was cutting into his stomach.

Everything was a blur of movement and shouting. He took a blow to the head. He felt something sharp in another man's hand. Paul's hand. The knife.

'Alex?' he croaked. 'Get back up. We're too close to the edge.' The words came out garbled, and of course no one was listening to him.

With a supreme effort, he managed to get both hands onto a knotted, partially exposed root. He couldn't get his fingers all the way around it, as it was still embedded in the earth, but it gave him something to grip. Straining every muscle, biting down hard on his lower lip, he tried to shift his body further up the slope, away from the edge, but now both men were hanging onto him. Their combined weight was dragging him down.

With a ripping sound and a sudden release of tension, his belt buckle snapped free – it was a couple of years old and the leather had been fairly worn. Hands grappled at his leg, and there was a shout. Not words. Just fear. Another yell. Unbearable pain in his arms and shoulders. He was completely out of breath. He was on his side and he pedalled with his legs, desperate to get them back onto solid ground. He heard stones crunching, falling. A scream. The clatter of metal on concrete. No one was holding on to him now. He stopped moving, pressing his body into the ground, his muscles still tense and shaking.

Back beyond the fence there was the sound of running footsteps.

'Sir? Sir, are you okay?' It was one of the PCs arriving, severely out of breath.

He raised his head and looked around. He was alone on the cliff edge.

'Fuck!'

For ten long seconds he couldn't breathe, then he felt a pair of hands under his armpits, pulling him up. His fingers released their white-knuckle grip on the root, and he felt ground under his feet. He couldn't stand, but the PC dragged him up to the fence and rested him against it.

'Where are they?' said Francis, though of course he knew.

'Over the edge.'

He pulled himself up using the railing at the top of the fence.

'Alex?' he yelled.

He couldn't give a shit what had happened to Paul.

Beneath him, there was nothing but silence.

He edged forward and looked over the edge.

In his pocket, his phone buzzed angrily.

65

Francis

On the flat concrete of the undercliff path lay a body. Francis knew it was dead from the angle of the head and the splatter of blood around – like a ripe fruit dropped from a height. He peered hard, but the light was fading.

Dear God . . .

But only one body. And the glint of the metal blade, the knife lying next to it.

Why couldn't he see the other?

He dropped onto his hands and knees so he could lean further out.

Now he could see the steps leading down to the path below. There was someone hanging precariously to the outer edge of the railings, halfway down the cliff.

'Alex?'

Alex groaned.

'Are you okay?'

He didn't make a sound – he was hanging on with one arm, the other one hanging limp by his side, blood dripping from his fingertips to stain the white chalk red just below where he hung.

'Officer, get down there. Help him.'

The PC had started down the steps before Francis had even got the words out of his mouth. It took him seconds to reach

Alex and he was able to hold the boy until the second PC arrived to help. Together, they lifted him up, over the railing, and sat him on the steps.

'Are you okay, Alex?' called Francis, from the top.

'What about Mum?'

'DC Albright's with her. I'll go and see.'

He pulled himself back over the fence, and turned to watch the two PCs helping Alex up the steps. The boy was cradling his bleeding arm across his chest. Then he remembered the insistent bleeping of his phone. Robin . . . the instructions . . . He checked the phone as he half ran along the clifftop back towards the caravan park.

There was a series of text messages from Kyle.

Fitz is here. We're opening the scroll.

Francis clicked through to the next one. It was a photo of a familiar-looking roll of papyrus. He had to stop jogging so he could focus on the writing.

could.grants.palms
Come alone, go to the top on your own
or this dear, sweet hostage dies.

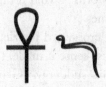

It was finished off with the two hieroglyphs.

'What the fuck?' The beginning of the message made no sense.

Francis jogged the five hundred metres back to the mobile home where he'd left Gavin with Marni.

'Gavin?' he called out as he got close.

'Boss?' Gavin appeared in the doorway.

'Is she okay?'

'She's fine. Maybe concussion. I've called an ambulance.'

'Good. Get another – Alex is injured. Call in the CSIs.'

'Where's Alex? What's happened?' Marni's voice was laden with fear as she pushed past Gavin in the doorway.

'He's fine. He's safe,' said Francis. 'The constables are bringing him up.'

'And Paul?' said Gavin.

Francis shook his head. 'He's dead. We need to go.'

His first thought was to take the Suzuki, but Marni didn't have the keys.

'Paul has them,' she said, ruling out that idea.

He and Gavin set up off the hill to where they'd left Gavin's car at the top. As they jogged, Francis told Gavin about the message.

'Could. Grant. Palms. What do those words at the beginning mean?' he said, after Gavin had heard it. 'Where does he want us to go?'

Gavin shrugged. 'Could. Grant. Palms. I've no idea.'

'Just like three random words. A clue, maybe? Where are there palm trees in Brighton? Somewhere on the front?'

'But the other two words – what do they signify?' Gavin repeated them several times.

It was like a cryptic crossword puzzle, and the more Francis thought about it, the less sense it made.

'Got it,' said Gavin suddenly. 'Geocoding. It might be What3words.'

'What?'

'Geocoding. It's an app. Every three metres square of the earth's surface is represented by three words.'

'Seriously?'

Gavin nodded. 'I've got the app on my phone.' He pulled out his mobile. 'Could. Grants. Palms.' He typed in the words.

They had reached the car.

'I'll drive,' said Francis. 'Just tell me where to go.'

He felt suddenly light-headed. Coming out here had been a huge mistake. He should have stayed in Brighton and sent Gavin here with Kyle. What if he got to Robin too late?

'It's the i360,' said Gavin. 'That's going to take us at least twenty minutes to get to, even blue-lighting it.' He looked at Francis, who was about to get into the driving seat. 'You're a fucking mess, boss. Let me drive.'

They swapped sides and seconds later gravel was spraying out from behind the back wheels as Gavin turned the car around at speed. They hit the main road with lights flashing and siren blaring and kept both on continuously until they reached the centre of Brighton fifteen minutes later.

Was Robin still alive?

The i360 observation tower stood on the seafront opposite Regency Square like a giant needle, reaching more than one hundred and fifty metres into the sky. A doughnut-shaped viewing platform rose up and down the tower to give visitors spectacular panoramic views of Brighton, the South Downs, the Sussex Coast and the sea with its gently curving horizon. Francis had taken Robin and his mother up it when it had first opened. It had been one of his mother's last outings, before she became too ill for such frivolities. The huge platform, complete with champagne bar, could accommodate more than two hundred passengers.

The message had demanded that Francis come alone, so Gavin dropped him around the corner in Cannon Place, and he ran the rest of the way. He looked up at the tower. The viewing platform was halfway up, and still rising. He didn't bother to go into the street-level ticket office to buy a ticket, but went straight down to the beachfront embarkation area.

'Ticket?'

Francis pushed past the girl checking tickets on the door, flashing his warrant card.

'Wait, sir. You need a ticket. You can't just come barging through . . .'

'Police,' said Francis. 'Get me whoever's in charge.'

The girl's eyes widened with surprise, but she stood rooted to the spot.

'Go on. This is an emergency. I need the platform brought down now.'

The girl turned and hurried inside, Francis following her. She led him to a door marked 'Staff Only'.

'Mr Parry, Mr Parry?' she said, knocking and entering.

A man got up from behind a desk. 'What is it, Stacey?' He was frowning.

'My name's DI Francis Sullivan. I need you to bring down the viewing platform immediately.'

The man looked at him askance. 'I'm sorry, but what exactly's going on?'

'Your name?'

'James Parry.'

'Mr Parry, we have an ongoing situation . . . I need to go up the tower.'

'Why?'

Francis felt a muscle tighten in his jaw. 'I'm sorry, but I can't go into that. Please have the platform lowered immediately.'

'I can't do that.'

'Why not?'

'People have paid. If they don't get their full time, I'll have to refund all the tickets.'

'And you'll be able to make an insurance claim for that.

However, I need it down and cleared of people right now.' Francis was struggling not to raise his voice.

James Parry didn't look convinced.

'You don't want to be charged with obstruction.'

Finally, the message got through.

'Stacey,' he said to the girl, who was still lingering in the doorway, 'tell Ron to lower the platform now. I'll go and make an announcement.'

'Can you get the whole waiting area cleared too?' said Francis.

Parry gave him a pained nod.

They went back to the area where people were queuing to get on.

'Sorry, ladies and gentlemen,' yelled Parry above the general hubbub. 'We've got to cancel the next ride and clear the building. Keep your tickets and we'll sort out a refund or a replacement . . .'

The rest of what he said was drowned out by upset and angry voices.

'What's going on?'

'Why can't we go up it?'

'Must be broken.'

'Maybe there's a bomb!' This last exclamation fell in an unfortunate moment of silence. Then a woman screamed and panic blossomed. People stampeded for the door and Francis only just managed to step to one side to avoid being mown down. The platform itself made a steady descent – it hadn't quite reached the top, and when the doors opened, there was a tide of moaning as the disgruntled passengers were shepherded towards the exit. Francis pushed through the throng to get onto the platform.

A few minutes later, he finally had the viewing platform to himself. He'd even insisted that the two barmen wait at the bottom, while he went up on his own. He gave James Parry the thumbs up through the glass door, and the ring-shaped vessel started its slow climb. Francis paced from one side to the other, watching the ground closely as it fell away from him. Was the killer down there somewhere, watching?

Brighton shrank beneath him as the world expanded. He could see far along the coast to the east, to the marina and, way beyond it, the cliffs at Beachy Head. To the north, the city gave way to the soft undulations of the Downs, while the view west encompassed Hove Lawns, with its angel statue, and gold, sandy beaches curving away into the distance. Returning to the east side of the pod, he looked down on the silverskin onion domes of the Pavilion, then picked out the squat 1960s building that housed the police station in John Street. What was he looking for? He went to the southern side. With the sun so low in the sky now, the sea shone like a mirror, making him squint and turn away.

As they climbed higher still, a familiar feeling weighed in against his chest. He stepped back from the curved glass with its steel railing. He couldn't look straight down now, only out to the distance. He carried on back until he could feel the firm edge of the bar behind him. He put his arms out to either side to grip its reassuring surface.

He'd always suffered vertigo, but it seemed even worse with the vestiges of a hangover. He turned away from the view and watched the steel grid-like surface of the tower passing as the platform continued to move – it was like being inside a glass lift. He took deep breaths and went around the bar to help himself to some water.

Finally, the i360 juddered to a halt. It was silent and he was completely alone, more than one hundred and fifty metres above the city. It didn't make sense. No one could meet him up here, unless they'd come up with him. He walked all the way around and checked behind the bar. For a second, paranoia got the better of him. Could there be someone, on the other side of the central tower, moving round silently to always remain out of sight? He sprinted around the platform a couple of times until he was convinced he was alone.

Sweat ran from his brow into his eyes and he wiped it away with a gesture of frustration.

What was he meant to be doing up here?

He walked around the platform again, more slowly this time. He'd missed something. There was something here he was supposed to see. To find.

Under the bar there was a row of cupboards. He opened them one by one. Glasses. Cleaning products. Paper rolls for the till.

A Canopic jar . . .

'No!'

He grabbed it from the bottom shelf of the end cupboard. A crude clay jar with a falcon-head top.

No. Please God, no.

He turned it this way and that, looking for the killer's message, but there was no scroll attached to this jar. He didn't want to think about what was inside it, but he couldn't stop himself. He retched as he tried to prise the lid off, grasping the bird's beak and trying to twist it. It was stuck fast.

He staggered to his feet, clutching the jar.

'Robin . . . ' It came out as a sob. He was supposed to have looked after her.

Seized by a tremendous rage, he threw the jar against the curved window. The jar shattered and fell to the floor. The thick glass window was unmarked.

Francis stared at the shards of clay, expecting to see a mess of blood and natron. But there was nothing except dried, orange pottery. And a small, creamy roll of papyrus. He dropped to his knees and snatched it up, not caring as he knelt on the sharp edges of the broken pot.

He unrolled it.

*You're on top of the world, but not for much
longer.
On a clear day, you can see for fifty miles in
every direction.
You can even see where I'm holding your hostage.
It's time to come down and find us.
The clock is ticking.
damp.amber.normal*

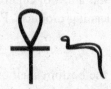

Of course, it was signed with the snake and the ankh hieroglyphs.

'Fuck you!' Francis got up and pulled his phone out of his pocket. He was being played. It seemed so obvious now – why hadn't he seen it before he had wasted time coming up here? Someone down on the ground was laughing up at him. He scurried to the edge of the platform, his stomach lurching as he caught sight of Regency Square far below, and quickly dialled the number James Parry had given him.

'Get me down. Now.'

66

Francis

Francis ran from the exit of the i360 to where Gavin was drawing up by the kerb. He hurried around to the passenger side of the car and climbed in.

'What happened?'

'Bastard's playing cat and mouse with us. Did you get my text?'

Francis had sent Gavin the three words from the message on his way down the tower.

'Yes – they're for the Pavilion.'

'Go.'

It was pouring with rain and almost dark by the time they screeched to a halt at the India Gate of the Pavilion. A black bollard in the middle of the gateway prevented them from getting any closer to the entrance, but Francis was out of the car practically before it stopped.

'Get uniformed backup out here, and an ambulance,' he yelled over his shoulder to Gavin, as he set off at a run.

He hadn't told Gavin of the plan that had come to him as they drove across town at breakneck speed – that he would offer himself in Robin's place. He didn't have time for an argument with Gavin, or anyone else.

By the time he'd pelted the twenty metres to reach the door, his hair was plastered to his head and his already mud-stained suit was soaked.

The girl at the ticket desk looked up with alarm as he rushed in.

'Sorry, sir, you can't buy a ticket now. We're closing in ten minutes.'

Francis pulled out his warrant card.

'Who's in charge? The building needs to be cleared.'

'What . . . ?'

'Now!' he added sharply.

The girl picked up the phone on her desk.

Francis looked around, catching his breath. Ornate mouldings, carved pillars, dragon lanterns and a painted ceiling – it was all familiar from childhood visits. Where would the Embalmer be? How could he be holding a hostage in a building that was open to the public? Not in the public areas . . . behind the scenes, somewhere.

'Have you got a map of the building?' he said to the girl.

She pulled a leaflet from a plastic caddy on the counter and started to unfold it. Francis could see a diagram of coloured blocks showing the visitor route through the building.

'No, no.' Francis shook his head. 'I need a plan. I need to see the whole building, all the floors, even where tourists don't go.'

The girl stared at him, eyes wide, mouth a little open.

A middle-aged woman in a black shift dress appeared from a doorway behind the ticket desk.

'What's going on? Who are you?'

'Police,' said Francis. 'Close up and get the people out. We have reason to believe there's a wanted man in the building.'

She glanced at the warrant card he was still holding up.

'Right,' she said. 'Elizabeth, get onto the PA and say we're closing.' She unclipped a radio from her belt. 'Attention, calling all staff – evacuate the Pavilion now. I repeat, evacuate the entire building.' She looked at Francis. 'What else can I do?'

'I need to check all your non-public areas, from top to bottom.'

'I'll come with you,' she said.

'No. The man is dangerous. How could someone sneak into the building?'

'The outside is covered by CCTV cameras, so no one could sneak in unseen,' she said.

'What about the secret tunnel?' said the reception girl.

'What tunnel?' said Francis sharply.

'It runs from here to what used to be the old stables – now the Brighton Dome.'

'There's a secret tunnel between here and the Dome?' said Francis.

'Yes. But it's locked,' said the woman. 'No one could just wander in through it.'

Unless they had a set of keys . . .

'Tell me how to get to it.'

It took the woman less than a minute to tell Francis how to find the entrance to the tunnel, and she gave him her keyring, holding out the key he would need to open the door. He ran from the entrance hall and went immediately right through the Red Drawing Room. A door on its opposite side led through a vestibule to a small, curved staircase that took him down into the basement. It was dark, the air instantly cooler, and he could smell the damp fustiness of an old building. The manager had explained to him that this passageway ran the whole length of the building, where, at the far end, it gave access to the secret tunnel to the Dome.

Francis turned on the torch on his mobile and ran down the corridor. There were doors on either side, which he tried as he passed. Most were locked, one or two opened into empty rooms, and others into rooms which contained cleaning supplies and old bits of furniture. No Embalmer. No hostage.

'Robin?' he called. 'Are you down here?'

His voice echoed off the grimy brickwork, but there was no answer.

His phone buzzed. An email with a photo of a handwritten message. This one wasn't on papyrus, just on a page ripped out of a notebook.

Where are you, Sullivan?
My patience is wearing thin and my blade is sharp

Francis felt sick. There were no hieroglyphs – it had clearly been done in a hurry. He glanced at the top to see who it had come from, but it just said XXXXX.

He ran on and came to a door at the end of the corridor. It wasn't locked and swung open easily when he pushed it. He peered down the tunnel. It went dead straight, as far as the small beam from his torch could reach. He had no doubt that this was how the Embalmer could have brought a hostage in. But where were they now? He made a snap decision – if he went along the tunnel, he was leaving the Pavilion, and the What3words location that the Embalmer had sent him. He hadn't checked upstairs yet, so he turned back. The manageress had said there was a hidden spiral staircase – formerly used by the servants – that led from the basement right up to the domes on the top of the building.

He found it as she'd described it and took the stairs two at a time. There were small landings, with doors, at the ground and first floor, but these led to the staterooms where the public were allowed to wander. At the top, however, there was a series of rooms underneath the Pavilion's famous onion domes, once servants' quarters, now long abandoned.

Beyond the first floor, the ancient wooden stairs had obviously had no maintenance for years. The boards creaked under his feet

362

and the tight spiral banister shook when he placed a hand on it. He slowed down, testing each step with his foot. He didn't want to announce his presence before he needed to. He went a full circle, step by step, and saw a painted door at the top. There was a crack of light along the bottom of it.

His phone, set to silent, vibrated in his pocket. He answered the call.

'*You're too late,*' whispered an unfamiliar voice in his ear.

'But you might as well come in,' said the same voice, from beyond the door.

Francis didn't need a second invitation. As fear tightened its vice around his chest, he pushed down on the door handle and stepped inside.

'Welcome to the Bottle!' said the same voice.

The Bottle. It was a small round room with distinctive lozenge-shaped windows that he'd seen a thousand times from the outside – he was inside the Pavilion's main dome. Unlike the rest of the building, it was in a state of disrepair – faded floral wallpaper peeling off the walls, bare floorboards thick with dust, graffiti and rubbish wherever he looked. But while the architecture was extraordinary, it was the man standing in front of him that held his attention.

The speaker was the Embalmer.

He was short, almost a foot shorter than Francis, who looked down on him. His dark hair was shaved, apart from an inch-wide Mohican strip running from the front to the back of his head. The rest of his pale skull glinted in the harsh light of the bare bulb that hung above them, and on his forehead were two protuberances. Small horns – subdermal implants. His face was pierced more than a dozen times, silver glinting along his brow, in his nose, his cheeks, his lips, his ears – his skull studded like a Christmas orange covered with cloves. And there were tattoos up his neck and all over his head, on the v-shaped gap that showed his chest, and on his hands. His fleshy features were pale and freckled, and between his lips, Francis could see the end – the two ends – of his tongue. It was split, like a snake's tongue. But most disturbing of all, there was something . . . just something that seemed tantalisingly familiar about him.

Where the hell did he know him from?

The Embalmer stepped forward, quite deliberately invading Francis's personal space. He was bulky with an imposing musculature that Francis could see quite clearly under a tight-fitting white shirt. A white shirt speckled red with blood. Robin's blood?

He leered up at Francis and opened his mouth to reveal the full extent of the split in his bifurcated tongue. A cut had divided it into two halves, each of which was at least three inches long. Two halves that moved independently of one another, like tentacles, as he made a low hissing sound from the back of his throat.

A grunt from somewhere in the room behind him finally dragged Francis's eyes away from the monster in front of him.

'Take me instead,' said Francis. 'Please. Just let her go.'

The Embalmer ignored his plea.

'Do you recognise me yet?' he said. There was some innuendo behind his words, but Francis's mind was blank.

He pushed past him to try to get to his sister.

'Robin?'

A hooded figure sat in the centre of the room, tied to a chair that was precariously tilted back against an old table.

But as Francis came closer, he saw the person was wearing men's clothes, not women's, and men's shoes.

It wasn't Robin?

He darted forward and pulled the cloth bag off the man's head.

'Rory!'

His sergeant's bloodied head lolled to one side. He'd clearly taken a beating, and he seemed only half conscious. On the floor, next to the chair, stood a Canopic jar without its lid and a polythene bag of what was presumably natron. Rory's shirt was undone and had been pulled back over his shoulders to expose his chest and torso. *Was he about to be gutted?*

'Rory!'

'Step back.' The man was suddenly a menacing presence bearing down on him.

Francis stood his ground. 'You utter bastard.'

The Embalmer slipped deftly around him. He grabbed the back of the chair Rory was on and shoved it forward, so it was no longer resting on the table. He moved behind it and with one hand grabbed a handful of Rory's hair, yanking his head back.

'Look, he's not dead yet. I wanted to save that particular pleasure for your arrival.'

A blade flashed in his other hand, and he pressed it against Rory's cheek, just below his left eye.

67

Francis

Why in God's name had he been stupid enough to come up here alone? Because he'd blindly followed the Embalmer's instructions? Or because he'd wanted that moment of glory . . .

His brain made a snap decision with no time for thought.

Do the unexpected.

Instead of going for the Embalmer, he went for the chair. He bent and grabbed one of the front legs and yanked it forward and up. The chair swung backwards and Rory's head dropped away from the Embalmer's hand. The blade flashed as the monster plunged it into Rory's eyeball. Rory screamed as the chair crashed to the floor.

With a roar of anger, the Embalmer lunged at Francis, who dived to one side. As his opponent sprawled onto the floor, he pulled himself up into a crouch at Rory's side. He needed medical attention right away. But before Francis could do anything to help, the man leapt at him again, landing against his shoulder.

Then they were wrestling on the floor. All Francis's muscles burned. They hadn't recovered from the fight on the cliffs and now he was expecting them to perform again. The Embalmer was stronger and heavier than him and within seconds had him pinned down flat on his back.

'You offered yourself instead of him? Looks like I've got you both.'

He held Francis down with both hands gripping tightly round his neck. Strong muscular arms, thick stubby fingers . . . choking the life out of him. Keeping his weight solidly on top of Francis's body, he pressed down even harder. A few more seconds. Francis blinked as the periphery of his vision turned black and grainy. Then he felt the monster's balance shift to one side.

It's your only chance.

He jerked his knee up and jabbed it into the Embalmer's side. It was enough to pitch the short man over, but it also brought his hand right into contact with a potential weapon – a broken chair leg lying by the skirting board. Francis shuffled backwards, sitting up, as the Embalmer picked up the piece of wood and struggled to his knees. Behind him, Francis's hand came to rest on something, the Canopic jar. He closed his fingers into the rim and reached his other hand up to the edge of the table to haul himself up. He kept the jar behind his back as the Embalmer came at him, both arms outstretched, raising the chair leg ready to strike.

Now!

Francis swung the heavy clay pot around, taking full advantage of his longer reach, smashing it against the side of the Embalmer's head. The man screeched – an inhuman sound – and staggered. But he kept hold of the baton and he kept coming. Francis dodged out of his way and threw a punch. This time he missed, as the Embalmer ducked.

'Gavin!' he yelled, hoping beyond hope that the DC had ignored his instructions about going in alone.

There was the thunder of footsteps on the stairs.

The Embalmer stopped and blinked. Then he changed direction. Before Francis had worked out what he was doing, he'd unlatched one of the oval windows and was clambering through it. Cold air and rain gusted into the room. Francis looked down at Rory, still tied to the upset chair. His left eye was bleeding heavily and his right eye was closed, a dark hollow in his bone-white face. He was trembling and jerking against his bonds as if he was fitting.

The door behind him opened.

'Boss!'

'Get the paramedics up here now,' shouted Francis.

Then he put a foot on the windowsill and climbed outside to an alien landscape of leaded roofs and gullies, chimney stacks and skylights, domes and minarets, parts floodlit and shining in the downpour, and parts in deep black shadow.

He found himself on a tight ledge, with a considerable drop down to the flat roof from which the main dome sprouted. He looked around but he couldn't see the Embalmer anywhere. A sound of breaking glass caught his attention. There was a row of skylights at the end of a pitched roof some thirty feet away – and there was the Embalmer, scaling up the side of the giant cone-shaped roof at the far end of the building.

Francis squatted on the ledge and, holding onto the sill of the window, let himself drop down onto the flat roof. He ran along the guttered side of the pitched section, passing the smaller domes and minarets that gave the Pavilion its distinctive skyline.

The Embalmer waved at Francis provocatively. 'Do you remember? Hiding out on rooftops at school?'

The wind almost whipped the words away, but not before they'd set loose a torrent of memories. As Francis ran, a face flashed up in front of his mind's eye. A small red-haired boy. And a name. Euan Hornbuckle. Now he had the connection. A kid in the class below him at Brighton College. Whiny. Snot-nosed. Telling tales about things that had never happened ... Euan Hornbuckle, though only ever Hornbuckle at school, was Euan Drysdale. Denise Drysdale's son, given up for adoption. Now he knew who he was dealing with, and the shock made him stagger and trip.

He crashed down against the sharp edge of a rain gutter, the breath knocked out of him.

A few feet away, he heard the sound of laughter carried on the wind.

He looked up. The man that Euan had become was shinning up one of the tall minarets at the corner of the coned roof.

As Francis scrabbled to his feet, ignoring the piercing pain in his ribs, it all fell into place. The tattoo with the scales of justice and ACAB and the cricket stumps – that was for him. He was supposed to be one of the Embalmer's victims. But why? What grudge had this twisted boy carried through the decades?

He took a deep breath and it felt like a knife was cutting into his side. He gasped, and the pain dug deeper. The fall must have smashed a rib.

'Euan!'

The Embalmer looked down at him, a sour grin splitting his features.

'You remember. I'm touched. I thought you never noticed me at school.'

You can't talk him down.

Pursing his lips together and trying to keep his breathing as shallow as possible, Francis hobbled across to the bottom of the minaret. He put his arms around it – they didn't quite reach all the way around – and pulled himself up onto its square base. There was no way he'd be able to climb it as Hornbuckle had. He simply didn't have the strength left in his arms, and he was already feeling lightheaded with the pain from his ribs. But Hornbuckle didn't know that.

'Come down,' he called. 'Let's talk this through.'

'I'm not an idiot, you goody-goody police boy. Hand myself over to you? Forget it.'

'You can trust me.'

Hornbuckle made his feelings known, and a large glob of spittle hit Francis on his upturned cheek. He bent his head to wipe it away on his shoulder, causing another detonation of pain.

Down below, sirens and blue lights were filling up the paved area in front of the Pavilion entrance. There were shouted instructions as the backup arrived. But up here on the roof, it was just him and Euan Hornbuckle.

He started to climb. It was up to him to get Hornbuckle down. The arrest was his to make.

Above him, Hornbuckle realised what was happening. With a roar of anger, he let go of the minaret and dropped, his feet glancing off Francis's shoulder as he leapt onto the steep slope of the adjacent cone. Francis lost his grip on the minaret and his footing on the base. He felt himself falling, then landed on the narrow sloping sill that edged the cone. The pain in his side was electrifying.

Hornbuckle looked at the activity at the front of the Pavilion and without a second's hesitation scurried across to the other side of the roof. Francis watched, fighting for breath, as the Embalmer lowered himself over the edge and dropped down onto the dark, deserted lawn at the back of the building.

He had no choice – he couldn't let him get away.

Practically biting through his lip to combat the agony that was spreading through his chest, he crawled across to the side of the roof where Hornbuckle had launched himself into the darkness. As he crested the edge, he saw a sprawled figure on the ground below, just starting to rise to his feet. He had one chance – he knew he was in no fit state to pursue Hornbuckle. He sat on the edge and pushed himself off with all the strength he had left. If he didn't hit his target, he'd pulverise himself on the hard ground.

The air rushed by his ears for a split second, then he crashed onto Hornbuckle, whose legs instantly gave way beneath him. As they tumbled into the wet grass with a sickening thud, Francis felt another immense explosion of pain. The breath shot out of him and his chin hit the dirt. He bit his tongue and tasted blood. But he still had the presence of mind to grab hold of the body writhing underneath him.

That's all he had to do.

Hold on for dear life.

For. Dear. Life.

Teeth sank into one of his forearms.

He wasn't sure he could hang on much longer.

Then a shout from above.

'They're round the back.' Gavin's voice, directing the men on the ground.

Footsteps.

People were dragging them apart. Three PCs – two men and one woman. The men grabbed Hornbuckle and pushed him down onto his front in the grass. Francis heard the snap of handcuffs. He was still fighting to breathe. The woman PC came to his side.

'You all right, sir?'

Francis looked up at her, unable to speak.

'Stay lying down. We've got paramedics coming.'

He closed his eyes.

It was over.

68

Wednesday, 22 November 2017

Francis

After twenty-four hours in hospital, Francis discharged himself. Three broken ribs. Cuts. Bruises. Blue-green toothmarks on his arm that luckily hadn't broken the skin. There was nothing lying in a hospital bed was going to do for him. He got a prescription for Tramadol and spent the rest of Sunday sleeping it off in bed. Euan Hornbuckle, born William Drysdale, adopted by Tom and Marion Hornbuckle, aka Euan Drysdale, was in custody. Rory was in hospital. Alex was in hospital. Paul Mullins was dead. Marni was recovering and had been reunited with Pepper. The planet could spin on its axis for a day without his intervention.

Robin had collected him, dosed him with soup and had apologised profusely for failing to answer her phone the day before. 'I forgot to charge it before I went out. We got talking over lunch and then decided to go shopping.'

By Wednesday morning, once the Tramadol had kicked in, he felt ready to face the world again. There was too much to be done for him to take time off – and more than anything he needed to talk to Euan Hornbuckle and find out what had happened to turn him into the monster he'd become. But first, he needed to go back to the hospital.

Rory's wife, Linda, was sitting by his bed when Francis arrived.

He'd met her a couple of times, but only very briefly. Rory kept his personal and professional lives well apart from each other. She stood up when Francis came into the room.

'Linda, I'm so sorry.' It wasn't just a trite apology. Francis couldn't underestimate his share of the blame for what had happened to Rory. 'How is he? How did the op go?' He looked down at Rory. His head and left eye were swathed in bandages. His right eye was closed, and Francis wasn't sure if he was dozing or completely out for the count.

Linda Mackay blinked a couple of times, and her eyes shone with bright, unshed tears. She sniffed. 'He's had a good night.' Her face crumpled. 'They couldn't save his eye . . .'

'Oh, God, I'm so sorry.' He should have realised it was Rory being held. His sergeant would never have gone missing for a day – not when they were in the middle of two big cases. 'What can I do? Anything?'

Linda looked utterly devastated. She shook her head, and her eyes told him she didn't want to be having this conversation. He supposed she'd been sitting by his bed all night.

'Look, Linda, let me sit with him a while. Get something to eat, have a shower, whatever you need to do, I can stay with him.'

Lips compressed, the woman nodded and hurried out of the room. She was barely holding herself together.

Francis sat down. With only one eye, what did Rory's future hold? He made a decision that moment that he'd fight Rory's corner with everything he had. He absolutely wanted to keep him on the team. If he wanted to stay . . .

'Linda? Is that you?' Rory's single eye flickered open.

'It's me, Rory.'

'Boss.'

'I'm so sorry that this happened to you. I should have got there quicker.'

Rory sighed. 'He jumped me from behind and overpowered

me. Shoved me down that tunnel under the Pavilion. I thought he was holding a gun to my back. So fucking stupid – it was a length of metal pipe.'

'Not stupid. If it felt like a gun, it was a gun.'

They were both silent for a moment.

'You'll come back to work, won't you?'

Rory shifted in the bed. He was obviously in a lot of pain. There was a jug of water and a beaker on the nightstand, so Francis offered him a drink.

He knew he was asking prematurely. 'The team needs you. I need you.'

'I don't know yet,' said Rory. 'This,' he indicated his bandaged eye, 'is going to take some getting used to.'

'I want you back. You'll be fine for most things.'

'Most things?'

'Well, probably no more fast response driving.'

Rory's visible eyebrow went up. 'From the man who crashed into a railway crossing?'

Francis grinned. 'I think it was your intervention that caused the crash.'

There was the glimmer of a smile on Rory's face, until he tried to shake his head and winced with pain. But it was enough for Francis to know that he was going to be okay.

'Haven't you got a killer to deal with?' he said, once he'd recovered himself. 'You shouldn't be hanging around here.'

'Just giving Linda a break. God knows, she's going to need them while you recuperate.'

Rory's two-fingered answer sent Francis on his way, and twenty minutes later a taxi dropped him off in front of the station. It was going to be a while before he could drive, too.

Gavin, Angie and Kyle were heads down at their desks and a subdued air hung over the incident room, despite the team having just wound up two major cases. But one of the team was in hospital. One of the men they'd been chasing had escaped justice at the bottom of a cliff.

'Hey boss,' said Angie, looking up as Francis went across the room to his office. 'How are you?'

Francis shrugged. 'Been better. A few broken ribs.'

'Ouch!' said Kyle. 'Been there.'

'How's Rory?' said Gavin.

Francis gave them an update on the sergeant's condition, then asked for an update in return.

'Okay,' said Gavin. 'I've tied up some of the loose ends. Turns out, like we thought, Euan Hornbuckle was Denise Drysdale's son. She gave him up for adoption at birth. The Hornbuckles were well off and childless, and took Euan in. They're both dead now – a house fire when Euan was twenty-one.'

'That might bear looking into,' said Francis, 'knowing what we now know about Euan.'

'You were at school with him, boss, weren't you?'

Francis nodded. He'd spent an awful lot of the last twenty-four hours trying to remember Euan Hornbuckle from the four years they'd spent together at Brighton College. But he only had the flimsiest recollection of the boy.

'He was in the year below me, so he hardly registered. You know what it's like at school – you look up to people in the classes above you, and studiously ignore anyone below. But he seemed like an outsider, even back then,' said Francis. 'Where is he now?'

'Downstairs. The psychologist's doing an initial assessment.'

69

Wednesday, 22 November 2017

Francis

The psychologist's preliminary report landed in Francis's inbox a couple of hours later. He opened it and devoured it quickly, searching for the answers he needed to understand what drove Hornbuckle to kill. It was only a first assessment, but first impressions counted, and he wanted to know what he was going to come up against in the interview.

Subject: Euan Hornbuckle

Date of birth: 5.2.1988

Age: 29

Birth parents: Denise Drysdale, father unknown

Adoptive parents: Tom and Marion Hornbuckle

Reason for referral: Euan Hornbuckle has been referred for psychological evaluation to determine his current cognitive and emotional status following arrest on suspicion of four counts of murder, one count of grievous bodily harm, resisting arrest, and a number of lesser charges.

Background: Hornbuckle has been known to social services from childhood and background information has been obtained from previous psychological evaluations and medical reports.

His fractured relationship with his mother is known to have contributed to poor self-esteem, confusion and an inability to form appropriate adult social relationships. It can safely be assumed that Euan Hornbuckle is suffering from an antisocial personality disorder. He exhibited a number of behavioural traits throughout his school history that have led to this conclusion. He does not deny these problems and was co-operative in discussing his issues. However, in keeping with antisocial personality disorder, he expresses no feelings of remorse or guilt for his actions and will always find other individuals to blame for his own failings and misfortunes.

The particular behaviours that led to the series of murders he is now charged with will have started during childhood, when he would have formulated his own code of conduct after rejecting society's expectations of him. In our discussion, he mentioned his belief in Kemetism, a neopagan religion of Ancient Egypt, the tenets of which he appears to have twisted to suit his own worldview. An event in his recent past will have triggered the mental crisis that led him to embark on a killing spree. This motivation will need to be explored more thoroughly before any meaningful conclusions can be drawn.

Damn right his motivation needed to be explored, but at least it was a start. Now it was time for Francis to face the individual that had not only wanted him dead, but who had even constructed a sarcophagus with his name on it.

Underneath the cold strip light of the interview room, even with one arm in a sling and with all his piercings removed, the Embalmer still looked like a man to be reckoned with. He glared at Francis with his split tongue resting provocatively on his lower lip. Francis eyed the small horns, jutting out at his hairline, and the gaping holes in his drooping earlobes from which the spacers had been removed.

As Francis took his seat, the Embalmer made a low hissing sound that reminded him of his encounter with the boa constrictor.

'I know you now,' said Francis, pulling out a chair from the table and sitting down. 'I remember – you were in the class below me.' Gavin, who'd followed him in, took the chair beside him silently. 'But we'll get to that later. First, tell me about your mother, Euan. Your real mother. Why did she put you up for adoption?' Everything pointed to this being the source of Euan's grief, and Francis felt if he pushed hard enough here, the cracks would begin to show.

There was a flicker of something in Hornbuckle's eyes – sadness maybe? 'She loved me. She did.'

'But she couldn't keep you?'

'It was hard for her. She just wanted me to have a better life.'

'Couldn't your father have helped her?'

Hornbuckle scowled. 'He ... ' He shook his head, unable to continue.

'You don't even know who he was, do you?'

'No.' He slumped in his chair, staring into the distance somewhere beyond Gavin and Francis.

'But your mother gave you up as soon as you were born?' prompted Gavin.

Hornbuckle snapped to attention. 'She had to. She couldn't keep me. She was a model – her life was too glamorous for a child. But she used to come and talk to me. When I was at primary, through the playground fence. She loved me. She said she'd come for me, when I was big enough.' He sighed.

'But she never did,' said Francis.

'One day she stopped coming.' Hornbuckle's mouth twisted with pain and Francis saw the ghost of the small boy still trapped inside him. 'I thought something must have happened to her. I thought she was dead.'

'But she wasn't, was she?'

'For years, I believed that she was. My adoptive parents told me she was dead. They told me that she hated me. They beat me. The woman would smack me and the man watched and laughed.'

'Did you kill them? Did you set the fire they died in?'

Hornbuckle returned his gaze unwaveringly, but he didn't answer. Francis took the answer to be yes. There would be plenty of time to revisit this now and establish what had happened.

'I didn't live up to their expectations.'

'So you searched for your real mother? We know you found her. Why did you kill her?'

Hornbuckle leant back and closed his eyes.

'Come on, Euan. You loved her. You thought she loved you. Something went badly wrong, didn't it?'

He opened his eyes and took a deep breath. 'I never stopped thinking about her, even when I thought she was dead. I honoured her memory with sacrifices to the goddess Isis.'

'Sacrifices?' said Gavin sharply.

Hornbuckle sat up straight, looking down his nose at Gavin. 'Don't question my religion. Sacrifice and death bring immortality. The great gods live forever.'

'Cut the mumbo-jumbo, Euan,' said Francis. 'Tell us how you came to find your mother.'

'I wanted to honour her grave. That's how I discovered she was still alive – there was no death certificate for her. It wasn't hard to track her down using the internet. She was still living in Brighton.'

'And how did you feel when you realised she was alive? Didn't you wonder why she'd stopped visiting you?'

'It wasn't her fault.'

Francis and Gavin remained silent, waiting for him to explain.

Hornbuckle clenched his fists and his mouth tightened into a thin line.

Eventually he spoke. 'She felt it wasn't fair on me, when she had nothing to offer me, so she decided to stop coming.'

'And you believed that?' Francis knew he was being cruel.

'It hurt her as much as it hurt me.'

'I see.' Francis took a sip of his cold coffee. 'So the reunion was all hearts and flowers?'

He wondered what it had been like for Denise Drysdale to have Euan come crashing back into her life.

'She was overjoyed when I made contact with her. She invited me to come and live with her in her flat. That's when I started to use her surname.'

'But later you killed her?'

Hornbuckle's breathing became suddenly faster. He glanced around the room, avoiding eye contact.

'Why did you kill her, Euan? I thought you loved her.'

'Apophis decreed it.'

'Apophis?' said Gavin.

'The Great Serpent spoke to me. He told me it was time to start down the path.'

'The path to what?'

'The path to immortality.' Hornbuckle's eyes rolled back in his head, then he snapped back to lucidity again. 'I didn't want to do it. I resisted it for a long time – I'd only just found her. But then,' his brow lowered and his face darkened, 'she killed one of my snakes. One of my daughters.'

Francis and Gavin exchanged glances.

'She hated them. She was jealous of the attention I gave them.'

'So she killed one of them?'

'She claimed it had escaped. She said she was scared.' His eyes glazed over, like he was retreating into his own private world. 'My girls would never have hurt her. They're harmless.'

Francis could hardly agree with this, but he stayed silent, waiting for Hornbuckle to continue.

'She said Wadjet had tried to strangle her.'

'Wadjet?' said Gavin.

'Wadjet was my oldest daughter, named for the snake goddess of Dep. Denise killed her with a kitchen knife. That's when I knew that I had to heed the message Apophis had sent me.'

Francis had lost patience with Hornbuckle's nonsense. He stood up.

'You killed your own mother because she defended herself against a snake? And then you tattooed her and mummified her body? Believe me, Euan, you'll be going to prison for a very long time.' He turned to Gavin. 'I need a break.'

'I am Apophis, the Great Serpent. You will feel my anger.' He hissed and pushed his forked tongue out between his lips.

Francis ignored him and opened the door to let Gavin out of the interview room.

'Your death will make me immortal.'

70

Wednesday, 22 November 2017

Francis

'Tell us about how you mummified the body, Euan,' said Francis. He was once more sitting across the table from Hornbuckle, but was now refuelled with caffeine and nicotine after a half-hour break. 'What were you trying to achieve? So, tell us about Alicia Russell, Luke Bridges and Ada Carmichael. Were they also sacrifices to your snake god?'

Hornbuckle smiled. 'They were the sacrifices to ensure my immortality. Denise was the first. You would have been the last, Sullivan.'

'How did you choose them?' said Francis. *How did you choose me?*

'They were people who had wronged me, put me down. By sacrificing them I was taking back my dignity. When you clear the haters, you become immortal.'

'Ada Carmichael. Why her?'

'Ada Carmichael always thought she was better than me.'

'You knew her?'

'We were at college together. She was a bitch. A slut.'

'I know what this is about,' said Francis. 'She knocked you back, didn't she?'

Hornbuckle's hands, resting on the table, tightened into fists again. 'I was good to her. We were friends.'

382

'You just called her a bitch and a slut.'

'She changed. She started seeing someone. Didn't want to be around me. I was her boyfriend, until she found someone better.'

Francis doubted that this was the case. It seemed far more likely that Hornbuckle had been a pest to her. He was almost certainly delusional about the relationships in his life.

'So you killed her? Because she preferred another guy to you?' said Gavin.

He shook his head. 'She had it coming – she was a cock tease. I asked her to a club and she said yes. Then she stood me up and turned up with this new bloke. Maybe if she'd realised the error of her ways and come back to me ... maybe I could have forgiven her. But she never did.'

'And the disembowelling? Part of your ritual too?'

Hornbuckle nodded. 'The sacrifices had to be made.'

Francis thought of Tom Fitz and how he was going to feel when he heard all of this.

'Why Luke Bridges?'

A shadow of regret seemed to pass across Hornbuckle's face, but it was gone almost as soon as it appeared. 'He was supposed to be my best friend.'

'When?' said Gavin.

'When we were kids. He lived next door. We went to the same primary, we played on our bikes, played football, ran around each other's houses.'

'And then what?'

'Then nothing. He found other playmates. He joined the cool gang.' The last two words were spat out with disgust.

'It's the same story, isn't it?' said Francis. 'Did you ever ask yourself why it kept happening?'

Hornbuckle locked eyes with him and made the familiar guttural hissing sound.

'Alicia?' prompted Gavin.

'That job at the museum should have been mine. But she gave it to her niece. Her gormless, stupid niece. The girl knew nothing about the birds on display there. She wasn't even interested in them. I've loved that place, all my life.'

So that was it. Euan Hornbuckle couldn't stand rejection. He'd never got over the fact that his mother had given him up.

'And each of the six tattoos on Denise represented a sacrifice? Denise, Luke, Alicia, Ada. Me. The tattoo with the Egyptian symbol for teaching – who was that for?'

'There was a teacher who used to beat me. I went to find him, but he was already dead.'

'Save you the bother, did it?' Gavin's voice could barely contain his anger.

'There's one thing I still don't understand,' said Francis. He kept his tone neutral, even though he was feeling every bit as angry as Gavin.

'What?'

'Why you chose me. Why was I set to be your grand finale?'

'Of course. You wouldn't understand,' said Hornbuckle, a sour look sweeping his features. 'Life has always been so easy for you, hasn't it? Every day in the sunlight, never lurking in the shadows.'

'I don't know what you mean. Can you explain?'

'Why bother? You're not really interested. You were never interested in people further down the pecking order.'

'Try me.'

Euan slammed a fist on the table. 'You have no idea, do you? Privileged, entitled white man.'

'You're white. You're a man. You went to the same school as I did, Euan. We're not that different.'

Mirthless laughter spilled from Euan Hornbuckle's mouth. He pushed out his bifurcated tongue and made the two points wiggle independently.

'Not that different? Fuck you, Sullivan.'

Gavin leaned forward across the table.

'Tell me, Euan,' he said. 'What's this all about?'

The Embalmer made a performance of angling his chair towards Gavin's end of the table.

'Your boss. The golden boy. Top of the class, captain of the cricket team. So, so popular. And now, the brilliant detective, solving murders left, right and centre.' His words dripped with bile. 'What he did to me? It makes him the perfect candidate.'

'Candidate for what?' said Gavin.

'Sacrifice.'

Francis locked eyes with him, keeping his expression impassive. 'What did I do to you, Euan? Remind me.'

Cold fury flashed in Euan Hornbuckle's eyes. 'You know what you did.'

'I honestly don't.'

This response made Hornbuckle angrier still.

'You don't even remember,' he said, through gritted teeth. 'You had me dumped from the team. You were captain of cricket. You went to the coach and told him I'd been cheating.'

It came back in a rush. It had been at an away match, against another local school. Hornbuckle had only just scraped into the team because one of the other players was ill. Like he said, Francis was captain. He'd seen Hornbuckle messing with the other school's kit in the pavilion and he'd called him out. Hornbuckle had been tossed from the team, but it wouldn't have made much difference. He was a weak player and wouldn't have lasted anyway.

'Because you had.'

'I was helping the team. Being picked was the best thing that ever happened to me – at last I had the chance to gain some respect – and you ruined it.'

Francis shrugged. 'You were in the wrong, Euan. Then, and now.'

'The cricket stumps? On the tattoo?' said Gavin. He looked at Francis. 'They meant you.'

'So you had planned to kill me right from the start?' said Francis.

Hornbuckle's chest expanded and he hissed. There was a dark malevolence in his eyes that seemed to suck the light from the room. Inside, Francis shuddered.

'You were on my kill list from the day it happened.'

Francis had had enough. 'Such a sad little life you've led, Euan. Everyone has it in for you, don't they?'

Gavin shot him a warning look.

'You wouldn't understand,' said Hornbuckle.

His voice had gone up in volume and pitch. He was becoming agitated. But Francis had lost any sympathy he'd had earlier – it was just one long whine of 'poor me'.

'Christ, Euan, you're not the first kid to have had it rough. But the others don't kill people for it.'

'I can't forget and I can't let go.'

Francis glared at him. 'You failed when it came to me.'

'I would still kill you, given half the chance.' He made the hissing sound and leaned forward. Francis could smell his breath, foul and rancid, and something inside him snapped. His fist landed squarely on Euan Hornbuckle's jaw, knocking him off his chair and onto the floor.

'That was for Rory,' Francis said, stepping over the sprawled body.

71

Friday, 8 December 2017

Francis

The parking area at the Woodvale Crematorium was almost full, but Francis managed to squeeze his Golf into a space a little way down the lane from it. Another car drew up as he was getting out of his. It slowed to a stop and the driver's window opened.

'DI Sullivan!' It was Tom Fitz.

Francis bent down to the window.

'You covering this for *The Argus*?'

'And paying my respects,' said Fitz.

He parked his car and Francis waited for him so they could walk up the lane together.

'It'll be a while before we get Ada's body for burial?' Fitz asked.

'I'm afraid so,' said Francis. 'But I'll check with Rose when I'm back in the office and let you know.'

'Thanks,' said Fitz.

They walked in silence for a moment, then the reporter stopped and turned to face Francis.

'Listen, Sullivan, I know we haven't always seen eye to eye ...'

Francis laughed at the understatement. 'But I wanted to thank you and the team for what you've done in bringing Hornbuckle to justice.'

Francis shrugged. 'It's our job. What we do.' Fitz had written up the story of how Euan Hornbuckle had been apprehended in the most glowing terms, casting Francis and Rory as the heroes of the piece.

'I mean it. I'm really grateful for Ada's sake. She was a good kid.'

'I'm sorry for your loss, Tom. If only we'd been able to bring him in sooner, she might still be alive.'

'Her death's not on you.'

They continued walking, almost at the chapels.

'You still want to take down Bradshaw?'

This time it was Francis who stopped walking. He waited as Tom Fitz seemed to weigh up exactly what he was going to tell him.

'There was a case. Back in the nineties, a missing boy. Bradshaw was in charge. You should look into it.'

People were starting to file into the left-hand of the two chapels and Tom Fitz strode off to do his job as a reporter.

Francis went to join the mourners at Thierry Mullins's funeral. There would be time enough to question Tom further another day.

He sat at the back. He didn't want to intrude on Marni's grief. Thierry had undoubtedly been the love of her life, even if they'd been divorced far longer than they'd been married. He saw her sitting next to Alex in the front pew, her head bowed, but defiantly wearing a red dress and red shoes. Alex, black-suited, hair freshly shorn, put a supportive arm around her shoulder. His arm was still bandaged from the knife wound he'd sustained in the fight with Paul. Francis hoped he'd move back home with her, at least for a while, so she wouldn't have to grieve alone.

On the other side of her was an elderly woman in traditional funereal black, just rising from her knees onto her seat. Thierry's mother, Francis surmised. Marni had mentioned that she'd be coming over from France for Thierry's funeral and to collect Paul's body to take back to Aix-en-Provence. He couldn't begin to imagine what she was going through – losing two sons, one accused of murdering the other. But at least there'd be no trial now. Liv was sitting on the other side of her, and beyond her was a middle-aged woman who looked enough like Marni to be her sister, Liv's mother.

Behind the family, Thierry's studio colleagues Noa and Charlie and their partners made up the first row of Brighton's tattooing community. Thierry had been a popular man and well known in the town, an organiser of the tattoo convention. Francis was probably the only member of the congregation without a tattoo ... then he smiled at his own stupidity, and thought about the half-finished octopus tattoo on his shoulder. It was time to get it completed.

The service was simple and brief. Alex stood up to give his father's eulogy in a clear, confident voice that still conveyed the depth of emotion he was feeling. Marni, Thierry's mother, Liv and plenty of others cried openly as he spoke about moments he'd shared with his father. Even Francis felt the heavy swelling of unshed tears and a lump forming in his throat.

Alex had spoken at too many funerals for one so young.

'A lot of you probably know that there's some doubt as to whether Thierry or Paul was actually my father. Today, I'm laying that doubt to rest. I can say with absolute certainty that Thierry Mullins was and always will be the only father I ever had and the only father I'd ever want. God bless you, Papa.'

As he went back to his seat, Francis saw tears glistening on his cheeks, too.

And then, to the accompaniment of Lou Reed's 'Perfect Day', Thierry's coffin slipped away behind the red velvet curtains. Francis looked away – it was the moment he hated more than any other. At the front, Marni's shoulders shook and Thierry's mother sank down into her seat, unable to stand as she watched her son's body embarking on its final journey.

Outside, Francis could breathe again. He hadn't expected to be so affected by Thierry Mullins's funeral – but then maybe he hadn't counted on being so pained at seeing Marni's very evident grief. He wanted more than anything to lend her a strong arm to lean on, but he knew it wasn't the time or the place for him to step in. She'd need plenty of support moving forward, and he could always be there for her during the long, dark days ahead.

Alex broke away from his family to come and speak to him.

'Last time I met you at a funeral, you said you owed me,' he said. 'This time, you don't. You saved my life out at Peacehaven.'

'I don't know about that,' said Francis.

'I do. Paul would have taken me down with him if you hadn't been there. Thank you.'

Francis shook his head, but didn't say anything.

Marni came over to them, and Alex went to find Liv. Her eyes were red-rimmed, her mascara clumped. She looked as tired and drawn as Francis had ever seen her.

'Thank you for coming,' she said.

'Of course,' he said. 'I'm so sorry for your loss.'

She nodded, unable to speak.

He gave her time.

'What will you do now?' he said, after a minute had passed.

Marni studied the ground at her feet.

'I don't know,' she said, with a shrug. 'Alex is heading off to art school in London. I might move up there, too.' She raised her head to meet his gaze. 'There's nothing left here for me now.'

There is. There is.

The words hammered through his brain, but he couldn't say them.

'Thierry's gone and I can't see myself with someone else.'

She waited for his response.

'But . . .' His mouth was dry. The words dried up. 'Don't leave without saying goodbye.'

'Of course.'

She reached up and touched the black scar on his cheek, just for a moment. His fingers caught hers. He leaned forward to kiss her, his lips brushing hers for a brief moment. Then she was gone, back to her mother-in-law and her son.

Francis turned and walked down the lane to his car. He could still feel the touch of her fingers on his face. But the scar Marni Mullins left inside him would run far deeper and last for far longer than the one on his cheek.

Acknowledgements

I'm approaching writing this with some trepidation, having managed to misspell people's names in the last two sets of acknowledgements I wrote!

Clearly, however, I won't spell my agent's name wrong. Once again, huge thanks to the wonderful Jenny Brown, of Jenny Brown Associates, who is both cheerleader for my writing and wise counsel for my writing career. I wouldn't have reached the end of book three without her unflinching support. A great deal of thanks also to my editor at Trapeze, Sam Eades, who early on gave me some excellent writing advice, which I follow in every book: 'Put you character in a bad situation, and throw in something that will make it worse. Then pile something else on top of that.' Gratitude is due to Phoebe Morgan, who guided this book through its early stages while Sam was on maternity leave, and to the rest of the brilliant Trapeze and Orion teams who all work so hard to produce and sell their authors' books.

As usual, I had expert input on policing matters from Superintendent (Retired) David Hammond of Staffordshire Police, who does far more to keep Francis Sullivan in line than DCI Bradshaw does!

Thanks are additionally due to, among others, my brother Nick Higgins for reading early drafts and to the members of my writing group – Jane Anderson, Jane Bradley, Gill Fyffe, Hannah Kelly and Lucy Lloyd – for critiquing and support.

As always, thanks and love to Mark, Rupert and Tim.

Credits

Trapeze would like to thank everyone at Orion who worked on the publication of *The Embalmer*.

Agent
Jenny Brown

Editor
Sam Eades

Copy-editor
Laura Gerrard

Proofreader
Kim Bishop

Editorial Management
Clarissa Sutherland
Charlie Panayiotou
Jane Hughes
Alice Davis
Claire Boyle

Audio
Paul Stark
Amber Bates

Contracts
Anne Goddard
Paul Bulos
Jake Alderson

Design
Lucie Stericker
Joanna Ridley
Nick May
Clare Sivell
Helen Ewing

Finance
Jennifer Muchan
Jasdip Nandra